A novel

By

Clay Hutto

Published by HARBINGER PRESS
5390 NE 35th Place
Portland, Oregon 97211

Library of Congress Control Number:
2015947727

Hutto, H. Clay, 1957 –
Wyo / Clay Hutto
ISBN 978-0-9799088-2-8
Satire – Movies – Graduate School – Wyoming –
20th Century – Fiction.

For Professor Ravage,
a capricious but entertaining instructor
and
Hedy Lamarr,
for her visual inspiration

Wyo

1

Dale Smith walks into the student newspaper office early Thursday morning. Before he can make it to the arts and entertainment desk, the newspaper's editor, Felicia Fernandez, accosts him.

"Here's another letter complaining about your movie review," she says. She hands him the letter.

Dale scans the written complaint. The writer didn't agree with Dale's sarcastic critique of *The Rose*. He especially found Dale's mockery of Bette Midler's performance to be objectionable. Rather typically for complainers, the writer hadn't read his review closely. Dale didn't fault Midler's performance as much as he objected to the character herself. The character was abrasive, self-pitying, and obnoxious. She was supposed to be based on Janis Joplin but Milder wasn't a Southerner and she didn't sing rhythm and blues. Midler, in spite of her talent, wasn't right for the role.

Dale thinks there is some kind of informal campaign against his reviews. Counting this letter the student newspaper, *The Branding Iron*, has received four condemnatory missives during the last four weeks. But the same two people seem to be taking turns denouncing his cinematic opinion.

"Spencer Dribble strikes again," Dale says. He hands the letter back to Felicia. "Or should I say Spencer Drivel. Because that's what he writes: drivel."

"Yeah, his letters aren't composed very well. That's why I didn't pick him to write movie reviews."

"You mean this guy wanted to be the movie reviewer?"

"He applied when you did."

"You never told me that."

"I didn't see any reason to at the time."

Dale gives Felicia a mock-critical look. She laughs.

"What about the other complainer. What's his name ..."

"Robert Baugh."

"Does he also want to be the newspaper's movie reviewer?"

"No, he just doesn't like your 'aesthetic perspective.'"

"His letters are sort of pompously written. Does he speak like that?"

"I don't know. I don't know him."

"I thought you knew everyone here at good ol' Wyo."

"Not everybody. There are twelve thousand students on campus."

Dale nods pensively. He's still thinking about the chiding letters. Then he notices that Felicia is smiling at him. She's a short, plump, dark-haired girl with pronounced dimples in her cheeks. Her dark brown eyes have a teasing look in them.

"Are you going to print that letter from Dribble?"

"We can't print every letter to the editor, can we?"

"What kind of name is Dribble, anyway?"

"I don't know. But his father is Dr. Dribble, the psychology professor."

"You got to be kidding."

"I'm not. I took a psychology class from Dr. Dribble."

"With a name like that he ought to be teaching basketball."

Felicia laughs. Dale thinks she has a pleasant laugh. He realizes that he's lucky to have a supportive editor. A less encouraging one would probably can him. He doesn't want that. He enjoys watching movies and since he's going to see them anyway he might as well write about them. He's even getting graduate credit for it. This fall he received grudging permission from his advisor, Professor Comstock, to earn one hour of credit in an independent study course by writing film reviews. Comstock only granted the request because Dale told him that he planned on being a movie critic at a real newspaper sometime in the future.

"There's also another letter. But it's not addressed to the newspaper. It's addressed to you."

Felicia hands Dale an envelope. He notices that the University of Wyoming Department of English is printed on the upper left corner. He hopes he's not going to be denounced by a professor.

Dale pulls out the typed letter and quickly reads it. It's not a complaint. It's a letter praising him for his "trenchant" film reviews. The letter is signed Dr. Stephen Schrag. The professor teaches the Modern American Novel class that Dale is in. Since it is a class with thirty students attending, and Dale rarely speaks in class, he wonders if Dr. Schrag knows his student is also the *Branding Iron* movie reviewer.

"Is it good or bad news?" Felicia asks.

Dale shows her the letter and she reads it.

"Well, at least you have one fan."

"Thanks."

"Actually, you have two. I like your reviews, too, even though I think you can be sorta harsh at times. But at least you're entertaining and you seem to know what you're writing about."

"Harsh? Did you like *The Rose?*"

"It wasn't so bad."

"Bette Midler isn't anything like Janis Joplin."

"But I don't really know who Janis Joplin is."

"Was. She died nine years ago."

"There you go. You sometimes forget that a lot of college kids don't remember the sixties like you do."

"I'm only a year older than you."

"Really? But you seem *so* much older."

She's teasing him. He plays along. "That's right. Older and wiser."

"Let's not get carried away. Do you want us to print that letter from the English professor?"

"No. He wrote it to me. No need to disseminate it to my critical public."

Dale walks over to the desk he uses and opens a drawer. He grabs the paperback copy of the novel *The Moviegoer* that he'd earlier forgotten. Felicia notices the book.

"How appropriate."

"I'm reading it for my Modern American Novel class."

"I've never read it. Is it any good?"

"Yeah, it's a good novel. And it's about a lot more than seeing movies."

"Such as?"

"Philosophy. The meaning of life. Why perceptive people are often unjustly attacked by their obtuse critics."

"You're joking."

"Only in part. Well, I got to go. By the way, I'm seeing *Dracula* this weekend. I think I can really sink my teeth into that movie. Want to run the review?"

Felicia wags an admonishing finger at him but she also smiles. Dale gives her a wave and leaves the student newspaper office. He walks down the stairs to the first floor of the Memorial Union and then proceeds out of the building and across campus until he come to the an old red brick building where the university radio station is located. He opens the door, walks down a gloomy hallway, and enters the newsroom where he sees Edward Darby, the assistant news editor, waiting for him.

"You're late," Darby says.

Dale points to the large clock mounted on the wall above the AP wire machine. "Exactly on time," he says as he and Darby stride down a hallway to one of the studios. Dale pauses, takes out the typed script, and hands it to Darby. Dale goes into the control room of the studio while Darby goes into the vocal booth. Dale sits at a chair in front of the console and prepares for taping. He looks through the large glass window at Darby who is perusing the script. Dale turns on the intercom and asks Darby if he is ready for a run-through. Darby nods and Dale put on the headphones. Darby reads the script out loud, his resonant baritone voice filling Dale's ears. Dale times the reading. Just a tad too long. He tells Darby to pick up the speed a little.

Darby goes through another run-through. Dale signals an okay sign and prepares for taping. When he turns on the reel-to-reel he nods to Darby. The news editor proceeds to read the script of the weekly installment of *The Buffalo Quotidians*.

The Buffalo Quotidians is a spoof news show that airs on the college radio station KUWR at 8:30 p.m. every Friday. It's a ten-minute show that Dale writes and produces. When he thought of the idea at the beginning of the fall semester, he didn't think Darby would approve. Darby, however, proved to have a sense of humor and after he read the first Quotidian, he'd agreed to air the mock news stories every Friday. He even agreed to serve as announcer.

Dale alternates watching the audiometer and Darby in the on-air room. Darby is a senior at Wyoming but he looks older than the usual undergraduate. He's tall, a couple of inches over six feet, with a slightly heavy build. He has shaggy brown hair, hazel eyes, and a square face dominated by a jutting jaw. He's not exactly handsome but has a distinguished look and a confident demeanor that he hopes will help him find a real radio or television job when he graduates.

While listening to Darby read the script, Dale detects a slight east coast accent to his voice. Darby is from Chevy Chase, a suburb in Washington D.C. Dale has noticed before that Wyoming has a surprising number of students from the East and Midwest. He supposes they come west for the skiing and scenic beauty more than the academics.

Ten minutes later, Darby finishes the script almost exactly on time. Two seconds to spare. That's fine. They can play the theme song a tad longer to cover the gap.

Dale signals that the taping is finished and Darby walks over to the control room.

"I think that's the best script yet," Darby says as he watches Dale splice the intro and the close to the program tape.

"Which story did you like best?"

"The Martin and Lewis one."

That spoof concerned the Cowboys' head football coach

whose last name was Martin. Dale turned the coach into Martin & Lewis, after the '50s comedy duo of Dean Martin and Jerry Lewis. Instead of teaching the football team football fundamentals, Martin & Lewis teaches the team pratfalls, one-liners, and other comedy techniques. The result is football ineptitude, resulting in the team's present 3-7 record.

"I still don't get the name of this show," says Darby. "Why *Buffalo Quotidians?*"

"I used to work on a newspaper in Buffalo City, Oklahoma. And quotidian simply means something that occurs daily. Something regular and mundane. So, *The Buffalo Quotidians.*"

Darby nods. "I get it. Say, has anyone ever asked you about the show?"

"Nope."

The show had been broadcast since the beginning of fall semester. But no one had mentioned it to Dale. He guesses very few students or faculty listen to the campus radio station. It plays mostly classical music. It also broadcasts National Public Radio programs. Darby has tried to get the station manager to switch the format to rock music but so far no luck. However, on Friday the station broadcasts fifty minutes of rock and roll, mostly oldies and alternative rock, to fill out the hour along with *The Buffalo Quotidians.*

"Me neither. I'm getting the feeling that we don't have an audience."

Dale, his task complete, hands the finished tape to Darby. "We labor in obscurity now, but one day we will make history."

Darby nods sardonically as Dale says he has to rush off to class. He departs and walks over to Gowdy Hall. He mounts the stairs until he gets to the third floor where the Mass Communications Department is located. He attends his screen-writing class for an hour and a half, has lunch at the school cafeteria then returns to the third floor to teach his class, Introduction to Journalistic Writing 101.

Dale is one of three graduate teaching assistants in the Mass Communications Department. All three teach one class in exchange for free tuition and a modest stipend. At the start of the fall semester he expected that some faculty member would give him pointers on how to teach the class. But no one volunteered any assistance. If it wasn't for his office mate, a graduate research assistant named Neil Nordberg, Dale would have been completely lost. Nordberg helped him make up a syllabus and gave him a general idea of how to organize the class. But Nordberg couldn't prepare him for the unnerving experience of standing before a class of twenty students for the first time. During that first class Dale managed to avoid humiliation by keeping to a strict schedule he composed ahead of time and not looking at any student too directly. Nevertheless, as he stood in front of class going through the class roster, reading the syllabus, and providing general information about the class, he felt very self-conscious. He also felt hyper-aware of the students before him. He noticed minor facial changes. He became aware of slight variations in posture and body language. The entire classroom seemed narrow and claustrophobic and he was keenly aware of his dry mouth and sweating armpits. Somehow he got through that first day's eighty minutes of class time without making a fool out of himself.

As the weeks passed, his anxiety lessened and he grew more comfortable in front of the classroom. His voice didn't quaver any more and his mouth didn't instantly turn into a desert. But he sensed that he didn't command any genuine respect from his students. Some of them, in fact, were older than he was. But none of them gave him any real trouble and he learned how not to focus too much on their bored, indifferent faces.

After teaching his class, Dale walks to the office he shares with Neil Nordberg. Nordberg is not there so Dale puts his textbook, grade book and the students' feature stories that he will later grade in his desk drawer and walks down the hall to the largest classroom on the floor where his History of Cinema I class meets. It's his favorite class. Every Tuesday a classic film is shown and then class discussion is held on Thursday. Tuesday the class screened *Citizen Kane*. Dale saw it once before, but he was even more impressed with the film on a second viewing.

Dale arrives just as class discussion is beginning. He sits, as usual, in the back and listens as the instructor, Dr. Wagstaff, mostly lectures on the cinematic merits of the film.

Dr. Wagstaff, or Walt as he prefers to be known, is a middle-aged man of average height and regular build whose most salient feature is his completely bald head. The skull itself appears larger than normal and since it has nary a trace of hair the smooth, prominent cranium attains an almost classical kind of beauty. Dr. Wagstaff's facial features are rather ordinary. His mouth and nose are of a kind seen on thousand of male faces, completely undistinguished. His blue-gray eyes are almost as unremarkable except that the color seems to vary according to his mood: more blue when jovial less blue and more gray when bilious. But the most interesting feature aside from his bald head is Wagstaff's well-trimmed Fu Manchu beard. If it wasn't for the vaguely reddish cast of the facial hair and his round blue-gray eyes, the bald head and neatly groomed mustache and beard would give Wagstaff an Oriental cast to his appearance.

Class ends and Dale realizes that he hardly listened to the lecture. Instead he was thinking about the scheduled publications board meeting at 4 p.m. This semester's literary magazine editor, Anna Cappelletti, decided to transfer to Indiana University to complete her undergraduate degree and therefore she will not edit the magazine next semester. The publication board is meeting that afternoon to pick a new editor and Dale is one of the two applicants.

Dale, lost in thought, doesn't notice Wagstaff standing next to his desk.

"Was it my incisive lecture that prompts your pondering or is it something else altogether?"

Dale glances up and sees Wagstaff's grinning visage. The professor fancies himself something of a wordsmith; a somewhat unusual notion considering his specialty is the cinema.

"I was just thinking about deep focus photography," Dale says with complete pseudo-earnestness. They walk out of the classroom and proceed down the hallway.

"Yes, you and Gregg Toland. But somehow I suspect your mind is riveted on something else. Maybe a young lady?"

"If only that were true. No, I was thinking about the upcoming publications board meeting."

"Ah, yes. You are pursuing the position of editor for next semester. But tell me, Dale, don't you ever wonder if you're spreading yourself too thin?"

"I like being busy."

"Taking fifteen hours instead of the recommended twelve. Teaching your class. Working at the campus radio station, the newspaper, and the literary magazine. And how many films do you see a week?"

"Six or seven."

"I've even caught you down at the film library watching rusty reels of old silent movies."

"I've never seen them before. You know, there are some Charlie Chaplin movies down there."

"Not any of his best. But if you don't watch out you might end up burning yourself out. Like Edna St. Vincent Millay's candle: Burning at both ends."

"I didn't know you liked poetry."

"I prefer film but I used to read quite a bit of poetry. It's becoming an obsolete art form. We no longer live in a verbal world; we live in the era of the image."

"Maybe. I've always loved literature but right now I'm more interested in seeing as many movies as I can. I'd like to see all the good films eventually."

"And how many films do you calculate that would be?"

"Worth seeing? I don't know. Maybe five hundred."

"Say there are twenty worthy films per year. We've had cinema for about seventy-five years. Exclude the first fifteen years of mostly amateurish silents. That leaves sixty years. Multiply by twenty and you have one thousand and two hundred films worth seeing."

"Wow, that many. How can anyone see all those films?"

"You could start by moving to Denver. There's a movie repertory theatre there that shows two classic films every night. If you saw a double feature twice a week it would only take you six years to reach your goal. Of course, even that theatre doesn't show every *worthy* film."

"How many of those films have you seen?"

"Quite a few. I grew up in Muncie, Indiana but there was a repertory movie theatre there. Yes, Gertrude, in Muncie there is a there there. Anyway, I saw hundreds of old films before I left for college. Then I saw more films during my graduate days in Champaign-Urbana. Living in Laramie has hampered my movie going, of course. I have to drive to Cheyenne or Denver once a week to sate my cinematic appetite. Even so, I'm probably only half way to your imagined worthy film total."

"That's discouraging. It'll take decades to reach my goal."

"You're young. By the time you reach my age perhaps films will be as easy to access as books are today."

"Wouldn't that be great? I could have a movie library and a book library. Then I wouldn't have to depend on television to see old movies."

"You certainly seem to have a rapacious appetite for movies. Why is that?"

"I've always liked watching them. In the last few years I've become more serious about film as an art. Of course, I still love reading books."

"Books are becoming obsolete. Stick to film."

Wagstaff nods a good-bye to Dale then enters his office. Dale walks farther down the hall to his office. As he walks, he thinks about Wagstaff's question. One of the reason he likes movies so much is that when he was growing up that was about the only entertainment his family engaged in. When his father was away from home, either serving on a navy ship or stationed at a base, Dale, his mother, and his sister, would go to the drive-in to watch a double feature every Friday. They'd sometimes go on Saturday, too. It was the highlight of the week. Dale remembers that simple pleasure of going to the drive-in and seeing mostly mediocre movies and yet enjoying the experience of seeing the magnified images on the screen and smelling the scent of popcorn on the night air, hearing the crunch of gravel as a car crept over the small hills in the parking lot. His mother never took them to a theater to see a movie. She was crippled in her right leg and didn't like going out in public.

Dale opens the door to his office and sees Neil Nordberg sitting at his desk. They exchange greetings as Dale tosses his film textbook on the desk and takes a seat. He glances over to Nordberg. He has the better desk. It faces the only window in the office.

Nordberg is an inch or two shorter than average, perhaps five eight, about the same height as Dale. He has a lean build, almost slender, and probably only weights one hundred and forty pounds. He has black hair, which initially puzzled Dale. He always imagined Scandinavians as having blonde or red hair. But Neil's eyes are very blue and he has fair skin. His features are well defined and angular. If Nordberg didn't have a sharpness to his look, a calculating narrowness, he might have been considered handsome. But his dark blue eyes often seem to be squinting in a shrewd way as if he were a poker player and he is trying to read the other players' hands by examining their expressions.

From the beginning Nordberg was unusually friendly. He was the only person to offer Dale any advice about teaching. Dale appreciated that but there is something in Nordberg's manner that bothers him a little. His friendliness seems a little practiced, not spontaneous. Even when Nordberg smiles Dale detects a glint of cunning in his narrow eyes.

"How'd it go in class today?" Nordberg asks.

Dale glances over and sees Nordberg now facing him, with that analytical look lurking in his eyes.

"It went okay. I wish I had more poise in class, though."

"It'll come with practice. You can overcome your natural shyness if you try."

"Were you shy when you taught last year?"

"A little. But I overcame it."

Dale nods, although he doubts that Nordberg was ever shy. He seems to be too self-aware for that. Nordberg was a GTA last year while earning his master's. This year he works as a research assistant for the department head, Dr. Schneider. Neil told Dale that he was either going to go to a doctoral program in mass communications or go to law school. Maybe both.

"Too bad there is another applicant for editor of the literary magazine," Nordberg says.

"I don't mind the competition."

"No, of course not. However, it would have been simpler if you'd been the only applicant as it appeared you would be."

"What do you mean?"

Nordberg is one of five people on the publications board. The other four are a senior named Pamela Partridge; two faculty members, Professor Wilson, a female art professor; Professor Comstock, the journalism professor who also serves as Dale's advisor; and one administrator, Dr. Woolfson, Dean of Student Services.

"The other applicant was recruited at the last minute," Nordberg says in an insinuating kind of way.

"Recruited? By whom?"

"By Professor Comstock."

Dale leans closer to Nordberg so no one would hear although the office door is closed. "You mean Comstock got someone else to run against me?"

Nordberg nods. That shrewd look is even more apparent in his eyes.

"Why would he do that?" Dale asks.

"It's obvious, isn't it?"

"Yeah, I guess so. He doesn't want me to be editor."

Dale wonders what Comstock has against him. The professor has never been friendly but Dale hadn't thought that Comstock disapproved of him.

"Don't worry. I think you'll have the votes." Nordberg rises and dons his Herringbone jacket in preparation for leaving.

"That is, as long as you don't blow the interview."

Dale nods, now feeling a little worried. He hadn't been nervous before.

"See you at the pub board in a few minutes," Nordberg says as he walks out of the office.

"Right."

Dale sits at his desk and contemplates the words of Wagstaff. Maybe he is burning the candle at both ends. However, he wants to take full advantage of the opportunities of a graduate school at a state university. He went to undergraduate school at his hometown college, Galilee Nazarene, and there wasn't a literary magazine, a radio station, or a film society on campus. GNC didn't even screen movies on campus until his senior year when they showed one film, *Oliver!* during homecoming weekend. Most Nazarenes didn't approve of seeing movies, especially the R-rated kind. Dale was a Nazarene for a short time, mostly because his college girlfriend was a devout Nazarene girl. That was the first reason why he transferred to GNC: to pursue her. The second reason was that he needed to stay at home until his sister finished high school. Their mother was frequently mentally ill and Dale thought he should remain at home until June graduated. At present, June was in her second year at GNC living in the dorm, and their mother was living with their grandparents. So far, his mother hadn't suffered another schizophrenic episode.

Dale graduated college in three years, had worked one year at a small town daily newspaper, and now was almost halfway through graduate school. He missed out on certain campus activities by attending GNC and he was determined to make the most of the opportunities offered at a state university. He wanted to see as many movies as possible, learn about film as an art, and participate in other campus activities that he was interested in, such as the radio station and the literary magazine. He wanted to "seize the day" and live this opportunity to the fullest. He wanted to be a renaissance man even if he was living in Laramie, Wyoming in 1979 rather than Florence, Italy in 1579.

At ten minutes to four Dale leaves his office and walks down the hall. He notices that the door to the other GTA's office is open. He pauses there and sees Gary Grabowski and Deborah Pierson sitting at their respective desks. They exchange greetings and Deb invites him in but Dale says he has a meeting to attend. They say their farewells and Dale proceeds out of Gowdy Hall on his way to the Memorial Union.

As Dale walks across campus, he feels a spark of jealousy that Grabowski got to share an office with Deb Pierson. Grabowski is his roommate – they share an off-campus townhouse – and he's an okay guy, a little on the boring side, but not obnoxious. But Dale doesn't think it's fair that Grabowski, a married man, gets to share an office with Deb. She's a pretty girl, one of the prettiest he's seen on campus, and she has a pleasant personality to boot. She has long light brown hair, bright green eyes, and a soft smiling mouth. Dale suddenly realizes one of the reasons he finds Deb attractive is because her natural charm reminds him of his ex-girlfriend. Unlike his former girlfriend, Deb is rather tall, perhaps 5-8, and she has a slender figure. Thinking of those differences makes his jealous throb fade. Still, Dale finds Deb attractive and he would rather have her for an office mate than Neil Nordberg, even if Nordberg had been friendly and helpful these past months.

Dale walks into the Memorial Union and heads to the student council offices when he encounters a young woman at a hallway intersection. He slows down to avoid bumping into her and she turns her head to look at him. He recognizes her as a girl who is in his Modern American Novel class. Her name is Marsha Martin.

Marsha recognizes him, too, and she isn't pleased to be in his company. She offers an insincere smile as they both continue walking to the student council offices. As they walk, he discreetly scrutinizes her. He's never been this close to her before. In their lit class she sits at the front, he in the back. He notices that up-close she is even less attractive than from far away. She's fairly tall, as tall as he is, thin, and dressed in a more proper way than most students, a sartorial fact that has little to do with the interview since he's noticed she often dresses in a "preppy" way. She wears a long beige skirt and a shapeless green cashmere sleeveless sweater with a beige blouse underneath. The sweater appears shapeless because she doesn't have much of a bosom. But at least she fills out her skirt to some degree.

The most noticeable quality about her above the neck is her billowing, medium brown hair. It radiates around her head like the feathery fronds of a dandelion. The features of her face are unappealing for the most part. Her eyes are olive green in color and rather small and lusterless. Her mouth is long but the lips are not full or pouty. Her nose is prominent, aquiline in shape, and it unfortunately dominates her face.

When Marsha participates in their lit class, she speaks in a tight, quiet voice as if it hurts her to produce sound. Since Dale sits in the back of the class, he has a hard time hearing her but what little he has heard has not impressed him. Just ordinary observations and obvious questions.

Rather abruptly, Marsha stops walking and stares at Dale. He notices again that her eyes are strangely green like olives and that within them seems to be a kind of intensity of emotion that the rest of her, except for her hair, tries to repress.

"How badly do you want to be editor of the literary magazine?" Marsha asks.

Her voice, even this close, still has that reluctant sound to it, as if it is wheezing out of her like the tepid heat of a malfunctioning radiator.

"I want to be editor or I wouldn't have applied. I don't know if I feel badly about it though."

Marsha nods doubtfully. Apparently that isn't the answer she seeks. "Don't you also work on the *Branding Iron?*"

"That's right."

"You write movie reviews."

Her voice grows tighter and quieter, almost down to a hiss, obviously indicating her lack of appreciation for his work.

"That's right."

"And you're not an English major?"

"No, but I took a lot of lit classes as an undergraduate. Why are you asking all these questions?"

"I'm just wondering why a person of your background would want to edit the literary magazine."

"What about you? If you are so interested in editing the magazine why aren't you on the staff this year?"

Marsha purses her lips in annoyance. Her thin body slumps. He notices that all her energy seems to go into her hair.

"I intended to but I knew I would have artistic differences with Anna Cappelletti."

"Artistic differences? It's just a campus literary magazine not the *Paris Review*."

Marsha blinks her eyes at the mention of esteemed literary magazine in a way that suggests that she's vaguely heard of it before, has the impression that it's important, but doesn't really know what it is. She abruptly starts walking again. Dale lets her proceed for a few feet then he follows.

They arrive at the student council offices and are instructed to take seats. After a brief interval, Marsha is summoned into the conference room for her interview. Fifteen minutes later, Marsha walks out of the conference room, her face immobile as a mask, and exits the student council office without a word. Dale notices a middle-aged lady signaling him that it is time for his interview.

He enters the conference room and sees five people sitting behind a long Formica table. He immediately recognizes Neil Nordberg and Professor Comstock. He guesses the plump blonde young woman is Pamela Partridge. He recalls that she's a senior majoring in journalism. He's seen her around campus. Once he saw her talking with Felicia Fernandez in the *Branding Iron* office. He's had no personal contact with her; they haven't been in any classes together.

One of the other two people is a tall, bearded man dressed in a navy blue business suit. Dale imagines he must be the dean of student services, Dr. Woolfson. The other person, a middle-aged woman, has long flowing red hair and a big-featured but not particularly pretty face. Dale surmises that she must be the other faculty representative. He finds out her name when introductions are made. She's Regina Wilson, a professor in the art department. Of the five, she is by far the most flamboyant. It's not only her wild red hair and her colorfully made-up face, it's also her yellow and red peasant dress and the purple bead necklace hanging around her neck. Her garish dress and animated face reminds him of a gypsy woman.

Dr. Woolfson mentions that the committee has reviewed his application materials, the resume, transcripts, and work sample. The fact that he is currently on the *Owen Wister Review* staff is a point in his favor. He obviously knows how the magazine is organized and how it functions. Then Dr. Woolfson and the four other committee members proceed to ask all the perfunctory questions which Dale concisely answers: he wants to edit the *OWR* because he's keenly interested in literature; he has the necessary qualifications because he's taken several literature courses and has diligently tried to developed his literary taste and judgment; and he has the added benefit of having experience in journalism, not only editorial work but also knowledge of printing techniques and layout and camera work.

As far as Dale can tell, the interview is going well. Four of the five committee members seem impressed with his answers. Only Professor Comstock appears to have doubts. Dale occasionally glances in his directions and notices that Comstock's expression is a sour one as if he's bitten into a lemon expecting an orange.

During an interlude in the interview, when Dr. Woolfson has to discuss some administrative matters with his secretary, Dale ponders why Comstock seems to disapprove of his application. Dale remembers when he first met Professor Comstock several months ago when he arrived at the University of Wyoming to attend graduate school. Dale had left his newspaper job in mid-May so he could take six semester hours during the summer term. The day after arriving on the fairly small but attractive campus, he walked into the Mass Communications Department office seeking information about his degree requirements and other matters. He was told to see his advisor, Professor Cyrus Comstock, who happened to be in his office. Dale walked down the hall and saw a man in his early fifties sitting at his desk. Comstock was dressed in dark corduroy pants, red suspenders, and a white dress shirt with an open collar. He had short brown hair, graying at the temples, and an undistinguished face except for a rather large, somewhat beaky nose. To Dale, he appeared to be an ordinary looking middle-aged man.

Dale knocked on the partly open door and Comstock glanced in his direction in an annoyed way. Dale noticed that the professor seemed busy making calculations in a notebook, but it wasn't a grade book and besides spring classes had been over for two weeks. But there was something in Comstock's manner as he hovered over his desk that puzzled Dale. The professor seemed somewhat anxious, as if he were adding up a long serious of important figures and the result kept coming out wrong and he couldn't figure out the mistake.

Dale rapped on the door again, this time slightly louder, and Comstock peered in his direction. His beaky nose and relatively small mouth and eyes definitely gave him an avian appearance, perhaps a look of a parrot or a parakeet. The expression on his face was not welcoming.

"All right, come in," Comstock said in a squawky tenor voice, which further confirmed the parrot image.

Dale entered and introduced himself. Comstock did not seem pleased to see him.

"I was told that you're my advisor," Dale said, hoping that this information would improve Comstock's attitude.

"Yes, yes, what do you want?"

"First, I need you to approve and sign my class schedule."

Comstock motioned for Dale to bring him the form. He took it and was about to sign his consent when he noticed something.

"You're taking broadcast law and film theory?"

"Yes."

"I thought you were a journalism student."

"I'm a graduate student in the mass communications program. I'm concentrating on film studies."

"Film studies! I don't teach those courses. I teach journalism. News writing and editing. Why am I your advisor?"

"I don't know. The secretary in the mass comm office told me you were my advisor."

Comstock shook his head and grumbled some words that Dale couldn't make out. He signed the form, however, and Dale noticed that he signed his name in a very slow, deliberate way as if he were actually forging his own signature.

Comstock extended the signed form in Dale's direction without further comment. Dale paused. He knew he hadn't made a favorable impression with his advisor so he thought maybe some additional conversation would help. However, he didn't know what to say to this rather cantankerous man. He glanced about the professor's office. It was a very clean, neat, and well-organized office. The furniture consisted of a desk and cushioned chair, a second wooden chair, a lamp, a filing cabinet, and a large bookcase filled with mostly journalism texts. Dale also noticed several pamphlets on the top shelf. He leaned closer to get a look at the title: *The Journal of North American Mass Communications Programs*. That didn't interest him. He looked at the lower shelf and noticed other publications that did interest him: several literary magazines lined up in a row and a dozen yearbooks. Dale noticed that the last yearbook was the 1971 yearbook.

"Does Wyoming publish a yearbook anymore?"

Comstock swirled around in his chair and stared at Dale.

"Our last yearbook was the 1971 one. It was a disgrace! Upon my recommendation, in fact, insistence, the university stopped publishing one after that."

"The university hasn't published a yearbook for almost ten years?"

"As I just informed you, the 1971 yearbook was the last one."

Dale knelt down at the lower shelf and pulled out the 1971 *Wyo*. The cover looked inoffensive. A silhouette of a cowboy on a brown background with the year 1971 embossed in golden letters.

"So what was wrong with it?"

Comstock opened his rather large hand and Dale deposited the book in his palm. Comstock flipped through several pages of the yearbook until he came to the yearbook staff photo. He showed it to Dale. The staff members were dressed like hippies, maybe they were hippies, and they lounged in the yearbook office in provocative poses: a guy and a girl slumped together on a tattered couch, their hippie attire disheveled, their vaguely smiling faces giving off a post-coital look of satisfaction; another female staffer sitting open legged in a chair, her skirt rising above her knees, her eyes closed as if in slumber; a male staffer squatting on the floor looking like he was about to defecate although his holey jeans were completely pulled up; another male staffer sitting on the desk, his whiskered face smiling in a disagreeably weary way as he extended a middle finger to the camera; Dale guessed the idea of the picture was to suggest how overwhelmed and tired the staff was from working so hard to make deadlines but when the viewer looked more closely he would see the vaguely obscene parody.

"Disgraceful!" thundered Comstock.

He quickly flipped a few more pages and showed another offensive photo. A fraternity picture that showed several of the members discreetly giving the camera the finger. Another photo of some guys making faces, leering actually, as their hands framed the crotch area of their jeans. Then Comstock pointed out several sexually suggestive headlines and cut-lines. He also pointed out several drug references in the body copy and headlines. The review of the yearbook took thirty minutes. Ninety percent of the yearbook was conventional; but it was obvious that the other ten percent, the naughty and offensive parts, still disturbed Comstock.

"And do you know how the staff got this objectionable material into the yearbook?"

Dale shook his head no.

"They showed me the innocuous version of those pages. The pages without the obscene photos and lewd copy."

Dale thought he was exaggerating. There wasn't anything really obscene in the yearbook. No profanity or nudity. Some of the photos were definitely rude. Some of the headlines and copy were suggestive. There were drug references. The humor in the yearbook was sophomoric and the attitude was a knee-jerk anti-authority kind. Dale didn't find those qualities interesting. Actually, even in 1971 he thought such attitudes were already becoming passé and counter-culturally conventional. But Dale had seen worse displays of counter cultural mores. When he'd attended a seminar at the University of Oklahoma he'd visited the yearbook office and looked through yearbooks from other schools. Some of the late '60s and early '70s yearbooks had profanity in them. Some had nudity, too, although nothing too explicit. Dale had noticed that most of those yearbooks were from fancy private schools in the east.

"You were the advisor to this yearbook?"

Comstock's leathery face turned a livid shade of scarlet. His eyes, a murky greenish color, narrowed and Dale noticed that there was an odd look in them, a strange intensity that he'd seen before. His mother sometimes had that kind of expression in her eyes before she went crazy. The enlarged pupils produced an almost shiny, eerie look of approaching lunacy.

"They hoodwinked me. They deceived and falsified. They produced a travesty without my knowledge or consent. I exacted revenge, however. I confiscated as many of the reprehensible yearbooks as I could lay my hands on. I would have burnt them if I had my way!"

Comstock's vehemence startled Dale. He took a step back and eyed his advisor rather warily. He wondered why Comstock would keep the notorious yearbook in his office if he despised it so. That fact seemed to suggest that Comstock perversely wanted to be agitated.

"Is the literary magazine still published?"

"Oh, yes. I couldn't get rid of that."

"That's too bad," Dale said with only a trace of irony.

Comstock gave him a searching look. Dale returned his gaze and noticed again that the professor's eyes had an agitated quality in them as if whatever they beheld would soon prove to be unbearable to witness. As soon as Dale thought of that, the professor averted his gaze to the floor. Dale also noticed that Comstock was vigorously rolling his ballpoint pen against the palm of his clenched hand.

"Is there anything else you want?" Comstock's voice no longer had any energy in it.

Dale said no and thanked the professor for his time. Comstock returned to the work on his desk, his shoulders noticeably slumped.

As Dale walked down the hall, he wondered why in the hell he'd been assigned Comstock for an advisor. The man taught news writing and editing not film courses! He thought Comstock was an odd bird but since the professor taught journalism writing and editing courses Dale thought he wouldn't have much contact with the Queeg-like professor.

Now as Dale sits in his chair waiting for the publications board to conclude his interview, he realizes that he can't avoid Comstock. As his advisor, Dale has to get his signature for his class schedule. Worse, Comstock supervises his independent study courses. Dale complained to Wagstaff several times about Comstock being his advisor and especially about his role as supervisor of his independent study work. But Wagstaff was jovially indifferent. Dale suspected that Wagstaff didn't serve as any graduate student's advisor. There were only ten graduate students in the department to begin with. Somehow, Wagstaff had escaped the onerous duty of advising a graduate student. Dale knew he'd never consent to be his advisor since it meant a few more hours of work. So, it looked like he was stuck with Comstock. So far, it hadn't been too bad. Comstock had no interest in Dale's independent study since it involved reviewing movies (his radio station work was evaluated by the station manager). Only once did Comstock comment on the nature of his independent study project. He told Dale that he had been gratified to read his disapproving review of the horror film *Nightwing*. Dale asked if Comstock had seen the film. The professor huffily replied, of course not! I don't see trashy movies!

Of course, Comstock's position on the publications board might prove detrimental to his desire to be editor of the literary magazine. Dale remembers what Nordberg told him: that Comstock had personally recruited Marsha Martin to run against him. That obviously meant he favors her application. Dale wonders why Comstock was even serving on the publications board. Why had he been appointed advisor to the yearbook when the university had one? It's obvious to any sensible observer that Comstock dislikes if not disapproves of literary and artistic expression. Having him sit on the publications board made about as much sense as having a vegetarian judge a BBQ eating contest.

Dr. Woolfson returns and apologizes for the delay. He says he believes it's Pamela's turn to ask questions.

Dale looks at Pamela Partridge. Once again he notices she has very white skin, fairly short blonde hair, and a round, plump face that matches her rather short, plump body.

"How would you describe your aesthetic philosophy? And with what criteria will you judge the submissions?"

"I don't know if I have an aesthetic philosophy except that I admire work that is original and convincingly presents a particular point of view. In other words, stories and poems that have their own integrity. I don't care for writing that is derivative or obvious. I would use that criteria in selecting work."

"So you don't subscribe to any current aesthetic philosophy or school of thought? Such as feminism or Marxism or deconstructionism?"

"No. I try and evaluate creative works on their own terms."

He's not sure if that's the answer Pamela wants to hear. He can't tell if she subscribes to any of those "aesthetic philosophies" just by looking at her. She dresses rather outdoorsy. Tan slacks and a thick blue sweater. On her feet are brown Timberland hiking boots, which a lot of students wear at Wyoming. Her hair isn't long but it doesn't have a severe kind of cut that some of the more overt feminists seem to sport. He thinks such a hairstyle is called a Page Boy. But even if he could deduce her personal philosophy by her appearance, he wouldn't alter his answer.

Pamela offers a small, somewhat ironic smile but says nothing in response.

Dr. Woolfson asks if anyone else has a question.

Comstock raises one finger and the dean nods for him to go ahead.

"Dale, I have one essential concern about having you serve as editor of the literary magazine. Will you have enough time to perform your duties? Since I serve as your advisor in your course of study, I know you are presently taking fifteen hours of coursework instead of the recommended twelve. In addition, you're working on the campus newspaper and the campus radio station. I also remind you that in the spring you will assist me in proofing *The Journal of North American Mass Communications Programs*. How can you possibly edit the literary magazine with all those responsibilities already before you?"

"I think I'll have time. I'm not going to work at the radio station next semester. I'm ahead of schedule on some of my class work, the screen-writing class in particular. Essentially, I've finished the first draft of the script that is required in next semester's class. By the time I need to assist with *The Journal of North American Mass Communications Programs*, most of the editorial work on the literary magazine will be finished. And I'll have a very good staff supporting me. I've already tentatively asked a couple of people to be on the staff next semester if I'm appointed and they've agreed. And if I'm selected I will do whatever is necessary to produce the best literary magazine in the university's history. I'll make the time."

That answer prompts small smiles of approval and agreeable nods from three of the board members. Comstock, however, looks unconvinced. He stares down at his notebook with a frown on his rather weathered face. Dale also notices that Nordberg doesn't smile or nod his head. But he's not frowning either.

A couple of more perfunctory questions are offered and Dale answers them satisfactorily and the interview is over. The Dean says the board will notify him of its decision by tomorrow by mail. He thanks Dale for applying for the position and attending this interview. Dale nods at the pub board members and exits the conference room, feeling that he's done pretty well. He walks across campus to his office. Once he arrives there, he sits at his desk and reviews some of his answers. He doesn't want to guess who will vote for him. He recalls their facial expressions and body language and the only person who clearly opposed him was Comstock. Dale doesn't know if the professor had much pull on the committee. He hopes not. Surely the four other members have some suspicions about Comstock's anti-literary impulses and therefore won't take his opinion too seriously.

Dale decides not to think about the vote. He'd done his best. Whatever happens will happen. He's not a fatalist, but he doesn't believe in worrying about things he can't change.

Just as Dale is about to go home, he hears footsteps echoing down the hall. Dale rises from his seat as Nordberg appears in the doorway.

"I thought I might find you here, Mr. Editor."

"I've been appointed?"

"That's right. You'll get the letter tomorrow."

"Good."

"It was a three-to-two vote in your favor."

"Who voted against me?"

"Comstock –"

"Of course."

"And Dr. Woolfson. But that was only because he preferred an undergraduate as editor. After you won the vote, he said you'd make an excellent editor."

"Did Comstock try and sway the others?"

"He only tried to sway me. The other two, Pamela and Professor Wilson, were definitely on your side."

"Sounds like you were the decisive vote then," Dale says, noticing once again that rather cagey look on Nordberg's face.

"Let's just say you owe me one."

"What?" Dale doesn't like the way that sounds. It's as if they had been colluding before the vote, which obviously wasn't the case.

"I'm joking. I was on your side from the beginning."

In spite of Nordberg's reassuring words, Dale notices he still has a rather insinuating expression.

"Well, thanks," Dale says. "I better get going."

"Say, Dale, what are you doing tomorrow night?"

"I'm going to the campus movie."

"I mean after that."

"I don't know. Probably nothing much."

"Would you like to go somewhere off-campus for a drink?"

Dale is not sure how to respond to the invitation. Nordberg stands there, his eyes narrowed, his mouth set in a slight grin. Nordberg seems to be an interesting, intelligent fellow but he has a quality about him that Dale mistrusts.

"Maybe. I don't know."

"Well, think about it. I'll be attending the movie too and afterward you can decide if you want to join us."

"Us?"

"A couple of other friends will probably join in."

Dale nods. For some reason he doesn't fully understand at that moment, Dale feels reassured that if accepts Nordberg's invitation they would be part of a larger group.

"Okay, we'll see," Dale says but with a more optimistic tone to his voice than before.

Nordberg grins and waves and departs the office. Dale wonders why Nordberg is so friendly. Even though he has shared an office with him for two months now, he doesn't know him that well. Neil Nordberg is a post-graduate student assisting the department chairman with a research project. Nordberg seems like an interesting guy and Dale appreciates how Nordberg helped him, especially in regard to teaching his class, but there is something about Nordberg that bothers him.

Well, he thinks, maybe if he gets to know Nordberg better that slightly uneasy feeling will fade.

It only takes ten minutes for Dale to traverse campus and approach the townhouse he shares with Gary Grabowski. Actually, they share only the bottom half of the house. A woman, Connie Bailey, is the owner of the house and she resides in the upper half.

The townhouse is located just across the street from the west end of campus. It's a white wooden house with a slanted red roof and Dale likes living there. Since it's so close to campus he can easily walk to all his classes and activities and doesn't have to worry about finding parking. He parks his car, a 1975 red Chevy Monza, on the street curb and only drives it a couple of times a week, usually to go to the grocery store or see a out-of-town movie in Fort Collins or Cheyenne. The rent is a little higher than he'd like to pay (he was used to paying cheap rent when he lived in Buffalo City working on the newspaper) but the bottom half of the house is spacious and everything works well.

Dale spent the summer living in a student dormitory, which wasn't a bad experience since he had a single room. He had lived in a dormitory twice before for short periods. The first time was in high school when he stayed in a dorm while attending Boys State for five days. The second time he lived in a dormitory was at the University of Oklahoma when he attended the Student Leadership Conference, also for five days.

Dale decided to stay in the dorm that summer because he thought it would be easier to find a place of his own in the late summer rather than at the beginning. When Grabowski arrived in August and asked him if he'd like to share a place together, Dale agreed. He'd only known Grabowski for a short time but he seemed like an okay guy. At least he practiced normal hygiene and didn't have any obvious personality problems so Dale reckoned he'd make an acceptable roommate.

And he has so far. The fact is that Dale is so busy with his classes and his student activities that he isn't home much at all. When he does arrive at their place, he doesn't stay for long. He eats a quick, simple meal, then goes back to campus to see a movie or he spends time at the newspaper office or radio station or he ventures downtown to see a current movie.

After tonight's quick dinner, he plans on going downtown and seeing a classic movie at The Trout Theater, which is sort of Laramie's repertory movie theatre. The owner of the theatre, Shane Starrette, shows current mainstream films during most of the week but on Thursday nights he screens a classic Hollywood or a foreign language film. Occasionally, he also shows "art" films, those low-budget, independent movies that generally don't attract large audiences. Dale enjoys going to the Trout Theatre. It is a cozy and intimate theatre, well maintained and not run-down, and once Shane found out that he was reviewing films for the campus newspaper he gave Dale a free movie pass.

Dale walks down the steps that lead to the lower half of the house, opens the door, and walks inside. It's only five p.m. but the November sky is already darkening outside and inside the house the living room is gloomy, the only light coming from the glare of the television set.

Gary Grabowski sits in the easy chair only ten feet away from the television screen. Dale walks over and says hey and Grabowski mutters hi in return.

Dale glances at the TV to see what his roommate is so avidly watching. It's not the news, it's not sports, instead Grabowski is watching some dumb game show, *The Family Feud.*

Dale doesn't understand why Grabowski likes watching television so much. Since Laramie is fairly far from any large metropolitan center – Denver is 120 miles to the south and Cheyenne is 80 miles to the east – television is transmitted by cable and that means there are a few more stations to watch than the usual network ones. But as far as Dale can tell the additional stations broadcast similar junk. When he has time, Dale occasionally watches a sporting event, the World Series or college and pro football, but otherwise he wishes that the television didn't exist.

Grabowski, however, often spends part of his evenings watching TV.

Dale studies his roommate as he sits in the easy chair gazing at the inanity on the television screen. Ordinarily, a game show as stupid as *The Family Feud* wouldn't interest him. He prefers cop shows and risqué sitcoms like *Three's Company*.

Grabowski is of average height but appears somewhat taller because of his long legs. His trunk is thick and he doesn't seem to have a waist. His long legs just seem to lead to his hips, which lead to a shortened torso then to fairly broad sloping shoulders. Grabowski also seems to lack a neck, but that's because he tends to droop his chin close to his chest as he sits and watches television. He has a very white complexion with pale blue eyes and fairly long blonde hair. His hair has a very fine texture and when Dale looks down on Grabowski's head, as he is doing now, he can see tiny pink patches of his scalp peeking through the fine strands of hair. The rest of his features are fairly nondescript. A rather ordinary nose and a smallish mouth that rarely smiles. His light blue eyes are small and slightly beady and he wears stylish spectacles with large lenses.

Dale waits for Grabowski to say something. Perhaps he will ask about his interview for editor of the literary magazine. Grabowski knows Dale is vying for the job. In fact, Grabowski told Dale just yesterday if he became editor then he might be interested in serving as photography editor. That's because Grabowski is a photographer. He worked on a small daily newspaper as a photographer after getting his B.S. in journalism from Dickinson State College in North Dakota. Grabowski wasn't raised in North Dakota, however. He's from Chicago. From the Polack section of Chicago (that's what Grabowski said with a kind of defiant note of pride in his voice when they first met). He has a fairly large family – he's one of six kids – and his father is employed by the city's public works. That's about all Dale knows about Grabowski's background. Gary doesn't talk that much about himself.

In fact, Grabowski is rather taciturn by nature. Dale is beginning to think that Grabowski's laconic nature is more of a pose than a genuine reflection of his personality. He saw him once sitting in an off-campus bar having an animated conversation with another young man, whom he later found out was a history grad student by the name of Pablo Mesa. After speaking at length in a strangely loud way, Grabowski had quaffed the remaining half of the mug of beer in one long gulp.

Maybe that's what it takes for Grabowski to get gabby: drinking lots of beer.

But Dale has never seen his roommate so uncommunicative. Dale realizes that something is wrong.

"Did something happen?"

Grabowski continues to watch the television. It's as if he's been hypnotized by the stupidity.

"Gary, did something unfortunate happen?"

Grabowski snickers. "Unfortunate? Yeah, I guess you could say that."

"Well, what?"

"I got a call from Christina. She wants a divorce."

"Your wife called? When?"

"An hour ago. She couldn't even wait until after five when the rates go down."

Dale has met Christina twice. The first time was when he rode along with Grabowski when they drove up to where she was living in Cody. They left Laramie at sunrise in Grabowski's Ford Ranger pick-up truck. Dale had worked a night shift at the dormitory desk and he only got three hours of sleep. Grabowski's truck had a camper shell and Dale could have taken a nap during the trip but Grabowski never suggested that although he knew Dale had worked overnight at the dormitory desk.

Instead, Grabowski drove the pick-up down the highway mostly in silence only offering an attempt at conversation when Dale threatened to fall asleep.

They made it to Cody after seven hours of driving. As soon as Dale met Mrs. Grabowski he knew coming up with Gary was a mistake. Christina was as blonde and fair as her husband with the same kind of thin, fine straight hair. She didn't really have a pretty face. Her lips were too thin and her nose too long and narrow but she did have attractive blue-green eyes. She was tall with long legs but a skinny figure. She wore small pink shorts with a blue T-shirt but even the small shorts didn't make her appealing. When she turned around, Dale, as he almost instinctively did with girls, glanced at her bottom and even though the nether curve of her pale buttocks protruded out of the shorts, he hardly felt a thrill.

The problem was that Christina was unhappy and she didn't disguise it for Dale. She didn't want Gary to go to graduate school in Laramie. The university was all the way down at the southern part of the state. It was so far away that they would only get to see each other occasionally. Christina didn't want to move to Laramie. She had a good job in Cody working for the state tourism office. If she went down to Laramie what would she do? As Dale observed the two of them together, it was evident that Gary didn't really want his wife to come to Laramie either. He made no attempt to persuade her.

Somehow Dale, exhausted from lack of sleep, made it through the evening. He slept on the couch of their little rented house and woke up to a sullen husband and wife. Why had he consented to go on this trip? To see more of Wyoming. He'd never been out of the southeastern part of the state. The trip hadn't been that scenic, however. Most of the journey they traveled through barren semi-desert until they got to the more attractive area around Cody. When they drove into town, Dale had looked west and saw the hazy outlines of the Grand Tetons Mountains. Dale hoped that Grabowski would suggest a trip west the next day so he could see the magnificent mountains. Instead, Dale accompanied the Grabowskis and an unattractive female friend of theirs on a trip to a small town on the Montana border so Gary could play in a softball tournament with his old team. Dale sat in the stands with the two women and watched Golden Boy ground out into a double play, pop up, and hit a sacrifice fly. The sac fly did tie up the game but Grabowski's old team, even with his inspirational return, lost in extra innings.

The next day Grabowski and Dale drove back to Laramie. Dale tried to make conversation but Gary wasn't in much of a mood to talk. Christina hadn't been very friendly to either one of them before they set off on their journey back.

The second time Dale encountered Christina was one month later when he drove to Cheyenne to pick her up at the airport and bring her back to Laramie. Grabowski couldn't make the trip because he had a court date. He'd received a traffic ticket and instead of paying the full fine he wanted to contest the ticket. So, it was up to Dale to pick up Gary's wife. When Dale arrived at the airport, Christina didn't seem pleased to see him. She didn't seem to appreciate the fact that he was driving a 160 mile round trip to pick up his roommate's wife. For that matter, Grabowski didn't seem too appreciative either. He hadn't volunteered to pay for the car's gasoline, which Dale was beginning to realize was characteristic of Grabowski's lack of roomie propriety.

At first, Christina treated Dale with as much warmth as he suspected she would later demonstrate toward her semi-estranged husband but as the trip progressed and Dale patiently asked her questions she seemed to grow to tolerate his presence. She even told him a little about herself. Christina met Gary at college in North Dakota. Unlike Grabowski, she was a native North Dakotan. Her father was a wheat farmer. She told him her maiden name, a strange Norwegian name that he had a hard time pronouncing accurately: Gudmundsdottir. It was the kind of Scandinavian name that had a slash through the O. Christina said her family disapproved of the match. Gary was

Polish and Catholic and they were Norwegian and Lutheran. But they were married during their senior year in college and first lived as a couple in a small hamlet in North Dakota where Gary got his first newspaper job, then later in a small town not far from Cody.

When Dale turned off the interstate to head into Laramie, Christina looked very seriously at him and asked if he knew whether Gary was having an affair. Dale said that he didn't know, but he did know. Not that Grabowski was having an affair with a woman exactly; it was more like he was having brief sexual liaisons with as many women as he could find. Dale guessed he was trying to make up for lost opportunity. After all, Gary married while still in college. Still, Dale didn't like it when he came home in the evening and heard a female voice murmuring from behind Grabowski's closed door. Dale had to admit that his displeasure was more a consequence that he wasn't having any sexual affairs, even the brief kind. He'd met several girls so far but only a few had taken his fancy and they had steady boyfriends. And the one he really found appealing, Deborah Pierson, he knew he had no chance with.

After talking with Christina on that ride back to Laramie, Dale was even more disapproving of Grabowski's tomcatting around. Dale was old fashioned enough to believe that a man ought to keep his marriage vows, and besides, it was obvious that Gary's adulterous behavior was hurting Christina.

That weekend Dale managed to keep himself as scarce as possible. He stayed away most of her visit except to sleep in his room, spending even more time than usual at movie theatres and the newspaper office and the radio station. However, he was present when Christina was about to leave for the airport Sunday afternoon. This time Gary was going to drive her to Cheyenne. When Dale said goodbye to Mrs. Grabowski he had a feeling he wouldn't be seeing her again. He just didn't think it would be a result of a divorce.

"Do you think she'll go through with the divorce?"

Grabowski shrugs his sloped shoulders. "Yeah. In fact, she

said she's seeing somebody else."

"That's too bad."

Grabowski removes his gaze from the television screen and looks at Dale. "Ehh, no biggie."

Dale has often heard Grabowski use that expression. When he got a flat tire, or when the kitchen drain clogged, or even when he got the speeding ticket, all those minor misfortunes were labeled a "no biggie." Well, getting divorced certainly seems to qualify as "a biggie." But Dale realizes that this is Grabowski playing his laconic, down-to-earth, unflappable persona where life's misfortunes whether major or minor could be dismissed with that simple-minded phrase.

"Okay," Dale says. He turns to go to his room when he pauses. "I'm going to the Trout theatre to see a classic movie. An early David Lean film, *Brief Encounter*. Do you want to come?"

Grabowski's beady eyes have returned to *The Family Feud*. "No thanks."

"It's supposed to be a good movie."

"You're the movie expert, Dale. I think I'll just stay home tonight."

"Okay. I'll see you later."

Grabowski nods and Dale, instead of going to his room for an hour, decides he'll just go ahead and leave and spend some time in the town library before the movie. He walks over to the closet to fetch his flannel jacket, the nights are turning cold now, and as he is about to open the front door to leave he hears Grabowski's voice. He's talking on the telephone. To one of his paramours.

2

Walking down the hall in the Mass Communications Department Dale hears an unusual sound coming from Professor Comstock's office: laughter.

Dale pauses outside the partly closed door. A male voice, Comstock's, is producing a sound that resembles the braying of a mule. A female voice dances an octave higher but the laughter is not much more appealing. It sounds something like a squeal.

Dale, curious to know the cause of Comstock's uncharacteristic good humor, moves closer to the door and peers through the crack. He sees the same young woman who had attended the publications board meeting yesterday, Pamela Partridge. She's dressed in the same outdoorsy way as if she's just returned from an invigorating hike: blue jeans, a red lumberjack shirt, a green feather down vest, and brown Timberland hiking boots. She's sitting in the wooden chair at a perpendicular angle to Comstock's desk. On her plump, almost porcine face, a broad smile remains. She has good teeth. Her fair complexion looks rosier than before, no doubt a consequence of her hearty laughter. Still smiling, she pushes the strands of her blonde hair back behind her pink ears.

Comstock is leaning forward in his leather chair gazing at Pamela in a strangely avid way, as if she were a nicely roasted piece of pork that he'd been offered after a three day fast. Dale had never seen his advisor look so animated. Pamela says something that Dale can't quite hear but the quip produces a roar of laughter from Comstock. They chat for another minute then Pamela rises to leave. Comstock jumps up from his seat, puts a paw on her shoulder to give it a friendly squeeze then abruptly turns to his desk, and opens a side drawer.

"What color would you like, my dear?"

"Red."

Comstock produces an old fashioned red lollipop and gives it to Pamela. She giggles, takes the candy, says "bye bye" and leaves his office.

She exits so quickly that Dale is caught standing outside the door. He doesn't even try to pretend he wasn't peeking. The whole scene has been so peculiar that he feels more curiosity than embarrassment at having witnessed it.

"Oh excuse me," Pamela says as she side steps Dale.

He moves out of her way and follows her as she walks down the hallway. He glances at her and sees she is blushing. A crimson wave creeps into her pale face and her earlobes in particular are glowing red.

"What was that about?" he asks.

"What do you mean?"

"I've never heard Comstock laugh. I didn't think he was capable of such a spontaneous emotion."

"He's a very nice man once you get to know him."

"He's nice to you. He gave you a *lolly*."

Pamela's rather small mouth frowns but her green eyes don't show any disapproval. In fact, they seem to twinkle in merriment.

Dale remembers another odd scene a few months ago when he was leaving his office and he saw a couple of female undergraduates leaving Comstock's office. They were giggling and holding candy. When he walked by them he noticed they were clutching Tootsie Rolls.

"Tootsies and lollipops. I didn't know Comstock operated a candy store. He's never given me any sweets."

Pamela's mouth now smiles to match the mirth in her eyes. "I've always suspected that you were a naughty boy. Making fun of a nice old gentleman like Professor Comstock."

"What do you mean suspected?"

They walked down the outside steps of Gowdy Hall and Dale opens the door that reveals the student quadrangle before them.

"From the way you write your movie reviews. Always making fun of things you don't like."

"I just happen to have a sardonic sense of humor. Anyway, some things ought to be made fun of."

"Is that so?"

"Of course. We should deflate the pompous and ridicule the pretentious."

Pamela gives him a skeptical look.

"Yeah, I know. That sounded a little pompous and pretentious."

Pamela laughs. She doesn't have a musical laugh but he is glad to know she has a sense of humor. Before today he wasn't so sure.

"By the way," she says, her laughter now completely gone, "congratulations on being selected as the editor of the *OWR*."

"Thanks. I'm looking forward to editing it."

"I voted for you in spite of your lack of political awareness."

"Yes, I'm aware that I lack political awareness."

She doesn't laugh this time; only a small and not entirely convincing smile appears on her face.

"Why aren't you writing for *The Branding Iron* or helping with the *OWR*?" Dale asks.

"Actually, I edited the *BI* last year. This year I'm working on my senior honors thesis. I also have an internship with *The Boomerang*."

She means the *Laramie Boomerang*, the town's daily. He nods and tries to look impressed. However, the newspaper isn't very good.

"Well," Dale says, "I'm headed over to the English department. I have my Modern American Novel class. Where are you going?"

"To the *Boomerang*."

Dale starts to walk away. "I guess that means you'll soon be returning."

"Very funny," she says, "but I've heard that before."

Dale gives her a wave and she nods a goodbye and heads in the opposite direction toward the student parking lot. As he walks away he glances back and sees Pamela Partridge's retreating figure, in particular her rather broad behind. He's not sure if he finds her appealing or not. She seems bright; they probably have similar interests. He doesn't think she's especially attractive. Even though in general he likes fair women, and prefers the plump over the skinny, she might be a little too porcine. In addition, there was something about her manner, her attitude, which irked him a little during the publications board meeting. In spite of the laughter he's heard today he thinks she might be too serious, too "aware" about socio-politics. And her attire. Even though he dresses in a rustic way – today he's wearing his usual duds, Levi's and a lumberjack shirt and cowboy boots – he isn't sure if he appreciates that look on a girl.

He shrugs. He isn't even sure she was flirting with him. In fact, he has a vague feeling that Pamela Partridge officially disapproves of flirting.

But Mimi, on the other hand, definitely doesn't disapprove of flirting.

Dale walks out of the classroom with her. Their Modern American Novel class is over and she's walking sort of close to him, occasionally swinging her hip out so it bumps against his thigh. He isn't sure what to do in this situation. If she were his girlfriend, he'd give her a friendly grab or maybe playfully slap her rump but she isn't his girlfriend. Mimi claims she has a boyfriend back in Denver. They've been going together since their senior year in high school. He's attending Denver University on an academic scholarship. Mimi wanted to go to DU, too, but it's a private university and the tuition was too high. She didn't get into the University of Colorado, so she came to

Wyoming. She goes back to Denver every other weekend.

That's her story and maybe it's true. All Dale knows is that she's the flirtiest girl he's come across in a long time. She flirts with just about every guy on campus it seems. Lately, it's been him. Which is okay; he likes her. She has a good sense of humor, loves literature and movies, and isn't pretentious or snobby. He thinks she's sort of attractive, too. She has long, dark, curly hair. She wears it in a wild, tangled way. Her face is more cute than pretty with big brown eyes and an animated mouth. Her nose is a little large and her face doesn't have a well-defined curvature that the prettiest girls seem to have but on the whole he thinks she is rather attractive.

Mimi also has a figure that she describes as "old fashioned." Instead of a slender figure that is preferred in contemporary culture, she has more of a '50s figure: big breasts and big hips. Actually, Dale thinks she's a little on the heavy side but he would never tell her that. She's self-conscious about being fat and she is always babbling about her diets and weight gain and losses. She's a very talkative girl. If he didn't like her rather zany personality he probably wouldn't be able to tolerate her loquacity.

They walk outside together and Mimi – that's her nickname; her real name is Miriam Morgenstern – stops and gushes: "What a wonderful day! Look at that azure sky. So clear and crisp and clean!"

For a mid-November day in the Rockies, the weather is unseasonably warm.

"Yeah, it's a fine day."

"Fine? Dale you are so understated. Don't you ever want to exclaim over the joy that is living! Just smell the pine trees. Doesn't that musky odor awaken something deep and primal inside you?"

"Yeah, my allergies."

"I mean, we should adulate nature. We should rhapsodize about the natural world. That's one reason why I came to Laramie. To live in a medium sized town that still basks in the bosom of nature. I suppose Denver used to be that way fifty years ago. Now, the steel and pavement and concrete and gas exhaust and pollution overwhelm its natural beauty. I might as well be living in Cleveland!"

Miriam aspires to be a poet.

"Are you going to tonight's movie? Of course, you are. You're Dale, the movie critic, who sees every film he can. I can't wait to see tonight's flick. The divine Miss M!"

"I didn't know Bette Midler starred in *Some Like It Hot*."

"No, I'm speaking about the original divine Miss M. Actually, the divine Miss MM. Marilyn Monroe!"

Mimi is an ardent fan of Marilyn Monroe. That's how he and Mimi became friends: when she discovered that he enjoyed watching her movies.

"One MM going to see another MM," muses Dale with only a slight irony to his voice. He doesn't want to tease Mimi too much. She's too sensitive. "Isn't that deeply meaningful?"

"You're so right! Must be fate. To share the same initials with my favorite movie star of all time."

"You do know that Marilyn Monroe is her stage name."

"Of course I know! I know everything about Marilyn. Her birth name was Norma Jean Baker and she lived in orphanages and foster homes and suffered horrible abuse! I know all about the most lovely leading actress of all time."

Dale isn't sure about all of Mimi's details. For instance, he doesn't think Marilyn's last name was Baker but he isn't an expert on such matters and he doesn't want to dampen Mimi's enthusiasm.

"Well, I must be off! I'm supposed to meet Spencer at the union. He's promised to help me with my psychology class. Oh, I do wish I were as studious as you are, Dale."

"Wait a minute. Did you say Spencer?"

"Yes, Spencer Dribble. Do you know him? Oh, he's so intellectual! He wants to be my beau but as you know I am always faithful to my Joe DiMaggio."

"I only know Spencer Dribble through correspondence."

"You two are pen pals? Astonishing! But Spencer is such a man of letters. I must be off! But promise me one thing before I go. Sit next to me at tonight's screening. I need your calm demeanor next to me or else I might loose complete control."

"Okay. If you wish."

"Goodbye, Dale! I look forward to tonight's sweet meeting."

Mimi waves and sashays down the sidewalk on her way to the Memorial Union. Dale watches her retreating figure thinking if she lost ten pounds she'd have dimensions more like her movie idol. Aside from her weight, her only other drawback was her glossolalia. Nevertheless, he finds her somewhat attractive. He even asked her out on a date a month ago, the first girl he'd solicited since arriving in Laramie. She said ordinarily she would love to go out with him, he was so cute! but she had a steady boyfriend, Joe DiMaggio. Dale later found out that her boyfriend didn't have that name. Mimi was joking or fantasizing. But his name was something Italian. Maybe D'Amato. Oh, well. That's how it went. The few girls he found attractive have boyfriends or are married or were too tall for him. But something has to change. He's getting increasingly frustrated at not having some romantic activity. He doesn't think he'll resort to Grabowski's behavior: Picking up chicks in bars or settling for unattractive but receptive coeds. But who knows?

As Dale approaches his residence he notices the tops of several letters sticking out of the black mailbox. A good sign. Perhaps Will Whitaker or Teri Boswell has written.

Dale pulls out the mail and shuffles through it. Two bills, some junk mail, and two letters, both addressed to him. What a pleasant coincidence. Letters from both of his regular correspondents.

Dale throws the bills and junk mail on the kitchen counter then goes into his bedroom to read the letters from Will and Teri. In addition to a mattress on the floor, his room is furnished with a table and a lamp, an old wooden chair, and a small desk where he keeps his manual typewriter. He settles down in the chair and reads Teri's letter first. He's known her since his college days. When he edited his undergraduate newspaper, she served as assistant editor. After he graduated and took a job at the *Buffalo City Stampede*, a small daily in western Oklahoma, Teri wrote occasionally, usually regaling him with the latest news at Galilee Nazarene College. But since she graduated last May and found a newspaper job herself, also on a small daily in Duncan, Oklahoma, she has written with more regularity.

Teri was a fairly good friend while Dale attended GNC. They shared similar interests: journalism, literature, movies. She had something of a sardonic sense of humor (for a Nazarene girl) and a candid personality that he liked. What brought them closer as platonic friends was when she joined him when he drove from Oklahoma to Wyoming. The trip took two days and they had plenty of time to talk and catch up on what had happened during the past year when Dale was working on the newspaper in Buffalo City and she was enjoying her senior year at GNC.

Now, at his desk Dale quickly reads her five page letter, penned in her own spiky handwriting. Most of the letter concerns two scandals involving GNC people. The first scandal happened last spring just as classes had concluded. An unmarried female English professor's contract had not been renewed. Essentially, she had been fired. The professor, Bronwyn Ayers, had been suspected of hanky panky. Specifically, she had been dating a married man who actually was separated from his wife. Such behavior wasn't adultery but it was close enough for the Nazarene administration and she'd been relieved of her duties. Dale knew Bronwyn. During his senior year, he'd been in the poetry writing class she taught. She also advised the college yearbook and Dale occasionally ran into her in the student union. She was a young woman, in her mid-20s, and fairly attractive. Her most noticeable features were her very long, partially braided auburn hair, the boots she wore, her tall, slender figure, and most prominent of all, her large breasts. She often wore sweaters, which, of course, made her breasts even more noticeable even though the sweaters were modestly styled. Dale had always been partial to the female posterior but he definitely appreciated Bronwyn's magnificent mammaries.

The second scandal involved a former GNC student that Dale had been friendly with during his senior year, a fellow named David Hawkins. Hawkins had been something of a BMOC at GNC. He started on the varsity basketball team, made academic honor societies, and was involved in several campus organizations. Soon after he graduated last spring, he married his girlfriend, Hope Jorgenson. Dale had known her, too; in fact, she'd been his ex-girlfriend's roommate for two years. The happy couple moved to the Tulsa area where David got a job coaching junior high athletics and teaching English. Most people at GNC, although not Dale, thought they were a perfect couple.

Teri reveals the nature of the Hawkins scandal on page three of her letter:

You won't believe this, Dale! But David turned out to be a homosexual. I heard a week ago that one day he just left Hope. In a note he apologized to Hope for misleading her about his true nature. He apparently drove to Colorado to stay a short while with his brother Joseph (remember we stayed the night at Joe's and Emily's house in Longmont?) and rumor has it that he's now in San Francisco. Weird, huh? Who would have thought that he'd turn out that way? Not Hope, I bet. I feel really sorry for her. She's back in Galilee now. She's handling the break up fairly well. They were only married for five months. Rumor has it that she's going to try and get the marriage annulled. Apparently, they never had, ahem, successful relations.

The rest of Teri's letter discusses her duties at the newspaper. She's graduated from copy editing and writing obits to actually writing news stories. She likes her job although she was surprised by how many of the newspaper staff cursed and smoked. Especially the sports writers. (She underlined sports writers since Dale had been the sports editor at the *Buffalo City Stampede*. However, no one smoked in that newsroom.)

Dale feels a little strange reading her letter, especially the part about David Hawkins. He knew Hawkins true nature; that is, he suspected he did. For a few months they had been fairly good friends even though they traveled in somewhat different social circles. Hawkins had been in many of the same classes as Dale and David's girlfriend, Hope, was a roommate of Dale's girlfriend, Amanda. But one incident made him question Hawkins' "nature." It was when he played racquetball with Hawkins. Dale thought he had noticed Hawkins sneaking looks at him while changing in the locker room. He wasn't sure, however. Afterwards, David made some suggestive remarks on the drive back to campus. From that point on, Dale refused Hawkins' offers of racquetball and their friendship cooled.

Now Dale wonders if he should have warned someone, maybe even Hope, about David. Of course, he didn't know for certain that Hawkins was a homosexual (or maybe bisexual; that was the implied subject of Hawkins' suggestive remarks). He didn't know that Hawkins would marry Hope. However, Hawkins was going steady with Hope when he made his pass at him so maybe he should have warned her. But what would he have said? Don't marry that guy because he'd rather be a peeping Tom in the men's locker room rather than the women's?

It was a sad turn of events. Dale liked Hawkins and he thought Hope was a nice girl. He felt sorry for both of them.

To get his mind off the Hawkins' scandal, Dale decided to read Will Whitaker's letter. Dale especially liked corresponding with Will. He'd met him while working at the *Buffalo City Stampede*. Will had been a "special" reporter for five days to help with the paper's coverage of President Carter's visit to the rather small and colorless town of Buffalo City. Before Will had arrived to help out, Dale had been mostly a lonely and bored young man. All his co-workers at the newspaper were older than he was. He didn't have any real friends and most of the time he simply worked long hours and then went home and read novels. Will's arrival changed that, at least for a few days. They immediately hit it off. They had a similar kind of sense of humor, they liked the same kind of things, and they were interested in books and movies and culture. They were curious about intellectual matters. In short, they seemed like kindred souls. There were some obvious differences. Will's background was more sophisticated than Dale's. He'd gone to a prep school. He knew a lot more about politics and cultural matters. Will was two years older so Dale didn't mind that his friend knew more about certain things. In fact, Dale regarded Will as sort of a mentor. They only spent five days in each other's company, but Dale felt that he'd found a true friend, especially a kind of friend that he'd been looking for since high school: an intellectual friend.

At the time of their first meeting, Will was finishing his master's degree in journalism at the University of Oklahoma. He'd gotten his undergraduate degree there as well and had edited the student newspaper his senior year. After Will returned to Norman to finish his studies, he wrote a fairly short but highly entertaining letter and Dale responded. They had been corresponding ever since.

After graduating from OU last spring, Will moved to Minneapolis where his parents were living. He found a part time job as a dispatcher at WCCO, a television station in Minneapolis-St. Paul. That fall he started graduate studies, this time in political science, at the University of Minnesota. One of the recurring themes of Will's letters had been what direction he should take: should he work in journalism, preferably as a newspaper reporter, or should he remain in academia and perhaps earn his Ph.D.? Dale had responded that Will would be successful at either occupation, but he thought Will had remarkable skills as a reporter. His work for the *Stampede* had been consistently excellent.

One of the highlights of the past year occurred in mid-August when Will and a friend of his named George Alexander drove to Wyoming to visit Dale. They stayed three days and their lively presence had dispelled Dale's gloom over his relative isolation on campus. They drove down to Denver, saw a funny movie, *The In-Laws*, then later drove down to Fort Collins and saw another good movie, *Breaking Away*. After the movie, they drove west into the mountains and hiked into the forest. And during these adventures the three of them engaged in clever banter and intellectual speculation. Dale never had so much cerebral fun.

George, a short man who was going prematurely bald at twenty-five, was almost as perceptive and witty as Will. He was certainly as intelligent. George primary interest was political philosophy. After graduating from OU with a degree in history and political science, he attended Georgetown University's law school. He was on track to receive his degree next year. Dale enjoyed being in George's company but he continued to feel a special kinship with Will.

After Will and George left Laramie to drive to Minnesota, Dale felt that familiar sense of isolation and loneliness return. He'd not made one real friend during the summer at Wyoming. He was the only GTA on campus at that time and the two classes he took only had a few other students in them, all undergraduates.

Fortunately, he had Will's and Teri's letters to look forward to. They got him through the rest of the summer and when fall classes started he became very busy so he didn't feel that lonely isolation as much as before.

About half of Will's new letter described his graduate school courses, his relationships with his professors and fellow grad students, and his work at the television station. The other half discussed what books he'd been reading (he still read novels and non-fiction books in addition to the demanding required reading for his classes), the movies he'd seen, and the magazine and newspaper articles he'd perused. Enclosed in this letter was a photocopied article from *The New Republic*. Will had mentioned that magazine so often that Dale had begun regularly reading it, too, along with *The Atlantic* and *Harper's*.

But the most interesting part of the letter detailed plans regarding a trip they would take together during Christmas Break. Will planned on flying down to Denver where Dale would pick him up and they would drive back to Minnesota and Dale would spend Christmas with Will and his parents.

Dale hears Gary Grabowski coming in. He leaves the letters on his desk and walks into the living room. He sees his roommate removing his parka and hanging it in the closet.

"What's up?" Dale asks. That was his usual greeting.

"S.O.S.," says Grabowski. That was his favorite acronym: same old shit.

He walks over to the television, turns it on, and sits down on the sofa. Grabowski isn't watching the tube, exactly. He just wants it on.

Dale glances at the TV. He doesn't recognize the show nor does he care. Just S.O.S. to borrow Grabowski's phrase.

"I'm thinking about making kielbasa for dinner," Grabowski says. "Want some?"

"Those big sausages?"

"Yeah. I bought some at the supermarket. Make some kasza and kapusta kiszona to go with."

"Sounds like a special K kind of meal."

"Huh?"

"All the K's."

Grabowski nods. "Yeah, Polack food has a lot of K's in it."

Dale thinks it's sort of odd that Grabowski likes that ethnic slur. "What kind of food are those last K's?"

"Kasza is a grain. Kapusta kiszona is sauerkraut."

"Sauerkraut?"

"Yeah, it's good."

"I think I'd rather have a chicken fried steak."

"I never knew what a chicken fried steak was until I moved to North Dakota."

"The best chicken friend steak is in the Southwest."

"I'll take your word for it."

Dale thinks they've had enough discussion about cultural

differences in cuisine. He doesn't want to eat Grabowski's kielbasa again, though. Those sausages were too fatty the last time. Actually, he and Grabowski rarely eat together. They share expenses for the rent and utilities but not groceries. Grabowski wanted to split the food cost in half and Dale went along with it for a couple of months but he soon learned that his roommate had a rather voracious appetite. Also a taste for odd food, not only kielbasa, but also some strange soup, a kind of Polish borscht. Dale paid his half of the food bill but ended up eating only about a quarter of the food. So, he decided the two should abrogate their original agreement. Grabowski occasionally tries to entice him in partaking in one of the meals he cooks. Dale acknowledges that Gary isn't a bad chef. Gary has told him that he often cooked when living with his wife but Dale has no interest in sharing food again. He'll continue to eat his simple fare, sandwiches and canned soup and TV dinners (minus the TV viewing) and when he needs a larger meal he'll splurge by going to a diner and getting chicken fried steak or biscuits and gravy.

"We could order delivery pizza," Grabowski says.

"Yeah. But half of it has to be simple. Just Canadian bacon. Not all that stuff you get."

"Would I have to pay more?"

Grabowski's half, with all the extra ingredients, boosted the price quite a bit.

"No, we'll share even-Steven."

"Okay then, let's get pizza. I'm not in the mood to cook a big dinner anyway. Especially for one."

Dale sometimes thought they were the Wyoming equivalent of *The Odd Couple*.

"Let's order it soon," Dale says. "I'm going to the campus movie tonight at eight."

"What's showing?"

"*Some Like It Hot*."

That information does not impress Grabowski. He shrugs his sloping shoulders. Sometimes Dale can't believe that his roommate is a graduate student in journalism. Well, photographic journalism. He doesn't seem to have much intellectual ambition or curiosity. Dale has never seen Grabowski reading a book except for a textbook for one of his classes. He's never seen him reading a novel. He doesn't appreciate movies, at least not classic films or art films or foreign language films. Grabowski once said he liked "popcorn movies." He doesn't like going to a movie and thinking about what it means. Grabowski doesn't have much taste in music either. He doesn't have many albums but what he has consists of two genres: country and heavy metal. He said he grew up listening to Led Zeppelin, Black Sabbath, and AC/DC. He liked loud music. But when he moved to North Dakota to attend college he acquired a taste for some country music. Willie Nelson, Waylon Jennings, Johnny Cash, and some of the "outlaw country music." Dale shared his taste for one country musician, Johnny Cash, but not the rest.

It surprised Dale to learn that Grabowski grew up listening to heavy metal bands. Grabowski has such a lackadaisical attitude, and goes through his daily routine in such a dull if not lethargic manner that Dale can hardly imagine him as a headbanger in his younger days.

Dale wonders if Grabowski smoked dope while listening to his Led Zeppelin records. He has never seen his roommate puffing pot. As far as he knows, he doesn't indulge. But marijuana costs more than beer and Grabowski is definitely frugal in his habits. He drinks beer but not to excess. Grabowski never gets drunk. Not even tipsy. About the only thing he seems to rouse himself for is seducing unattractive coeds and bored waitresses. That is another quality that puzzles Dale. Grabowski isn't much to look at and he doesn't have a dynamic personality and doesn't have much money and doesn't make scintillating conversation and he completely lacks charm. And yet he seems to find bedmates fairly regularly. He found one last night. Dale saw her slipping out of the house around midnight. She was somewhat more attractive than his usual plain playmates. Dale was surprised and a little envious. What did that young woman see in Grabowski? Maybe she likes men with long legs and no necks.

"*Some Like it Hot* is a really funny movie," Dale says, trying to forget about his roommates' perplexing sexual prowess.

"It's a comedy?"

"A farce. Very funny."

"Maybe I'll go then. I don't want to see some serious, arty film though."

"It's not. It's a film by Billy Wilder."

Grabowski shrugs his sloping shoulders to indicate he's not impressed.

"You don't seem to have much interest in movies."

"Depends on the movie. I like movies that don't preach, don't teach, and don't philosophize."

"That's most Hollywood movies." Dale wonders what Grabowski really likes. He's never heard him get excited about anything except for food and maybe photography. "Tell me something, Gary. What are your three most favorite things to do?"

A look appears on Grabowski's face that is almost thoughtful. His rather beady pale blue eyes narrow and he reaches a hand up to rub his chin that shows little nubs of a blonde beard.

"It can be anything?"

"Yeah, anything. Your three very favorite activities."

"Sleeping. Photography. Eating." Grabowski sits up straighter. "I forgot one. Sports. I like sports, too."

"That's okay. I'll give you four."

"Okay. Those are my favorite activities."

Dale waits for Grabowski to ask what his favorite three or four activities are, but he doesn't. Grabowski isn't very curious about other people. However, Dale is almost appalled by his roommate's answers, although not surprised. Grabowski does sleep a lot. At least nine hours a day. He sleeps so much that he must be good at it. Dale has seen how much he likes to eat, especially Polish cuisine. At least Grabowski mentioned one activity that requires some mental effort. Dale has seen some of Grabowski's photographic work. It wasn't bad. It was more journalistic in nature than artistic but Gary knew how to compose a competent photograph. As for sports, sometimes they watched a football game together although Dale had been too busy of late to watch many games. Grabowski hadn't played any organized sports in high school. He said he went to a big high school on the south side of Chicago and he didn't have the size to play. At college, he played intramural football and basketball and performed fairly well. For a few weeks, Dale and Grabowski went to the old gym to play basketball and racquetball. Dale easily beat him in racquetball the first time so Gary didn't want to play that again. In basketball Grabowski had played better. He had a fairly good outside shot and he used his long legs and thick trunk to position himself strategically under the basket. They had teamed up against two other guys in a game of two-on-two. They won even though Dale didn't have a good shot because of two crippled fingers on his right hand. Instead he fed the ball to Grabowski who scored most of the points. They played a couple more times then his roommate stopped asking him to accompany him to the gym. Dale guessed he found a better partner.

The only other athletic competition they engaged in was a foot race. Grabowski once bragged about how he was rather fast for a bigger guy. Dale said let's find out. So they raced a hundred yards on the quadrangle one evening and Dale smoked him. Won by ten yards. Instead of congratulating him, Grabowski asked in a rather resentful way if Dale used to run track. He said yeah. He'd won over two dozen medals running track in high school. Grabowski only said in response that his knee was bothering him.

Thinking over Grabowski's answers Dale wonders why his roomie didn't mention another physical activity, namely sex. Grabowski seems to engage in it fairly often. Then again, maybe he and his partners just sleep when they go to bed.

If Grabowski asked him his three favorite activities Dale would say: One, creating something. A story, a poem, a drawing, a spoof radio show. Two, communicating. Not just having meaningful talks with someone but also reading a good book or watching an interesting film or listening to engaging music. And three, sex. He's never had many sexual experiences; he's never been promiscuous. In fact, he thinks that kind of behavior is reckless and immature. He still has something of an old-fashioned moralist inside him. But what sex he's experienced he's mostly enjoyed, at least on a physical level. Sometimes the encounters were awkward and early on he'd been self-conscious. So that third favorite thing he likes to do is more a hope that in the future he'll find a woman he finds physically attractive and also likes and then he's certain the sex will be really good. In fact, passionate. He'd like to have a passionate affair with a woman who didn't have the inhibitions of the Nazarene girls he grew up with but also doesn't have the jaded or weird attitude toward sex like a couple of girls he got to know later. So, his third favorite activity is not rooted so much in his experience or perhaps even in reality. It's sort of an idealized version of sex that he hopes he will one day experience. A kind of sex that will transcend the perfunctory, the ordinary, and the awkward kinds. Therefore, it will be more than sex. Perhaps it will even rise to the level of eros.

Like Grabowski, Dale forgot sports. Okay, he'll have four favorite activities, too, and add sports.

"Ready to order the pizza?" Grabowski says, interrupting Dale's reverie.

"Sure," says Dale.

At fifteen minutes to eight, Dale and Grabowski walk across campus to the Memorial Student Union ballroom. As they enter, they see a large crowd. Almost all the seats have been taken. Grabowski scans the back section of seats and apparently sees a friend.

"I'll catch you later," he says.

Dale watches Grabowski walk over to a girl with fluffy brown hair. Dale realizes that she's the same young woman he saw leaving their place last night. She's not as pretty as he thought when he got a glimpse of her last night. In fact, she looks a little like a gopher when she smiles. Her two front teeth are quite a bit longer than the rest. She's also skinny and with her bushy brown hair she looks like an inverted mop. Grabowski hasn't mentioned her name. He never tells Dale the names of his partners.

Dale hears someone calling his name from the front. He turns and sees Mimi waving at him.

"Dale! Over here!"

Her rather brassy voice cuts through the low rumble of voices. Dale walks over to her. She's sitting on the front row.

She pats a vacant chair with her hand. "I saved you an seat right next to me."

Dale says thanks and sits down. He looks down the row and sees several people he knows. Felicia Fernandez, Ed Darby and Pamela Partridge are sitting on the far end of the first row. Next to Mimi he sees another person he recognizes, Marsha Martin, the girl he'd defeated for the OWR editorship. She's talking to a tall fellow with dirty blonde hair and a long, arrogant face. Almost immediately, Dale feels an antipathy for the guy, which he know is unjust because he doesn't know who he is. But he's apparently a friend of Marsha's, which is damning enough.

"Oh, isn't Spencer Dribble dignified looking tonight," Mimi says, noticing the direction of Dale's stare.

She must think that because he's wearing an Oxford blue shirt and tan slacks rather than the more usual casual attire of jeans and a flannel shirt like Dale. Dale glances at Dribble's feet. Rather than boots he's wearing some dressy kind of loafer.

"As dignified as a certified public accountant."

"Wwwhat?" Mimi croons.

Before Dale can clarify his comment, the cartoon starts. The audience applauds at the sight of Bugs Bunny's appearance.

Two cartoons later, *Some Like It Hot* starts. The movie casually establishes its story and doesn't veer into farce until ten minutes into the film. But when it does, the audience roars its laughter. Throughout the movie, the audience responds with hearty guffaws at the absurd situations and the clever dialogue. Dale is gratified to hear the laughter and he joins in. He's seen the movie before on television but it's even more delightful on the semi-large screen without commercial interruption. Watching with a pleased audience adds to the sensory pleasure of sight and sound in service of the zany antics and often non sequitur dialogue.

One hundred minutes later, the film reaches its absurd ending. It's perfect.

The audience bursts out in applause. Mimi actually leaps out of her chair, giving the film a standing ovation.

"Didn't you just love it! Wasn't Marilyn just divine!"

Dale nods as the applause ebbs away and satisfied viewers start to shuffle out of the auditorium.

Mimi continues to rhapsodize about Marilyn. Who says she can't act? She's a great comedienne! Not only is she gorgeous but she has perfect timing. And such vulnerability. And of course, Venusian beauty!

Dale patiently listens. He likes that line about her Venusian beauty. Maybe Mimi will make a fairly good poet. However, his reaction to Marilyn's performance is more nuanced. She certainly gives a good comic turn and yet there is something about her acting that seems to suggest that she's not fully in control. Dale wonders how much Billy Wilder had to do with her performance. In addition, he wonders if Wilder purposely wanted Marilyn to look a little too plump, a little blowzy in fact, to make her character even more absurd. She becomes a caricature of sexiness. A Venus of Tits and Ass. The film has a cynical satirical undercurrent to it and that makes it more than a hilarious farce. It's comically subversive.

While Dale thinks these profound thoughts, Mimi continues to babble and he only tunes her in when she introduces Spencer Dribble.

"Oh, but wait! You two already know each other. Dale says you correspond with each other. Of course, I don't know why you two would do that since you both live here but writing letters is a much more meaningful form of communication!"

Dale focuses his gaze on Dribble. Standing, he looks like he's an inch or two over six feet, which makes Dale dislike him even more. Dribble is not well built. He's slender and rather narrow-shouldered and his chest has a pathetic concave quality. His face is elongated and ascetic looking with a long, narrow nose and a grim mouth. His dirty blonde hair is combed back off his forehead but is quite long in back. His eyes are small and have an indistinguishable light color and poised on the bridge of his thin nose are a small pair of round spectacles. Dribble stares intently at Dale through the lenses of his spectacles as if he is inspecting an amoeba under a microscope.

"Did you find favor with *this* film?" Dribble asks. His voice is clipped and rather high-pitched and flutey.

"Yeah, it was funny."

Dribble glances at his companion, Marsha. She's looking at Dale with the same kind of resentful disapproval she employed yesterday on their way to the pub board meeting.

"He says it's *funny*."

"How would you characterize it?" Dale asks.

"I would say it is a predictable but plausible submersion of the arbitrariness of societal gender roles."

"Oh, you two!" interjects Mimi. "It's simply hilaricus! And what about Marilyn's amazing performance? What do you two intellectuals have to say about that?"

Dale is tempted to voice the thoughts he'd recently formulated but he resists. He knows Mimi wouldn't like it and Dribble would twist it into some kind of sexist put-down. Dale can already tell he is that kind of guy.

"She was luminous," Dale says, remembering in particular the scene near the end of the film where Marilyn is singing and the spotlight illuminates her voluptuous figure.

"Oh, exactly! Dale you couldn't have said it better. And what do you think, Spencer?"

Dale can tell that Dribble is reluctant to disagree. He wonders if that's because Dribble is also concerned about Mimi's reaction. Maybe he really does want to be her beau.

"An obvious but aptful assessment."

Their agreement seems to defuse the tension. Mimi gives more praise of her favorite movie star and Dale watches Dribble and Marsha, trying to see if they are a couple or just friends. They don't seem to be romantically involved with each other but he's not sure.

"Dale," Mimi says, "we're going out for a drink. Would you like to join us? I'd be delighted to have you along. I'm sure Spencer and Marsha feel the same way."

Dale sees both of them pursing their already rather thin lips in disapproval. They needn't worry. He has no desire to remain in their company.

"Thanks, Mimi, some other time. I already made plans for after the movie."

"Oh, that's too bad. I did want you and my other friends to get to know each other better. We're going to a very fashionable bar, well, it's more like a nightclub really. I'm sure the conversation would prove stimulating!"

"Like I said ..."

"Of course, I understand." Mimi pauses for a moment and gives Dale something of an inquisitive look. "Well, another time! I'll see you in class Monday."

Dale says goodbye and nods a farewell to Dribble and Marsha who, of course, don't return his semi-friendly gesture. Dale watches them as they encounter a young man and a young woman of their ilk, pause for a brief chat, then the five proceed out of the auditorium.

Dale doesn't really want to go home. He enjoyed the movie and he would like to talk about it with someone. But not Dribble. He starts to leave when he sees Neil Nordberg standing close to an exit. Nordberg sees him and waves.

3

Dale discreetly watches Deb Pierson as she sits before her desk grading the latest class assignment for her Introduction to Journalistic Writing. She sits in the cushioned chair in a very lady-like way, with her posterior lightly sitting on the seat; her spine curves forward just enough to maintain her perfect posture. She wears an attractive beige skirt that covers her knees even while seated and on top she sports a pink cashmere sweater. Her light brown hair is of medium length and as he focuses on the way it becomingly frames her attractive profile she reaches a hand toward her face and deftly places a loose strand of hair behind her ear. That simple act gives eloquent testament to a natural grace.

Dale decides it's not only her refined features that makes her so appealing; it's also those more subtle qualities of style and poise and charm that attest to an old fashioned ideal of being a lady. She reminds him, in fact, of the pretty Nazarene girls he knew growing up in his hometown of Galilee. Maybe it's the nostalgia factor that adds to her overall appeal, because when he critically examines her person he realizes that she's not a beauty and her figure is too tall and willowy for his taste. And yet, as he secretly peers at her, he feels the same melancholy yearning he used to feel as an adolescent when he stealthily gazed at his future girlfriend.

Dale arrived in her office ostensibly to talk to Grabowski. That was just a pretext, of course, and now he is as silent as his roomie who sits at his desk fiddling with his 35 mm camera.

It's a fairly expensive camera and when Dale glances over to envy its quality he notices that Grabowski is also staring at Deb.

"All finished," Deb announces as she drops her ink pen on the table next to the graded feature stories. She leans back in her chair with a soft satisfied smile.

Dale likes her voice. It has a pleasant feminine lilt to it. It's as refined and charming as the rest of her.

She glances at her two male colleagues and smiles. "I wish I were as fast as you two at grading papers."

Dale glances at Grabowski who is pretending to be examining his camera. As soon as Grabowski noticed Dale looking at him as he looked at Deb, he shifted his full attention to his camera as if he were an expert repairman appraising an especially difficult job.

"That's because you're a conscientious grader,' Dale says.

"And you're not?"

"No, I whip through them as fast as I can. I'm of the Wagstaff School of grading."

Deb smiles, then thinking better of it, she hides her grinning mouth with a delicate hand. She's seen their mentor grading papers, too. Wagstaff doesn't even sit at his desk. He stands at a podium with a red marker in his hand and dashes through the papers as if he were conducting "The Flight of the Bumblebee."

"What does that mean?" Grabowski asks.

"Haven't you seen Wagstaff grading papers in his office?"

Grabowski shakes his head no.

"You ought to some time. If there were an Olympic event for grading papers he'd have the record. I once saw him grade all the essays for the film class in one hour. He spent an average of three minutes on each paper."

"What were you doing in his office watching him grade papers?"

"Admiring his technique, of course. I want to emulate the Fastest Grader in the West."

Grabowski gets that slightly peeved expression on his pale, bland face the way he does when Dale indulges in satirical quipping. He raises his camera and snaps Dale's picture.

"Oh, I think Dr. Wagstaff is just as conscientious about his grading as I am. He simply has a different method."

Grabowski turns his camera to Deb and takes her picture, too.

"Gary, I've asked you before to please not do that."

Grabowski lowers the camera and shrugs. "No biggie."

Dale surmises he means her request will be honored because whether he takes her picture or not is of little importance to him. Dale also wonders how often he's done that in the past.

"What do I see? All three of the department's GTAs gathered together to plot the overthrow of the Mass Communications Department?"

It's Wagstaff. A hand against the door-frame supports him as he leans into the room. He is smiling a mischievous grin, his Fu Manchu mustache framing his strong, white teeth. Dale notices again his gleaming, glabrous skull completely devoid of even one single follicle of hair. Dale imagines he must shave off the remaining patches of fuzz every morning in order to produce such an immaculate cranium.

"Oh, hello, Dr. Wagstaff," Deb says. "I mean, Walt."

Unlike the other professors, especially those with Ph.Ds, Wagstaff prefers students call him by his first name. Instead of speaking his first name, Dale and Grabowski nod their greetings.

"Actually, it's just the opposite," Dale says. "We're meeting to decide which one of us will become the human sacrifice to appease the departmental gods."

Wagstaff laughs his whooping, hiccuping laugh. His cackle, high-pitched and reedy, sounds like a Kookaburra.

"Very good! And which of you is to become the sacrificial victim?"

The three GTAs say nothing but Dale points an unobtrusive thumb at Grabowski. Gary glowers at him in response.

Another Wagstaff whoop.

"Unfortunately, Dale, there is a traditional requirement for the sacrificial victim. She or he must be a virgin. I doubt that any of you qualify."

Dale and Grabowski immediately glance at Deb whose fair face blooms a rosy blush. Her bright green eyes open wide with a mixture of shock and embarrassment.

"Time to dispense with such silliness," quickly adds Wagstaff. "The reason I invaded your territory is to extend an offer for a Thanksgiving repast at my humble home. That is, if any of you scholars will be remaining in town?"

Deb, her dignity now restored, says she's going home to Cheyenne for Thanksgiving break. Grabowski says he will be out of town, too.

"That leaves you, Dale. How about it? Can you stomach a Thanksgiving feast at my abode?"

"I not going anywhere," Dale says. "So, okay."

"Superlative," Wagstaff says. He never simply says "super." He starts to go then stops. "I forgot to mention the time of the affair. Come over at 6 p.m., Dale. At present, there is only one other anticipated guest: Neil Nordberg."

Wagstaff strokes one long strand of his Fu Manchu mustache, raises one of his thinning eyebrows, and then disappears down the hall.

The three GTAs look at the empty doorway where moments before their mercurial professor stood. Wagstaff often makes impromptu visits. He suddenly appears, banters for a few minutes, and flees as abruptly as he appears.

"You know," Dale says with mock-thoughtfulness, "I'm looking forward to a nice, quiet Thanksgiving meal at the Wagstaffs."

Wednesday afternoon Dale drives Grabowski to the Denver airport so he can catch a flight to Chicago. Grabowski informs Dale that he hasn't been back to Chicago since last Christmas. Polacks tend to make a big deal about the holidays, he adds.

That constituted most of their conversation on the drive down. The taciturn Grabowski hadn't exactly asked Dale for a ride to Denver in the first place. Instead he dropped hints. He stated that it cost $12 a day to leave a vehicle at long term parking at Stapleton Airport. Later he affirmed that the shuttle van from Laramie to Denver totaled $25 for a one-way trip. Then a day before his scheduled flight, he casually mentioned that a commuter flight from Laramie to Denver cost $50 one-way.

"Look," Dale said after that last bit of information, "I can drive you to Denver if you want."

"No biggie," Grabowski said.

Now Dale drives into the big international airport and slowly negotiates his Chevy Monza through the heavy traffic. Ten minutes later, he drops his roommate off at the curb of the departures area outside the terminal. Grabowski says thanks, hefts a duffel bag on one of his sloping shoulders and heads off to the terminal.

Ten minutes later, Dale gets out of the airport traffic and makes it to the freeway. Instead of returning to Laramie, he decides to see an old movie at The Rialto, the repertory movie theatre. That's the only reason why he didn't object to driving Grabowski to the airport. He didn't even mind the fact that the niggardly Grabowski didn't, as usual, offer to pay his share of the gas.

Dale sees a Billy Wilder double feature at The Rialto, *Sunset Boulevard* and *Ace in the Hole*, a.k.a *The Big Carnival*. As he drives back to Laramie, he thinks about the two films. He saw *Sunset Boulevard* before on television and the movie had impressed him, but seeing it on the big screen without commercial interruption made the viewing experience even more engrossing. He also noticed on a second look more of the irony and ambiguities contained in the film. He missed some of the significance of the film the first time he saw it. For instance, he hadn't really understood the decadence involved in William Holden and Gloria Swanson's relationship.

Even more provocative was *Ace in the Hole*. The film applied a cynical, sardonic perspective on the newspaper and radio businesses that disturbed and fascinated him. He never saw the lead actress, Jan Sterling, before and he was impressed by her performance as the calculating, embittered wife who eventually can't stomach Kirk Douglas's heartless exploitation of her husband's perilous predicament. Dale was even more mesmerized by Douglas' acting. He knew Kirk mostly from his '60s films in which he usually played a crafty cowboy or heroic slave leader or a tough cop. He'd never seen an actor demonstrate such controlled fury and contempt for civilizational restraints as Douglas did in his daringly callous role.

But what excited him even more was the genius of Billy Wilder. How could a man who'd made the hilarious *Some Like It Hot* have also made those cynical black comedy masterpieces? Then he remembered his thoughts about *Some Like It Hot* a week ago. That film was a farce and definitely had a lighter comic touch but lurking within its lunacy was a hint of the same derisive black humor.

Another quality that he admired about Wilder's films was how he got understated performances from his actors. Even Gloria Swanson didn't overdo it. She was grotesque and weird but only in the last amazing scene did she let it all hang out. Dale always appreciated acting and film-making that was understated in its approach. Even in comedies and farces, he thought that approach made the wackiness more effective. He saw *Bringing Up Baby* in an undergraduate film class and he thought what made that comedy even more hilarious was the understated acting. Take out the more overtly goofy elements, especially the screwball complications, and the acting and direction seemed characteristic of a drama. Wilder in *Some Like It Hot* used an understated approach. Even Jack Lemmon's overtly comic performance was mostly naturalistic. Very little mugging, no telegraphing the absurdity, no self-conscious winking at the audience to point out the obvious that they were all engaged in a wild and wacky comedy. Dale was very impressed by that approach. He wished more contemporary films employed that style.

Dale was surprised by how much he liked those two films.

68

Ordinarily, he preferred comedy that was more good-natured. He especially liked the films of Frank Capra and the novels of Charles Dickens. Both of them had a more optimistic and life-affirming sensibility. But Dale thought Wilder's sensibility, which reminded him a little of Evelyn Waugh's bitter satires in literature, was equally compelling and certainly more in tune with today's zeitgeist.

By the time he arrives home he feels a keen need to talk his ideas out. But there's no one around to have a discussion with. Well, it's time for him to answer Will Whitaker's letter. He'll discuss those ideas in his epistle. He knows Will will find them interesting and he'll understand.

Dale and Neil Nordberg follow Walter Wagstaff into his study. Down the hall in the dining room they hear the cater-wauling of the Wagstaff children: Lionel, ten; Ethel, eight; and John, six. The three moppets have terrorized the household the entire evening. They ate their Thanksgiving dinner in a small room adjacent to the dining room where the grown-ups, Wag-staff and his wife, Kitty, her parents, Mr. and Mrs. Dumont, and Dale and Nordberg, had theirs.

Kitty, a tall, dark, very dignified woman of thirty-five, didn't spend much time with the adults during the meal. Often she left the room to adjudicate some dispute between the children or to issue dire warnings that if their behavior did not improve they would be sent to bed without their holiday feast. Her warnings had no effect. The children screeched and hollered all through the meal. They engaged in food fights. More than once, Ethel broke into tears over the brutality she suffered at the hands of the boys only to exact revenge by hiding the drum-sticks, the only part of the turkey that John would consent to consume. At one point, Kitty returned to the adult table oblivious to the fact that she'd forgotten to wipe off a dollop of mashed potato at the crown of her raven hairdo. When her mother informed her of that embarrassment, Kitty excused herself, left the room, soon to return with her hair all in place and without any potato embellishment.

All during the children's Gotterdammerung, Wagstaff remained nearly oblivious to the domestic disarray. He remained seated at the head of the large table, made light conversation with his in-laws and guests, and heartily devoured large portions of the traditional Thanksgiving fare. Dale was quite impressed with the professor's sangfroid. Even when the worst miscreant, John, galloped into the dining room demanding to know where his drumsticks were, Wagstaff remained unflappable. Upon receiving no intelligence to the whereabouts of the turkey's appendages, John kicked his father on the shin. Only then did Wagstaff's composure – or indifference – crumble. He bolted from the table, swooped up his surprised son and carried him rather roughly to the children's room. When he returned, he made no mention of the contretemps but simply resumed his duties as affable host.

Now, Wagstaff takes a seat in a leather chair and invites his two guests to do the same. Nordberg settles on an old sofa while Dale walks over to the bookshelves and scans titles. Aside from the expected books about journalism, film, and related professional concerns, Dale notices that several of the shelves contain books about history, political science, general philosophy, biology, astronomy, and literature. In fact, quite a few books are poetry and short story collections and novels.

Upon closer inspection, Dale notices that all the literature tomes have a thin coating of dust on them.

"Like a true bibliophile, Dale goes right to the library," observes Wagstaff.

"The way you dismiss the importance of books I thought you wouldn't have any."

"In my younger days I used to be quite the bookworm. I especially enjoyed poetry and short fiction. But the demands of work precluded literary pursuits. And, as I've mentioned before, I became increasingly convinced, with the passage of time, that the printed word is destined for obsolescence."

Dale glances at Nordberg to see his reaction. Neil doesn't

seem particularly disturbed by that remark.

"I think books will always exist," says Dale.

"Exist certainly, but with diminished cultural importance."

"That's already happening," says Nordberg. "People are getting more and more of their news from the electronic media."

"And film has replaced the novel as the dominant narrative art form."

"But isn't there something in a novel that you can't get in a movie?" asks Dale.

"Yes. More words."

Nordberg laughs but Dale doesn't.

"I know what you mean, Dale," says Wagstaff. "There are certain particular virtues contained in a novel that you can't duplicate in a film. But perhaps those virtues, introspection, a deeper understanding of psychology and human thought and feeling, just aren't as relevant for a society such as ours."

"We live in a fast-paced electronic world," Nordberg says. "Who has time to read?"

"You don't read?" asks Dale.

"Of course. For professional and work related reasons. But I don't read for pleasure much anymore."

"Neither do I," Wagstaff says rather ruefully. "I can't remember when I last read a serious novel."

"But you're missing deeper artistic meaning," says Dale. "Meaning that's contained in literature."

"That's a curious thing for you to say, Dale," says Wagstaff. "You've confessed to seeing at least one film a day. You consume them like they're apples."

"I like seeing movies but as you said they don't have certain qualities that a book, a novel, has. And I'm really just catching up on seeing films. I've always read novels but I didn't get the chance to see many good older films at my undergraduate college."

"Where did you go to college?" asks Nordberg.

"At my hometown school, Galilee Nazarene College."

"A religious college?"

"Yes. It was the only college in my hometown."

"There's nothing necessarily deficient about attending a religiously affiliated college," Wagstaff intones. "Although I must admit I've never heard of a Nazarene college until we received your application."

Dale doesn't want to talk about his college or hometown so he asks Wagstaff what colleges he attended.

"I received my Ph.D. from Illinois. They have a highly respected film theory department."

"Tell Dale where you went to undergraduate school, Walt."

Dale thought it was interesting that Nordberg used Wagstaff's first name. Even though he invited students to do so, few did.

Wagstaff hesitated for just a moment. "As an undergraduate, I attended Ball State."

"Ball State?" Dale asked.

"Yes, and don't bother making any jokes. I've heard them all before."

"That's in Muncie, Indiana, isn't it?"

"Congratulations on your geographical acumen. Like you, I also attended my hometown college."

"Walt already knows this Dale, but as an undergraduate I went to St. Olaf's. Do you know where that is?"

Dale thinks about it. "No, I've never seen a football score about that college."

"It's in Minnesota," Wagstaff says.

"In Northfield," adds Nordberg. "About forty miles south of Minneapolis-St. Paul."

"Is it Catholic?"

Nordberg chuckles. "It's affiliated with the Lutheran church but it's no longer a religious college."

Dale nods. He's never heard of it. He wonders if Will Whitaker has heard of it.

"Now, gentleman, to change the program so to speak, would you two like to see a film to conclude our evening's festivities?"

Dale and Nordberg give each other puzzled glances.

"You mean on TV?" Dale asks.

"No, I mean a film shown in this room on my own personal projector."

"Sure," Dale says. Nordberg agrees as well.

Wagstaff instructs Dale to pull down the film screen from the opposite wall while he gets the projector ready. Dale does as instructed and turns to see Wagstaff rolling a genuine film projector mounted on a portable carrier out of a closet. Two canisters of film lie on the bottom shelf of the carrier. Dale goes over to assist the professor in getting the film ready. In five minutes, everything is ready to go.

"I doubt that either of you have seen this film before," Wasgstaff says.

The last time someone showed Dale a movie in his home was back in Buffalo City when an older friend screened X-rated features for him. But surely Wagstaff wouldn't do that. Not on Thanksgiving.

The film starts. It's not X-rated. But it appears to be rather risqué. It's entitled *Ecstasy*.

The three watch in silence. The film's dialogue is in German and the quality of the film is rather grainy. The sound lacks clarity. There's not a great deal of story but the old black and white film is about a frustrated but beautiful young woman named Eva who leaves her older husband. Eva, hot from walking during the warm day, decides to cool off by skinny-dipping. She leaves her clothes on a horse that wanders away and she runs through the forest in the nude trying to find it. A handsome young man named Adam finds the horse and clothes. He teases her about not giving them back but eventually does. Later, she goes to his isolated home and they become lovers. Her estranged husband finds out about them but instead of confronting them he shoots himself. It appears that the young lovers are free, but while waiting for a train to take them to their happiness, Eva leaves her sleeping lover and departs on a different train.

The film isn't very long. Dale doesn't find it that interesting except that the actress is young and beautiful and she appears nude. She's seen at a distance but it's obvious that she's really naked. In another scene, a close-up of her face shows her in the throes of passion.

As the film ends, Wagstaff calls for the lights. Dale turns on a lamp and he and Nordberg watch Wagstaff rewind the film.

"Did watching *Ecstasy* make you ecstatic?" Wagstaff asks.

"It was interesting," Dale says. "When was it made?"

"Made in 1933. It became a *success de scandale* due, obviously, to the nude scenes and the close-up of Hedy Lamarr's face during orgasm."

"That was Hedy Lamarr?

"One of her first films. She came to Hollywood in the late thirties and made mostly inferior films for two decades."

"I think I remember seeing her in *Samson and Delilah*," Dale says. "I saw it on TV."

Wagstaff chuckles. "First Eve then Delilah. The lady has a thing for playing Biblical dames."

"How did you come to acquire this film?" asks Nordberg.

"That I cannot say. Let it suffice that it wasn't easy. There are very few copies available. When the filmmakers tried to show it in the U.S. in 1935 the Catholic Legion of Decency denounced the film and the Hays Office refused to give it a seal of approval. So it only showed in a few art theatres in New York."

"I guess back in 1935 a movie like that really shocked people," Dale says.

"It was not the first film to depict nudity but it might have been the first to suggest sexual intercourse. Definitely the first film to show a woman's face while she's having an orgasm. So, yes, it was scandalous."

"Was she really having the big O?" asks Nordberg.

"Not according to her autobiography. She said her facial expressions were a result of her acting skills and being jabbed on the ass with a safety pin."

The three of them laugh. Wagstaff returns the film to its canisters and puts the projector back in its closet.

"Just think," Dale muses out loud. "Instead of watching that film we could have been watching *The Sound of Music* on TV."

"I'm thankful that we didn't," says Nordberg.

Wagstaff proceeds to tell them a few interesting facts about *The Sound of Music*. The three of them chat for ten more minutes then Dale and Nordberg decide they should leave. On their way out, they thank their hostess, Mrs. Wagstaff, who is patiently waiting for her husband to emerge from his study. The kids and the grandparents are all in bed.

As Dale and Nordberg leave Wagstaff's home, Dale glances back at the handsome two-story Tudor house a lit in the night by porch lights. It's in a good location, too, only a block away from Washington Park. Wagstaff has done all right for himself.

They walk to their cars in the brisk, cold night air. Dale, still thinking about the movie, looks at the three quarter moon shining in the nitid night.

"She was really beautiful," says Dale.

"Who?" asks Nordberg.

"Hedy. Now that I think about it, I remember seeing her in a couple of other movies. I think one was with Bob Hope. She had fantastic full lips."

"Yeah," Nordberg says but not with the same sense of awe that Dale feels. Nordberg is the first to reach his car. Before he opens the door, he asks Dale what is doing tomorrow.

"I don't know. Probably just catching up on things."

"Would you like to do something together? We could meet over at campus. Hardly anyone will be there."

"I don't know. What would we do?"

"I'll think of something. So what about it?"

Dale notices that Nordberg has that insinuating look on his face again. His dark blue eyes narrow in a knowing way that Dale, in a good mood after the dinner and the special movie, no longer finds annoying.

"Okay. What time do you want to meet?"

"Noon. Outside Gowdy Hall."

Dale nods and he walks on. He hears Nordberg starting his

car and then driving away. As he thinks about Nordberg's invitation, he's glad he accepted. Otherwise, he would have gone through another lonely day.

As Dale walks across campus, it starts to snow. He glances up at the glassy gray sky and watches as thick white flakes plummet toward him. This isn't the first snowfall of the season. That happened in late October, a week before Halloween. It snowed only three inches and the bright sun melted most of it the following day. In early November it snowed again, this time dumping almost one foot of snow. The snow lasted more than a few days that time but once it disappeared the weather had been dry and mild until now.

As Dale approaches Gowdy Hall, he sees Neil Nordberg waiting for him at the entrance to the building. Nordberg is wearing a blue ski jacket along with his jeans and snow boots. He waves and Dale trudges over, the snow already beginning to accumulate and stick on the walkways.

"We picked a great time to meet outside," says Dale.

"Yes, the temperature is dropping fast."

"Well, we can't stay here and talk. My mouth is already turning numb."

"That's because you're not dressed warmly enough. You're not even wearing a winter coat. May I remind you that this is Wyoming and not Oklahoma. It gets really cold here."

"So I've heard. Are all the buildings locked up for the holiday?"

"Yes. They won't be open until Sunday."

"Even the student union?"

"That's right. Most undergraduate students go home for Thanksgiving."

"Do you want to walk over to my place?" Dale asks.

"I have a better idea. Let's go to the old gym and explore."

"I thought you said all the buildings are locked."

"They are, but I have keys to the old gym."

As they walk over to the old gymnasium, Nordberg explains

that the keys belong to a friend of his who works as a custodian on campus. He looks after the old gym and since he was going to be away for Thanksgiving he gave the keys to Neil. Neil is supposed to check out the building every day to make sure no pipes break or anything else goes wrong.

They arrive at the rear entrance and Nordberg uses a key to open the door. They enter. The gym is strangely quiet and dark. The only time Dale has been here was to play basketball with Grabowski. He likes the rather eerie sense of emptiness. It reminds him of when he was a campus policeman during college and he'd patrol the empty halls of Cimarron City High School.

They go into the weight room and look at the weight machines and the free weights. The room has the smell of stale sweat hanging in the air. They go over to the windows and peer at the snow hurtling down from the skies. Dale likes standing in the warm old gym staring out at the cold snowy day. He feels that secure feeling he used to feel when he was a boy and he'd be inside his home looking out at the inclement weather.

"You never talk much about yourself," says Nordberg. "I just found out last night that you went to a religious college."

"Like I said, it was in my hometown."

"So, you're no longer religious."

"Not really. I have spiritual beliefs but I'm not formally religious."

"Me neither," Nordberg says. "I think religion is mostly a way of inhibiting people. To prevent them from experiencing life to the fullest."

"Sometimes I used to think that. Some of the Nazarenes I grew up with wouldn't even attend movies."

"Think how they'd react to the movie we saw last night."

"Yeah, they would want to ban it even now."

"And by today's standards it wasn't even that provocative."

"That's by today's standards," Dale says. "Back then it was quite daring."

"I'm glad I don't live back then. Think of all the things you couldn't do. The things you couldn't experience. For people like us, that would be poisonous."

"During the conversation last night, you didn't seem to care about reading books that much. Were you always that way?"

"Yes, I noticed that bothered you. I've always read books. But now I'm more of a visual person than a verbal one. But there are still some novels that I like to read."

"Like what?"

"I like D.H. Lawrence. Have you read any of his novels?"

"I've read *Sons and Lovers*."

"Have you ever read *Women in Love*?"

"Not yet. But I saw the movie on TV."

"You need to see that film without it being censored by television. In it's own way, it's as provocative as *Ecstasy*."

"In what way?"

"Maybe I'll get the film committee to show it next semester then you'll see for yourself. In the meantime, I'll give you the paperback novel to read."

"Okay. Why do you like Lawrence so much?"

"He revels in the senses. In nature. He tells us to throw off the false restraints of civilization and connect with what really matters, the visceral part of life."

Dale nods but he thinks he hasn't read enough of Lawrences's work to make that assertion. He looks out the spot in the large window that isn't frosted over. The snow continues to fall in big clumps from the slate gray sky.

"Speaking of nature," Dale says, "It's good to be inside on a cold, snowy day like this. I sort of get a special feeling."

"What kind of special feeling?"

"A sense of physical well-being and contentment." Dale glances at Neil. "Does that make sense?"

"I know what you mean. I think I feel it too." Nordberg looks around the gymnasium. "Did you used to play sports?"

"Yeah, I played them all in high school. Football, basketball, baseball, and track.

"I thought so. You have an athletic build. But why didn't you wrestle?"

"My high school didn't offer wrestling. Did you play sports?"

"Not team sports. Not even ice hockey." Nordberg grins. "I grew up in Minnesota, you know. I played tennis and swam instead."

Dale nods. "I was never very good at swimming."

"Maybe you just didn't practice enough. Hey, let's look around the rest of the gym."

Dale says okay and they leave the weight room and walk down a gloomy hall. They hear the echo of their footsteps on the concrete floor. They come to a door and Nordberg stops.

"Let's go see the pool."

Nordberg unlocks the door to the pool and they go in. Nordberg flips on one light switch and part of the room is illuminated. They walk over to the edge of the pool and peer at the chlorine blue water. They smell the slightly astringent smell.

"We ought to go for a swim," Nordberg says. "The pool is heated."

"We don't have our swim trunks."

"Who needs them? The warm water will feel good, especially thinking how cold and snowy it is outside."

That idea appeals to Dale. He feels a sort of excitement grow inside him, a desire to express his physical self in this quiet gym, sealed off from other people, the world itself, on the outside.

"Come on, Dale," Nordberg says. "Let's skinny-dip."

That word conjures up last night's movie and the scene of the ravishing Hedy Lamarr and her nude bathing. Thinking of her intoxicates his senses.

They begin to undress. Nordberg throws his clothes off first and Dale hears him dive into the water. Down to his shorts, Dale hesitates for a moment then he rips them off. He walks over to the pool and jumps in.

The water is pleasantly warm. He surfaces and sees little waves of steam appearing on the surface. He tastes the almost citric flavor of the water in his mouth.

He sees the blurry image of Nordberg swimming under water. Dale's mind, however, is focused on images of Hedy Lamarr as she swam in the lake in the movie. He turns and does the backstroke. He enjoys the sensation of the warm water bathing his bare body. The sensual experience seems both wholesome and daringly naughty. He wonders if this is what Nordberg meant when he spoke about D.H. Lawrence. Did Lawrence mean that one should immerse his self in the realm of the senses and just live for the moment?

Dale swims over to the side of the pool and lifts himself out. He walks over to the springboard and mounts the steps. He's very aware of his body and ordinarily he would be embarrassed by this display. He's always been shy. But the quiet, almost isolated surroundings and the soothing water encourages him to shed those inhibitions. For the first time in his life, he enjoys being naked in a non-private situation. He feels strong and confident and full of life. As he stands on the diving board, he's aware that Nordberg is looking at him. But he doesn't care. He isn't thinking of him.

"Let's see how well you dive," says Nordberg.

Dale dives headfirst into the supple, tepid water and lets the momentum of his dive carry him through the water for ten yards. Then he thrusts his arms and legs and that propels him down the pool for twenty yards before he surfaces. He hears a splash. It's Nordberg diving in.

Dale gets out of the pool again and walks over to the diving board. As he walks he feels his genitals swaying but it's not an erotic feeling as much as a sensuous one. As he climbs the steps, he hears the patter of wet feet. He senses Nordberg behind him. Dale ascends to the top and pauses before he walks out onto the diving board. Suddenly, he feels something strange against his hip. It's a sensation he's never felt before but the touch sends a bolt of panic through him. That touch is hard but spongy. And Dale knows what it is.

He turns his head back and sees Nordberg standing right behind him with an odd expression on his face. It's not his usual insinuating look. It's more a look of entreaty. Dale's eyes look lower and then he sees Nordberg's erection. The sight disgusts him. That previous feeling of panic disappears and is replaced by a surge of fury. His hands clench into fists but instead of attacking Nordberg, he turns and dives hard into the water.

He quickly swims to the side of the pool and gets out. He glances over to the diving board. Nordberg stands there but Dale only looks at the disturbed expression on his face. Dale gathers his clothes and starts to swiftly walk out of the swimming room.

"Dale!"

Nordberg's voice echoes in the natatorium. Dale pushes open the door and suddenly realizes that he's not in a locker room. Instead he's standing in the hallway. He quickly gets dressed even though it's difficult pulling his clothes over his wet skin. He's tugging on his socks when the door opens and a fully dressed Nordberg appears.

"Don't go out in the cold all wet," he says.

Dale says nothing. He's still angry. He's having trouble pulling his socks on. He knows Nordberg is watching him with his cool blue eyes.

"I won't say that I'm sorry," Nordberg says.

Dale still says nothing.

"Okay, maybe I'm sorry it happen that way. I didn't mean to sneak up and surprise you. It just happened."

His boots now on, Dale considers tramping out of the building into the cold but his hair is still wet. He probably would catch pneumonia.

"Let's go into the office and I'll get a towel for you to dry off with. And we can talk."

"Talk about what?"

Nordberg starts walking down the hallway. Dale reluctantly follows. What anger he still feels is now directed at himself. He should have known better. There was something about Nordberg, his slyness, which should have warned him.

Nordberg unlocks the door to the office, turns on the lights, and fetches two towels out of a drawer. He tosses one to Dale.

Dale vigorously dries his hair and rubs his face.

"I was hoping that you would be more open to life's experiences," Nordberg says. "I got the impression from our recent talk that you would be."

"We weren't talking about that stuff."

"We were talking about living life to its fullest. Experiencing everything. Including sensual experiences."

"No, you were talking about that. Not me."

"Do you think it is wrong?"

"Yeah, I think it's wrong."

"Have you ever experienced it before?"

"No I haven't."

"Then how do you know you won't like it?"

"Like what?"

Nordberg smiles a frustrated grin. "Do I have to spell it out for you?"

"No you don't." Dale pauses. He's getting angry again. He takes a deep breath and slowly exhales it. "Look, I'm not a homosexual."

"Do you think that I am?"

"No, I think you're Peter Pan. Of course, I think you're a homosexual. And I'm not. So there's no point to any of this."

"It's true that I'm gay. But we don't have to do anything right away. I like looking at you. Just let me do that."

"No thanks." Dale tosses the towel on the counter.

"You still have too much of that religion in you."

Dale doesn't reply. He walks out of the office and heads for the rear exit.

"You're too inhibited, Dale! You need to learn how to experience things!"

Dale pushes on the bar handle and the exit door opens to a world of utter whiteness. Snow is still falling from the pale sky. Snow completely covers the ground. The only colors other than white are the brown tree trunks and branches of the exposed evergreens.

He tugs his jacket closer to him. The wind has died down but the air is still frigid. He walks in the direction where he thinks the walkway is. His boots spray snow as he marches across campus.

He shoves his bare hands into the pockets of the jacket. He needs to buy gloves. He thinks about those mundane concerns for a few minutes to keep his mind off what happened. He's almost back home when he considers the strange encounter. He should have known better. He's been in a similar situation a couple of times although it never went that far. When he went to Boys State his city's counselor appeared in the shower room when he was taking a shower and later made suggestive comments. At GNC, David Hawkins spied on him in the locker room while they dressed. Later he made tacit entreaties. When Dale traveled to Europe the summer after college graduation, he'd been accosted several times by men of varying ages. And just last spring in Buffalo City his older friend, Byron Mors, a guy he played chess with and once viewed X-rated movies with, told him he would like to "watch him," meaning he wanted Dale to masturbate while they watched the porn films together. After that bizarre request, Dale avoided Byron. What made Byron's behavior even stranger was that he was married with one kid and he was one of the town's prominent citizens.

Dale wonders why he seems to attract weirdos. He doesn't know. But he does know one thing: he needs to find a girl.

4

Tuesday, the last week of fall classes, and Dale strides into the *Branding Iron* office with an urgent question: where are all the newspapers?

On his way to campus that morning he didn't see any newspapers on the racks in the lobby of the Downey Classroom Building where most of the undergraduates take their humanities and English courses. None were available at Gowdy Hall. Even the racks and kiosk shelves in the Memorial Student Union were devoid of the *BI*.

Dale scans the newsroom and sees only a couple of people present. That's the usual situation on a Tuesday morning. Most of the staff doesn't arrive until the afternoon. The night before the editors were up late pasting up the copy and then they took it to *The Boomerang* to be printed. Dale sees one young woman that works on the editorial side, the head copy editor, Dallas Kincaid. When he first met her, he asked if she was born in Dallas or Texas. She said no, she was born in Cheyenne. Dale said that's interesting. My sister was born in Dallas and her name is Cheyenne. He was kidding, of course, but for several weeks

Dallas believed his story. When he finally told her the truth (he did have a sister but her name was June and she'd been born in Hawaii), Dallas didn't resent having her leg-pulled. She smiled and said she would be sure to double-check all facts in his copy from then on. He liked her good-natured personality and the fact she could take a joke. They became friends but more of the casual variety since she has a steady boyfriend.

Dale goes over to Dallas. She's fairly tall and slender with fluffy blonde hair and a cute face.

"Hey, Dallas, have you noticed there aren't any newspapers in the racks?"

"No, I haven't. Not anywhere?"

"I didn't check the dorms but the I didn't see any in the classroom buildings. There's not any in the student union either."

"We have papers in our kiosk," she said, pointing to the wooden structure next to the front door.

"Yeah, I saw that. But that's the only place with papers that I've seen."

"That's strange."

He's about to agree when Felicia Fernandez walks in. As soon as she sees Dale, she shakes her head in a reproving way as if she's caught him doing something naughty. Dale can't think of anything impropriety that he's committed recently so he's curious to know what's on her mind.

She walks over to them, with an annoyed expression still on her face.

"Dale says that newspapers seem to be missing around campus," Dallas says.

Dale notices that Felicia looks not only irked she also tired. Her eyes are blood-shot and puffy. Her disposition, normally cheerful, is glum.

"I got this letter this morning," Felicia says. She gives it to Dale.

He reads:

To the Editor of the Branding Iron:

We, the enlightened readers of the student newspaper, have confis-
cated several bundles of newspapers and are holding them ransom until
you relieve your movie reviewer, Dale Smith, of his duties. We care
deeply about film and culture and we cannot bear his exerable reviews
to be run in your otherwise adequate tabloid. Unless our demands are
met we will continue to persecute as many BIs as possible. Please heed
our request and fire that SOB before any more papers are lost.
Sincerely,
The Committee to Stop Dale Smith (CSDS)

"I guess whoever wrote this meant to write execrable instead of exerable. Also, how can they persecute a newspaper?" Dale hands the communiqué to Dallas. She quickly peruses it.

"Is this a joke?" Dallas asks.

"Does it look like a joke?" Felicia asks. "A lot of papers are missing. The dorms don't have any. And I received an anonymous phone call early this morning telling me to check my mailbox. I found that letter."

That explains her lack-of-sleep look, Dale thinks. She probably only got a few hours of slumber before receiving the phone call.

"I'm sorry they're taking this out on you and the newspaper," Dale says. "You ought to go back and get some sleep."

"I can't sleep until I find out who did this. I've already been to see Dean Woolfson. He said they might start a campus investigation."

"The Committee to –" Dallas stops out of deference to Dale's feelings. "I mean who are these CSDS people?"

"I can guess."

Felicia and Dallas look at Dale.

"I think there's at least four of them. I saw them together at the Friday night campus film a month ago."

"Well, tell us," Dallas says.

"Can't you guess one of them, Felicia?"

"You mean Spencer Dribble?"

"Yep. And his female friend, Marsha Martin, is another miscreant. I don't know who the other two were."

"Bob Baugh and Patti Montag," says Dallas.

"You know them?" Dale asks.

"They're in my lit class. They're friends with Spencer and Marsha. But I think there's a fifth person, too."

"Well?" asks Felicia.

"Neil Nordberg. I had to come to campus early this morning and I saw him walking away from the student union with a big bulge underneath his jacket. I now think he was hiding newspapers."

When Dale heard Dallas say Nordberg's name he felt his stomach drop. Now that the initial surprise has faded, he feels angry. He'd like to go over to his office and punch Nordberg in his smug face. But he probably wouldn't find him there. Since their strange interlude at the old gym almost two weeks ago, he's hardly seen his office mate. Dale only stays in his office during his office hours now. Nordberg has office hours much earlier in the morning and doesn't drop by any more. Dale got a glimpse of him working in the department chairman's sub-office a few times. Nordberg is Schneider's research assistant so apparently Neil moved the center of his research work there. That's fine with Dale. He has no interest in talking to Nordberg anymore. When he thinks about what happened at the old gym, in particular Nordberg's sneaky and manipulative behavior, he still feels angry. Dale wonders if Nordberg planned the whole thing from the beginning; that his friendliness and helpfulness was just a ruse for an eventual seduction. The whole episode disgusts him. It isn't so much that Nordberg is a homo but that he was duplicitous. If he'd been honest about his intentions Dale still would have rejected him but Nordberg's manipulative behavior especially angered him. Now it appears that Nordberg is exacting some kind of adolescent revenge on him. It's ironic. In the past, Nordberg praised Dale's movie reviews. Now, he's one of the plotters.

"I wonder what made them do this now?" Felicia says.

"I think it was last Friday's review of *Manhattan*," says Dallas. "I heard Spencer and Marsha criticizing it in my modern drama class."

"So instead of writing another complaining letter he decides to steal the whole newspaper?" Felicia asks.

"You didn't print his last complaint," Dale reminds her.

"We printed the first two," says Felicia. "Spencer doesn't have an automatic forum to criticize our staff. But stealing newspapers is not just a harmless prank. We have advertisers who pay for their ads to be seen. The students pay an activity fee. They have a right to read the *BI* for themselves and decide if they think a review stinks." She glances at Dale. "I don't mean to say that your review stunk. I liked it. But even if it did stink we make the editorial decisions not Spencer and his gang."

"What did they find so objectionable about the review?" Dale asks Dallas. "I didn't pan the movie. I pointed out its good qualities and its weaker elements."

"I think Spencer is a big Woody Allen fan. He didn't like it that you said Woody can't act."

"I didn't say that. I said that he's effective in the comic scenes but strains a little in the dramatic ones. It amazes me how people misread things."

"Spencer takes Woody very seriously," Dallas says.

Dale thought there was a joke in that statement somewhere but he isn't in the mood to find it. "I don't know why people take film criticism so seriously," he says, forgetting momentarily that he took it seriously too.

"So what are we going to do?" asks Dallas.

"I could resign," Dale says.

"Do you want to?" asks Felicia.

"No, I don't. I haven't done anything unethical or displayed blatant ignorance. I write my opinions. I try to be fair-minded and informative. Maybe readers don't understand that reviewers don't have a lot of time to analyze their ideas and polish their copy. I see the movie then I come to the newspaper and write the review. I'm not writing magazine essays where I can take weeks to refine my thinking and language."

He knows he spoke too forcefully. Both Felicia and Dallas understand the process. But the more he thinks of CSDS actions the more indignant he feels.

"And it's more than objecting to your movie reviews anyway," says Felicia. "Spencer wanted to be the movie reviewer and I picked you instead."

"And Marsha wanted to be the literary magazine editor and she lost," Dale says. He doesn't mention Nordberg's personal reasons for his vendetta.

"Right, I forgot about Marsha's ulterior motives." Felicia jabs at the letter. "Of course we're not going to give in to their stupid demands. I'll speak with Dr. Woolfson again today and tell him about our suspicions about who these people are." She looks at Dale and Dallas. "I might need the two of you to provide some information, too."

Dale and Dallas both say they will help when needed. Felicia takes the letter and puts it in her notebook. She says she's going home for a short nap and then she'll come back and set up an appointment with the dean. She'll keep them informed.

They say their farewells and Felicia leaves. Dale walks over to the rack with today's newspapers in it and takes one. He flips to the entertainment section and stares at his review.

"What movie did you review for today?" Dallas asks.

"*Apocalypse Now*," he says.

Dale walks over to the Roripaugh Hall where the English department is located. The three story stone building is situated in a nice part of campus, on a small hill overlooking a field that features deciduous and evergreen trees and a flower garden that has a floral arrangement in the shape of a large W. Ordinarily, he would sit on one of the benches atop the hill and gaze in appreciation at the small pastoral scene, but now as he takes his seat he hardly looks at the natural beauty before him.

His mind is concentrated on the CSDS gang. He's especially incensed with Nordberg. He wonders, however, if his reviews are seriously flawed. He's tried to develop his understanding of film these past few months. During the summer term he took one of the required core courses for his film concentration, Film Theory. He's never been especially interested in theories, not literary theories or philosophical theories, but he tried to comprehend the abstract ideas contained in the textbook. He read about the different critical perspectives, tried to divine the meaning of the different schools of thought in regard to film. Some ideas compared film to dreams; others to drama; still others thought film was best understood in a technological context. He read Siegfried Kracauer's theories and the Auteur Theory and ideas by other European thinkers. He had been reading more thoughtful reviews in magazines for several months before the course. Ever since Will Whitaker educated him about more serious, perceptive journalism as found in magazines of opinion, Dale read the film reviews of Stanley Kauffman and John Simon. He thought both reviewers were excellent. He also read reviews by the critics of the large circulation big city newspapers. All this work improved his thinking. He no longer passively sat in the theatre simply enjoying a movie. He trained himself to see more details and to be attuned to more subtleties in the film-making process itself. He was more aware of how a film was produced. He now knew that it was a rather intricate process that coordinated technical elements (cinematography, set design, costume design, sound, lighting, etc.) with more artistic or expressive elements (screen-writing, acting, direction). He became especially interested in the art of direction. He knew it was more complicated than what it appeared to be from simply watching a film. Since a film, especially a good film, immediately seduced the viewer into accepting its fictional world, it was easy to get absorbed with the sights and sounds before him. Dale couldn't escape from that experience, and didn't want to if he liked the film, but he tried to train his mind to also see the film as a work of cinematic art with particular attention to how the film was being directed.

In the spring, Dale would take a directing course and create his own film. He was looking forward to that course. He thought the only way he could really understand film as an art was to try and make one. It would be a very short film, of course, but he thought it would allow him to delve deeper into the aesthetics of film.

Since he read so much literature, especially novels, he knew he had a tendency to focus too much on the story elements of a film. He didn't think that was a mistake, but he was beginning to better understand that film had more than story to it. Perhaps form was as important as content. He still liked best the films that told good stories, with well-developed characters, and memorable dialogue. But he wanted to develop his understanding of the more cinematic elements contained in a film.

As for his theory on film, he still didn't have one. He thought that films most resembled narrative fiction. And yet, the more he thought about a film in relation to a novel, or when he saw a film adapted from a novel and then later read the novel (or vice versa), he realized that there were significant differences between the novel and the film, even when they were dramatizing the same story. He still didn't understand how those differences developed. He comprehended obvious differences: movies had to be shorter than novels so events were condensed or eliminated; some characters were excised out of the film version; sometimes two characters were combined into one for the sake of brevity, and so on. But there were other, more subtle differences between novels and films of the same story and he aimed to understand that process better.

One idea, however, that he is formulating is that a novel can be told from several different points of view: first person, third person, omniscient, even second person. That approach colors the nature of a novel. But film only has one point of view and that is the camera. Even when a film makes use of subjective shots or tries to give an approximation of a character's thinking process in a voice over, the real controlling intelligence in a film comes from the camera.

The camera as point of view should produce a more objective quality to a film. And in some films it did. But most films, especially those from Hollywood, created a subjective response in the viewer. Why was that? Because people tend to impute their own emotions to the characters they are watching. That's why the actors are so important in a film. They are the source of an audience's subjective identification. That's why casting is so important. For his master's thesis he might develop that theory more than he had when he wrote his final paper for the Film Theory class.

In the meantime, he tries to see a variety of films. He reads about them, not just reviews but more substantial essays. He likes the sillier qualities about the movie business, too, the awards and film personas, and other superficial but fun qualities. But he wants to refine his thinking so he can see films in a larger context, the historical, intellectual and artistic. He knows he has a long way to go. As he remarked to Wagstaff several weeks ago, there were so many films he wanted to see, especially the better older films, and he felt impatient that it would take years to do so.

He's serious about studying film. That's why the criticism of Dribble and his gang disturbs him. Rather than approach their differing perspectives and tastes as something to discuss, even argue, those Cinematic Goths attacked him. Stealing newspapers to try and silence him! Well, he wouldn't be intimidated. He'd be glad to debate Dribble and the rest of them. And if they preferred pilfering to reasoned debate then the hell with them.

"Oh, my! You look so serious lost in thought."

Without looking up, he knows it's Mimi. For a moment, he wonders if she was part of the CSDS. She seems to know all those people. She plops her Rubenesque figure next to him on the bench. He looks at her. She's smiling so broadly, so sincerely, that he knows she wasn't one of the conspirators.

"Did you get a *BI* today?" he asks.

"No, I didn't. There didn't seem to be many around. Why? Did you have a movie review in it?"

"Yeah."

"What movie?"

"*Apocalypse Now.*"

"Oh, Von Goebbels wanted to take me to that movie. But isn't it a war movie? I don't like violent movies. Too much blood and guts. So, I said no. Besides, I don't go to movies with other guys as a couple because of –"

"Joe DiMaggio."

"That's right! But if I were to go to a movie with a guy to make a couple I'd pick you over Von Goebbels. You sort of remind me of Arthur Miller, Marilyn's other adoring husband. You're so intellectual! But didn't Arthur Miller wear glasses?"

"Yeah. And he had false teeth too."

"Really? You can't tell that from the photos. But maybe they retouched those photos back in the '50s. But I hope not! I don't like to think that maybe Marilyn's photos were doctored."

"Who is this Von Goebbels you keep referring to?"

"Just a guy I know. He loves movies like I do. He keeps on imploring me for a date. He's a senior majoring in film. He's very talented. But not very good looking. Of course, Joe DiMaggio and Arthur Miller weren't handsome. But I like for a man to have at least a tolerable appearance. Maybe I shouldn't have compared you to Arthur Miller because you're so cute! But Von Goebbels, I'm afraid, is a little strange looking. More like Peter Lorre than Tony Curtis."

"Is his name really Von Goebbels?"

"Why, certainly. Mark Von Goebbels. He's very German. I mean, he's an American. Born here, lived here all his life. But his attitude is very Teutonic if you know what I mean."

"Yeah, I know what you mean."

"Anyway, instead of seeing that war movie a gang of us went to see *Kramer vs. Kramer*. It was simply marvelous. So touching. I bawled like a baby at the end. But you know that I'm emotional especially in regard to children. Have you seen it yet?"

"No, I'm going to see it tonight. But Miriam –"

"Mimi!"

"Right. You mentioned that you went to see *Kramer vs.*

Kramer with a gang. Who comprised this gang?"

"Von Goebbels, his brother, Matt, Anna Cappelletti, Ed Darby, and me."

"Not Spencer Dribble?"

"No, he and Marsha and a few others went to see that Apocalypse movie."

"How well do you know Dribble?"

"I know Spence very well. But only as a friend, although he's always pleading for a date. Anyway, we both started at Wyo the same time. Now, we're seniors!"

"What's his major?"

"One of those combined majors. He takes a lot of English classes, including film classes in the English department. He takes many psychology classes too but that's because his father is a professor there and he thinks the other profs will be easy on him."

"Yeah, he's the son of Dr. Dribble."

"That's right! But why are you asking all these questions. I thought you and Spence corresponded?"

"Yeah. In fact, I just got a letter from him today."

"Dale, I still don't understand why you and Spence correspond if you're both on the same campus. I can understand it if you two were going to different colleges, although even then, I must admit, I'm a little puzzled as to why two men would want to correspond with each other, although both of you are very intellectual so I suppose in your letters you write about all kinds of cerebral stuff and that's why you know so little personal information about him."

"Actually, I'm beginning to learn more personal stuff about him."

"Well, I hope so! Oh, look at the time. I think class is about to start. Did you finish *Catch-22*? It's sort of a long book isn't it? Did you think it was funny? I didn't so much. I'm not very fond of that black humor stuff."

Dale gets up and Mimi walks with him toward Roripaugh Hall. On the way she asks him what topic he is picking for his final paper. Before he can answer she says she's going to write about how *The Catcher in the Rye* is the most censored novel of our time.

"Do you know how many schools have banned *The Catcher in the Rye* since it's publication in 1951?"

"Three million, seven hundred thousand and twenty-two."

"I don't think there are that many high schools in the entire country, Dale! No, according to Literature Watch it's around two thousand! Can you believe it? Some people tried to get *The Catcher* banned at my high school when I was a junior. They didn't succeed but boy did they try! And that was Denver. Well, Littleton. But I mean, it's not some country bumpkin school in Alabama or Oklahoma or someplace like that!"

Dale nods ignoring the insult to his home state. He continues to nod as Mimi expounds on her thesis for her paper, explaining in some detail and with several asides about her great project as they enter Roripaugh Hall to attend their Modern American Novel class.

It's almost ten at night when Dale comes home and finds, as usual, Gary Grabowski reclining on the couch watching television. He's watching one of his favorite shows, *Three's Company*, and Dale waits for five minutes until the show ends to speak.

"Your pick-up has a flat on the left rear tire."

Grabowski shrugs. "No biggie."

"You ought to buy some new tires instead of just patching your old ones."

"Man, who has the cash for that."

In spite of Grabowski's rather frugal habits, he never seems to have any extra money. Since Dale doesn't have much either, he doesn't offer to loan him any.

"You didn't go anywhere tonight?"

"No. Stayed home. I didn't feel like going out. Did you see another movie?"

"Yeah. *Kramer vs. Kramer.*"

"Doesn't interest me," Grabowski says without a hint of irony in his voice.

Dale notices that three empty bottles of beer stand on the coffee table. Ordinarily, Grabowski doesn't have more than two.

"Well, I guess I'll head off to my room."

"Okay. Oh, yeah, something else. The divorce is final. I got the papers today."

"That was fast."

"I didn't contest anything. No fault divorce, something like that. Even so, I got to pay those goddamn lawyers. Now, that's the racket to be in! You play the middleman, type up a few forms, witness them, and charge the suckers a couple of thousand dollars."

Grabowski must be upset. He spoke more than two sentences in a row.

"You should go to law school," Dale says, half humorously.

"Yeah. Maybe."

"So no more Mrs. Grabowski. The wife I mean."

"Christina is Miss Gudmundsdottir again. Well, for a while at least."

"She's going to be married again?"

"Looks like it."

"Wow, that was quick."

"Who knows how long she's been seeing the dickhead."

Dale thinks: probably almost as long as you've been seeing your chicks.

"If the guy has money," Grabowski says, "maybe I can go back to court and get her to pay alimony."

"To you?"

"Shit, yeah. She already makes more money than I do as a GTA."

Dale thinks: probably another reason, in addition to your philandering, as to why she divorced you. Then he thinks: I hope Grabowski doesn't read minds.

"You know, that new actress on *Three's Company* is even better looking than Suzanne Somers."

Obviously Grabowski doesn't.

Grabowski stands and stretches. "You want a beer?"

"No, thanks."

"Good, there's only one left anyway." He starts to lope into the kitchen but stops. "Oh, yeah. I was supposed to tell you something. Deb's going to have an end of semester party at her place Friday. Want to go?"

"I guess so."

"Good. You can give me a ride."

Dale hands a file containing all his newspaper clippings to Professor Comstock. Not only did he write twenty-five movie reviews, he also wrote fifteen advance stories describing the movies the film society were screening on weekends. He thought those stories had more than earned him the one-hour class credit for his film independent study.

Comstock, however, is not impressed. He accepts the folder, opens it, and idly flips through the clipped newsprint.

"Dale, I'm afraid I was premature in agreeing to this project for your independent studies class."

"Why?"

"Submitting a batch of movie reviews hardly qualifies as work for a college course."

"Why?"

"*Why?* Why do you think?"

"I don't know."

"If you don't know then how can I explain it to you?"

Dale thinks: you're not explaining it to me. That's the problem.

"Nevertheless, since I foolishly agreed to this project in the beginning, I'll accept it as credit for the course. However, I'll just award you a P for passing."

"Will that affect the degree requirements?"

"No. You can receive up to three hours on a pass/fail basis."

"Professor Comstock, are you sure about that?"

"Of course, I am! I've been teaching in this department for almost twenty years. I know all the degree requirements."

"Okay. But I want to point out that the work in those clips constitute over 200 column inches of writing. I didn't add up the word count but I imagine it's more than a typical research paper in an independent studies course."

"That's another concern I want to bring up with you. If you decide to do another independent studies course by writing movie reviews as I suspect you are planning on doing, then I'm going to have to require that you also submit a ten page research paper."

"A research paper?"

"Yes, and on a suitably journalistic topic. Not about movie reviewing!"

"Professor Comstock, every major daily newspaper in the country publishes movie reviews. There are journalists who write only movie reviews. Why doesn't that count as valid work in a college course?"

"We've discussed that topic before, Dale. I'm not interested in subjective kinds of journalism like movie reviews or sports columns. I'm interested in the nitty gritty! In the writing and editing of news."

"But I am interested in subjective kinds of journalism. That's what I want to do when I get a newspaper job again."

Comstock, who had been rolling his fairly expensive ink pen in the palm of his hand, suddenly clutches it as if he were about to wield a dagger. Dale notices that Comstock has a rather large, bumpy-knuckled, almost gnarled hand. As he observes that quality, Comstock raises his hand and stabs the padded armrest of his chair with the pointed end of the pen.

"Those are the conditions of my accepting your independent study next semester!"

Dale isn't alarmed by Comstock's sudden attack on the armrest but he does grow wary. "Okay. That means even more work."

"That's the problem you made for yourself. I warned you

about taking on so many responsibilities, especially frivolous ones like writing movie reviews and editing literary magazines."

Dale decides to stop agitating Comstock. Who knows, if pushed any further, the professor might not just stab the armrest.

"I understand, Professor Comstock. But I can get an hour of independent study by working on the campus newspaper writing movie reviews if I also write the research paper?"

"That's what I just explained to you."

Dale stands up. If he'd been in a better mood he would have hinted about his sweet tooth. While waiting in the hall for his meeting with Comstock, he heard the cooing of the two female undergraduates behind the half-closed door. When they emerged ten minutes later they were clutching candy. Not Tootsie Rolls or lollipops, though. Licorice sticks. Dale wonders if Comstock favored those candies when he was a kid. Although at that moment, it is almost impossible to imagine the professor as a candy-loving child.

"Thanks for your time, Professor Comstock."

"I'll return your clips in a few days."

Dale nods and walks out of his office and almost runs into two more female undergraduates. They're already smiling in anticipation of their sweet conference with the avuncular professor.

Dale and Grabowski arrive a little late to Deborah Pierson's party. They walk up to the second floor of a brick and stone building that looks somewhat like the kind of house they rent. Dale rings the doorbell and Deb greets them.

She's dolled up, wearing a green dress with her light brown hair styled above her delicate neck, and wearing more make-up than usual. She smiles a broader smile than her typically demure one and when her lips come together again Dale notices that the lipstick makes her lips look fuller and more alluring.

Dale and Grabowski enter into a noisy, festive room. Dale

scans the crowd of about a dozen people and sees several people he knows: Felicia and Dallas from the *BI*, Ed Darby and Jerry Sibelius from the radio station, Anna Cappelletti, the *OWR* editor, and Pamela Partridge. The only older person present is Regina Wilson, the art professor who also serves on the publications board.

Dale appraises Anna Cappelletti for a few seconds. She is dressed snazzily, too, in a becoming dress, similar to Deb's but the color is burnt orange. She's also done her hair and applied tasteful make-up. She looks quite attractive with her symmetrical features and slender but shapely figure. He got to know her while working on the *OWR* staff. She has a fairly reserved personality, but nice enough. Maybe she was a little pretentious at times. She aspires to be a poet. While working late on the literary magazine one night back in late October, the night of the first snowfall, he walked her back to her sorority. They engaged in a pleasant conversation about literature and fictional muses like Dante's Beatrice, Petrarch's Laura, and Sir Philip Sidney's Stella and when they paused in their walk Dale impulsively kissed her. That was quite unlike him but he hadn't kissed a girl for a long time and Anna looked so comely standing beside the sorority gate with snow falling gently on her gleaming long blonde hair that he acted almost on instinct.

Anna wasn't offended but she didn't respond. She stood as still as a statue of Dante's Beatrice until he removed his hands from around her waist. "Don't you know that I have a steady boyfriend?" she informed him. He didn't know. She never mentioned him. But she spoke the truth. He was back in the Hoosier state, attending the University of Indiana. (Later Dale discovered that he'd competed in the Little Indy 500 just like the guys in *Breaking Away*. When he learned that he found himself liking Fred, even if he had a dull name, and he never made any additional advances to Anna.)

Dale thinks that's the primary reason Anna is leaving Wyoming: so she can join Fred at Indiana.

He's not glad she's leaving although her departure allows

him to edit the *Owen Wister Review*. He liked talking to her, although their conversations after his impulsive smack on the lips resolutely remained in the realm of the literary.

Thinking of the *OWR*, Dale sees several copies lying on a table next to the bookcase. The fall issue came out last week. Contained in it are one of Dale's short stories, "Bodies of Water" and two poems that now rather embarrass him. The work of three other people he knows (or knows about) were also printed: Mimi has one poem, a rather obvious ode to Marilyn Monroe; Spencer Dribble has a critique, a pseudo-intellectual analysis comparing Woody Allen's *Interiors* to a Chekhov play; and Pamela Partridge published an essay on hiking through the Rocky Mountain National Park and observing the appalling degradation of the ecosystem there. He didn't share Pamela's environmental passion exactly, but the essay had been well written.

Now, looking farther in the back, Dale is annoyed to see two more people in attendance: Neil Nordberg and Marsha Martin. Fortunately, those are the only members of the presumably now defunct CSDS. No pilfered papers today, the last newspaper of the term.

"Dale, Gary, I want you to meet my boyfriend, Chris Calloway."

Dale sees a tall, lean, rather rustic looking fellow standing next to Deb. He smiles good-naturedly and extends a hand. Dale shakes it, noticing the strong grip. Grabowski does the same and Dale almost grins at Grabowski's look of mild surprise at the strength in Calloway's handshake.

They chat for a few minutes. Dale learns that Calloway is a second year law student. He's originally from Rock Springs, a town in western Wyoming with a reputation as a rough place. Dale asks him what kind of law he intends to practice and Calloway grins and says, "criminal."

"For the defense or the prosecution?"

"Prosecution. But I'd make more money practicing defense law."

Someone calls Calloway's name over the pleasant noise of rock music and conversational chatter and he excuses himself. Dale glances at Grabowski who looks grumpy. Grabowski asks Deb if there is any beer. She says there's a keg in the kitchen. Grabowski lumbers through the crowd heading for the suds.

"What do you think of him?" Deb asks. She's wearing high heels and stands an inch taller than Dale. A second reminder tonight of why she is not attainable.

"Grabowski?"

Deb laughs. Dale has never heard her laugh like that before. Her voice is as musical as the old Chicago song, Colour My World, which is being played on the stereo. He thinks maybe she's had a beer or two.

"No, Chris."

"He's an impressive guy," Dale says. He means it. Even across the room, because of Calloway's height, Dale can see him as he talks to another fellow, probably a law school buddy. In addition to his six-foot plus height, Calloway has a strong build, exudes a quiet kind of confidence, and has rugged good looks. He's bright, too, at least bright enough to get into law school. He has qualities (his height in particular) that Dale, who is generally content with his identity, sort of envies.

"I've been at Wyo for five years now and he's the first man I've met that really impresses me."

Dale nods. He tries not to take Deb's evaluation personally, although he now hopes that Calloway lacks something, maybe a sense of humor, even though he knows that's spiteful.

"I better resume my hostess responsibilities. Mingle, Dale. There's beer and soft drinks in the kitchen."

Dale nods and watches Deb float away. He smells the lingering scent of her sweet perfume.

As he negotiates his way through the crowded living room, he stops and talks with people he knows. The party is a little raucous to really carry on a conversation. But Ed Darby asks him how he likes the music. Playing now is a record by a group called Blondie. Dale knows about them, of course, the group had a hit album last year, but he never heard the group's early albums until he started working at the radio station. He discovered two other groups that he likes just as well, the B-52s and Devo. When Dale asked Darby about those two groups Darby said that they were a couple of New Wave bands. Dale had never heard of that term so Darby explained. It was a new sound that was coming out of New York and the United Kingdom, although the B-52s were from Athens, Georgia. Darby also introduced him to two other New Wave groups, The Knack and Bram Tchaikovsky, and Dale liked those groups, too. He remembered that Bram Tchaikovsky had a hit single earlier in the year, "Girl of My Dreams." He'd liked that song a lot but he also was fond of the album's title track, "Strange Man, Changed Man." Darby said that New Wave was something of a throwback to '60s music but with a more ironic attitude. After listening to albums by Blondie, The Knack, Bram Tchaikovsky, the B-52s, and Devo, Dale thought Darby's analysis was right.

Dale also liked the absurd sense of humor present in the music, especially Devo and the B-52s. So much of the '70s music lacked a sense of humor that Dale relished the comedy contained in New Wave. Dale mentioned to Darby that there was funny music in the early '60s, especially from Doo Wop groups and R & B bands like The Coasters. Oddly enough, Darby had never known that and hadn't even heard of the Coasters. So Dale went into the storage room and brought out an old LP of the Coasters and played "Little Egypt" for him. Darby thought it was great and later that week he even played the song on the radio just before *The Buffalo Quotidians* were broadcast. KUWR ran a classical format but Darby had talked the station manager into broadcasting one hour of rock music on Friday nights.

"That's not a record," Darby says, almost shouting. "It's KUWR."

"The radio station is playing the song?"

"Yeah. It's my New Wave play-list. The show just started."

Dale strains to listen to the second song now playing. "Rock Lobster."

"Great choice," he yells back.

"There's another surprise," Darby says. He motions for Dale to follow him over to the table where the radio stands.

As "Rock Lobster" winds down, Darby yells, "Attention everyone! Attention!"

The subdued roar of conversation fades. Darby raises his arms and repeats the command. He now has everybody's attention.

"I want you to hear a program that most of you have never heard because you don't listen to KUWR. But I want you to listen now."

Darby turns up the volume on the radio and the stirring sounds of the "Washington Post March" spring forth. Dale grins. It's the beginning of *The Buffalo Quotidians*, his and Darby's mock news radio show.

A few people give modest laughs at hearing the incongruous Sousa theme song; a few other people resume their conversations. Then the dulcet baritone voice of Edward Darby intones the title of the show.

Dale listens with most everyone else. He's never heard the show broadcast because he's always been at the campus Friday night movie. Even though he and Ed just recorded the last *Buffalo Quotidian* for the semester two days ago, and he knows every word since he wrote the spoofs, hearing them spoken aloud and broadcast on the radio gives the silly spoofs an almost Allenesque quality.

This edition of the *Quotidians* concerns the fictional crisis of the "Hollies," a group of wealthy Californians, escaping their gas-starved state as they trek to Oklahoma where the price of gas is cheap and the supply plentiful. The three-part series is called "The Gas of Wrath" and the climax occurs when an ex-Beverly Hills family, the Roads, is nearly trapped by a mob of belligerent Okies near Buffalo City, Oklahoma when their Rolls Royce runs out of gas. Fortunately, the family's pregnant daughter, Fossil of Fuel, saves them all by filling up the tank with gasoline from her own breasts.

Some of the audience laughs, getting the reference to the "Grapes of Wrath." For the last few months California and much of the rest of the country had been suffering from a gasoline shortage. Dale thought it would be funny to reverse the Dust Bowl journey that the "Okies" took to California.

At the conclusion of the radio show, a few people actually clap. Darby takes a bow then says, "and now let me introduce you all to the writer, producer, and mad inventor of the show, Dale Smith!"

Dale, abashed by the attention, feigns an air of sophistication. A couple of people around him laugh and offer their mostly mocking congratulations. Then Devo's "(I Can't Get No) Satisfaction" comes on and everyone forgets about the radio show and him.

Dale walks into the kitchen to grab a 7-Up when he sees Neil Nordberg filling a plastic cup with beer. It's been three days since Dale found out about Nordberg's treachery, but he's no longer angry. He still thinks Neil is a rat but with distance he also sees a little of the absurd humor in the theft and prankish note.

"Now you're a radio show producer, too," Nordberg says with an unconvincing smile.

"Well, at least you can't steal the airwaves."

It's Nordberg who now looks abashed. "Oh, that."

"If you dislike my movie reviews so much why don't you just write a complaining letter to the editor like Dribble does."

"Your friends at the BI won't print any more complaints. That's what prompted the revolutionary act."

"Some revolutionary act. More like an junior high school act."

Nordberg shrugs. "Okay, it was stupid. But I was sort of mad at you. However, I really don't dislike your movie reviews."

"Okay. Let's call a truce."

As Nordberg glides by, he has that insinuating look in his cool blue eyes. "There never was a declared war. You just need to loosen up. You're not even drinking beer."

Nordberg points to the bottle of 7-Up that Dale holds then he ambles out of the kitchen. Dale shrugs. So much for live and let live.

The party begins to thin out by ten p.m. The noise abates and people, mostly the student journalists and GTAs, begin to gather in smaller groups to talk. Felicia and Dallas, who were sitting on the couch talking to Dale, excuse themselves and Dale glances around the room wondering how long he should stay. It's been a fairly fun party, made even better now that he sees Nordberg and Marsha leaving. Before she exits through the front door, Marsha turns her head, looks at Dale looking at her, and sticks her tongue out at him.

He shakes his head in semi-amusement. She must be tipsy.

"One reason she dislikes you is because you made fun of her father."

Dale glances to his right and sees Pamela Partridge taking a seat next to him.

"I made fun of her father?"

"In that radio show you do."

Dale thinks about Marsha's name. Marsha Martin. Then he gets it. In a previous *Buffalo Quotidian*, Dale had satirized her father as being "Martin & Lewis," a coach so laughable in his coaching abilities that even a comedy duo could do better. "She's the daughter of the head football coach?"

"Ex-head football coach."

"Well, I warned him."

Pamela looks puzzled.

"I told Coach Martin to stop running the wishbone offense. Defenses have figured it out. But he persisted in his folly and the administration had no recourse but to can him."

"You're sort of a strange guy," Pamela says.

She's not drunk but he can smell beer on her breath and her eyes have that heavy-lidded, glazy look of semi-intoxication.

"Yeah, I know. But I'm cute."

Pamela laughs. "You *are*." When he frowns she laughs again and bumps her hip at him.

Dale thinks it's sort of odd that some girls (Mimi and now Pamela) flirt with their hips. Well, maybe that's not so odd. He especially likes female hips.

"What's your ethnic background?" she asks.

"Scots-Irish, German, and Apache Indian."

"Apache? Really?"

"Not Apache. Some Creek Indian though."

Pamela leans forward to get a better look of him. When she does so, she slops a little beer out of her full cup onto his lap. She giggles then apologizes.

"That's okay," he says. "I like the smell of fermented grain on my clothes."

"You *do* look a little different. Creek Indian?"

"That's right. One of the five civilized tribes."

"I hope you're not *too* civilized." She smiles in a suggestive way.

Dale turns and appraises her fully for the first time. She's dressed in her usual style, with jeans, flannel shirt, a goose-down vest and those lady-like Timberland hiking boots. Maybe after the party she plans on hiking in Rocky Mountain National Park. She's still smiling in that naughty way but her eyes are droopy now so her expression is more of a woman falling asleep than falling in lust. She's not bad looking, he thinks, with her blonde hair and blue eyes. However, he doesn't like her wilderness attire and her nose is a little too puggish. It's small and turned up and that along with her cheeky face reinforces a porcine portrait. But she has a nice smile and he prefers plump women over skinny ones and her figure doesn't look too bad. Maybe her waist isn't narrow enough to really set off her (rather small) bosom and hips but he liked it when she hipped him before.

"I have my savage moments," he says, looking into her bright blue eyes.

Her eyes widen and he can see some tiny bloodshot threads around the whites of her eyeballs. Not an especially seductive sight.

"Have you ever heard of basketteering?" she asks.

"You mean mouseketeering?"

"No. Bas-ket-teer-ing." She enunciates each syllable, ignoring his silly jest.

"No, I haven't."

"Well," she says in something of a purr, although it sounds more like a lisp, "it's the technique of sizing up a man by looking at his groin."

"Now, why would anybody do that?"

He ought to be shocked because he knows what she means but the evening is growing late and he is getting goofy.

"You can get a more accurate idea if you know his ethnic or racial background."

"Really. I never knew that."

"Whites aren't the biggest. Northern Europeans tend to be larger in that area than southern Europeans."

"Do Germans have big schlongs?"

"Fairly big. Around six inches."

"We *are* talking about the same thing."

"I think so."

"Have you ever seen *Young Frankenstein?*"

"What?"

"The movie ends with Madeleine Kahn being schtupped by the Monster who apparently has such a large phallus that she sings in ecstasy. The Monster is German. At least his parts. But who knows? Maybe Gene Wilder assembled all his body parts from Germans except for his bratwurst. Maybe that came from Africa."

"You're making fun of me."

"Not at all. Just trying to figure out what you're getting at."

"Trying to estimate *your* size."

Dale has never met a girl with as much penis envy as this one. But at least Pamela wasn't as weird as Louise Henderson, the cosmetician for the deceased, the last woman he'd had sex with. That was back in Buffalo City eight and a half months ago.

"Well," he says, "there's only one sure way to find out."

"We could leave."

Dale considers the implications. He hardly knows Pamela Partridge. He certainly would like to engage in some intimate activity that wouldn't be happening in a swimming pool with the wrong sex. But he isn't sure. He feels that pleasant rush of blood inside him. It's churning in the direction of the beer stain on his lap. He thinks of uttering a terrible cliché, your place or mine, when an unannounced derrière deposits itself onto his lap.

"Dale, dahling! I'm ready for my close-up!"

"Miriam, I mean, Mimi. What are you doing here?" He knows he was speaking another cliché but that's all he could come up with.

"I'm crashing the party! I only came to see *you*." Mimi throws her hands around his neck and gives a snide glance to Pamela, who is brushing off spilled beer from her lap.

"That's very naughty of you, crashing a party. And it appears that you are intoxicated, too."

"I'm drunk with love. For you!" She kisses Dale on the cheek, a big, wet, sloppy kiss that he does not like. It's more like someone trying to suck out poison from a snakebite than a kiss.

"Excuse me," Pamela hisses, as she rises from the couch. She glares down at her jeans where a large blotch of beer is soaking into them.

Dale starts to ask her to stay but she storms off. Mimi gives her retreating figure a Medusa-like stare.

"Pamela Partridge! We don't want her. Away with you, wench!" Mimi waves one hand while the other clutches Dale's neck.

He shrugs disappointedly. His bird has flown. But there is another possibility.

"Mimi, what about Joe Dimaggio?"

She scrambles off Dale's lap. "Oh, Dale. Thanks for reminding me. I would never be unfaithful to my Joe."

"Glad to be of help."

Mimi smiles and bends over and gives him an affectionate kiss on the other cheek.

"Bye bye," she says.

Dale watches her walk out with a guy who must be Von Goebbels. At least judging by his Lorre-like appearance: short stature, dark hair, googly eyes.

He looks for Pamela. He doesn't see her. He guesses she's left too.

How frustrating. Another party out of bounds.

5

Dale and Will Whitaker get out the car and walk toward the fence so they can get a better look of Devil's Tower. Fortunately, it's as clear day and not terribly cold for mid-December in northeastern Wyoming. The butte rises like an upturned milk bucket into the bright, azure sky. Even from where they stand, five miles away, they can see the rocky ridges on it sides.

"Looks like it did in *Close Encounters*," says Dale. His breath crystallizes in the cold air.

"Yes, but I don't see any extraterrestrial spacecraft hovering close by," says Will.

"Maybe they're using a cloaking device."

They walk down the road while still gazing at the geographic monument. A pick-up truck drives by but they don't look at it. They both stare at the butte, the sky, and the brown fields with patches of snow that surround Devil's Tower.

They made good time getting here. They left Laramie at five in the morning because they wanted to make it to Devil's Tower and Mount Rushmore before dark. The day before Will had flown to Denver and Dale had picked him up and they drove back to Laramie. Dale showed him around the nearly empty campus, presented the *Branding Iron* offices, the college radio station KUWR, the *Owen Wister Review* office, and his office in the Mass Communications Department. Then they returned to Dale's place and sat around and talked for a few hours before retiring early in preparation for the big trip. Dale didn't get a chance to introduce Will to Grabowski. His roommate had taken a short trip to Cheyenne but he'd be back the next day and would remain in Laramie until after Christmas. Then he was going to fly to Chicago for a post-Christmas gathering with his family. Waiting until an after-Christmas flight had saved Grabowski a couple of hundred dollars, money he needed to pay his attorney fees. Dale rather wanted Will to meet Grabowski. He was curious to see how Will would react to his dull roomie. But as Grabowski often said, no biggie.

The trip from Laramie to Devil's Tower took six hours. They drove on Interstate 25 to Douglas then turned off on state highway 59 and made it to Gillette by ten a.m. Back on Interstate 90, they drove for ten miles then took two more state roads, highway 14 and highway 24, to get within viewing distance of the tower. They knew they were taking a risk by driving in this part of the country in winter. But the weather gods were propitious and they encountered clear roads and clement weather.

Dale, who brought his 35 mm camera, gets his friend to pose in the foreground as he takes a shot of Will and Devil's Tower. Then Will snaps Dale's photo and after a final examination of the geographical erection, still no saucers in sight, they take off for the Black Hills and Mount Rushmore.

Two hours later they arrive in Rapid City and it takes half an hour more to arrive at Mount Rushmore's tourist center. By the time they walk to the viewing area the sky is turning a little gloomy. Sunset comes earlier in the northern climes during winter and although it's not yet 2 p.m., the sun is already down halfway to the horizon from its earlier zenith.

It's an impressive sight, the busts of the four presidents displayed in the rocky formations of the cliff. And yet, as Dale scrutinizes the monument, he feels a tad disappointed.

"It looks smaller than it does in the movies," he says.

"You're always comparing things to movies," says Will. "And I thought I was mad for cinema."

"I mean, it's spectacular, but it's smaller than I imagined. In *North By Northwest* it looks bigger."

"Those are mostly sets, you know."

"Yeah, I know. It's funny how fiction can be more real in our minds than reality."

They take pictures of themselves and the monument. Dale even obliges one of the few other tourists by taking his photo with his wife.

As they prepare to leave, Dale asks Will which presidential head he likes most.

Will examines the large grayish faces. All of them have noble and wise expressions.

"I admire Lincoln the most as president and I think he has the best head."

"Me, too," says Dale. "His craggy face looks good in stone."

They hustle back to the car. The sun is sinking lower in the sky and they can see some stars beginning to appear in the higher and darker parts of the sky.

They drive back to Rapid City then turn east on Interstate 90. The Twin Cities are 570 miles away. If they drive the 55 mph speed limit, it will take over ten hours.

"Damn this speed limit," Dale says as he scans the long, straight highway and the vast, flat land spread out before it. "No wonder the ranchers were angry at Carter back in Buffalo City. All this open land and hardly anyone on the road and you can't go fast."

"Yet another asinine federal government regulation," says Will.

Dale pushes down on the accelerator and watches the needle of the speedometer rise to sixty, then sixty-five, then seventy. "If we average 70, we'll shave off two hours. Think it's worth the risk?"

"Yes I do. But slow down when you approach a population center. That's where the cops hide out."

As the Chevy Monza zips down the highway, Dale and Will talk about their respective experiences in graduate school. Dale tells him about all the activities he's involved in, the classes he's taking, and his encounters with Comstock and the members of the now defunct CSDS. The tactics of the group amuses Will but he understands how such actions are a kind of censorship, which he abhors.

"And I don't think my reviews were all that harsh," Dale says. "Imagine what a group of reactionaries like that would do to John Simon? They might burn him at the stake."

John Simon is the notoriously acerbic film critic that currently writes for *The National Review*. Will laughs at the idea of capital punishment for caustic critics.

When they stop for gasoline in Sioux Falls, they switch and Will does the driving and most of the talking. He tells Dale about his courses, his work at WCCO, one of the television stations in Minneapolis-St. Paul, and what movies he's seen when he has free time, which is not often. All these topics are covered in their lengthy letters to one another but being in each other's company enables them to elaborate on certain experiences and ideas.

Dale settles into the passenger seat and gazes at the black highway and the surrounding dark land. The lighter sky, a dark purplish gray, hovers above it all. He feels a sort of contentment as he sits in the warm, speeding car knowing that it is cold and dark outside. He listens to Will's voice, not deep but with a fine clarity, as he speaks about his life these past few months. He feels again that kinship to Will, and it brings a reassuring inner warmth, and he remembers the first time he felt that connection to him, back when Will came to Buffalo City to help with the newspaper coverage of President Carter's visit. Even though Dale has been very busy these past months and he's met a few people that he likes, there still are moments of lonesomeness. Most of his friendships at Wyoming are circumstantial and so far he's not met anyone he feels he could talk to in depth. For a short while, he thought Neil Nordberg might offer that possibility but he was misled. Dale hasn't told Will anything about the rather bizarre swimming pool incident with Nordberg because remembering that strange day still embarrasses him. The fact is that Dale doesn't write about his personal feelings that

114

often nor does Will. Most of their correspondence centers on intellectual and cultural concerns. They have a cerebral friendship and at this stage Dale is satisfied with that. He thinks Will, although he is only two years older, lives a more sophisticated life and he knows more about certain matters. Dale wants to learn as much as he can from him and when he has caught up a little with Will in those areas then they could enlarge their friendship by talking about more personal matters.

"You didn't take this route last summer, did you?" Dale asks.

"No, we drove through Nebraska then up through Iowa." Will's boyhood friend, George Alexander, had been with him during that trip.

"Why did you do that?"

"Both my parents are from Nebraska. I wanted to travel through that state again."

Dale asks where in Nebraska. Will says his father's family had resided outside Grand Island, which is located in central Nebraska. They were farmers. Both granddad and grandmother Whitaker are deceased. His mother grew up in Omaha. Her father was a businessman. His grandmother Foster is still alive and living in a nursing home in the Twin Cities. His parents met at the University of Nebraska in Lincoln. They married after graduation. They lived in New York City for three years back in the early '50s. When they decided to settle down for good they drove west with the intention of living in California but when they arrived in Tulsa they liked it so much – it's small city charm as his mother often puts it – that they stayed there.

"My parents will be back before you leave," Will says. "You'll get to meet them."

Will's parents are in Hawaii taking a holiday vacation. They are scheduled to return home the day before Dale's planned departure.

Dale thinks about his parents. In a few days when he drives back from Minnesota he could detour south and visit them in Oklahoma. Of course, that would result in doubling the mileage of an already long trip so he isn't going to do that. Going back to Oklahoma to see his parents was sort of awkward anyway. His mother is living with her parents. His father lives with his second wife, a woman Dale dislikes. He could see his half brother, Marlon, who was a year and four months old now. He could also see June, his sister. During Christmas break she is staying at a friend's house until the dorms open again. But, truth be told, he really has no great desire to see any of his family. Instead, he telephoned the day before Will flew out and spoke briefly in separate conversations to his mother, father, sister, and grandparents wishing them a Merry Christmas.

Making good time and not seeing any cops, they leave I-90 at Worthington and angle northeast on Minnesota state highway 60 then highway 69. Taking that route will save fifty miles. Even though the road is no longer an interstate, they speed along. They discuss books and movies and some of the New Wave bands that Dale likes. Will, not as interested in rock music as Dale, tries to understand his friend's enthusiasm.

Highway 69 takes them right into Bloomington, the pleasant Minneapolis suburb in the southern part of the metro area where Will's parents live. They pull into the driveway of an attractive condominium just before midnight. They drove from Laramie to the outskirts of Minneapolis in nineteen hours and both young men are exhausted.

When they enter the condo, Will doesn't even bother to give Dale a tour. He'll do that tomorrow. They just wash up and go to bed, Will in his own room, Dale in the guest room.

As Dale lies in the comfortable bed, snug under the old fashioned quilt, he thinks how strange it is to wake up in one part of the country and before that day is over to be in a very different place. He imagines not only traversing vast territory via cars and airplanes but actually time traveling. Where would he like to go? Like H.G. Wells, he'd pick the unknown, the future, and as he visualizes what his future would look like ten, twenty, even thirty years from now, he falls deeply asleep.

Dale wakes the next morning when the family cat jumps on

the bed and sniffs his face. Dale pets the mostly black cat for a few minutes then he looks out the window and sees a foot of thick, wet new snow covering the streets and the lawns of the condos. He thinks that's appropriate since Christmas is only four days away. When he sees Will at breakfast, Will tells him that Minneapolis has a fleet of snow plows and by noon most of the major streets and highways will be clear.

After breakfast of juice and cereal (neither of them cooks), Will gives Dale a tour of the condo. It has two stories and the interior is tastefully furnished and handsomely designed. The floors are covered in a thick, aqua blue shag rug and the walls display tasteful art of still life and landscapes and black and white arty photographs. Dale asks who designed all of this and Will says his mother. She was an art history major in college and she had decorated the condo herself.

Dale had never been in so splendid a household before except the times he visited his college girlfriend's house. He had certainly never lived, even briefly, in such a genteel and attractive home before. He's very impressed but Will is modest about his family's good taste.

In the afternoon they start the first day of their vacation together. Will first shows him the University of Minnesota campus, in particular, the student union and library. Then they see a movie matinée, *Being There*, a satire on contemporary politics and culture that features an excellent by performance by Peter Sellers. They both enjoy the movie and have a stimulating discussion about it afterwards while enjoying an early dinner at an unpretentious downtown restaurant. That evening they see another movie, *The Graduate*, at the Walker Fine Arts Center. They both enjoy the film immensely. Both of them saw the film when it showed on television several years ago but seeing it in the theatre is a more fulfilling experience. Both young men identify with Ben Braddock and the uncertainties he has about his life and his reluctance to join the corrupt adult world.

The next day they repeat the process except Will takes Dale to WCCO. They watch the noon broadcast from the viewing room and afterwards Will shows him the dispatcher's shack where he works. Dale asks him if he ever thinks about working in broadcast journalism. Will says he never would. It pays better than print journalism but the actual work is superficial and full of pressure to maintain decent ratings. They see *The Jerk* for the movie matinée and both of them are disappointed. The Steve Martin film is mostly a series of inane gags and contrived skits and it never materializes into a developed comic story. They both rather like Steve Martin the stand-up comic so they had expected a better movie.

That evening they see *Soldier of Orange*, a foreign language film from Holland. They both are impressed with how the Dutch film is more candid and naturalistic about the war than typical Hollywood films. It's about what happens to four Dutch young men before and during World War II in the occupied Netherlands.

Back at Will's parent's home, they have a lively discussion about the film and how they think they would have responded if they had lived in Holland during the war. Neither one is convinced they would have acted as heroically as the major characters.

The third day of their shared vacation begins with a tour of the galleries of the Walker Art Center. Dale likes the Renaissance paintings best; Will is more attuned to the abstract expressionists. Dale is puzzled by those paintings so he listens as Will describes the aesthetic intentions of the artists. In the end, Dale still doesn't like them much but he thinks he understands that school of art better due to Will's tutoring.

For the matinée they go see *Kramer vs. Kramer*. Dale has already seen it a few weeks ago but he agrees to see it again since Will didn't have time to see it when it first came to the theatres. They both like it and Dale sees things on a second viewing that he didn't fully appreciate on a first viewing. For example, he is more impressed with how the film is directed. Robert Benton, the director, skillfully frames scenes and gives a certain distance to most of them. He also uses music cleverly to cool the emotions of the viewers, that is, until the end when the previous restrained style gives way to a more emotional final scene. On the other hand seeing the film a second time makes the story seem a little less impressive. Dale notices more of the film's contrivances. For example, neither Kramer seems to have any family. Dustin Hoffman's character only has one friend, the ex-friend of his ex-wife. The film's world is quite small. Also, he begins to question if the Kramers would resolve their legal battle so amicably. Upon reflection, he's more aware of the soap opera elements in the episodic story. Nevertheless, he still likes it. The film features excellent acting by Hoffman, Meryl Streep and the little kid and it's deftly directed in a concise, almost ironic style.

That night they see *Apocalypse Now*. Will didn't have time to see it when it was first released. They both like it but as with *Kramer vs. Kramer*, a second viewing enables Dale to scrutinize the film more thoroughly. Now he thinks that the story is rather weak, mostly because the man who goes in search of Kurtz is psychologically disturbed himself. Dale thinks the film's story would have more resonance if Willard had been uncorrupted, more of a straight arrow, and then as he travels deeper into the Asian version of *The Heart of Darkness*, his moral decline would have been more dramatic.

Dale mentions some of these observations to Will. He understands Dale's points, but he is more focused on the amazing cinematography, brilliant direction, and superb acting. Will does concede that the ending is somewhat anti-climatic. The Brando-Sheen confrontation isn't as dramatic as it should have been.

During dinner they discuss the source material for the movie, Joseph Conrad's The *Heart of Darkness*. They both have read the novella, but they decide they need to read it again to fully evaluate the parallels between novel and film.

On their last completely free day, the day before Will's parents arrive, Will drives Dale around Minneapolis and St. Paul showing him the landmarks and points of historical interest.

They visit F. Scott Fitzgerald's boyhood home in St. Paul and are allowed to wander in the old but well-maintained house. Both Dale and Will are fans of Fitzgerald, especially his best work, *The Great Gatsby*.

As usual, they attend another afternoon matinée and see *The Electric Horseman*. Neither Dale nor Will is particularly impressed. The film is a rather conventional drama with Jane Fonda playing yet again a role of an ambitious but ultimately decent television reporter pursuing a story. Robert Redford plays, of course, the electric horseman, who has stolen a retired thoroughbred racehorse because he can't tolerate the horse being exploited by greedy capitalist bastards.

Again, they have dinner at a fairly inexpensive but tasteful restaurant and afterwards go see another movie. This time it's *Manhattan*, another film that Dale saw weeks ago but Will hasn't seen. And as with the case of the other two films he's seen twice, a second viewing gives him an additional perspective and he is more aware of the film's weaker qualities. Will, however, loves the film and is quite impressed with the ethical issues its raises and the artistic way in which it is directed and filmed.

Back at the Whitaker's pleasant home, Will and Dale engage in their first disagreement. Will thinks *Manhattan* is the best film of the year. Dale isn't so sure.

"You were impressed with how it was filmed, right?" Will asks.

"Yeah, the black and white cinematography by Gordon Willis was superb."

"You have to agree that the musical score was evocative."

"I do."

"And doesn't the ideas in the film appeal too you? Aren't they meaningful and treated in an ironic way?"

"For the most part."

"Then I don't know why you don't love the film?"

"Maybe because I've seen it twice, unlike you, and it's weaknesses are more apparent."

"What kind of weaknesses?"

"Well, first I don't think it adds up thematically. At the end of the film, Tracy says that everyone gets corrupted. And it's supposed to be a poignant moment because now Woody doesn't want her to leave and become compromised. But hasn't having an affair with a much older man already corrupted Tracy? I mean, she seventeen and he's forty something."

"You think that's corrupt? Having an affair with an older man?"

"Yeah, sort of. I mean she's a lot younger. She's sleeping with him at his apartment."

"But she's in love with him."

"That's hard to believe too. I mean she's this cute seventeen year old and he's this repulsive older guy."

"You think Woody is repulsive?"

"In those bedroom scenes I did. Seeing scrawny Woody Allen smooching on a nubile girl. Yuck."

Dale notices that Will seems disturbed by his reaction. He's puzzled as to why. It's obvious that Woody Allen is no Adonis.

"Go on."

"We have no idea how Tracy and Woody met. The romance seems implausible. But thematically, as I said before, it doesn't add up because Tracy's already been corrupted by Woody so she's not losing her innocence and he's not losing her to the corrupt adult world because that's already happened."

Will says nothing for a few moments. He's thinking. "I don't see it that way. It's a matter of degree. Tracy hasn't been corrupted because she's been in love with Woody. She retains an innocence in spite of the sexual affair."

"Yeah, that's what the film wants us to think. But I don't think that is grounded in reality."

"The only reality is the reality that the film establishes for itself."

"I mostly agree with that. *Manhattan* creates its own world really well in a sight and sound way: The cinematography and music. But reality in a dramatic film has to correspond to reality in the world to some degree. And that's where *Manhattan* fails."

"Sounds like you're writing a review."

"I already did that. I had those concerns when I first saw it, but seeing it again makes it more obvious. I didn't believe that Tracy would fall for Woody. And what about her parents? They don't mind that their teenage daughter is sleeping with a creepy middle aged man?"

"Creepy!"

"Yeah, it is sort of creepy. I mean Woody's character is funny and bright and he's affectionate to Tracy but the age difference is still a problem."

"Not to me."

"If Isaac had been played by somebody else, an actor who is more physically appealing and younger, then their romance would have been more plausible and interesting."

"Like who?"

"Maybe Dustin Hoffman."

"You think Dustin Hoffman would be better in that role than Woody?"

"He's certainly a better actor."

"Yes, but doesn't Woody bring something to that role that Dustin couldn't?"

"Maybe. But that was another problem with the movie. Woody Allen is pretty good as a comic actor but in the dramatic scenes he isn't so convincing."

"I thought you liked Woody Allen."

"I do. I just think he's better as a writer and director than as an actor."

"You don't seem to have liked *Manhattan* at all."

"I liked it. I guess I just noticed more things I didn't like as much on a second viewing."

Will remains silent, thinking. Dale knows he is like he is: that he wants his friends to like what he likes. Instead of reassuring him that he liked *Manhattan*, Dale instead adds another criticism.

"And Diane Keaton's character was annoying."

Will nods. "Yeah, a little."

"Sort of an anti-Annie Hall."

Will smiles wryly.

"I know you like Woody Allen," Dale said in a more conciliatory voice. "I like him too. But no one makes a perfect picture."

"What about *Annie Hall*?"

"Okay. That was close."

That concession makes Will feels better and he asks if Dale wants something to drink before bed. Cocoa maybe?

Dale says sure and follows Will into the kitchen and watches as he makes the cocoa.

"At least you can make something," Dale says.

Will grins. "I'm not bad at instant coffee, too."

The next afternoon, Christmas Day, Will and Dale drive to the Minneapolis International Airport to pick up Will's parents. They wait at the TWA gate and soon see Will's parents as they walk into the terminal.

Dale's immediate reaction is that the Whitakers are a dignified, respectable middle-aged couple. Mr. Whitaker looks older than his wife. He is a little taller than average, with a regular kind of built, maybe a bit of a paunch, and is mostly bald. Will greets his parents. His father shakes his hand and his mother kisses him. Then Dale is introduced. He gets a better look at Mr. Whitaker. He notices that he has a fairly handsome face with a straight nose, shrewd hazel eyes and a strong chin. His mouth, however, has a sort of pursed, dissatisfied look. When Dale puts those features all together he realizes that Mr. Whitaker reminds him of Ray Milland's character in *Love Story*.

Mrs. Whitaker reminds Dale of a movie person, too: June Allyson. She has a similar petite figure, cute, smiling face with bright blue eyes and perky personality. Her hair is silver in color and stylishly cut. When she speaks her voice doesn't have June Allyson's feminine throatiness; instead it has a slightly nasal sound to it, which is common in the upper Midwest.

She greets Dale warmly. Mr. Whitaker is more aloof.

They all get into the Whitaker's family car, a silver 1979 Buick Electra, that Will drove to the airport instead of his Volvo. Mr. Whitaker takes the wheel and drives at moderate speed back to their condo. On the way, Will asks his parents questions about their vacation in Hawaii and it's apparent that his mother is cheerfully talkative whereas his father is more reserved. That reinforces their screen personas for Dale.

When they arrive home, Dale and Will carry the luggage. Instead of having more conversation, Mr. Whitaker and his wife decide to take a nap. They need one. They left San Francisco at 5 a.m. that morning after flying there from Hawaii the day before.

"Now, you boys enjoy yourself but don't eat anything. I'm going to cook all of us a delightful dinner when I get up after a refreshing nap."

"But mother, you just got home. Don't you want to relax?"

"I've been relaxing for a week! I'm also tired of restaurant food. Besides, I enjoy cooking, However, if you are so concerned about my kitchen duties, then you can load the dishwasher afterwards."

Will frowns at that idea and Mrs. Whitaker laughs. She kisses him on the cheek and reminds them not to eat anything.

"We'll open our presents before dinner," says Mr. Whitaker.

He and his wife leave for their bedroom. Will suggests that he and Dale go into his room and listen to some records.

Dale thinks Will's bedroom is an accurate reflection of the Will he knows: neat, clean, organized, and intellectual. The bed is made, no clothes in sight, and the desk is organized in an orderly fashion with a typewriter, notebooks, pens and pencils. A dresser bureau is in one corner and he notices a framed photo of Will with his parents. There is a large cork bulletin board on the wall opposite the bed. All kinds of things are pinned to it: move ticket receipts, play programs, class schedules, newspaper clippings, essays ripped from magazines, and Xeroxed photos from magazines of jazz musicians, writers, politicians, and journalists. A rather large bookcase is located next to the desk and Dale examines the contents: mostly textbooks and scholarly tomes about academic subjects of history, political science, economics, law, literature and journalism are located on the lower two shelves. In the middle shelves are his movie books. Several reference books and texts covering film history and criticism. Also biographies of filmmakers and a few stars: Orson Welles, Alfred Hitchcock, David Lean, Billy Wilder, Fellini, Bergman, Kurosawa, and Woody Allen. When Dale sees the three books about Woody, he rather wishes he'd been less critical of *Manhattan*. On the top two shelves are dozens of novels. Dale is surprised to see several mysteries among the classics. The authors featured most are Hemingway, Fitzgerald, Thomas Woolfe, and Sinclair Lewis. Dale approves. He likes all those writers, too.

Stacked next to the bookcase are magazines. When Dale glances at them, he notices most of them are from this month only. But the stack looks to be a foot high with issues of *The New Republic*, *The National Review*, *Harper's*, *The Atlantic Monthly*, *The New Yorker*, *Esquire*, and three others that Dale isn't familiar with. Will must have past issues neatly bundled up somewhere else.

"What?" Dale asks. "No *Playboy*?"

"I have that tucked away under my bed."

Dale grins at the jest and joins Will at the other end of the room where the stereo and records are located. The stereo is a fairly expensive model and stands on a sturdy wooden platform. In addition to the receiver and turntable there is also an old eight track. The two fairly large speakers are positioned in two corners in the spacious bedroom. In a gray crate, dozens of album are filed alphabetically. Dale notes to himself that the books were also arranged alphabetically within their respective genres. So, Will, is an alphabetizer. Dale, on the other hand, organizes his books and records chronologically. That's not as precise a system and Dale's bedroom is not nearly as fastidiously organized. In fact, he tends to be rather sloppy with his clothes and personal belongings but not his books and records.

Will asks Dale what he'd like to listen to. Dale shrugs. What do you got?

Will kneels and flips through the albums while Dale looks over his shoulder. A lot of jazz. Dale's heard of some of the artists, Louis Armstrong, Count Basie, and Glenn Miller and Benny Goodman in particular because he's seen their biopics on television. But most of the other musicians he's never heard of: Dave Brubeck, John Coltrane, Miles Davis, Dizzy Gillespie, Billie Holiday, Thelonious Monk, and Charlie Parker.

Will also has quite of few classical albums. Dale has heard of most of the composers. Then in the back of the crate are the popular music albums, including sound tracks of Broadway shows and movies. Will appears to have all the Chicago albums, some Carole King, The Manhattan Transfer, Joni Mitchell, Paul Simon (and Simon and Garfunkel), James Taylor, and, of course, the Beatles.

"Play some of that jazz," Dale says. "I've never heard much."

Will selects the Dave Brubeck album, *Count Five*. He puts it on the turntable, only after carefully cleaning the record, and Will takes a seat on his bed while Dale sits in the chair.

They listen and Dale is surprised that he likes it. Will plays more records this time by the artists Dale has never heard of before and he doesn't like the music as much. It doesn't seem to have as much melody. Afterwards, he asks Will questions about it and he gives thoughtful replies. Will's analysis of the jazz records helps Dale understand some of the underlying principles and concepts but when they listen to more jazz records he finds himself still not liking the music much better.

Of course, Dale realizes part of his problem is that he's never had any musical instruction. He never played an instrument in school. While in college, Dale listened to a series of records in the library discussing the principles of classical music. The recordings also gave a concise history of classical music and biographical information on the major composers. He tried to educate himself on his own mostly because his college girl-friend was a music major and he wanted to understand music on a more technical, intellectual level. Maybe he thought that would impress her. But he realized after a while that he'd never fully understand or appreciate certain kinds of music, the more complex kind, because he didn't play or read music. He concluded that some endeavors, such as serious music, required direct experience to fully understand it.

So, he is content to be a casual listener and that means he mostly listens to rock and pop music, although he enjoys quite a lot of classical music especially compositions from the Romantic era.

After the jazz, Will put on an album by The Manhattan Transfer, "Pastiche." Dale nods with approval. Will then turns the volume down a little.

"What do you think of Pater and Mater?"

"Your parents are interesting. Your mother is very nice."

"Yes, she is."

They hear someone walking down the hall. The footsteps are soft and barely discernible. Must be Mrs. Whitaker. The master bedroom was at the end of the hall.

"That's Mother getting up. She's going to prepare the Christmas feast."

"I hope she's not to a lot of trouble on my account."

"Not at all. She'll defrost a turkey breast in the microwave and she'll fix all the trimmings and bake an apple pie and it will all be ready in a few hours."

"Sounds good." Dale is hungry although he and Will stopped at a place called White Castle for a hamburger before going to the airport. But the hamburger was surprisingly small and square-shaped.

"What do you think of my father?"

Dale isn't sure what to say. He'd only spent ten minutes in his presence. Will has never written much about him in his letters. "Well, he seems like an intelligent, dignified kind of man."

"He's that all right."

"He reminds me of Ray Milland. You know, in *Love Story*."

Will nods. "There is a vague resemblance. I haven't seen that movie in several years but isn't Ray Milland disappointed in his son?"

"For marrying a poor, Italian girl."

"At least I haven't done that."

"But maybe you will."

Dale says that in a pseudo-earnest tone of voice as if he is a professional prognosticator and the mood lightens. Will, now grinning, remarks that the Manhattan Transfer is a very talented group.

Dale agrees.

Before dinner, the Whitakers and Dale open presents. Mr. Whitaker gives his wife a lovely white cashmere sweater and matching kid gloves. Mrs. Whitaker presents her husband with a London Fog overcoat. Will gives his father a new leather briefcase and his mother a pink wool sweater. Mrs. Whitaker laughs at the coincidence but Dale can tell that neither the father nor the son is amused.

Dale realizes he's made a faux pas for not bringing a gift for the Whitakers. They don't seem to mind since they don't have gifts for him. They do have a gift for the cat, Tuxedo. It's a felt mouse sprinkled with catnip. Tuxedo, named for his white chest and black everything else, springs to life. He wrestles the mouse into submission and rubs his whiskered face on the rug.

He did remember to bring gifts for Will, two books: *Darkness at Noon* and *Cry, The Beloved Country*.

"I hope you don't have them already," Dale says after Will tears off the sloppily made wrapping.

"No, I don't. Thanks very much. The Koestler novel is especially appropriate. I'm taking a course in Soviet history next semester."

Dale notices that Mr. Whitaker suppresses a frown.

Will gives Dale his presents: a University of Minnesota

sweatshirt, baseball cap, and pennant.

"I probably would have given you books too," Will says to Dale, "but I thought you'd have any novel I could think of."

"I like this Gopher paraphernalia. I'll wear it at Wyoming and see how all the Cowboys fans react."

The gifts given, they all go to dinner in the dining room. Just as Will predicted, the meal consists of a large turkey breast and all the traditional trimmings. During the dinner, there isn't much conversation. Mrs. Whitaker speaks the most and the topics are consistent with polite conversation. For desert, they have apple pie. All the food is delicious. Dale is impressed with Mrs. Whitaker's cooking skills and compliments her once the meal is finished.

"It was nothing special," she modestly says. "We usually have this kind of holiday meal."

"It was very tasty just the same. I haven't had such good food in a long time."

"Don't you cook?"

"Not at all. But my roommate sometimes makes kielbasa and other Polish dishes."

"Is he a good cook?"

"He thinks so. But my stomach tells me otherwise."

Mrs. Whitaker and Will laugh but Mr. Whitaker manages to only give a wry smile. The dinner concludes and they retire to the living room. Mr. Whitaker makes a fire. Mrs. Whitaker brings coffee for all except Dale ~ he doesn't drink coffee ~ but she thoughtfully includes hot apple cider for his consumption.

Mrs. Whitaker talks about the Hawaii vacation. Will mentions the movies that he and Dale have seen. Mrs. Whitaker is a movie fan. She asks which movie was the best that they saw. Dale sees Will giving him a wry look.

"*Manhattan*," Dale says. That brings a smile from Will. "But I think you'd like *Kramer vs. Kramer* a lot too."

"Yes, I've heard that is a good movie," Mrs. Whitaker says.

"Did you and Dale do anything else but see films?" Mr. Whitaker asks.

Will tells him about all the other things they did. When he mentions visiting F. Scott Fitzgerald's home, Mr. Whitaker nods thoughtfully.

"Dale," Mr. Whitaker says, "I understand that you're also a graduate student. At Wyoming?"

"Yes, sir. Wyoming."

"What are your plans after you receive your degree?"

"I'll probably find a newspaper job."

"Didn't you have a newspaper job before you went to graduate school?"

"Yes, sir, I did."

Mr. Whitaker nods. "Sometimes it seems that young men are going to graduate school simply to postpone building careers. For example, William here, is now attending his second graduate school. That's not counting law school. If he'd remained in law school, he'd be receiving his degree this spring and then could embark on a law career."

Dale doesn't take umbrage at Mr. Whitaker's observation because he knows it's really directed at Will. However, he didn't know that Will attended law school. He glances over to Will who sits on the sofa next to his mother with a slightly vexed look on his face.

"Dear, boys today take more time to decide on what they want to do with their lives," says Mrs. Whitaker.

"Obviously. But we didn't have that luxury in 1944."

"My father served in World War II," Will says, "before he went to college."

That explains why Mr. Whitaker looks several years older than his wife even though they met at college. Dale doesn't say so but his father served in Korea in the Navy. He saw action on a cruiser as a seventeen year-old kid.

"When I got back to the States, I didn't have time to decide what I wanted to do with my life. It was decided for me. I went to college on the GI Bill, graduated, started a career, and married."

"Bill," says his wife.

"I know. Things are different today. More complicated."

Mrs. Whitaker steers the conversation back to more polite and therefore more boring topics. They all talk for another thirty minutes before Mr. and Mrs. Whitaker decide to retire for bed.

After the family members all say goodnight to each other, Dale expresses his thanks for their hospitality.

"I'll be leaving very early tomorrow morning so I probably won't be able to thank you then. But I appreciate your allowing me to stay in your attractive home for these past few days."

Mrs. Whitaker smiles graciously and says he was entirely welcomed. Mr. Whitaker tells him to be sure to drive safely back to Wyoming.

Dale and Will watch them toddle up the stairs to their bedroom.

"That was a certainly an exciting evening, wasn't it?" says Will.

"It was fine. Your mother is a good cook."

Will nods. He looks disgruntled.

"You never told me that you went to law school," Dale says in a slightly teasing tone of voice.

"There wasn't much reason to. I only lasted one year."

"Why did you leave?"

"Simple. I hated it."

"That's a good reason to leave."

They walk over to the fireplace. Will takes a poker and stabs the smoldering logs. He gazes intently at the embers as they spark.

"Going to law school was my father's idea." Will gives the logs one more poke. "Of course, he has a valid point. I should be starting a career. The question is what kind of career? Should I get my Ph.D. and teach college? Or should I try journalism?"

"Well, what do you really want to do?"

"I'd like to travel around the world. Work at odd jobs. Experience things. Do that for a few years then I'd have a better idea of what to do for the rest of my life."

"Makes sense."

"Did I tell you that the summer before law school, George and I bummed around Europe for six weeks?"

"Yeah, you mentioned that in one of your letters. Did I tell you that I also went to Europe? But it didn't last for six weeks."

Will walks over to the couch and sits down, while looking at Dale with a pleased expression on his face. "You didn't tell me that. When did you go?"

"May 1978." Dale sits on the chair opposite the couch.

"That's interesting. George and I went over in June of that year. How long did you stay?"

"A month. I left the U.S. May twelfth and returned June tenth."

"That means we were in Europe at the same time. For a week, anyway. Why didn't you stay longer?"

"I ran low on money." Dale didn't add that the reason was he'd been swindled in Paris.

"Where were you during the first week of June?"

"By then, I was probably in Germany. Then I went to Amsterdam. Then Paris. Then back to London."

"George and I were in Paris from June fifth to the ninth. Were you there then?"

"Yeah, I think I was. I got there on June sixth. Left on the seventh to go to London."

"That's amazing. Then we were both in Paris for two days in June. We didn't know each other then but we were there. In what part of Paris did you stay?"

"Somewhere close to the Left Bank."

"So did we!"

"Who knows, maybe we passed each other in the streets."

"Maybe walking the Montparnasse. Or browsing for books at Shakespeare & Company."

"Why not? I went there!"

"So did I!"

Will gives an abashed smile at their enthusiasm and glances at the stairway that leads to the upstairs bedrooms.

"It's remarkable that almost two years ago we were in Paris at the same time and now we're sitting here," says Dale.

"Yes, remarkable."

Dale gets up at six in the morning to start his journey back to Wyoming. Will gets up, too, and they meet in the kitchen for juice and cereal.

"What route are you taking driving back?" Will asks.

"This time I'm going through Nebraska."

Will grins. "Is that right?"

"If I stop off in Grand Island should I look up some of your relatives?"

"There aren't many left there. Just an uncle."

"What does he do?"

"He sold the family farm and now operates a pet store."

"Okay, I'll stop off and buy a newt."

"Why a newt?"

"I like them and they're portable."

"You know, you're rather goofy early in the morning."

Breakfast finished, Dale hefts his grip (that's what he likes to call it; it's really just an old gym bag) and heads for the door. Before Will opens it for him, he sticks out a hand. They shake.

"Hey, I had a really good time," Dale says.

"So did I."

"I enjoyed talking to you. We had a lot of good conversations."

"Yes, we did." Will pauses, his face thoughtful. "You know, after you graduate from Wyoming, you ought to come out here for a while. You could get a job, find a cheap place to stay."

"Maybe two jobs. Save money for that trip."

"What trip?"

"The trip around the world we could take together. You know, work odd jobs, experience things, and figure out what we really want to do with the rest of our lives."

"That would be great," Will says sincerely, without even a trace of irony that usually appears in his voice.

"Well, I'm off."

Will opens the door and Dale walks out into the cold early morning. He turns and waves at Will whom waves back before closing the door. Dale walks to his car and looks at the deep dark of early morning. It's a clear night. He can see tight pinpoints of light in the inky canopy of sky. A glimmering crescent moon seems to linger at the horizon.

He gets in his car, starts it up, and drives away, thinking that these past few days have been some of the best of his life.

6

Sitting in the *Owen Wister Review* office the day after New Year's, Dale looks through staff applications. There aren't that many. Just twelve. He had expected more since he'd written a story in *The Branding Iron* about the literary magazine wanting assistant editors; he also got Ed Darby to air a PSA on the campus radio station; and he'd posted flyers all over campus announcing that the OWR was taking staff applications. He guessed most people didn't care about the lit magazine. Maybe Wagstaff was right; we were living in a visual not a literary culture.

As soon as he got back from Minnesota, he started planning the *Owen Wister Review*. He wanted to get a head start because spring semester would be a busy one. He'd carry fifteen classroom hours again; teach his Intro class; write movie reviews for the *BI* again; and he planned on still working at KUWR even though he knew Comstock wouldn't like it. There was a strategic reason for it. By working at the campus newspaper and radio station he had influence and could disseminate news more easily about OWR.

Since he was now editor of the literary magazine, Dale thought he had better found out who the heck Owen Wister was. So, he spent a few hours in the public library and discovered that Owen Wister was an Easterner who came out to Wyoming for his health in 1885. He returned to Philadelphia but continued to make trips to the west and Wyoming in particular. In 1902 he published *The Virginian*, thought to be the first cowboy novel. The book proved to be a huge success. Wister, however, never wrote another western novel and died thirty-six years later in Rhode Island.

Dale checked out the novel a few days ago and has already finished it. It was an okay book, perhaps a little corny by today's standards. He remembered the early '60s television show of the same name that he used to watch when he was staying with his grandparents. The TV show was pretty corny, too.

He's been back in Laramie for six days now. When he arrived home from Minnesota, he was surprised to see three letters in the mailbox. One was from Teri Boswell who was doing fine in Oklahoma. In her letter she wrote about going to Arkansas to see her family during Christmas. The other letter, actually a Christmas card with a note included, was from Anna Cappelletti. The note said she had enjoyed having him as a staff member and she knew he'd do an excellent job as editor of this semester's *OWR*. Dale had been surprised and gratified to get Anna's card and note. Maybe she didn't mind the kiss so much after all.

A few days later, Dale received a long letter from Will Whitaker. In the letter he mentioned how much fun he had during Dale's visit. He also said he was busy reading *Darkness at Noon*. He also discussed some of the movies he has seen. Dale wondered if Will saw them with anyone. He forgot to ask Will if he has any friends in Minneapolis. So far, Will hasn't mentioned anyone in his letters. He knew Will's good friend from high school and college, George Alexander, was attending law school at Georgetown. Will mentioned in a previous letter that he drove to Washington, D.C. to visit George last Christmas break. Now, as Dale sits in the literary magazine office, he wonders if Will is sometimes as lonely as he is.

Dale found one more letter (the third) waiting for him

when he returned. It was an invitation to attend a New Year's Eve party at Marsha Martin's apartment. The note hadn't been signed. It was just a Xeroxed invitation stating the party would start at 8 p.m. Of course, he didn't go. In fact, he thought it was a joke. Instead, he stayed home and watched Alabama win the Sugar Bowl and the National Championship. Dale, as a life-long Oklahoma fan, wanted the Sooners to win the mythical national championship. That season they won eleven and lost only one, to Texas in the annual meeting at the Cotton Bowl, but Alabama finished the season undefeated. That wasn't so bad Dale thought. His father's relatives all lived in Alabama so he knew his uncles and cousins would be happy.

Dale hears a soft rapping on the office door. He wonders who it could be. Classes won't start for another week and there are very few people on campus. He gets up and opens the door and sees Pamela Partridge standing before him.

"I saw the office light in the window," she says.

"Okay."

He's surprised to see her. Her cheeks are flushed and she's dressed in her typically outdoorsy way with the addition of a stocking cap and a parka.

"May I come in?"

"Sure, sorry."

He opens the door and she scoots in. She removes her forest green parka and red stocking cap and tosses them on an old armchair.

"The warmth feels good," she says as she rubs her now gloveless hands together.

"Yeah, it's cold outside."

"Frigid. It's supposed to hit twenty below tonight." She stares at an ordinary cloth jacket also lying in the chair. "Is that your coat?"

"Yeah."

"You're crazy. You need to wear something heavier than that. You'll freeze out in that weather."

"I'm also wearing thermal underwear in addition to my

flannel shirt, sweater, and jacket."

"Thermal underwear?" she says. Her voice sounds more than just normally inquisitive.

"Even though I'm a Southerner, I understand the importance of layering."

"Is that so? Well, you still need a heavier coat. Preferably one that is resistant to snow and rain and has goose down in it."

"Expert advice."

"That's right. You're a Southerner? You don't have an accent."

"The Yankees rubbed it out of me when I lived for a while in Rhode Island. Actually, I'm a Southwesterner. I grew up mostly in Oklahoma. But all my relatives are real southerners. Where did you grow up?"

Pamela takes a seat on a wooden stool. "Evanston, Wyoming."

"Where is that?"

"In the very southwestern corner of the state."

"So you're a Southwesterner, too."

She smiles for the first time. Not a big smile, but it's fairly nice.

"I ought to be miffed at you."

"Miffed?" He likes that word. "Why?"

"Because you didn't come to the New Year's Eve party last night."

"Did you send that invitation?"

"Yes, I did. Why didn't you show?"

"Because it was held at Marsha Martin's place. You remember that she stuck her tongue out at me at Deb's party last month."

Pamela giggles. "Oh, yes. I forgot about that. But I didn't forget other matters we discussed at that party."

Her smile is suggestive. He remembers that conversation as well.

"How did the party go?"

"It was rather dull. But at least Miriam Morgenstern wasn't there."

Dale tries not to smile. He remembered Miriam calling Pamela a wench. "I take it that you and Mimi don't get along."

"Mimi! What a silly nickname."

"She's a little silly sometimes. But I won't ask what the source of your disaffection is."

"Good." Pamela repositions herself on the stool. In fact, she sort of rubs her plump bottom against it. "How long are you planning on staying in this office, mister editor?"

"I was about ready to leave when you knocked."

"Did I mention how cold it is going to get tonight?"

Dale notices that look in her blue eyes again. For some reason, she's looking more attractive than before. Maybe it's the rather dim lighting in the old, musty office.

"Is Gary Grabowski at your place?" she asks.

"No, he's still in Chicago. He won't be back until tomorrow."

"Good."

Dale gets up and grabs his inappropriately light jacket. "Shall we go?"

"It's freezing in here," says Pamela as they enter the townhouse.

Dale goes over to the thermostat and turns it up. "Yeah, I like it cool."

"It's certainly that. Turn it up high, please." She removes her parka but not her gloves or stocking cap. She walks around the apartment inspecting it. "It's about what I expected."

"How so?"

"The lodgings of two bachelors. Spartan, functional, and charmless."

Dale nods. "That's an accurate description." He tosses off his jacket and peels off his sweater.

"Too bad you don't have a fireplace. Do you have anything hot to drink?"

139

"Would you like some coffee?"

"I don't drink coffee."

"I don't either. Grabowski does. How about hot apple cider?"

"Perfect."

They walk into the kitchen and Dale pours the cider into a pan and puts it on the stove. He turns on the burner and watches the flame caressing the bottom of the pan.

"Why don't you drink coffee?" Pamela asks. "Almost everyone does, especially in Wyoming in the winter."

"I don't like the taste. It's too bitter."

"You don't drink alcohol either."

"No." Dale thinks the cider is ready. He takes down mugs and pours the liquid into the cups and hands one to Pamela. "But I drink apple cider. Not the hard stuff, of course."

Pamela smiles and they walk back into the living room. She takes off her stocking cap and gloves and sits on the couch where Grabowski is usually perched when home. Dale sits in the easy chair.

"Would you like some music?"

"That would be nice." She sips the cider.

Dale flips through the albums. Since Dale keeps his albums in his room, most are Grabowski's. You'd think a stud like him would have something romantic and seductive. But no.

Dale finds his Manhattan Transfer albums in the back of the stack. He almost selects the group's second album, *Coming Out*, the one he likes best, but he remembers that two of those songs he still fondly associates with his old college girlfriend. So, instead he selects *Pastiche*. He doesn't like that album as well although it has a couple of good songs on it, especially the Cole Porter tune, "Love For Sale." He puts the album on the turntable and turns the volume down moderately low. He walks back over to Pamela as the mellow sounds of the jazz/pop group disseminate in the room.

"That's a good choice," Pamela says.

"You're familiar with the *Manhattan Transfer?*"

"Oh, yes. I have some of their albums."

He's about to ask her what kind of music she likes when she asks if he has any playing cards. He says sure. He walks over to an end table and grabs a pack of cards. He thinks it sort of odd that she wants to play a game.

Pamela tosses her parka and Dale's jacket on the floor rug. She turns off the lamp next to the chair, which leaves only one light on, the one farther away next to the couch. He thinks that's odd, too. They won't have good light to play cards.

She sits down on her parka and he sits down on the rug. He takes the cards out of the package and asks in a somewhat disappointed voice what game she wants to play.

"Let's play strip twenty-one," she says with a sly smile.

"What?"

"Strip poker will take too long. You know how to play twenty-one?"

"Sure. It's simple." He shuffles the cards. He's beginning to like this game. "So, the loser has to remove an article of clothing?"

"That's right."

In the subdued light, he thinks she looks cute when she smiles. Now that he knows the objective of the game he would like to have more illumination in the room. But there's enough light to read the cards.

They play the first hand. He wins by getting twenty-one. Pamela removes her shoes, those lovely Timberland hiking boots.

Dale wins the second hand when Pamela goes bust by drawing a third card. She removes her socks.

"You sure this is quicker than strip poker?" he asks.

She smiles but says nothing as they play another hand. This time Dale loses. Off goes his boots. The next several hands they trade wins. She removes her sweater and her blouse. He removes his socks and flannel shirt. When he sees her in her bra he's reminded that she's not very busty but seeing her pale belly and soft shoulders takes some of the sting out of his disappointment.

The next hand Dale loses. He could take off his jeans but he decides to take off the thermal top. When he wins next, Pamela stands up and unzips her slacks. Now this strip twenty-one is getting fun. In fact, he's never played a game like this. None of his former girlfriends would ever do something like this.

He watches as she wriggles out of her slacks. She's wearing fairly small pink panties that reveal all of her plump thighs. His arousal, which had been slowly building, takes a leap into full flowered lust.

She wins the next hand even though she took a risk by taking a fourth card. They all add up to twenty-one and beat his seventeen. She could have stuck with seventeen, too, but she went for it.

Dale has no choice but to take off his jeans. He doesn't really want to. His natural shyness comes over him. She has to coax him.

"Come on."

He stands and quickly pulls off his Levi's not performing the act slowly like she did with her pants.

"You *are* wearing thermal long john's," she says.

He sits down before she makes a comment about the bulge in his thermals. He feels sort of silly and he's annoyed that he's losing.

He wins the next hand. Again, Pamela takes an extra card and it puts her over. He wonders if she's playing recklessly for a reason.

She reaches behind her and unclasps her bra. It falls off her chest and he sees her rather small breasts. But in the subdued glow of the room, they look pretty good. From his position, he can't tell exactly what kind of areolas and nipples she has.

The next hand he also wins when Pamela conveniently goes bust. He anticipates her final act of stripping. She stands and peels off her panties. Her blonde pubic hair is not thick or bushy. He rather likes that. Maybe she is a little too plump. Her waist isn't small enough to make her completely curvy. But she looks attractive. She stands naked before him without any embarrassment. He's impressed by her composure.

"I lose," she says.

"That's what's good about this game," Dale says. "In the end no one really loses."

He stands up and she giggles at seeing his tumescent condition. He walks over to her and they embrace. His hands feel her back and waist and his bare chest rubs against her naked breasts. They kiss and even though her mouth seems a little small the kiss is pleasant. She reaches down with her hands and pulls at the waistband of his long johns. He pulls them down instead and they embrace again in the nude.

She looks down at his erect penis. "May I touch it?"

He's too excited and slightly embarrassed to speak. He nods. When he feels her small fingers encircle the shaft he tenses. When she caresses the head he has to summon all his self-control not to explode.

"Are you uncircumcised?"

"No."

"Are you Jewish?"

Dale grins. "No. Why?"

"No reason."

Before an unfortunate thing happens, he takes a half step back and her hand leaves his phallus. She leans closer to him and rubs her hands against his chest.

"You have a good body," she says softly. Then she looks down at her own naked body and shivers. "But I'm getting a little cold. Let's go to your room."

He nods and he leads her to his room. When he starts to turn on the light by the bed she asks him not to. She says it will be too bright. He gropes for the bedspread, finds it, tosses it to one side and they topple onto the bed. They immediately start kissing and caressing and Dale thinks how odd this is, being with a girl who is so willing. He's not experienced that too often.

Pamela starts moaning when he starts nuzzling her breasts. He reaches behind her and strokes her buttocks. They feel larger than they looked when they walked into his room. He's getting really worked up and he moves his pecker toward her vulva but when he touches her there she moves away.

"Do you have condoms?" she whispers.

Dale doesn't. But Grabowski does. He's not sure where. Besides, the idea of using one of his rubbers sort of disgusts him.

"Not any handy."

"Well, we can't go all the way then."

Dale feels frustration building inside him. His phallus is touching her soft thighs and he wants more.

"You not using anything?" He's whispering too, although there's no reason to. They are the only two people in the house.

"No."

That's it. This is worse than high school. At least back then he knew he couldn't go all the way because none of the girls he dated thought it proper. It happened once anyway, at Girls State of all places. His then girlfriend, Wendy Wainwright, had gone to Girls State and he'd gone to Boys State. When he came to pick up her to take them back to their hometown of Galilee, he'd arrived late and she was the only one left. Well, they couldn't help themselves and later she thought she was pregnant but she wasn't but the false alarm had scared both of them so they didn't do it again. In their hometown, you couldn't get contraceptives. So they kept on getting close but no cigar.

He sighs in frustration. He gets off her and lies on his back.

"Sorry, but I thought you'd have something."

He guesses he should but he hates wearing condoms. He doesn't like being encumbered. He doesn't wear a wristwatch or his high school class ring either because he doesn't like things clinging to his fingers or wrist. Of course, who needs those things? This was more urgent. He could go into Grabowski's room and search. But just thinking of Grabowski and his unattractive chicks makes him feel that the situation has turned sordid. His thinking of the awkwardness of it all has taken care of the situation anyway; he's no longer aroused.

Pamela snuggles up close to him and he reluctantly puts his

144

arm around her. He hears her murmuring. She relaxes in his arms and in a few minutes she falls asleep. After a few minutes, he hears her softly snoring.

He continues to lie there in the dark holding a snoring almost-lover. The frustration is gone and instead he feels foolish. He wonders if Grabowski has ever experienced this unsatisfying conclusion. Maybe so. Maybe that's why he didn't list sex as one of his favorite activities. If this sort of thing continues then Dale might have to revise his list, too.

7

On the first day of spring semester the weather remains implacably cold, so cold that the gray overcast sky seems frozen and can't release any snow. The rock-hard ground is covered in snow and the tops of the drifts have hardened into an off-white crust. The campus walkways are mostly clear but when Dale leaves one to take a short cut to Gowdy Hall his cowboy boots have a difficult time breaking through the hard crust. When he slams his foot down, his leg sinks down a foot and he has a hard time extricating it.

When he makes it to Gowdy Hall he expects his boots to be soaked but the snow is so dry there is only the grainy film of moisture on the leather.

On his the way to his office he sees that the other GTA office door is open. He pops his head in and sees Deb Pierson sitting at her desk, a sympathetic look directed at Grabowski, who slumps in his chair.

Deb smiles when she sees him. However, when she sees he is only wearing a corduroy coat, her expression changes into disapproval, the way a mother looks at her misbehaving boychild.

"Dale, you need a heavier coat than that. It's sub-zero out there."

"It's okay. I practice the layering principle."

Deb, apparently aware of the principle, smiles and asks how his Christmas break went.

"It was good. How was your break?"

"Delightful. I enjoyed seeing my family again."

"In Cheyenne, right?" Dale has an uncle, an aunt, and cousins living in that city. He's thought about calling his uncle but so far he hasn't.

"That's right. I spent three marvelous weeks home."

Dale glances past Deb's smiling face and sees a framed photograph of Chris Calloway perched prominently on her desk. In fact, the photo seems directly aimed toward Grabowski's field of vision.

"You didn't see Chris?"

"He came to visit several times. He stayed in Laramie to get a head start on his studies. He has a heavy schedule this spring."

Dale nods. He notices that Grabowski hasn't uttered a word. Usually when Dale comes by to talk to Deb and him (mostly Deb), he interjects a few terse sentences. But today he has been even more uncommunicative than usual.

"Anything wrong?" Dale asks his roomie.

Last night Grabowski seemed like his usual self: watching some prime time TV, quaffing a couple of beers, resolutely refusing to engage in any advanced cogitation. Dale notices that Grabowski is slumped in his chair, his long legs extended forlornly past his desk, his pale face morose. Behind the large lenses of his spectacles his pale blue eyes seem to be sadly staring at his big feet shod in winter boots as if realizing he will never accomplish his dream of becoming a ballet dancer.

"Oh, my yes," Deb sadly intones, "Gary's writing class has been canceled."

Dale glances at Grabowski who remains in his inert posture. "Why?"

"Only five students enrolled in his section," Deb says.

According to his preliminary class roster, Dale's section of Introduction to Journalistic Writing has sixteen students. The class limit is twenty. His class doesn't meet until tomorrow so there will probably be a few drops and adds.

"How many students do you have in your class, Deb?"

She says she has seventeen.

"Do you still keep your GTA?" Dale asks Grabowski.

He nods.

"Well, then lucky you."

Grabowski finally rouses himself. "I'm not lucky. Unlike you, I want to get a job teaching after I get my degree. You just want to get another newspaper job."

As soon as Grabowski makes that rather resentful sounding statement, he lapses into a sullen state again. Dale glances over to Deb. Her expression is caught between socially mandated sympathy and impatience with her office mate's self-pity.

"Okay, then. You can have my class."

Grabowski remains slumped but his beady pale blue eyes turn in Dale's direction. "Can we do that? Switch?

"We can try."

Grabowski stands up and stares at Dale with an expression that he has never seen before; an expression that approaches gratitude. "You would do that for me?"

Dale almost smiles at his roommates' uncharacteristic humility. Of course, he is doing this not just to help out Grabowski. "Sure, Gary. If it will help you in your quest to become a professor." He glances at Deb who beams an admiring smile his way. Her goodwill is almost a reward in itself. "Besides, I have to help Comstock with that damn *Journal of North American Mass Communications Programs*."

Dale notices that Deb's smile fades. In fact, she turns back to her desk as if she suddenly remembers she has an important assignment to prepare for. For some bizarre reason that no one has yet explained to him, he was assigned to be Comstock's assistant. In a few weeks he will be assisting the great professor in proofreading and editing a massive academic journal. All the GTAs have one additional duty besides teaching their section of Introduction to Journalistic Writing. Grabowski's is to help supervise the photography lab. Given his photojournalism experience, that makes sense. Deb's chore is to help Wagstaff operate the film and television library. Mostly, she helps keep track of who checks out instructional films and what few feature films the department has. It's an easy job. She clerks five to ten hours a week. What puzzles Dale, however, is why he, as the only GTA who has a film concentration, wasn't given that assignment. Instead he has the proofreading and editing job for Comstock, a job he hasn't the temperament or aptitude for. When Dale learned of this at the beginning of fall semester, he went to Wagstaff and told him he would be much better suited to helping in the film library. In fact, he confessed to being a poor proofreader. He wasn't very good at such detailed work. Wagstaff jocularly dismissed Dale's concerns. Hadn't Dale been a sports *editor* at his newspaper? He obviously edited and proofread copy there. Dale tried to explain that the newspaper didn't have any copy-editors so he had to proof his own copy and he didn't always do that very well. But Wagstaff waved his hand and said that it was too late to make any changes. So Dale was stuck being an editorial assistant to Comstock.

Dale glances over to Deb who appears to be perusing her class syllabus. He doesn't blame her exactly. Her concentration is advertising and public relations. She isn't studying news writing or editing either. But he knows she is a much better proofreader than he is. In fact, Grabowski often has her proof his papers. Dale has never stooped to that level but he's seen her correcting Grabowski's mangled prose. She has a knack for editing.

Dale suspects she simply doesn't want to assist Comstock (who could blame her although she'd probably get some tootsies and lollipops). Assisting with the film library is less time consuming and easier. Plus, Dale is certain that Wagstaff wanted her. Deb was a mass communications major at UW as an undergraduate. She didn't take that many classes with Wagstaff but they knew each other. Wagstaff certainly shows a paternal, if not more personal, interest in Deb. He'd rather spend what little time he devotes to student interaction with Deb than with Grabowski or him. As Dale glances at Deb's attractive profile and her becoming attire (a baby blue cashmere sweater and a long, winter dress but one that clings rather appealing to her slender figure), he realizes that he can't exactly blame Wagstaff.

"Let's go talk to Schneider," Dale says to Grabowski.

Grabowski agrees and they say so long to Deb and venture down the hall to the department chairman's office.

Schneider is present and his secretary conveys their message and in five minutes they are in his office explaining the situation. Dr. Schneider is a tall, lean, rather severe looking man with short black hair, brooding dark eyes, and needle-like nose. In contrast to his appearance, his personality appears to be affable and thoughtful. He listens to the problem. Grabowski speaks with more energy than usual explaining how he wants to find a college teaching job next year and how teaching two classes instead of one would greatly help his chances. Dale says he doesn't mind switching. He adds that he will be busy assisting Professor Comstock with the academic journal.

After they make their appeal, Schneider says there is no problem. Grabowski can teach Dale's section. Dale will retain his GTA and assisting Professor Comstock will be his only departmental responsibility. They need to do nothing else. His secretary will notify the registrar about the change in instructors.

Dale and Grabowski thank the chairman and leave. Grabowski almost struts down the hall, he is so pleased. Dale ambles along until he comes to Comstock's office with its partly open door. Comstock is in. He is almost always is. Dale has never seen Comstock's office door locked and shut. Every time Dale has been in the Mass Comm Department, even in the late afternoon to pick something up, Comstock is occupying his office. Dale facetiously wonders if the professor lives there.

Dale tells Grabowski he needs to speak to Comstock. His roommate nods and continues on his way. Dale waits outside the partly open door. He hears Comstocks's hectoring voice. It's not loud but it is grave and insistent and Dale knows he is chastising some hapless male undergraduate. Comstock's female students are never reproved. If they are cute and sweet they are suitably rewarded. But male students, especially those who are difficult and unruly and contrary, in other words, students sort of like Dale, are often subjected to Comstock's harangues.

A few minutes later, the chastened undergraduate ducks out of the office. Dale knocks, Comstock says come in, and Dale enters and sees the professor in his usual winter duds, corduroy pants, flannel shirt, red suspenders, and bolo tie. His corduroy jacket is hanging on the back of his chair. Dale thinks he ought to like the guy; after all, they sort of dress alike.

"What may I do for you?" says Comstock, his voice flat. He hasn't even look in Dale's direction.

"I got my fall semester grades today." They were late getting to him because the registrar sent them to his grandparents, the address listed on his application. His mother took a week before she forwarded the mail. "My independent study class has an incomplete grade listed instead of passing. What happened?"

"Yes, I tried to notify you last month but apparently you had already left for the break."

Dale waits. Comstock still refuses to look him in the eye. "What does the incomplete grade mean?"

Comstock gives him an annoyed glance as if he's asking an impudent question. "It means you cannot receive a pass/fail grade as a graduate student."

"But you said you could give a pass/fail grade."

"Apparently, the policy has changed."

Dale wants to upbraid him in the same way Comstock had just rebuked the undergraduate, but he knows that would only make the situation worse. "Okay. Are you going to assign a grade for the independent study course?"

"That's what I wanted to talk to you about."

An odd thing to say, thinks Dale, since he's the one who initiated this discussion not Comstock.

"I've decided to award a B to your independent study class."

"B?"

"Yes. I think that's a fair grade. As I've said before, the work you are doing in those independent studies really isn't academic or traditionally journalistic."

Dale bets Comstock didn't even read the movie reviews. But what was the point of arguing? He made A's in his other courses, including the one-hour radio practicum. He'd simply given Jerry Sibelius an audiotape of the *Buffalo Quotidians*. Sibelius recorded an actual grade. But Dale reckoned one B wouldn't hurt. Grad students could receive a few hours of B grades. If that happened in too many classes, of course, that could be reason to withhold the advanced degree.

"Since you will be writing a paper in addition of your work at the *Branding Iron* for this semester, I don't foresee anything to be concerned about in the future."

"Okay," Dale says.

He thinks about telling Comstock about changing sections with Grabowski. The professor might be pleased. Dale will now have more time to assist him with his academic journal. But he decides not to. He doesn't want to reassure Comstock.

"Well, thanks Professor Comstock for all your assistance on these matters."

Dale doesn't care if the professor detects the sarcasm in his voice. But apparently, Comstock doesn't because his "not at all" is spoken in his usual flat, dismissive way. Dale departs his office wondering if Comstock deliberately misled him by stating that the independent study class could be evaluated on a pass/fail basis. Dale, who has never trusted his advisor, now realizes that Comstock might be capable of sabotaging his degree.

"Aren't you excited to be taking this class?" whispers Mimi. "I mean, the professor is a *real* writer. His background is *so* distinguished."

"I'm excited," Dale says, using his understated, almost indifferent voice that he employs in the presence of Mimi. He likes plays the ironic straight man in relation to her Lucille Ball.

"What did you do over Christmas break? Was it thrilling?

My break was absolutely marvy because I got to spend most of it with my Joe. Did you –" she suddenly stops because that *real* writer walks in.

Dale is not surprised to see that he's a black man. He's seen Professor James Wilkins walk around campus on a few occasions; he's seen him sitting in his office in the English Department. He's never had any personal contact with him. A few students told him that Wilkins is a good teacher; a little distracted at times but that's because he's working on a new novel.

Professor Wilkins says hello to the class with a neutral tone of voice. His voice is moderately deep and has no accent. He's a tall man with a lean, muscular build. He appears to be in his early forties. He's wearing dark slacks and an Oxford blue shirt, a gray crew-neck sweater, and a dark blazer but no tie. His collar is open. He hands a small stack of syllabi to the first seated student. He moves to stand in front of his desk. There is something unhurried if not nonchalant about his manner and movements.

He's not a handsome man but he has a dignified bearing. His facial features are a mixture of the European and the African. His skin is medium brown in color. His brown eyes are rather arresting. They are large and heavy-lidded and he peers at the class in a perspicacious way that indicates an observant, analytical mind at work.

After Dale received permission to take this fiction writing class as one of his electives, he went to the library and researched Wilkins. He discovered that he has quite an impressive background. He attended the University of Pennsylvania as an undergraduate on a basketball scholarship. He made Phi Beta Kappa and All-Ivy (for basketball) his senior year. He went to Cambridge as a Rhodes Scholar. All this happened in the late '50s and early '60s when it was rare for black Americans to attend any college let alone an Ivy League institution.

Wilkins published his first novel a year after receiving his advanced degree at Cambridge. The novel, entitled *The Camp*, was about a middle-aged Jewish professor who teaches at a prestigious college but is haunted by memories of the concentration camp he was imprisoned in during World War II. *The Camp* received good reviews but didn't sell many copies. His second novel, *Shooting for the Moon*, published five years later, is more autobiographical. It is about a bright, ambitious young black man who uses his athletic skills to escape the poverty and squalor of his hometown. That novel won a literary award, although nothing major, and it was highly regarded by critics. It sold more copies than the first book but didn't come close to hitting the best-seller lists. A third novel, *Sojourner*, published five years ago, is something of a literary historical novel. It's about a freed slave who, soon after the Civil War, goes in search of his wife (she's not legally his wife because of the slave laws) and two children. That novel won another minor literary award and sold about the same moderate amount of copies. That novel was published in 1978 and Wilkins hasn't published anything in the interim except a couple of essays in *The New Yorker* and two book reviews in *The New York Times*. However, there seems to be a lot of speculation that he is working on his magnum opus.

Professor Wilkins speaks about the class requirements. There aren't many. Students will write two stories and submit them to a class workshop then they will revise one of them for a final assignment. Students are expected to attend all classes, especially the workshops. That's it.

Dale has never had a class with black professor before. He doesn't think there are many at Wyoming. The only other one that he's aware of is a geography professor who is an actual African. The middle-aged man is supposedly from Nigeria.

Wilkins asks the class if anyone has brought a story for next week. Mimi eagerly raises her hand. Wilkins comes over and she hands him the sixteen Xeroxed copies and as he accepts them she smiles an almost adulatory smile.

The rest of the class consists of Wilkins answering students' questions. Unlike most classes, several students have queries. Wilkins gives thoughtful, concise answers about class procedures and his own experiences as a writer, teacher, Rhodes scholar (and basketball player).

Class is dismissed a few minutes early and Dale walks out with Mimi. He hasn't seen her since the end of last semester but she's still the same loquacious, exuberant, eccentric kind of girl. Her hair looks even longer and wilder and her clothes are just as eclectic. She wears incongruous outfits consisting of Capri pants underneath a billowing skirt, a man's dress shirt along with a very feminine sweater. Today, however, she's dressed less for style and more for warmth. She tells him she's wearing her ballet tights underneath her blue jeans, which are underneath her long peasant dress. On top she wears a thermal undershirt, a sweatshirt, then a sweater, and her big, bulky winter coat that she hates to wear because it is so unbecoming!

"I'm surprised you're taking this class," says Dale, as they enter the bitter chill. "I thought you were a poet."

"Oh, but I am! I prefer poetry to express my turbulent and dark emotional life. But I also write what I term prose poetry. You know, narratives with highly figurative language and ambiguous symbolism."

"Sounds interesting."

"What about Professor Wilkins? I've never had him for class but I can tell from this one that he is going to be a towering influence on my writing. He's so intellectual! And tall, dark and handsome. You know, I wonder if he feels out of place here? I mean, there are so few African Americans! There aren't many in Denver either, but a lot more than here. Of course, maybe Professor Wilkins doesn't think in so crude of terms as skin color. After all, he has a white wife."

"He does?"

"Oh, yes. I've seen her. She teaches in the sociology department. She's not particularly attractive but very cerebral! That's what I've been told anyway. She's Jewish, too. I sure she must feel a little isolated here as well, maybe not as keenly as her husband, but she is definitely also a minority. They have two children, too!"

"Really?" Dale says in a mock-surprised way.

"Yes, really. Those kids are even more of a minority than their parents. Imagine being a bi-racial, half Jewish, half agnostic, intellectuals-to-be in benighted Laramie, Wyoming!" Mimi takes a breath. She looks at Dale. "Tell me. Weren't you impressed with Professor Wilkins?"

"Yeah, I was."

After the first meeting of the Film Directing class is over, Dale walks up to Wagstaff. Dale holds in his hand the class syllabus and another piece of paper listing the estimated expenses for the class. While he waits for Wagstaff to finish speaking with a male undergrad student, Dale again checks the expense sheet:

Super 8 mm camera rental: $20 an hour
Super 8 mm b & w film stock: $100 for 20 feet
Super 8 mm color film stock: $150 for 20 feet
Super 8 mm b & w film processing: $150 for 20 feet
Super 8 mm color film processing, color: $200 for 20 feet

Fortunately, the students are allowed to use the editing room without charge. But even so, it appears that making a 10-minute film would cost several hundred dollars and that is a conservative estimate and only if the director doesn't shoot too much footage.

"Greetings Dale," Wagstaff says. "I'm eager to hear what you think about this class. All of last semester I heard how much you were looking forward to being the next Cecil B. DeMille."

"You know, I was thinking about following in the footsteps of the man who made *The Ten Commandments*. But that was before I saw *Ecstasy*. Now, I'm more interested in making a film about breaking one of the commandments."

Wagstaff doesn't blush hearing a reference to the naughty film he screened for Dale and Nordberg at his home on Thanksgiving, but his bald head does seem to turn a deeper shade of pink. He gives an impish grin, strokes one strand of his Fu Manchu mustache, and chuckles.

"I think Hollywood has beaten you to the punch on that score."

"You've got a point, Walt." Dale notices that Wagstaff's eyes widen just a smidgen upon hearing Dale refer to his Christian name. "But I have another concern." He extends the expense sheet. "Making this film, even as short as it is, is going to cost a lot of money."

Wagstaff shrugs and grins. "Ask any producer and he will tell you that film is an expensive art form."

"Even if I plan the shooting script to the last detail and story board it, and don't waste any film stock, the project is still going to cost at least a month's salary."

"Unfortunately, your estimate is low. It will probably cost two month's salary."

"How am I going to pay for it all?"

"Do what filmmakers have been doing since the beginning of movies. Beg, borrow, and steal."

Dale shakes his head.

"It's not too late to drop the course."

"This is the course that my whole program is leading up to."

"Then you're going to have to find a way to finance the venture. I know it seems to be a daunting task. But look at it this way, you're learning how film-making really works. Not only artistically, but financially. Even Orson Welles struggled most of his career with financing his films."

"Okay. Thanks for your advice, Dr. Wagstaff."

"Not at all, Dale. That's why I am here. To dispense advice along with my cinematic expertise."

Dale trudges out of the classroom when he notices two other students in his class standing in the hallway. One of them is Von Goebbels. He does, unfortunately, resemble Peter Lorre: short, stocky, black hair, with eyes that seem to bulge out of the sockets. But Dale notices that the color of those eyes is dark blue.

"Aren't you Dale Smith?" Von Goebbels asks.

157

"Yeah."

"Mimi talks about you often."

"She's mentioned you, too."

"May I introduce my brother, Matt."

Dale looks at the young man standing next to Mark Von Goebbels. There isn't much resemblance. Matt is taller, about average height, with a regular build, and a more ordinary face although he does have a noticeably big mouth with a top lip larger than the lower one. In fact, the top lip sort of hangs over the other one.

When Dale and Matt Von Goebbels exchange greetings, Dale notices that Matt speaks with a slight lisp.

"I like reading your movie reviews," says Matt.

"I do, too," says Mark.

Well, the Von Goebbels brothers might be a tad strange looking but they obviously have good taste. The movies he has lately reviewed haven't been very interesting; releases early in the year usually weren't. But he did review *Being There* and mostly praised the film.

"Thanks," says Dale.

"This class does cost a lot of money," says Mark.

"So maybe we can team up on some things," says Matt.

"Okay. Sounds like a good idea."

"We could also rob a bank," says Mark.

"The First National only has one security guard. He's sorta old, too," says Matt.

Dale thinks they are joking but they speak so earnestly and without any inflection in their voices that he's not sure if they're being ironic.

"I don't think Wagstaff meant it literally when he said to beg, borrow, and steal," Dale says. "At least not the steal part."

"We just wanted to let you know that we are committed to film," says Mark.

"We take it very seriously," adds Matt.

"That's good. Well, I got to go."

Mark and Matt say so long and they march in the opposite

158

direction from Dale. After a few strides, Dale stops and turns and looks at the Von Goebbels brothers as they exit the building. They might be strange looking, and potentially dangerous, but Dale has a feeling they could be of use to him.

Dale and Pamela Partridge walk through campus after seeing the Friday night film, *Don't Look Now*. They're headed back to her place. She doesn't want to go to Dale's residence because she doesn't want to encounter Grabowski when he comes home. Dale hasn't asked her yet what she has against Grabowski and she hasn't yet volunteered the information.

As they walk, Dale kicks up snow with his boots. He likes watching the white stuff spray forth. The sub-zero cold wave broke yesterday and it snowed. The flakes were fluffy and more wet than usual and the fresh snow covered campus and made it beautiful again.

He's not holding Pamela's hand as they walk. So far they haven't done that. They really have done any conventional making out either. He's not even sure if this encounter tonight counts as a date. He didn't pick her up; he didn't pay for her cheap ticket. He did buy her a cup of cocoa at the campus grill after the movie but that only seemed like an act of friendliness. But it appears they are headed to her apartment for an intimate encounter and that's fine with him.

"How did you like the movie?" he asks. They haven't discussed it so far.

"It was interesting. I thought the Venice location was especially apt for the nature of the film."

"You know, I suggested they show that film last semester."

Both Dallas and Felicia were on the campus film committee and once he found that out he gave them a short list of films for the committee to consider showing for next semester. Five students made up the committee. Beside Felicia and Dallas, the only committee person he sort of knew was Spencer Dribble.

The film committee did a fairly good job selecting films last semester, Dale thought. They picked films mostly from the '40s and '50s. While growing up, he saw several of the selections on TV but he liked watching them again on the semi-big screen. In addition to *Some Like It Hot*, the committee screened three Hitchcock films: *Notorious, North By Northwest*, and *Psycho*. Seeing *Psycho* with an audience was fun. People actually screamed during the gruesome (but fairly non-explicit) murder scenes. Mimi screamed the loudest. He sat next to her and his left eardrum ached the entire night afterwards. She also made nail impressions on his left wrist when she grabbed his arm in fear.

Mimi hadn't attended *Don't Look Now*. She was apparently back in Denver seeing her Joe D'Amato, a.k.a. Joe DiMaggio. Dale thought that was just as well. He wasn't sure what he'd do if she wanted him to sit with her. After all, Pamela was with him.

This semester the committee was going to show mostly '60s and '70s films. Three films he recommended were going to be shown: *Don't Look Now, A Clockwork Orange*, and *Midnight Cowboy*. He never saw them because he was underage to see them at the theatre and they have never shown on television. All of them were R-rated, another reason why he wanted to see them on the semi-big screen and not have to depend on television to eventually show the censored version.

"A very good choice," Pamela said. "I have to admit that you have taste in films."

"Thanks."

He thought *Don't Look Now* was excellent. He usually doesn't care that much for films about the supernatural but this film was more subtle and plausible in establishing its fatalistic, bizarre story. He was especially impressed with the objective, almost impersonal direction. The filmmakers cleverly made a visual connection between the little girl and her red slicker and the evil dwarf and his red coat. He wonders what other films Nicolas Roeg has directed. He'll have to find out.

The film also featured an extended nude scene. When it lasted for more than a few seconds, he glanced at Pamela. She didn't seem disturbed at all. Her attitude was just the opposite of his previous girlfriends in high school and college.

"Dale, do you believe in fate?"

He's thinking of that nude scene, specifically of Julie Christie, so he doesn't quite hear her. "What?"

"Fate. Do you believe in it?"

"In a way. I believe there are certain patterns in life. Also, coincidence and serendipity. But I don't think fate determines everything. We have free will."

"That's a religious concept."

"No. Free will is a philosophical concept as well. Do you believe in fate?"

"I'm beginning to." Pamela begins spraying snow with her Timberland hiking boots, too.

They walk into her apartment and Dale sees why Pamela was so critical of his place. Her apartment actually looks like a civilized person lives there. It's very clean, the air has a refreshing scent, and the furniture isn't ragged or second-hand. It also has shag carpet, a pink color that he doesn't like but otherwise her apartment is attractive and cozy.

It's also not far from his place. Only two blocks. Dale thinks it sort of odd that he never saw her coming or going last semester.

They take off their coats and Dale makes a survey of the apartment in the same manner that she did last week with his place. He walks over to her small bookcase and examines the books: most of them are about journalism, photography, mass communications, sociology, travel, nature and the outdoors. A few collections of poetry and short stories. Not that many novels, but he notices that most of the authors are women: the Bronte sisters, Edith Wharton, Willa Cather, Katherine Ann Porter, and a few writers he's never heard of such as Anais Nin. He also notices half a dozen of books that appear to be about politics and feminism.

Next to the bookcase is a magazine rack. He sees *The New Yorker*, *The Nation*, *The Atlantic*, *Cosmopolitan* and a couple of other magazines that he's not familiar with. Then he sees another periodical lying on her coffee table next to the magazine rack that surprises him: *Playgirl*.

Pamela walks over and stands next to him.

"Why do you have that magazine?" he asks.

"Why shouldn't I? You probably read *Playboy*."

"Well ..."

"Because I'm a woman? I shouldn't be interested in such things?"

Dale's not sure how to answer. He's never known a girl who would want – let alone admit to – reading *Playgirl*. He's not sure if he likes that or not. He feels that it's a sign of open mindedness and sexual liberation, which he is in favor of as long as it benefits him, but it also seems out of character for a woman. Does she really like looking at that stuff?

He asks her. She picks up the magazine and opens it. She flips through a few pages. He sees the nude men. He doesn't like it. They look too polished and posed. When he sees their flaccid peckers he feels embarrassed. Of course, if they had erections then the magazine would be hardcore and even Pamela wouldn't have one of those around. However, this was bad enough. Having those images displayed before him was like being in a locker room with handsome soap opera actors who are violating the locker room etiquette by parading around.

"I don't get it," he says.

"You're not supposed to."

He glances at her and she seems to be enjoying the nude images. He wonders if she is putting on a bit of an act. After all, last week it appeared that she was eager to get nude first. That seemed normal to him. But now he's wondering what she really thinks in regard to seduction and sex.

"You know," she says, "you could be one of these models."

"I would never do that," he says, feeling offended rather than gratified.

She shrugs. "Seeing pictures like these takes the mystery away a little," she says. "In a way it's more fun to see a man clothed and guess his size."

"Oh, yeah. The practice of mouseketeering."

"Basketteering," she says. "And we never got around to determining your size." She peers down at his jean-clad groin. "I'd say six."

"No, that's my hat size."

"You always joke about sex. Why is that? Are you afraid?"

"Afraid? Of course not." He's annoyed that she used that word which he knows was her way to motivate him. It's a silly question, anyway. What about last week?

"Well?" she says, with a suggestive lift of her right eyebrow.

"What? Right here?"

"Why not?"

"Just disrobe?"

"Sure. You do that and I'll get a measuring tape."

"That's crazy."

"I knew you would be afraid."

"I'm not afraid. I just not used to stripping at the drop of the hat."

"I'll tell you what. If I'm within one half inch of my guess then I win. If I'm not then you win."

"And what are we playing for?"

"Whatever you *want*. Or whatever I *want*."

He's beginning to feel motivated. "All right. But you have to be within one quarter inch not one half."

"It's a deal."

She promptly leaves the room and he picks up the *Playgirl* and flips through a few pages. He still has a hard time believing that she likes looking at these photos. Well, maybe she's one swinging bachelorette.

She returns with a yellow felt tape measure. Dale is amazed that she actually wants to go through with it.

"Okay, now," she says with a strange enthusiasm as if she were trying to earn top honors in a science project, "come over to the dining room table."

He hesitates. She reminds him that the prize will be worth

163

it. He walks over to the dining room table and observes that height of his hips is about even with the top of the table.

"Time to drop them," she says.

He decides not to be embarrassed. If she's that interested, then okay he'll show her. He unbelts then unbuttons and unzips his Levi's. He hesitates for only a moment. He pulls his jeans and his shorts down in one quick jerk. His fully erect penis thrusts out.

He glances at her. She gazes at his erect member in a manner that is more thoughtful than lustful.

Move as close to the table edge as you can," she says. "You might want to lift your balls up, too."

He's a little shocked at her language but he lifts his scrotum with one hand while moving flush against the edge of the table. His phallus is lying extended across the light blue Formica table like a kielbasa.

"You do have a well-defined head. Sort of bulbous. That's more appealing that the other shapes."

He can't think of anything to say in response. He's never heard such talk. She takes one end of the tape measure and presses it against the base of his penis, her fingers touching his dark pubic hair. He tightens his muscles. He tries not thinking about how silly he feels standing before the dining room table with his britches around his thighs and his pecker being scrutinized by a tape wielding seductress.

Pamela pulls the other end of the tape forward. He looks at the black numbers as they ascend higher in numeration. He's growing curious as to the actual length himself. She extends the tape to the tip of his penis. They both see the size: five and five eighths inches. Just shy of five and three quarters. Pamela loses, again.

"I almost got it," she says, with a sigh. She rolls the tape up and deposits it on the kitchen table. Dale begins to pull his jeans up but his erection prevents it. She comes up behind him and places a small hand on one of his taut buttocks. "Don't pull them up. You'll just be taking them off again."

"Right," he says.

He follows her down the hall and his erect penis bobbles like a divining rod seeking water. He's not sure how much longer he can take this. When they arrive in the dark bedroom, she turns on a small lamp beside her bed and starts removing her clothes. He removes the rest of his. When they're naked she turns to him and asks what he wants to do.

"What we didn't do last time," he says.

"I thought so." She opens the drawer of the nightstand next to her bed and retrieves a small shiny square package. He knows what it is.

"Hey, I brought one, too," he says.

"That's fine. We might use both of them."

But they only use one condom and the experience does not go well. He dislikes how the condom feels around the base of his penis as he tries to thrust with enough precision to arouse her. But Pamela lies mostly unresponsive, an expression of discomfort on her face. The preliminaries were so unusual and confusingly erotic that they quickly aroused him. As a result, he doesn't last very long. After ten minutes, he ejaculates into the prophylactic.

He dislikes the next part even more. He walks into her bathroom and removes the used condom and deposits it in the plastic trash bin. When he returns to bed he feels sort of depressed. It's more than a post-coital melancholy. The whole build-up was exciting but the actual deed turned out to be sort of mechanical and messy. He glances at Pamela. She turns on her side and faces him. In the dim light, he discerns an expression of relief on her face.

"Don't blame yourself," she says. "I always have a hard time achieving orgasm."

165

8

Dale has never been to the Jackson Fine Arts Center before. He walks down the hall where most of the classrooms are located. At the end of the hall he comes to a closed door that opens to one of the art studios, a large room where student artists paint, sculpt, and draw. He glances at a small white card posted beside the door listing the class in session: life drawing 302.

He considered taking an art class for one of his electives. He took a drawing class when he was an undergraduate at GNC but it hadn't been an interesting class. All of the assignments were drawing landscapes, objects from still life, and facial portraits. Not one assignment focused on the human figure. The GNC administration obviously prohibited the use of nude models since it was a religious college. But he knew the life drawing class at Wyoming had a few weeks of drawing nude models.

But Dale isn't here for that. He walks into the lobby and goes over to the student gallery. He examines a series of black and white etching and drawings, this month's exhibit. One particularly interests him. It's a drawing of the top half of a Minute Man nuclear missile erupting from its silo. But what makes the drawing more compelling is instead of the USA symbol on its side there is a picture of JFK. The image of Kennedy is classic Kennedy: the wavy brown hair, the rather square shaped face, the high cheekbones, and the confident expression of a young political visionary.

It's an odd, almost surreal drawing. It's not historically accurate. Kennedy never launched any nukes. But Dale remembers that he almost did during the Cuban Missile Crisis.

Dale glances down at the signature: Matt Von Goebbels.

Matt is in Dale's film directing class. He'll have to mention his drawing. In fact, he's thinking about asking him to serve as the art editor of the *Owen Wister Review*. That's why he's at the fine arts center. He's looking for possible candidates to fill the last staff position.

"Hello. Aren't you Dale Smith?"

It's a feminine voice and Dale turns to see a middle-aged woman looking at him. She smiles. He recognizes her.

"I'm Regina Wilson. I'm one of the faculty members on the publications board."

"Right. I remember."

She's not an especially attractive woman, at least not at first glance, but as Dale studies her face and figure he thinks there is something appealing about her. She wears her long red hair in a ponytail rather than free and almost disheveled as she had the first time he saw her at the pub board meeting. She has a large nose but her green eyes are large, too, and round-shaped and heavy-lidded. Her mouth is wide but the lips aren't particularly full but when she smiles, as she does again under his inspection, he sees a very becoming smile, big and sincere that indicates a warm personality.

Her clothes are nearly as gaudy as they were at the pub board meeting: A long multi-color dress, beads, and a purple sweater. The long, loose dress doesn't fully disguise a full-bodied if not matronly figure. He tries to think of that phrase that describes her type. He thinks of it: an Earth Mother.

"How are you doing? As I remember, you're going to be one very busy young man."

Dale says he's doing fine but he is busy. She asks about the literary magazine. He tells her that he has selected all the staff except for the art editor. She gives him the names of a couple of students to call. He thanks her. She asks about his other classes and activities. He gives her a quick rundown of them and adds that the class he was most interested in, the film directing class, is rather expensive. He has to pay for camera rental, the film stock, and the film processing. She nods. She knows that film is pricey. In fact, the visual arts in general tend to be, unfortunately, expensive. That's one reason why so few people get involved. She fears that some students are discouraged from taking her art classes because of the additional cost.

"What classes do you teach?" he asks.

"I instruct the life drawing classes. I also teach a class in photography. An art class not a journalistic one."

"Right. I'm beginning to understand there is a distinction."

"Not to denigrate photo journalism," she says, again smiling that becoming smile, "but photography as an art is more expressive and subjective."

"That's how I think it is in writing, too. Journalism is more factual and objective but literary writing is more interpretive and subjective."

"Excellent analogy. The key to art is interpretation. How we see; how we interpret what we see."

"Or in writing how to write so the reader interprets more than just the words he reads."

"Or she." But she says it in a nice way. "I must say that is a perceptive point. I don't think a lot of people understand that."

Dale shrugs. "Well, I'm trying to learn."

She smiles again and says she has to go. She wishes him well in all his pursuits. He says goodbye and watches her stroll down the hall. He liked having that conversation with her. Maybe he should have taken an art class after all.

As Wagstaff ends his pep talk in the film directing class, Dale realizes that he has to completely change his film project. He planned on making a ten-minute dramatic narrative with a cast of three people. In fact, he already wrote the script. It was to be a takeoff on *The Graduate* except that it would depict the misadventures of a Ben Braddock-like character as a graduate student. The film's title: *The Post-Graduate*.

But Dale realizes that the things he planned will be too complicated and cost too much money. He is willing to dip into his savings to make the film but he doesn't want to use all his money. He needs to have enough left to finance his trip to Minnesota after he gets his degree. He'll need a nest egg for an apartment deposit and to tide him over for a few weeks until he finds a job.

Aside from the money, making a narrative film would present other challenges, primarily finding three actors who could convincingly play the roles of Ben, Elaine, and Mrs. Robinson. He was especially concerned about finding a Mrs. Robinson, although his recent meeting with Regina Wilson gave him the idea that she could play the role. (He toyed with the idea of asking Deb Pierson to play Elaine; as for Ben he had no one in mind. Ed Darby was too tall and mature looking for the role. In the back of his mind he thought he could play Ben although he was reluctant to follow in the footsteps of other actor-writer-directors like Orson Welles and Woody Allen.)

Aside from the problem with casting, he would also have to find locations and acquire props and costumes. He'd have to worry about the lighting and sound. He already scripted seven different scenes with three different sets and that set-up would complicate matters even more. Simply put, he didn't have the time or the resources, financial and human, to fulfill his plans for such an ambitious student film.

He has to simplify. First, he'll cut the time of the film. Instead of ten minutes he'll cut it to five minutes or maybe even less. That will save a lot of money. He won't have to buy nearly as much film stock or pay as much for processing the film. Second, instead of making a dramatic narrative, that is, a film with actors interacting with each another and speaking dialogue, he'll make a film that is mostly visual with very little interaction and dialogue between actors. That way he won't have to depend upon the actors too much and he won't have to make a soundtrack with synchronous sound. (All the film cameras don't have built-in audio anyway. A filmmaker has to make a separate soundtrack and overdub dialogue and sound effects and at a speed that matches the visual footage. The audio strip is then spliced onto the film during processing. Otherwise, films will have an asynchronous soundtrack, which was a lot easier to produce.) As he considers all these concerns, he realizes making a mock documentary or a spoof of some kind would be a lot easier.

Third, he could shoot his film in black and white, which would save money, and since some of his favorite films were in black and white that idea doesn't bother him. However, shooting in black and white or color depends on what kind of mock documentary or spoof he decides to make.

He needs to come up with an idea for a simple story and make the production as efficient as he can. If he can think of an appropriate story idea and plan it out to the last detail he might be able to make a cheap but engaging film. Instead of spending a thousand bucks or more he will only have to spend five hundred dollars. Still, considering his meager financial resources, that was a lot of money. He was learning about the financial demands of film-making and he didn't like it.

With the end of class, Dale sees the Von Goebbels brothers walking out. He hustles after them. They exchange greetings and the usual small talk until Dale gets to the point.

"Hey, Matt, I saw your drawing at the gallery. I liked it."

"Thanks."

"He has good a very good eye," says Mark, the shorter brother "He's going to be the cinematographer on my film."

"And Mark is very good with props and special effects," says Matt, the taller brother with a slight lisp.

"I'm especially good with small explosives," says Mark.

"A regular F/X man," says Matt.

"I could blow up a car," says Mark. "If you need that in your film, I can do it."

"Thanks but I'm not planning any explosions. Actually, I wanted to ask Matt if he'd like to be the art editor of the *Owen Wister Review*."

"What would I have to do?"

"Not that much. Your primary duty would be to select several photo reproductions of art for inclusion in the magazine."

"I think I could do that."

"Great. We're going to have a staff meeting tomorrow at 5 p.m. The office is in the student union on the third floor on the west end."

Matt says he'll be there then he and his brother depart. Dale walks away in the other direction wondering what would be involved in a car explosion besides the car and dynamite. No, he decides, that would be too expensive, too.

The *Owen Wister Review* office is small and cramped and hardly has enough room for the six staff members and the editor. The only good thing about it is that it's located in the corner room on the third floor and the window allows for an expansive view of the quadrangle.

The meeting ends and five of the staff members file out of the office, carrying flyers to be posted around campus advertising for submissions. Dale sits in the uncomfortable wooden chair before the rather rickety desk and reflects upon the meeting that has just concluded. It went well. He thinks the five staffers are going to work out fine. They all are knowledgeable in the areas of their expertise and, more importantly, they have agreeable personalities. No temperamental artist types. He thinks the staff will work well together which is what most concerns him.

The poetry editor, Millie Jansen, stands before an old filing cabinet. She's looking for paper clips. She holds in her hand the first manuscript, five pages of poetry written by Miriam Morgenstern.

"Any good?" asks Dale.

"A couple of poems aren't bad," Millie says.

She's a fairly tall, blonde young woman (she looks like Dallas Kincaid; Dale thinks they could pass for sisters) in her early twenties. Dale thinks she's rather cute with her thick medium length blonde hair and green eyes. He also likes her quiet, unassuming personality. When he first met her and she told him her name, he asked, "Are you thoroughly modern?"

Millie didn't get the movie reference. Instead, she looked a little offended and said, "I have a steady boyfriend."

Dale explained that he wasn't making a risqué inquiry but that he was referring to a '60s movie starring Julie Andrews, *Thoroughly Modern Millie*.

"I've never seen it," Millie said, but she smiled a forgiving smile. In spite of that odd interchange, she remained on the staff although she still hasn't seen the movie.

Now Dale wonders what Millie stands for. It's sort of an unusual, old-fashioned name. She's Scandinavian. So she could have one of those odd Norse literary names like Frigga and Snotra.

"Is your name short for Mildred?"

Millie smiles a frown. That is, her mouth turns down but her eyes look amused. "No."

"I hope it's not Millhouse."

"Of course not. It's Millicent."

Dale nods. He rather likes that name. "You ought to use it. It's classy."

"I do for my poetry." She paperclips Mimi's poems together and puts them in the cardboard box for poetry submissions.

"Do you know Mimi?" he asks.

"Oh, yes. She's in several of my classes."

"Does she have a steady boyfriend?"

"I don't know. She's not a close friend. Why do you ask?"

"She's always talking about her boyfriend back in Denver. Joe DiMaggio."

He waits to see how she will react to that name. Millie isn't puzzled. He guesses she doesn't know much about baseball or '60s musicals. But that's okay. She knows poetry.

"Is there anything else you need for me to do before I leave?" Millie asks.

"No, thanks."

Millie says goodnight and leaves the office. Even though he has a semi-regular girlfriend, if that was the right word for it, his mind focuses on Mimi and Millie and Deb. He finds all of them more attractive than Pamela. He wonders if Millie really does have a steady boyfriend.

"What a misogynistic film!"

Pamela Partridge throws her hands into the air. She shakes her head as if she can't believe the depths of depravity that is *A Clockwork Orange*. Dale, on the other hand, was very impressed with the film. He never saw a movie quite like it. It's not just the shocking subject matter but the way Stanley Kubrick shapes the film that fascinates him. The last time he remembers feeling such admiration and almost awe with the look of a film was when he first saw *Citizen Kane*.

"Weren't you appalled by that spectacle?" she demands.

"No. I thought the film was brilliant."

Pamela stops in her tracks. She stares at Dale. "How can you say that? A film that celebrates violence and rape and murder."

"It doesn't celebrate those things. It's a satire."

He starts walking but Pamela remains standing on the snow-streaked sidewalk. He motions for her to follow and she glares at him. He walks back to her.

"Are we going to your place or not?"

"I can't believe you approve of that film. It's a completely irresponsible film."

"It's shocking in many ways. But cinematically it's amazing." He glances at her. Her pale face is glowing with indignation. There are tears of vexation in her eyes. "Come on. We can talk while we walk. It's cold standing here."

They start walking across campus heading for her apartment. Along the way, Pamela continues to lambast the irresponsible film. She also denounces the behavior of the audience. Several young men actually cheered during the first rape scene.

"Yeah, that was disturbing," Dale says. "They didn't understand the film at all."

"They understood it all too well."

"Pamela, Kubrick isn't advocating rape or robbery or murder or any crime. He made a trenchant dystopian satire about State control of the individual. It raises a paradoxical question: should the State have the power to change human beings, in essence to remove free will, if it results in a safer, more ordered society? Ironically, that society would ultimately become mechanistic and soulless."

"All right, I don't want to argue about it," she says. "The whole experience was just revolting. Such films should be banned."

"Banned?"

"At least on college campuses. I wouldn't be surprised if some frat boy rapes a girl tonight."

"Aren't you overreacting?"

"Am I? Rape is a serious problem on college campuses."

"I didn't say it wasn't. But you can't blame a film for such crimes. And banning A Clockwork Orange would just make college kids want to see it all the more."

They arrive at her apartment. They go inside and take off their coats and other winter wear.

"I ought to write a complaint to the film selection committee. Whoever voted for that film ought to be kicked off!"

"Since I'm not on the committee, they can't kick me off," Dale says. "But that's one of the films I recommended they show."

Pamela stares at him. "You're joking? Did you know what kind of film it is?"

"Yeah, a good film. At least that's what I read."

"You knew how misogynistic it is?"

"I've never seen it before, Pamela. That's why I recommend the film committee show it. And you don't have to approve of everything in a film to admire it. That's the whole point of art."

"Art! You thought that was artistic?"

"Yeah, I did."

She crosses her arms across her chest and purses her lips. Dale doesn't like how she looks. He's beginning to lose his patience.

"Let's not discuss it anymore," he says. "You didn't like it and I did."

"I bet Mimi liked it as well. Too bad you didn't get a chance to sit with her."

They had seen Mimi sitting with the Von Goebbels brothers and a couple of other people that Dale didn't know well. She motioned for him to join her. He wanted to, but he knew Pamela didn't. He shrugged his shoulders in an apologetic way and walked toward the back with Pamela. When the movie ended, he saw Mimi with her friends as they were walking out. She turned and looked at him, but her expression was one of disapproval. She left without waving goodbye.

"I don't know why you dislike Mimi so much."

"She's a shameless flirt for one thing. Acting like a stereotypical female when men are around. And she's pretentious! Mimi! Her name is Miriam Morgenstern but she's ashamed to be a Jew."

"What do you mean?"

"She's a Jew. Didn't you know that?"

"No. She's never said. And how do you know?"

"Her name. And how she looks. All that curly dark hair and her big nose."

Dale thinks that Pamela shouldn't single out other people's noses. Hers was sort of piggy, after all.

"What does her being Jewish have to do with anything? She's eccentric and funny and friendly and I like her."

"Dale, sometimes you amaze me. You seem to completely lack social awareness. And I don't mean Miriam. I don't care about her. But you consistently don't take social issues seriously. Defending a film as politically dubious as that ... what we saw tonight."

"I don't care about politics. I care about art." He realizes he sounds pretentious so he adds, "and a lot of other things, too."

"All right, let's drop it." She turns to walk into the kitchen. "Do you want a beer?"

"No, thanks."

"I forgot you don't drink beer. Or anything else like that. When I first started knowing you I thought you might be a Mormon judging from your personal habits."

She goes into the kitchen and he hears her opening the fridge. This wasn't their first disagreement. Just last night she got in a bad mood, too. After an hour of increasingly testy exchanges, he finally figured out that she was upset because he forgot to spend Valentine's Day with her. Not that she approved of such sexist pseudo-celebrations. Then why was she upset? Because she would be pleased if wanted to give her flowers or candy or take her to dinner even though it was against her principles to accept. The argument became circular. She wanted a more traditional relationship but she really didn't. She felt like she did sometimes, especially during holidays, but she thought she shouldn't feel that way. They should have a completely equal relationship without all the conventional romantic trappings. If he didn't want to treat her like a girlfriend, then that was fine. She didn't want to be treated that way either. They both were free to do what they please. Each of them shouldn't make any demands on the other. If they got together just to have sex on weekends, then that was fine with her.

The only problem was that the sex wasn't very enjoyable. Initially, he liked the sex games she used to entice him. The games were fun but the end result was always disappointing. Dale thought Pamela really didn't like sex but pretended she did just so she could maintain this image of an independent, modern young woman who could engage in sexual affairs on a casual basis just as informally as any man. After all the fussing they did last night neither one of them wanted to go to bed together so he left. He thought maybe he wouldn't see her again but she called the following afternoon and wanted to know if he was going to the campus film (she always called movies films) that night. Now he wished he hadn't said yes.

He's never been involved with a girl like Pamela before. In high school and college his girlfriends were traditional in their behavior and views. He took them out for dates and they made out in his car or other secluded places when he could find them but there was no expectation that it would develop into a sexual relationship until marriage. His experiences had been centered around dating, courtship, and marriage although he had no intention of getting married at that time. His relationships were romantically based not sexually based. The only time it wasn't was the summer when he was nineteen and he had a short affair with a married woman, Sal, (he didn't know she was married at that time) who was the daughter of his father's girlfriend. That relationship had been essentially just a sexual one. Looking back on it, he realized that it hadn't been very satisfying either. He and Sal had sex three times and he had sort of enjoyed the experience physically but he hadn't felt any deeper feelings for Sal and she didn't have any for him. In fact, he suspected her mother (his father's girlfriend) had encouraged her to seduce him. But even though he thought the "affair" was a mistake it had been a novel experience, his first encounter where sex was the main priority.

This affair with Pamela is lasting longer than three trysts. It's now been six weeks. But it isn't anything official. They just get together on weekends to see a movie then go over to her place for some moderately enjoyable sex. They haven't had what he would call a real date yet. Apparently that bothered Pamela and the fact that it bothered her bothered her even more.

Pamela comes back into the living room holding two large glasses. Judging from the amber color and froth one is a beer. The other looks like a 7-Up.

She hands him the 7-Up. She walks over to the couch and sits down and takes a sip of her beer. He joins her on the couch and then remembers he had a question for her.

"What do you mean you thought I was a Mormon?"

177

"Like I said, your personal habits. You don't smoke or drink alcohol or coffee. And you seemed a little sexually inexperienced."

"No, I'm not a Mormon."

There weren't any Mormons in his hometown but he knew one guy who was one when Dale worked as an umpire for little league baseball in the Oklahoma City area. The coordinator was a Mormon and after Dale got to know him he talked a little about himself and his religion. Dale liked him.

"Well, you remind me of some of the Mormon kids in my hometown," Pamela says. She takes a big gulp of her large glass of beer.

"Back in Evanston?"

"Yes. It's not far from the Utah border. A lot of Mormons live there."

"My hometown has a lot of religious people in it, too. But no Mormons." In fact, the Nazarenes he knew consider Mormons to be similar to heathens.

"My parents are Mormon," Pamela says.

"But you're not?"

"Not any more."

"When did you stop being one?"

"In high school. And boy, did it bother my parents. They wanted me to go to BYU but I wouldn't. Talk about dull."

"What about your parents? You haven't told me much about your family."

"It's all boring. My father owns a drugstore. My mother is a homemaker, of course. Two older brothers. Both attended BYU and are now married with kids."

"So you're the youngest?"

"By five years. It's all so dull. I lived the Mormon life until I turned sixteen. Then I saw the light. I was determined not to be like my mother. She's taken for granted by everyone. She's never done anything for herself. And she's a bright woman. She could have done so much."

"Maybe she's doing what she wants."

178

"I don't think so although she's never said otherwise. But she's the type of person who wouldn't." Pamela finishes her beer. "But I don't want to think about all of that."

"Okay."

She leans against the couch and stretches her body. She looks at him in an inviting way, her eyes narrowing.

"Do you want to go to bed?" she asks.

"I don't know."

"Why?"

"I don't like using a condom."

"Why is it that men always expect that women should take care of everything? They just assume we will prepare ourselves for them."

"I'm not assuming anything. I haven't told you to go on the pill or use anything else."

"I'll grant you that." She traces the lip of the glass with one finger in a thoughtful way. "We could try something else."

"Like what?"

"Oh, it's something that Germaine Greer recommends."

"Who's she?"

"A celebrated feminist writer, of course. You haven't read any of her work?"

"If I had, then I would have recognized her name."

"Well, anyway, she recommends a sex act where a condom is not required. But we have to take a shower first."

"Together?"

"Would you mind?"

"Not at all."

The prospect of mutual bathing excites both of them. They rush to the bathroom and throw off their clothes. Pamela turns on the shower and they get in. The hot water splashes down on them and it relaxes them. They take turns soaping each other. When Dale starts working on her back, Pamela turns her head and whispers, "wash my asshole." Once again, he's shocked at her language but he complies. He first soaps her plump buttocks then he puts a dollop of soap on his middle finger and inserts it into her tight anus. They rinse off and get out of the shower.

"I think I know now what Germaine Greer was talking about," he says as they towel off.

Before they go into the bedroom, Pamela opens the medicine cabinet and takes out a jar of Vaseline. She leaves the lamp light on and positions herself on the bed by lowering her head and arching her back and presenting her round, full moon-like rump to him.

He opens the jar of Vaseline.

"Be sure and use a lot of lube," she instructs.

He covers his middle finger with the stuff as she reaches behind her and spreads the cheeks of her ass, revealing the pink oval of her anus. Seeing the small hole, he's not sure if this is going to work. But he generously lubricates her sphincter.

"Work your finger around to loosen me up."

He does and she groans. He thinks how weird all of this is. But in spite of that idea, he's excited at the idea of sodomizing her. When he thinks her anus is well prepared, he asks if she's ready. She nods her lowered head. He puts his penis against her anus.

"Go easy," she says.

He tries. He gradually inserts more of his phallus into her. It's a strange feeling. Her rectum is tighter and warmer than her vagina yet it feels emptier.

He gradually begins to thrust. She begins to moan and rock her hips. He quickens his strokes while trying to hold back. But the whole experience is too exhilaratingly decadent that he can't restrain himself any longer. While ejaculating he tries not to thrust too hard, concerned it might hurt her. Just the same he hears her groaning, not in ecstasy, but more in acute discomfort.

He withdraws and topples on the bed next to her. She's curled up in a ball, her pink butt toward him. He reaches over and pats one cheek watching the plump flesh quiver. Although he thinks the act was perverted, he can't deny that he enjoyed it. But he doesn't think Pamela did.

She finally straightens out and turns over. He sees that her eyes are still closed.

"Are you okay?" he asks.

"I guess."

"So this is what Germaine Greer recommends? Anal sex?"

Pamela nods. "And I now think she's one dumb bitch."

9

After their creative writing class, Dale asks Mimi to take a walk with him. They walk over to the bench that sits in the middle of a small stand of evergreen trees. She sits down, puts her big purple purse and purple backpack on the ground. She looks up at him because he hasn't sat down beside her. The expression on her face is one that he has never seen before: Not unfriendly but reserved and thoughtful as if she is a juror and she's not sure how she is going to vote.

"Is something bothering you?" he asks.

"Why do you ask?"

"Because you've been acting differently these past couple of weeks."

"How so?"

"Like you're acting now. Cool towards me. Not joking around and babbling like you used to."

"I used to babble, did I?"

"You used to talk a lot. About all kinds of things and without a lot of focus. But I liked it. It showed you felt comfortable talking to me. But that changed a couple of weeks ago. Why?"

He takes a seat now and looks at her face. At first, she won't look at him but before she speaks she turns in his direction.

"I don't like it that you aren't sitting with me at the campus movies."

"Yeah, well."

"And I don't like that you are seeing Pamela Partridge."

"What is it between you two?"

"Simple. We don't like each other."

"That's obvious. But why?"

"Different personalities. We used to be in some classes together but fortunately we have different majors so I don't have to be in same class with her anymore."

"Anything else?"

"Maybe you should ask her. She's the one who started it. A few years ago, we were sort of friends. But her attitude changed toward me. I never knew why. Then another thing happened that *I won't talk about* and that made everything worse."

"Okay. But what does that have to do with me?"

"You're *seeing* her. I can't believe that you're interested in her."

Sometimes he couldn't quite believe it either. Aside from the sex, they didn't have much in common. She kept trying to get him to do outdoor adventures with her: skiing, downhill and cross country, and lately hiking. They went downhill skiing a week ago and he liked it. She was impressed how quickly he took it up. He was naturally athletic and agile so he no problem learning quickly. But even though he liked it he couldn't do it again anytime soon. Skiing took much time and cost too much money. At at the ski lodge they went to, Happy Jack, he rented the equipment and paid a lift fee. Pamela used her own stuff, of course. And the trip, even though it was at the near-by Medicine Bow Mountain, still took all afternoon.

"Well, Mimi, I get lonesome sometimes. Maybe you don't know how that feels since you have a steady boyfriend, your Joe."

"I understand feeling lonely. What I can't understand is *her*."

"Just don't think about it. We're just friends, right? So, our friendship has nothing to do with Pamela.

He can tell that his logic hasn't completely convinced her, but she smiles at him for the first time that day. It's not one of her big, merry smiles, it's more tentative, but it's something positive at least.

"There's something else I want to ask you," Dale says. "Will you be in my movie? I need a pretty girl for an important role."

"You want me to star in your movie?"

"The film's only going to be a few minutes long, but yeah, you would be one of the stars."

"That's wonderful Dale! I've always wanted to be in a movie. And you are so talented. I mean, I loved your story today. You can write movie reviews and radio parodies and short stories and now you're making a movie. Why, I think you're even more talented than Spencer!"

He wishes she wouldn't mention his name. Well, she has Spencer and he has Pamela.

"How is Spencer Dribble doing?"

"You don't know?"

"I haven't received any letters from him lately."

"You two had a falling out? Strange that Spencer hasn't mentioned it to me. But that sometimes happens between two people with creative temperaments."

"That's it exactly. We couldn't get past our creative differences."

"I'm so sorry to hear that. Even though Spencer can be difficult at times, he has a brilliant mind and loads of talent, just like you."

"So, you're going to be in my movie? For certain?"

"Of course! I'll love being in it."

"Great. We're going to film next week during spring break. But we'll need to rehearse a couple of times before that. I'll let you know when."

"That's wonderful! I can't wait. I've never been in a movie before. I acted in high school plays and I even had a small role in one of the campus plays here but I've never been in a cinematic masterpiece!"

"Don't get carried away, Mimi. It's going to be a very short film."

"I don't care! I know you're immensely talented. Whatever medium you work in you display sheer brilliance!" Suddenly, she stops singing his praises. She looks at her wristwatch, a small, silver thing on her left wrist. "Oh, my, Dale. I'm late for my next class! I must be off."

Mimi jumps off the bench, gathers her things, and walks swiftly away. After a few quick strides, she turns and waves at him, a big smile on her face, a smile, in fact, of a starlet.

With the addition of Mimi he now has cast the major parts. The only problem is that Dale still doesn't have a shooting script. He nixed his first script because of length and complications and he only has a general idea for the second script. Right now, all he knows is that he wants to make a film about JFK. Ever since he saw Matt Von Goebbels' ink drawing of JFK's portrait on the nuke missile he wants Kennedy to be his subject. Maybe he'll make a parody about a press conference. He has other ideas just as boring. But at least he has Mimi as the lead actress (as Jackie) and he has Edward Darby cast as Kennedy. Darby, in fact, looks somewhat like JFK. If he got a Kennedyesque haircut, then Darby could pass for a plausible parody president.

Dale asked Darby yesterday to be in the movie after they finished producing that week's *Buffalo Quotidians*. Darby was in a good mood. He got word that the director of the radio station, Mike Sibelius, was going to Casper to head the public radio station there and Darby thought he had a good chance to be named his replacement once he graduated in May. When Dale told Darby that he would be playing JFK, he readily accepted the role. He was flattered to be compared to the great, martyred president.

So, Dale has his two leads and he thinks he can wrangle some other people to appear in his movie. He already has the Von Goebbels brothers signed on to help with technical concerns. Boy, he thinks, making a movie, even a student one, is a lot of trouble. He is now reconsidering his recent ambition to become a writer-director.

But he still has one problem: he needs to get a finished script and pronto!

Dale sits at his desk in his office in the Mass Communications Department reading about the films of Billy Wilder. He's decided to write his master's thesis on Wilder. Initially, Dale wanted to write about the films of Frank Capra, perhaps his favorite director of all time. But when Wagstaff didn't respond with much enthusiasm about that idea ("You know what the critics called his films? Capra-corn.") Dale reconsidered his decision. Wagstaff reacted more positively about Wilder. ("He's not much of a visual stylist but his films are amusingly acerbic.") Dale started his research several weeks ago and even managed to see a couple of early Wilder films that he hadn't seen before, *Five Graves to Cairo* and *Double Indemnity* both at the Trout Theatre's Thursday classics night. Now Dale reckons he's seen all of Wilder's major films either on TV or at theatres.

Professor Comstock suddenly walks into the office. Without even a hello, he drops a thick stack of papers on Dale's desk.

"Since you haven't stopped by my office, I have to come to yours even though you are hardly ever in."

Since Dale still keeps his office hours even though he's not teaching a class this semester he thinks Comstock is being his usual imperious, pompous self. He glances up and sees the middle aged professor staring at him with a look of contempt. It seems that Comstock expects Dale to behave with servile deference to him. After all, Dale is now his assistant on this major project. If Dale doesn't ingratiate himself with him then the professor regards his attitude as lack of respect or defiance or rebellion.

"Those are the proofs of the journal," Comstock says, pointing a horny finger at the thick stack of very white papers. "I expect you to start work on proofing immediately. Have you created the state folders yet?"

Comstock wants Dale to put the proofed pages into folders

according to state. Dale says yes, he's made all the folders. They are over on Neil Nordberg's desk. Comstock walks over to that desk and examines the folders. Written in black magic marker are the names of the fifty states and the Canadian provinces that have collegiate journalism programs. Dale returns to his reading when he hears Comstock's agitated voice squawking at him:

"You've misspelled one of the states! If this is the kind of inattention you'll bring to this project, Dale, then you are in for a very difficult time."

Dale turns and sees Comstock holding a light green folder. He tosses it on Dale's desk. It's the folder for Wisconsin.

"What's wrong?" Dale asks.

Comstock comes over and shoves a thick finger at the name on the folder. Dale notices that his finger has bulky knuckles. He still doesn't know what he's done wrong.

"Is that how you spell Wisconsin?" Comstock demands.

Dale looks at the word. It looks correct to him. "Yeah, I think so."

"What? With two O's?"

Dale looks more closely at the state's name. W-i-s-c-o-n-s-o-n. Oops. He now realizes that the he did indeed misspell the name. He remembers when he was writing the name in magic marker that he concentrated so much on the calligraphy that he didn't visualize the letters as he should and instead wrote the letters by hearing the word in his mind. That's how he pronounced the word. In fact, that's probably how his hillbilly relatives pronounced the word or perhaps they said Wis-con-*sun*.

"Sorry, Professor Comstock."

"Really, Dale, if you can't spell Wisconsin then how will you prove of assistance to me?"

Dale felt like saying: then get somebody else. But nobody else wants the job. He's stuck with it. Judging from the tall stacks of proofs it will take thirty or forty hours to proof the pages. Tedious work, too. He thinks it's unfair that he was picked for the job. Grabowski and Deb have much easier and more pleasant additional duties.

"You must understand that this is one of the most prestigious journals in North America. I expect you to devote yourself to proofing those pages. If you're uncertain about a stylistic point or grammatical usage or how to *spell* a *word*, then look it up!"

Comstock departs as suddenly as he entered. Dale can faintly smell the unpleasant odor of strong aftershave cologne and cigarettes. Comstock smokes but not in his office. The only time Dale saw him outside his office was once in the early morning as he stood under an awning at the back of Gowdy Hall puffing on a Lucky Strike.

Dale tries to defuse his anger. He almost wanted to jump up from his desk and punch the professor while he was berating him. So he misspelled a word? You'd think that he had tried to burn down the building.

He hears someone walking by the open office door. He turns and sees Neil Nordberg gliding by, an unsympathetic grin on his face.

Watch out, Nordberg, Dale thinks, flexing his fingers into a fist. I might just knock that grin off your face.

Dale strolls into Wagstaff's office without knocking. The door is wide open and Dale is still a little angry over Comstock's verbal lashing.

"I'd ask you to come in, Dale, but you're already in!"

Wagstaff leans against the back of his cushioned office chair, his long legs propped on his desk. Dale notices he's wearing argyle socks. Well, Walt *is* one snappy dresser.

"Does the film library have any footage of JFK?"

Wagstaff lifts his legs and drops his feet behind his desk. He sits up straight. "Unusual question. But then you're an unusual young man."

"Well, does it?"

"I think there are a few frames of our very late president."

"What's the footage about?"

"I presume the usual kind of material. Press conferences, news interviews. Why are you interested?"

"Just curious. Well, it's more than that. It's for research."

'If you're really interested in Kennedy then I might be able to help you. I have some movie footage that you might find compelling."

"You mean you have some film in your personal library at home and not in the department's film library."

"As a matter of fact, I do."

"Don't tell me. It's a sequel to *Ecstasy*."

Wagstaff laughs his whooping laugh. "That's what I like about you, your wicked sense of humor. But unfortunately, there is no sequel. However, there are rumors that JFK and Hedy Lamarr were lovers."

"You're kidding!"

"As I say, just rumors. But I know a lot about Kennedy. I am something of an aficionado. I'm especially interested in the Kennedy image and I don't mean his general persona but actual images of our late president."

"So you have a collection of Kennedy film footage and things like that."

Wagstaff nods in a self-satisfied way.

"Could I see some of it?"

Wagstaff pauses before answering. He appraises Dale in pseudo-thoughtful way as if he's considering a potential initiate to a secret club. "I suppose I could."

"Great. When can I see it? I'd like to see it as soon as possible."

"My, my, aren't we eager. What about Thursday evening?"

"No, I always go to The Trout theatre to see a classic movie on Thursday."

"Yes, I forgot about your amazing dedication to seeing old movies."

"What about tomorrow evening?"

"Wednesday? That means I won't be able to attend Wednesday church activities but ..." Wagstaff glances at Dale with a mischievous grin. He knows that Dale knows he's not a church-goer. "Okay, let's make it tomorrow evening. Come by at 9:30 p.m. The brood are in bed by then."

"Superlative! I'll drop by then. Thanks, Walt."

Wagstaff waves his hand in a *noblesse oblige* kind of way as Dale quickly exits his office. As Dale heads out of the department, he has a feeling that Wagstaff's personal stash of films might yield the inspiration he needs to finalize his movie's idea.

When Dale gets home that evening, he sees Grabowski sitting at the dining table using Dale's old manual Underwood typewriter. Grabowski glances up for a second then resumes his two finger pecking. Grabowski, of course, didn't ask permission to use his typewriter. Dale doesn't especially like his attitude that everything in the apartment belongs to him, or at least can be borrowed by him, since only his name his on the lease. But Dale isn't that possessive of his stuff.

"I'm just typing an application letter," Grabowski says. "You got some letters. I put them on the desk by the door."

Dale goes over and sees both Will Whitaker and Teri Boswell wrote. Judging from the thickness of the letters both penned their usual lengthy epistles. He grabs both letters and walks over to Grabowski. He watches as his roommate continues to hunt and peck at the keys.

"You ought to get Deb to do that for you," Dale says with only a touch of sarcasm in his voice.

"No biggie," Grabowski says. "Besides, she's not as cooperative as she used to be."

Grabowski used to have Deb proofread his class papers. She always complied. But maybe she has stopped doing that as she got busier with her own work. Grabowski, however, seems to have the knack for eliciting assistance. He also is a shameless sycophant with the professors in the department. On several occasions while walking down the hall, Dale spied Grabowski seated in one of the professor's offices nodding, smiling and chuckling at some comment. Dale also heard him flatter the same professors in his characteristically flat and nonchalant voice so he didn't sound too much like a toady.

"What are you applying for?"

"A teaching job."

"Isn't that premature? You're not going to receive your degree until the end of summer."

"Dr. Holznager said I should now start applying for any advertised position. I saw this job in the Chronicle of Higher Education."

Holznager was Grabowski's advisor. Since he taught the photojournalism courses that made sense. At least the department hadn't assigned Grabowski an inappropriate advisor like it had with him.

"What kind of job? Where?"

"Teaching photojournalism classes. It's at some regional college in Illinois."

"Okay, sounds good. When you get finished, let me know. I need to use my typewriter."

"Sure. No biggie."

Dale walks into his bedroom and reads the two letters from his friends. Teri's is mostly concerned with her job. She's frustrated that the managing editor isn't allowing her to have her own regular beat. She's thinking of looking for another job, maybe one in Arkansas so she'll be closer to her family. Will's letter is partly composed of his activities at work and in graduate school. He's going to finish his master's in political science this summer and he's working more hours at the television station to save money for their proposed tour of the world. He also writes two pages describing the latest films he's seen (not too many because of how busy he's been), the out-of-class books he's read (he just finished *Darkness at Noon*), and anaylzing several articles that he read in the dozen of journals that he subscribes to.

Will also regretfully reports that he won't be able to come to see Dale in Wyoming during spring break. He has a chance to pick up a dozen of hours at work and he's decided to do that. After all, he needed to save money for their trip. He's also a little behind with his grad studies and he wants to catch up over the break.

Dale's a little disappointed but he understands. He's going to be busy during spring break, too, hopefully filming his movie. And he's also going to do more work on the OWR and, if he can stomach it, work on Comstock's journal.

"Hey, bud," Grabowski says, his big blonde head popping into view, "I'm going out for a beer. Want to come?"

Ever since Dale gave his Intro section to Grabowski, Gary has been more overtly friendly, even calling him "bud" from time to time.

"No, thanks, I'm too busy."

"Man, you took on too much this semester."

"I like being busy."

"You're so busy you can't have any fun. What's school for if it isn't for fun?"

For Grabowski, having fun means drinking beer, watching TV, and bedding hopefully moderately attractive coeds. But he'll settle for the less attractive too as he's told Dale more than once. "In fact, man," he once confided, "those are the easiest chicks to bag."

Thinking of that conversation, Dale for a moment has the uncomfortable feeling that he might be emulating his randy roommate with his "bagging" of Pamela Partridge.

"Hey, what you doing over spring break?" Grabowski asks.

"Catching up. What are your plans?"

"I'm going to drive to Mexico."

"Really? Where?"

"Juarez. I've been told it's a wild place during spring break."

"Are you going by yourself?"

"No, I've been invited by Pablo."

Dale recalls that Pablo is the guy that Grabowski plays basketball with. Pablo Mesa, a graduate student in history, is originally from Mexico somewhere, perhaps Juarez.

"That's a long way to drive."

"Pablo's got a sweet ride. It's straight south. He said we can make it in twelve hours. He said the trip is on him. All I got to do is pay for my beer and tequila."

"Sounds great," Dale says trying to disguise the sarcasm. "Take in a bullfight while you're there."

Grabowski says so long and Dale goes back to reading Will's letter. When he finishes, he goes into the living room and sits down at the typewriter preparing to answer both letters. He's about to insert a sheet of paper when the telephone rings. He goes into the kitchen to answer the phone affixed to the wall.

After he says hello he hears a woman's voice ask for Dale Smith. He says he's speaking. She sort of chuckles, a pleasant female trilling really, and says her name as Regina Wilson. Dale remembers her name. He asks how she is and she says fine then she gets to business. She is looking for a male model and would like to know if he is interested.

"I couldn't stand up in front of a class," he says, embarrassed to even think about it.

"It's not for a class, it's for my personal work."

"You want me to model for you?"

"Yes, very much. Of course, I would pay you for your time. I remember that you were concerned about financing your student film. Well, you could earn quite a bit of cash for just several hours of work."

"I don't know. I've never done anything like that."

"I tell you what. Why don't you come out to my ranch early next week and we can discuss it. I'll show you some of my work and then you can decide."

Dale says he could do that. Regina gives him the directions to her ranch, it's just outside Laramie, and suggests that he stop by Monday afternoon, around one. Dale says okay. She says she'll be looking forward to their meeting and then says goodbye in her slightly husky but feminine voice that he likes.

He hangs up the phone and stares thoughtfully into space. Regina's phone call could be serendipitous. Even though he was going to cut down the length of his film, making a very short film would still cost several hundred dollars. He wants to use as little of his savings as possible now that he and Will have agreed to go on a trip overseas together. Working for Regina might be a lucrative proposition. But he still isn't sure. Posing for someone seemed like an effeminate thing to do. However, it's worth investigating. He'll decide after he speaks with her next week. Now, it's time to think about the theme of his film. In another hour he'll go over to the Wagstaff residence. There, he hopes he will find inspiration.

Wagstaff leads Dale into his den where he already has his projector ready. Dale takes a seat while the professor turns off the light and starts the projector.

"This film is the interview Kennedy did just a few months before his death. He talks about the Vietnam war and why he doesn't foresee sending American ground troops."

Wagstaff's description is accurate. It's an interesting interview within the historical context of the Kennedy administration and the Vietnam War but it provides no material for Dale to exploit.

Wagstaff shows several more short films, all of them press conferences or speeches given at various locales. Nothing especially interesting.

"Don't you have anything more out-of-the ordinary?" Dale asks.

"Indeed I do. But I will show it to you on the condition that you keep its existence confidential."

"Oh, come on. Is it a film revealing national security secrets?"

"Actually, it's been shown before on television but only a few times. And technically speaking, it's not a film but a video recording of a home movie."

"Okay, I'll keep mum about its existence. Let's see it."

Wagstaff threads the small roll of film into the projector and a couple of minutes later the images of a black Lincoln

Continental four-door convertible with five people riding in it appear on the screen. Dale quickly ascertains that the two people riding in the back of the limo are President Kennedy and his wife, Jacqueline. Somewhere in the back of his mind, he feels that he's seen this before. It's like seeing some image that evokes a nearly forgotten dream.

Dale and Wagstaff watch the film in silence. Only the whir of the projector is present in the room. They see the limo slowly driving down a street with a dispersed crowd of people waving as it passes. The car is obviously part of a motorcade. Some obstacle, perhaps a street sign, blocks the observer's view of the car containing the Kennedys and the other occupants of the car for a couple of seconds. A minute into the film, Kennedy appears to be in distress. His arms flap up, elbows extend. The expression on his face clearly indicates he is in pain. His wife glances at her husband in alarm. A few seconds later the right side of the President's head explodes sending forth a spray of blood. Kennedy lurches forward and to his right. His wife reaches for him as he slumps to his left. Then Mrs. Kennedy attempts to reach behind her, almost crawling onto the back of the limo. A secret service agent appears in view and prevents her from endangering herself. The limousine picks up speed and races down the street while people in the crowd stare in shock at the fleeing automobile. The film ends.

Dale says nothing for a few seconds. Wagstaff is equally silent.

"That's incredible," Dale finally says.

"Still shocking after all these years," says Wagstaff. "I remember exactly where I was when I heard the news. I was in the mass comm department lounge at Illinois."

"How did you get this film?"

"All I will reveal is that I have a friend who knew a man who worked at a New Jersey film lab. That lab, Manhattan Effects, made a 16 mm copy of the original 8 mm film shot by Abraham Zapruder in Dallas. My friend's contact made a few copies himself and my friend bought one from him. My friend, ill and with no family, sold me his copy. I do not care to disclose the price."

"Why hasn't this film or the original been shown in public?"

"It has. Still frames were published in *Life* magazine in November 1963. The actual film was broadcast on a late-night Chicago news show in 1970. Then in 1975, an ABC late-night show, *Goodnight America*, broadcast it."

"I think I saw that show. I was a senior in high school and for a reason I don't remember I was watching TV late that night. That's why it's seemed eerily familiar like a dream. I remember the shock I felt when I first saw it."

"That was the last time it was broadcast on television. And even then it was late night. So very few Americans have seen this film."

Dale turns back to Wagstaff standing at the projector. "Let's watch it again."

Driving away from Wagstaff's home, Dale decides to stop off at Gowdy Hall and get the proofs. It's almost ten at night so he doesn't expect anyone will be around. He unlocks his office door, not noticing a thin wedge of light seeping from the bottom of the door. He opens the door and sees Neil Nordberg and Spencer Dribble. Nordberg sits before his desk, Dribble at Dale's. Dale is surprised to see them. He says he's dropped by to get the journal proofs.

Nordberg narrows his cool blue eyes in his sly way and offers an insincere grin. Dribble doesn't smile at all. His tall, thin body is slumped in Dale's chair and the only reaction on his long, thin, pale face is a slight grimace. As Dale reaches his hand past him to collect the proofs, Dribble leans back in his seat as if fearful that Dale's touch might contaminate him. After Dale gathers the proofs in his hand, Dribble uses a long-fingered hand to adjust his spectacles as if to see more clearly his nemesis.

"Would you like to join us?" Nordberg asks.

"No, thanks, I've got to get home and do some proofing."

Dale holds up the stack of proofs.

"We're discussing Ken Russell's films in anticipation of seeing *Women in Love* next month. Didn't I once mention that I'd get the film committee to show that movie?"

Dale tilts his head as if considering the question. "I think you did. But I don't remember where. But now I'm surprised that you'd be interested in seeing a film with such a title."

"What does the title have to do with it?"

"It has the word women in it. I thought you didn't have any interest in women."

Nordberg says nothing but his blue eyes grow colder. Dale glances at Dribble. He sits there with the same slightly uncomfortable look on his face as if he's suffering from intestinal gas. Dale doesn't know how much Dribble knows about Nordberg's personal life. Obviously, they are friends. How close, he doesn't know or care.

"Got to go, boys," Dale says as he walks out of the office and shuts the door behind him. He remembers a few weeks ago when he received a paperback copy of *Women in Love* in his departmental mailbox. No note was attached identifying the giver. Dale read it over one weekend. It was an interesting novel, with the typical Laurentian intensity. Dale then returned the novel to Nordberg's mailbox with a note attached. It read: *As I once mentioned, my high school didn't offer (nude) wrestling.*

Dale watches Pamela walk to the bathroom. She's nude and he notices how pale and plump her buttocks are. She walks without any shame or, for that matter, any seductive charm. He thinks they are getting used to one another, maybe even a little bored, at least he is.

The novelty is beginning to wear off. He's never experienced a long-term relationship that was primarily sexual. But now that he's participated in a couple of new kinds of sex acts, he's finding the whole experience less exciting. In fact, they are sort of running out of things to do. After their misadventure in Greer-entry sex a week ago, Pamela vowed never to have anal

197

sex again. He didn't think she really liked having vaginal sex either. Early in their relationship, she once claimed after a rather perfunctory coupling that maybe her vagina was too small. He didn't like having intercourse with her that much either. He didn't like using a condom. She wouldn't use any contraceptives and he has never asked her to. Last night they tried oral sex and it didn't go that well either. After their shower, she climbed on top of him, her face hovering above his genitals while she straddled his chest, her plump rump positioned right before his face. He actually liked looking at her butt, she had a very demure looking natal cleft, pink and hairless, but when he saw a blemish on her right buttock his lust level fell a little. Her mouth and his tongue went to work. He felt his penis being licked and it sort of tickled then he felt her mouth trying to engulf it but it felt more like she was gumming it. The sensations confused him and the fact that he was flicking his tongue like a serpent in her nether regions distracted him even more. When he tried to concentrate on her clitoris, his awareness of the sensations at his groin grew vague and all he felt was moisture and warmth but no specific erotic feelings. If he concentrated on his penis being semi-sucked, his licking became more erratic and she'd squirm her ass to indicate his inattention.

The whole thing took too long. His mouth and tongue grew weary of their task and even his pecker was in danger of becoming bored with her rather mechanical ministrations. So he imagined he was having sex with Hedy Lamarr, not oral sex, but straight sex and as he thrust into her, he stared at her beautiful face, especially her voluptuous lips, and he grew extra erect and a few seconds later he ejaculated.

He heard Pamela sputtering at the other end. She rolled off the bed and dashed to the bathroom. He heard her rinsing her mouth, actually gargling, then spitting. She returned to the bedroom looking sheepish.

"Was it that bad?" he asked.

She lay down next to him. "I just wasn't prepared. You came so suddenly."

Of course, she didn't orgasm. She never has with him. (She hinted she's never achieved orgasm with any *man*. Then he wondered if she has with a woman.) At first, he didn't care so much. But now it is beginning to bother him. He doesn't want to be selfish. But if she can't reach climax then why should he deny himself?

Pamela returns with a bottle of massage oil that she forgot. He reclines on her bed as nude as she is. It occurs to him how casual he's becoming with being naked. In his younger days, he was bashful about his body and never would have lounged around in the buff. Now, he rather enjoyed lying in bed sans clothes. However, in the back of his mind he wonders if that's a good thing. He doesn't want to become narcissistic. He's secretly afraid that he could succumb to that vice the same way he's fearful about becoming pretentious.

Part of the problem is that Pamela is something of a nudist. When they first started having sex, he wanted to get dressed, at least cover his genitals, as soon as it was over. She objected. One of the things she liked best was relaxing in the nude after a sex session and she thought it was unfair that he wanted to put on his shorts while she remained naked. So he kept his clothes off and got more comfortable with it. Besides, she said she liked looking.

"I'll do you first," she says, "then you can do me."

He turns on his belly and she rubs oil onto his shoulders. He lies there and tries not to enjoy it too much. He still thinks this sort of thing is for women. He feels sort of silly lying there being rubbed with oil.

"You have such strong, broad shoulders," she says. "You must have been a good athlete. Of course, I rather disapprove of team sports. At least in theory. But it didn't do you any harm."

"I was all right. But even in high school I wasn't that big."

"You're big enough for me," she says with a throaty laugh.

Her hands move to the middle of his back. She rubs more vigorously, kneading the muscles around his backbone. She

199

says he has a narrow waist. She applies more oil to her hands. She says she loves the color of his skin. He really must be part Native American. The skin looks sort of dusky. And the skin is smooth without a lot of hair. She likes that too. Her hands move lower and start massaging his buttocks. He's not sure if he approves. But her fingers press into his firm flesh and she says in a quieter voice that he has great buns. He thinks that's a silly word but he says nothing in response. Then she moves on to his thighs. She briskly rubs them and remarks how big and muscular they are. Didn't he run track? He nods. She finishes with his thighs but doesn't go lower. Instead her hands return to his butt as she starts to rub again. You have dimples on your lower back, she says, pausing to touch them. Then her fingers move downward and rub the lower backbone before slipping into the beginning of his natal cleft. He tenses at her touch. He doesn't think he likes that but it's more of a mental objection than a physical one. But when her fingers slide farther down the crack, he lifts himself up and turns over.

"I don't like that," he says.

"Why? You did more to me."

"That's different."

She reaches a hand to grasp his erect penis. "Your cock seems to like it. Besides, you don't have to be so phallocentric."

"But I'm proud to be phallocentric."

She begins to pump his phallus. He rises on his knees and she reaches for a small towel. As she pumps his pecker, he rocks his hips. He puts one hand on her left breast and fingers the erect nipple. The other hand reaches down and cups one buttock. Just that additional touch results in a paroxysm of pleasure and he powerfully ejaculates into the towel.

He topples to the bed and breathes in loudly. He relaxes. But before he can get too comfortable, Pamela shakes his leg.

"I'm all ready."

He gets up, she reclines. He applies oil to his hands and starts massaging her pale and pink body. He starts at the shoulders, works down to her back, and then to her fleshy buttocks.

He thinks this is her best feature. Her ass is wide but also round and if he doesn't look at her waist, he thinks her bottom is quite fetching. He moves to her thighs and his hands rub them vigorously. She sighs and says he has strong hands. She likes that. Then he returns to her rump and slides a finger between her cheeks. She doesn't protest so he slides his finger all the way down her crack until he gets to her anus. He massages the tight, small opening.

"I think you like that area," she says.

He leans down to her ear and says she's right. He likes her asshole. Just saying the naughty word thrills him. He's never said that word aloud before.

"Remember a game we played several weeks ago," Pamela says. "The bet we made about my guessing your cock size? I said if I got it right you would have to do what I wanted?"

"Yeah, I remember."

"I lost so we did what you wanted. But do you know what I would have asked for if I'd won?"

"What?"

"For you to go down on me."

She turns over and gives him a frank look. "I want you to do that now."

"Okay."

She lies flat, raises her hips, and then spreads her legs. He looks at the white thighs, the blonde pubic hair, and the glistening vulva. He's not sure if he wants to do this to her; it didn't go so hot last night. But he lowers his head between her legs, opens his mouth, and first kisses her vulva before sticking his tongue in her vagina.

She moans loudly. He continues licking. He tries to flatten his tongue. He feels almost as if he's licking an envelope. The taste is sort of tart and the smell is pungent and he hears her moans while she rolls her hips. His tongue starts brushing against her clitoris. He's getting aroused again almost in spite of his reluctance to continue his oral efforts. Her moans become more impassioned and louder. She jerks her hips. He grabs her thighs and presses his tongue deeper inside her and she lets out a shriek of pleasure. She shudders and gasps then her body grows still. He lifts himself up and she closes her legs. She rolls on her side and extends her arms. "Hold me," she says.

He lies beside her and she snuggles up beside him. He puts an arm around her and she leans up and kisses him on the mouth, which he thinks is a little odd considering what they've just done. She leans her head against his shoulder and murmurs something.

"What did you say?" he asks.

"I finally came."

"Yeah, I noticed."

"That hasn't happened in a long time. I mean with someone."

Dale nods. He sort of wants to get up and get a drink of water but she's lying against him all contented so he remains put.

"We'll have to try this again soon," she says.

"Sure."

"You didn't mind doing it, did you?"

"No. I wasn't exactly sure what I was doing though."

"You did fine. More than fine."

They lie silent for several minutes. Dale almost drifts off when she asks what he is going to do over spring break.

"I have a lot to do. I have to make my movie."

"I was hoping we could go cross country skiing together. There's a lot of snow in the mountains."

"I don't have time for that. Besides, who wants to traverse snowfields all day."

"It's good exercise and you get to experience the beauty of nature."

"I like nature. But I don't like recreation that much. It's sort of boring and takes too much time."

"What do you like? Sports?"

"That's right. In sports you play intensely for a limited time and who scores the most wins."

"You're like so many men only concerned with scoring." If

she wasn't in a satisfied mood she would say that more critically. She has in the past.

"I like competition. I like scoring. I like winning."

"How very phallocentric of you."

"Tonight it was more tongue-o-centric."

Pamela giggles.

"Well, I'm going cross country skiing this week. With or without you. I could have gone to Cancun but I declined the invitation."

"Cancun? Well, that's better than going to Juarez."

"Why would I go to Juarez?"

"That's where Grabowski is going for spring break."

"Oh, him."

"What's your problem with the great Grabowski?"

"He hit on me once."

"Hit on you?" Dale wasn't familiar with that phrase.

"Wanted to go to bed with me. But I had no interest. He thinks he's some kind of stud. He's exactly the kind of man I dislike. Thinks he has property rights on women."

"Yeah, that's Grabowski."

"Anyway, I declined the invitation to Cancun."

"Who invited you?"

"Some friends."

"Who?"

"Patti Montag, Barbara Hughes, and Marsha Martin."

He recalls Patti and Marsha were members of CSDS. He raises himself and removes his arm from around her.

"Are they close friends of yours?"

"Only Barbara."

"Isn't Marsha Spencer Dribble's girlfriend?"

"Yes, in a way. They have a complicated relationship."

Dale looks down at Pamela. "You didn't have anything to do with stealing the campus newspapers as a protest against my movie reviews?"

"No, of course not."

"But you know them."

"Don't play guilt by association. I didn't help them."

He examines her face. She looks back not blinking her eyes. He believes her. "Okay. I was just wondering."

"Well, stop wondering. Anyway, I didn't want to go to Cancun. It's a tourist spot. A lot of college kids go there for spring break. But I'm not really into that scene. Too much drinking, too much casual sex. Too many silly women making fools of themselves over men."

"Hmm, maybe I should take your place."

Pamela bumps into him with her small shoulder. "You're not that way.'

"No, I'm not." Then he thinks: but isn't what we do casual sex?

"So you definitely won't go with me to cross country ski?

"I'll be too busy."

"What if I tell you that I'm going with another guy?"

"Oh, yeah? Who?"

She smiles slyly at him. "Would you be jealous?"

"I don't know."

"Well, don't worry. He has a wife. They both work at the *Boomerang*. They love to cross country ski. They have a cabin about fifty miles from here. They invited me to stay a couple of days. They said I could bring a friend."

"I really can't go. I have too much to do."

"Okay. But we can see each when I get back?"

"Sure."

Dale gets out of bed and starts to dress. Pamela turns on her side and watches. He glances at her. It sort of annoys him when she does that.

"You can stay over if you want."

That's the first time she's given that invitation. But he doesn't want to. In fact, although the sex was better than usual, he feels a desire to go back to his place and hear Grabowski snoring from his bedroom.

"Thanks, but I have to get up early tomorrow."

"Tomorrow's Sunday. You're not going to church are you?"

"You know that I don't go to church."

"But you used to, didn't you?"

"Not for very long. No, I have to get up early because I have a lot of work to do. The film, my thesis, the OWR, and maybe, if I can find the time, that damned journal that Comstock is so obsessed about."

"Don't be too hard on Professor Comstock. He has a troubled marriage."

"I'm not surprised. You seem fond of him. And it just can't be because he gives you candy."

"I've taken several classes from him. He's always been encouraging. I'm his favorite student."

"You know he's sort of crazy, don't you?"

Pamela smiles sadly. "Yes, I know that."

10

Dale follows Regina Wilson's directions and drives five miles out of Laramie toward Medicine Bow National Forest and arrives at her ranch a few minutes before one in the afternoon.

It doesn't appear to be a working ranch any longer. Her place consists of a two story stone and timber house, a barn, and a corral. A large expanse of pasture-land is located next to the house but he only sees two horses, a bay and an Appaloosa, grazing in the fields. No cattle or sheep.

As he gets out of his car, Regina comes out of her ranch house and waves. She dressed more rustically than on campus. She wears blue jeans, a western shirt, sweater and boots. They greet each other. He says he likes her ranch. She confirms his notion that it's not a real ranch. She inherited it from her parents and they had been actual ranchers.

They go insider her home and she offers him lemonade or beer to drink. He says he'll take lemonade and while he drinks they chat. She tells him a little about herself. She's a native Wyomingite, born and bred on this ranch. Although she loved Shiloh Ranch, she wanted to be an artist. She attended the art institute in Chicago then received a master's and along the way she got married, divorced, and five years ago returned to Wyoming to live on the family spread and teach at the university.

Dale's finishes his lemonade and she asks if he'd like to see her studio. He agrees and the two of them walk through the living room, past the kitchen where they see a middle-aged woman cleaning, and enter a spacious room with large windows on the north wall. He looks around. The room features a long worktable, a wooden bench, shelves stuffed with art equipment and instruments, a kiln, an elevated area with backdrops and a curtain, canvas boards and stacks of paper, plus a table with brushes and oils and watercolors and other kinds of art tools.

"The door to the darkroom is across the room."

Regina points in that direction and Dale sees an ordinary door with a red light hanging above it, a signal for when the darkroom is in use.

"You're also interested in photography?"

"That's my primary interest now. I've tried almost every media: oils, ink, watercolor, and sculpture. I still teach classes in those areas but my personal focus is in photography."

"This is a really nice studio," Dale says. He likes how the daylight streams in from outside and is diffused in the studio. He smells paint and turpentine and other artsy odors. He's always liked that smell.

"Thanks," she says. "Would you like to see some of my work?"

He says yes so they go over to a large open closet and she shows him some of her past projects. He examines the oil paintings, most of them feature portraits and nudes of women. A couple of paintings of horses. The watercolors are mostly of still life and the outdoors. Dale recognizes the subject of one watercolor: it's her Shiloh ranch.

"Let me show you my photography portfolio."

She takes a large black portfolio book from a drawer and the two of them sit down on two wooden chairs before the worktable. She opens the portfolio book. As with her oils, most of them feature faces and figures of people. The photos are in black and white and the subjects are mostly women but there are also a few young men. About half the photos are of nudes, all tastefully done, with more emphasis on light and shadow and texture than on the actual bodies.

Near the end of the series, Dale notices that one model looks like a younger version of Regina herself.

"Are these photos of you?" he asks.

"Self portraits," she says. "Taken a few years ago."

One is a close-up of her face. It shows that she's not pretty but her bold features displayed in stark and black and white are interesting. He likes the contrast between her long, red hair (which appears black in the photo) and the white, almost alabaster look of her skin. Regina turns another page and he sees two nudes of her. They were taken when she was younger all right. He can tell by the narrower waist. One photo is of the front of her. It shows her rather large breasts and substantial thighs. She's sitting on a stool, her torso twisted away from the light, and her legs are curved around the legs of the stool. She looks like she is trying to escape the light but can't quite make it.

The second nude photo is of her standing in a room, probably this one, in fairly low light, with her back to the camera. Her large buttocks and thighs are the most prominent feature of the photograph but her long dark hair descends down her back and she must have been holding her arms in front of her because the viewer can't see them. When he focuses on the white of her lower body, the top of her seems to disappear into the surrounding darkness, producing a rather surreal image. He likes that effect but his eye is also drawn to the broad hips and the meaty buttocks and thighs. Their whiteness and fullness are striking.

He glances at her, feeling a little embarrassed that he's seen her nude, even if it's just in an artistic photograph. But Regina shows no sign of self-consciousness at all.

"Impressive photographs," he says, as she closes the portfolio. "Did you ever model for another artist?"

"Yes, I did. That's how I financed my own work."

"Were you ever shy?"

"At first. I came from a middle-class ranching family so I didn't have any sophisticated notions about art, especially art that features nudes. But I soon grew more comfortable and confident and realized that my body was simply a means of expression. The artists who painted and drew me didn't even see me as a woman; at least not directly. They were always looking deeper than the bare skin."

"I like that idea. Using the body as a means of seeing past the body."

Regina smiles. "I think you have something of an artistic mind."

"Yeah, but I can't really draw. I'm good at drawing cartoons, but nothing more."

"Well, visual art is more than drawing. It's expressing what you see and feel. Maybe you ought to try your hand at it again sometime."

"Maybe I will."

"So what do you think, Dale? Would you like to model for me?"

"Well, maybe. I don't know what it involves."

"It's simple. I ask you to assume a pose. A look. Then I try and capture something interesting. "

"For a photograph?"

"That's right.

"I guess I could do it. But I wouldn't have to take off all my clothes, would I?"

"Not if you don't feel comfortable doing that. I'll tell you what. Let's start with a shot of the torso today."

"Just my shirt off?"

"That's right."

He agrees and Regina goes over to the desk and retrieves her camera. She says she will shoot photos in the studio without a back screen. She'll use natural light. She asks Dale to remove his shirt. He takes off his flannel shirt and T-shirt. Then she instructs him in a series of poses: standing with his arms crossed, lifting a hammer as if he's about to strike it, a back shot of him lifting himself up on a wooden beam as if he was doing a pull-up, and carrying two buckets of cement. The photographs take longer than Dale expects. Regina has to set them up, take light readings, consider the composition, and ask him to alter his pose or movements.

When she is satisfied with the studio shots, she asks if he'd pose for some shots in the barn. He says okay and they leave by the studio's back door and walk thirty yards to the old red barn. Only half of the building functions as a barn. It has hay bales and stalls for the horses. She takes photos of him lifting the hay bales and holding a pitchfork and other action poses. It's a warm spring day for Wyoming, almost seventy, and the exertion produces a sheen of sweat on his torso, which she says will produce a good effect. After thirty minutes, Regina says she has enough photos for this session. He puts his shirt back on and they walk past the other half of the barn that is now used as a garage for two old vehicles, one a tractor and another an old dark sedan.

Spying the car, Dale walks over to it. It's a big car from the early '60s, long and dark and best of all a convertible.

"Is this your car?" Dale asks.

"It is now. It belonged to my father."

"Does it run?"

"Yes, but I rarely drive it. I prefer my Volkswagen instead of that big, old thing."

"Could I ask you a favor?"

"Yes. But I'll grant it only if you do me a favor sometime."

"Okay. Do you think I could borrow your car? Just for a few hours. I'd like to use it in my student film."

"You're not going to blow it up or anything?"

Dale wonders if she knows Mark Von Goebbels. "No, I'll use it just to drive down a street and be photographed."

"I don't see why not. After all, one artist should help another artist."

Driving back to Laramie, Dale looks at the bright, clear

sky that stretches over the high plains outside Cheyenne. The weather has been perfect. Not too sunny but luminous enough so he didn't have to worry about the film's exposure. All his other concerns had worked out too. Now driving back, with the principal photography of his film complete, he is rather amazed that it worked out so well.

He glances over to Mimi sitting in the passenger seat. She's in a good mood. She liked being in a movie even if it was just a student film. She's dressed in her retro outfit. She wears a skirt, blouse, and jacket, with her hair is styled in an early '60s hairdo. She's no longer wearing her pillbox hat but he thinks she actually looks a little like Jacqueline Kennedy, albeit plumper. He appreciates that she was willing to cut and style her hair. She found the right period clothes at a vintage store in Denver. She even discovered a pillbox hat there, which she now holds in her hands on her lap.

"You did a good job," he tells her.

"Thank you. I wished I looked more like Jackie O."

"With you new hairstyle you look quite a bit like her."

"Really? You think so?"

"Sure. That's one reason why I cast you."

"But my figure doesn't look anything like Jackie's."

"The viewer won't notice that so much. The clothing, the hat, the general look was very Jackie K-ish."

Mimi laughs. "I have to admit that I have never been a big fan of Jacqueline Kennedy since she married that Greek tycoon. But after playing her in your movie, I find myself more interested in her tragic life."

Dale looks in the rear view mirror and sees the brothers Von Goebbels discussing the shooting. Both are dressed in old-fashioned looking business suits. They performed their roles well, too, and Matt's special effects, filmed earlier, went off without a hitch. Dale especially worried about the special effects not working.

The Lincoln Townhouse convertible drives up beside them in the other lane. The driver, Edward Darby, also wearing an old-fashioned early '60s business suit, honks the horn. Everyone in Dale's car waves. Darby waves back and the dark Lincoln Townhouse speeds up and passes Dale's Monza.

"Ed better watch out or he might get a speeding ticket," says Mimi.

"He just wants to get the car back to Regina," Dale says.

He keeps his Chevy Monza at sixty, five miles over the speed limit. He'd like to drive faster but he doesn't want to risk getting a ticket. He needs to conserve every penny for the film and keep his savings intact for The Trip. But he's anxious to get back to Laramie so he can mail the can of film to the processing lab. Then he has to work on his thesis and do more planning for the OWR.

As the Lincoln Townhouse pulls farther away, Dale remembers that the sedan is a 1963 convertible not a 1961 one, and, of course, Regina's car is a Townhouse and not a Continental but he doubts any viewer of his film would spot the anachronism. It wasn't a limo either, of course, and his film version would lack two people, Governor Connelly and his wife, but he thought viewers would be concentrating on the famous couple so they wouldn't notice too much the discrepancy.

Dale looks in his rear view mirror past the still conferring Von Goebbels brothers and spots the third car of their caravan, Grabowski's 1974 yellow and brown Ford pick-up. Driving it is the OWR fiction editor, Virgil Drury. Sitting in the cab are the two female staffers, Millie Jansen and Betsy Shore, the poetry editors. And Doug Trampas, the photography editor, and Lee Garth, the assistant fiction editor, huddle in the truck bed.

All five people were necessary for the shoot. Virgil and Doug drove the vehicles that blocked any traffic from getting into the camera's frame of the Lincoln Townhouse. Millie, Betsy, and Lee served as bystanders. All are dressed in clothes that sort of look like early '60s attire. Millie borrowed one of her mother's dresses and Betsy wears '60s era peddle-pushers. Lee sports his father's old suit.

Dale stares out at the rolling highway and thinks how difficult making a movie is. Even his very short film necessitated a lot of planning, and he cajoled people into helping. And then there was the logistics of the shoot itself. He had to find a location for the shoot. Laramie didn't have any streets that would fit the setting of the film. Fortunately, the Von Goebbels brothers were from Cheyenne and knew of an area that would serve. So the cast and the crew drove to Cheyenne. The brothers were right, however. The part of the city they recommended was a fair duplication of Dealey Plaza. They went through a couple of run-throughs. The cast had already rehearsed twice before in the student union ballroom. But Dale, who served as the cameraman, was still concerned. Everything needed to go right, to be timed accurately, and most of all, the special effects had to work.

And, amazingly, everything did go right. Dale's Chevy and Grabowski's borrowed Ford blocked traffic on the two-lane one-way street. The cars behind them honked in protest at the slow pace but that didn't matter because the film was silent. The Lincoln Townhouse proceeded down the street, being driven at only ten miles per hour, and Dale found the perfect spot and began filming. It whole process only took eighty seconds.

Dale now realizes he has another problem. A movie just one minute and twenty seconds long might not be long enough. The short length certainly reduces his production costs, but he has to think of something else to add to the film. He isn't sure what. He thinks he needs to increase the film's length to at least a minute. He needs another scene or an additional element, something that will add meaning. He isn't sure what that will be but he still has a week or so to come up with an additional idea.

The filming hadn't been fun. He worried the whole time. He also didn't like all the technical and logistical problems he faced. The cast cooperated but he wondered what would happen if he had to work with a difficult, temperamental star. A prima donna could cause all kinds of problems. He read about the filming of *Some Like It Hot* and how Billy Wilder contended with Marilyn Monroe's many emotional problems. Wilder tolerated her up-and-down moods because she was perfect for the role of Sugar Kane. But Dale now understands how a director would resent being dependent on the moods of a star. The more he learns about film, the more he doubts he could work in that medium.

The books he's been reading about the Hollywood system also discouraged his dream of being a filmmaker. The system sounded crazy. Producers scrambling for money, screenwriters having their work rewritten, directors having to placate demanding, spoiled, emotionally immature stars. Then there was the importance of advertising and how marketing a film sometimes undermined a film's integrity. Once a film was completed, the filmmaker faced the uncertainty of whether a fickle public would attend his film. Some producers would preview a film with a test audience and then make changes, another way of undermining a film's artistic integrity. Some studio heads would commandeer a film and make edits. Film was a collective medium. Even the rare individual like Billy Wilder who wrote and directed his films had to depend on a large crew of technicians. He had to rely on producers to finance his films. He had to work with volatile performers. The process sounded daunting and exhausting. And in most cases the end result wasn't art; sometimes the finished film wasn't even entertaining. Many times movies, in spite of all the money, time, and professionalism, turned out to be dreadful. Dale has seen a lot of those kinds of films already in his young life.

The whole process was complicated. The script, the crew, the director, the cast, and all the technical concerns, lighting, sound, costumes, sets, locations, film continuity, editing, scoring, the musical soundtrack, made making a film a formidable enterprise. Dale only dimly understood that from his reading. But now by actually making a film he understood the difficulty of making a movie and he's filmed only one scene!

And luck played a role, too. Dale has read enough articles and books to know that it takes more than a good script, a skilled director, and a talented cast; it took some serendipity, too. He was lucky on this shoot. First, he knew people who would help him; second, by becoming *OWR* editor he could persuade the staff to help him on the film; third, he got to borrow Regina Wilson's old car which was a much better choice of vehicle than the 1970 Oldsmobile Cutlass convertible, Ed Darby's car, that they were going to use. Even though his film was a parody, he wanted as many things as possible to match the originals.

Now, after this experience, Dale feels the rather disappointing realization that film-making isn't going to be in his future. He loves watching them. He would like to emulate his favorite filmmakers, especially the rare individuals who both write and direct their films. But he's beginning to realize that he's probably not suited to the film business. About ten percent of making a film is creative; the other ninety percent is technical. And screen-writing, which suits his solitary temperament better, is not really respected in Hollywood. In fact, that's the primary reason why some screenwriters (Sturges, Wilder, Allen) aspired to become directors: so they would have more artistic control. At least, that's what he's read.

"What are you thinking about, Dale?" Mimi asks.

"Just thinking how everything went okay today." He glances at her and appreciates her big smile. "And wondering what will go wrong tomorrow."

By the time they get back to Laramie, it's nearly four in the afternoon. The shoot interrupted everyone's spring break, but no one complained when they departed Cheyenne. Now back on campus Dale drops off the Von Goebbels brothers at their dorm. The brothers have decided to stay on campus for the night, and then drive back to Cheyenne where they will spend the rest of spring break. That leaves only Mimi.

Dale drives back to his townhouse and sees Grabowski's truck is back in its usual place, parked in the driveway. Dale stops his car long enough to get out and grab the keys from within the truck. Grabowski won't even suspect that his truck has been used. Since Grabowski has no compunction using Dale's personal stuff, Dale doesn't feel any remorse borrowing his roommate's truck without his knowledge. He even plans on filling the gas tank as a kind of rental payment.

"You can just take me to the bus station," Mimi says. She doesn't have a car on campus. She always takes the bus when she goes back to Denver.

"I'll drive you home," he says, parking his car on the curb, "but after a break."

"That's too far, Dale. I can take a bus. I always do."

"I don't want you do. I'll drive you. Think of it as payment for your excellent acting job as the former First Lady."

"Well, if you put it that way, then very well."

They get out of the car and walk into the house. Dale asks Mimi if she wants anything to drink. He has orange juice, 7-Up, and beer. She says she'll have a beer. Dale brings her one of Grabowski's Coors with a glass. Now, he'll have to go to the store and buy a beer because Grabowski always knows how many beers he has left.

"You've never been in my place. How do you like it?"

Mimi sits down in the easy chair and pours the beer into the glass as she glances around the spartan accommodations. "I'd describe it as austere."

"It's Grabowski's fault. He has absolutely no fashion sense."

"So where is your untalented roommate?"

Dale tells her about Grabowski's adventure in Mexico. How he's going there with a friend to sample the tequila and whorehouses of Juarez.

"Men," says Mimi. "They will drive one thousand miles to get drunk and get laid."

"The Grabowskis of the world will."

"You wouldn't?"

"I don't get drunk and I don't –" he almost said get laid but he caught himself in time – "visit whorehouses."

"You don't drink liquor at all?"

Dale holds up his glass of 7-Up.

"You're a very clean cut young man. In most ways."

"Now, what does that mean?"

"Oh, nothing." Mimi takes another drink of her beer.

"Is Joe off for spring break, too?"

"Yes, but he's not in Denver."

"Where is he?"

"He's on a spring break trip with a couple of fraternity buddies."

"Where?"

"Padre Island."

"Why aren't you with him?"

"He's with his frat friends. He didn't want me to go and I didn't want to go either. In fact, I'm going to break up with him."

"Haven't you two been going together since high school?"

"Since senior year. But I don't think it's going to work out."

"You've been together for over four years. There must be some reason why you two lasted so long."

"Because we're both Jewish kids."

"That's it?"

"No, of course not. But it's an important factor. My parents want me to eventually marry a Jewish man. I don't know if you've noticed, but there aren't a lot of Jews in this part of the world."

"Are your parents religious?"

"Not overly so. But being Jewish is important to them. They want me to honor the tradition, or something like that."

"And Joe is part of that tradition?"

"You could say that. I'm very fond of him, of course. But we've been dating for four years and maybe we're getting bored with each other already. Imagine if we got married!"

"Yeah, you wouldn't have anything to look forward to."

"You're funny. But that's the reason why Joe wanted to go on his own spring break trip. A change of pace. And without me."

217

"I can't understand that."

"You're teasing me again."

"And Joe is Jewish. He's not Italian?"

"He's both. You know there are Jews in Italy."

"Sure. Like Shylock in Venice."

Mimi smiles. "You do have a good sense of humor. But you have a lot of attractive qualities."

"Is that so?"

"If you drove me to Denver tonight you wouldn't get back until late. It's over five hours round trip."

"Yeah, that's true." Dale glances at Mimi. Her '60s styled hair gives her a more demure look. But her brown eyes are not looking at him in a demure way. "Of course, I *could* drive you tomorrow."

"Yes, I suppose I could stay in my dorm room."

"Or you could stay here."

"You mean stay overnight?"

"That's what I mean."

"Are you sure you would like that?"

"I'm sure I would."

"It *is* getting late."

"And the dorm would be rather lonely."

"You are a thoughtful young man, aren't you?"

"And you know what else we could do?"

"I'm almost afraid to ask."

"We could go see a movie."

"A movie?"

"Let's go see *All That Jazz*. You haven't seen it yet, have you? I haven't either. We've never seen a movie at a real theatre together before."

"Sounds almost like a date."

"No, it is a date."

Before seeing the movie, Dale stops off at the post office to mail his film to the processor then he takes Mimi to Zane's, his favorite diner. He orders chicken fried steak and she has French toast. She tells him that she's never eaten chicken fried steak. He says you don't know what you're missing. She says that sometime she will take him to Moe's Delicatessen when he's in Denver. They make a wonderful hot pastrami sandwich. He says this might be the beginning of a great cultural exchange.

In the theatre lobby of the Wyo they see Spencer Dribble and Marsha Martin. Mimi waves but doesn't go over to speak to them. They watch *All That Jazz* and Dale is very impressed with the film, especially the dazzlingly direction. Afterwards, they encounter Dribble and Marsha again and the four of them have a short conversation. Dale hasn't forgotten about Dribble's and Marsha's nefarious plot, but he isn't rude to them. All express their approval of the film. Dribble says even though it is derivative of Fellini's *8 ½*, Fosse still manages to invoke enough American iconography to avoid the copycat stigma. Mimi and Marsha nod in agreement but Dale doesn't.

"You don't agree with my assessment?" Dribble asks him.

"I don't know. I haven't seen *8 ½* yet."

"You haven't? And you call yourself a film critic?"

"I don't call myself anything. I just review movies for the *BI*. But I want to learn about the art of film. Maybe some day I will become a film critic."

Dribble's skeptical expression indicates he doubts that will ever happen. Dale returns his unfriendly stare. He's annoyed that Dribble has seen a significant movie that he hasn't. Marsha tugs on Dribble's arm and says they need to go. Dribble nods, says goodbye to Mimi, gives Dale a cold glance, and he departs with Marsha.

"It's too bad you and Spencer no longer get along," says Mimi. "You both have so much in common."

They return to Dale's place and since he doesn't drink coffee she makes them cocoa. They enjoy their hot drinks and they sit on the couch and talk about her English lit classes. They also discuss the creative writing class they are taking. Mimi admires Professor's Wilkins so much. What an impressive man. And what a great writer.

"Have you read any of his novels?" Dales asks.

"Oops. You caught me. I should say I hear that he's a great writer."

"I checked out one of his novels from the library. It's called *Shooting for the Moon*. I'm reading it now."

"Is it a work of genius?"

"It's a serious work of literature. I'm about half way through it. Tell you the truth, it's sort of difficult to read. He employs a lot of stream of consciousness. It reminds me of Faulkner but set in Pittsburgh. I like the basketball scenes. They're easier to understand."

"You amaze me, Dale. You've seen so many movies and read so many novels. I can't believe that we're the same age."

"In a couple of weeks I'll be a year older than you again."

"Twenty-three! You're getting *old*."

They talk about *All That Jazz*. Mimi especially liked the imaginative dance routines. Dale remembers in particular the one dance sequence where the cast disrobed. The lithe blonde takes her top off and even lying on her back her breasts don't completely flatten against her chest. He mentions the scene but he doesn't mention the blonde.

"Yes, I thought you would like that dance routine the best," she says.

Dale notices that Mimi has moved a little closer to him. He looks into her big brown eyes and sees that she's receptive. He puts his arm around her and she offers her lips and they start kissing. He likes her mouth; it's big and full-lipped and in the past he's wondered what it would feel like to kiss her. He likes the lingering flavor of cocoa and French toast in her mouth. The kissing leads to fondling and soon they are making out on the couch. When he puts his other arm around her waist, his touch confirms what his eyes evaluated, that she's lost some weight for the movie shoot. She's still a zaftig kind of girl, but there's not as much zaf as before.

They continue the foreplay for many minutes. When they come up for air, so to speak, Dale suggests they go into his bedroom. She nods and he leads her there. They start kissing again and Dale starts removing her vintage clothes. In addition to the dress she's wearing she also wears a slip, a girdle, and bra and panties. Because of the girdle, it takes him a few minutes to remove most of her clothing. When he finally gets down to her underwear he pauses to look at her Rubenesque figure. The hall light, which he deliberately left on, casts a soft beam of low light but it's enough to make out her generous curvature.

"Don't look at me," she whispers. "I'm too fat."

"You're not fat. You're beautifully abundant."

He can tell she likes that and she allows him to removes her bra. Her large breasts topple free. He sees that she has fairly large, dark nipples. Then he slowly pulls her baby blue panties down her big hips. He watches as her black pubic hair appears into view. It's abundant, too. In fact, he's never seen such a big bush.

She lies down on his bed while he removes his shirt and jeans. He begins to kiss and caress her but when he starts to engage in more serious foreplay, her mood changes. She stops responding and when he rises off of her to look at her face, she turns away from him. She curls up on her side and he hears her softly weeping.

He leans against her and tries to look at her face, but she's covered it with her hands. She's crying, all right, but not loudly and he's puzzled.

"What's wrong?" he asks.

"I don't know."

"Miriam, what's bothering you?"

"It doesn't feel right." She turns her head and looks at him. "It's not you. I just don't feel right."

He lies down beside her and puts an arm around her waist. He's feeling that frustration again. He's all worked up and his chick is weepy. And feeling her copious bare bottom pressing against his groin doesn't dampen his arousal.

"It's okay," he says. "We don't have to do anything more."

"You probably think I'm a crazy Jewish broad."

"No, I don't. I didn't even know you were Jewish."

"You didn't?"

"No, I never knew anybody Jewish until I got to know you."

Mimi turns just the upper half of her body toward him, while the lower half remains pressed against him. "You have never known any Jews?"

"No. I grew up in a small town in Oklahoma. There weren't any Jews there. Or for that matter, any Italians."

"Oklahoma. You mean like the musical, *Oklahoma*."

"Right, but the movie isn't an accurate representation of the state."

Mimi smiles for a moment, then her expression becomes serious. "The reason I started crying is that I've only been unfaithful to Joe once before. I'm not sure if I want to do it again."

Dale remembers her saying she is going to break up with Joe. If so, then she technically isn't being unfaithful to him. But he doesn't want to coerce her.

"Okay. I understand. We can just lie here."

Mimi nods and turns her upper body back to match her lower. She reaches for the bedspread and he helps cover her with it. His left arm resumes it's position around her waist. He thinks how quiet it is in the house. All he can hear is Miriam's soft breathing.

He hears her falling asleep. He thinks it's peculiar how the night turned out. He likes her; he likes her more than Pamela. The make-out session was enjoyable, too. He hasn't really made out with a girl in a long time. He's never really done that with Pamela. He thinks it's ironic that he's not going to have sex with the girl he likes. Instead, he'll have to wait to do that with the girl he doesn't like quite as much.

Pamela Partridge calls Thursday evening. Dale answers the phone, expecting it's her. She says that she got home Wednesday. Dale asks how her cross-country skiing went. She says it was fine. Ordinarily, she would wax poetic over her encounter with nature even though Pamela wasn't very poetic. Instead her tone of voice sounds peeved. Dale knows she's perturbed about something but right then he's not interested in finding out what. He's busy with his thesis. He wants to get the first draft finished before working on the final cut of his film.

"You want to do something Friday?" he asks.

"Do *you* want to do something?"

"Sure. Let's go see a movie."

Because of spring break, the university isn't showing any films over the weekend. They would have to see one off-campus, which they hadn't done together. He thinks it's rather odd that they only get together for campus events or go to her apartment for extracurricular activities.

Pamela doesn't answer right away. He hears her breathing on the line and waits.

"Okay, if you want," she finally says.

He says he'll come by her place tomorrow evening at 6:30 p.m. She agrees. He can tell she's waiting for him to say more, but he wants to get back to his work. He says he'll see her tomorrow and hangs up.

The next evening he arrives at her place and they walk to The Trout theatre in downtown Laramie. It's not a long jaunt, only eight blocks, and he likes how the evening air feels crisp and clean with a touch of warmth still lingering from the sunny day. He knows that it will get cold that evening. That's how spring is in the Rockies. Warm sunny days followed by cold nights.

Pamela isn't saying much as they walk. He knows she's still displeased about something but he doesn't want to talk about it now. He's in a mood to see a movie. He asks her questions about staying at her friends' cabin. She perks up a little and tells him about all the fun they had. Her friends, Mike and Linda Hogan, are a wonderful married couple. They both work at the *Boomerang*. Mike is the news editor and Linda the head copy editor. They have a cabin not far from the Medicine Bow National Forest and the three of them cross country skied through the higher elevations of the forest then hiked over the area without snow. On the second day, another guest arrived at the Hogan's, a former Wyo journalism student, Ward Hughes, who is now working at the *Casper Star-Tribune*. That made it a foursome. The cabin isn't that large but the four of them managed. They had a lot of fun.

Dale nods throughout Pamela's account. When she's finished he says he's glad she had a lot of fun. They arrive at the theatre. While waiting to buy their tickets, Dale chats briefly with Shane Starrett, the middle-aged owner and manager of the Trout. Dale starts to pay for his ticket but Shane says he should use his pass. Dale says he's not sure if he'll be reviewing the movie for the campus paper but Shane says that's okay. Dale offers to pay for Pamela's ticket but she, as usual, won't let him. She always insists of paying her share.

They find seats in the back of the cozy theatre. Dale glances around and notices that the theatre is almost filled. When he comes to the Trout's classic film screenings on Thursday, Shane is lucky to get half the theatre filled.

They watch *The Bell Jar* and Dale sometimes loses his concentration, his mind thinking about all the tasks he still has to complete. The movie isn't very good. It's slow-paced and features a rather sullen heroine. He's familiar with the story because he read the novel a year ago and he notices that the film departs from the novel in a couple of key respects.

After the movie, they walk briskly back in the direction of their residences, not talking much because the night has turned cold. Pamela asks Dale if they can go to his place, that is, if Grabowski isn't around. Dale says Grabowski is in Mexico, probably getting a venereal disease. Pamela frowns in disgust at that bit of information.

When they get to his place he asks if she wants anything to drink. She says something hot. They go into the kitchen and she makes them cocoa. Dale sits at the table and watches. Something is bothering her. She shuts the kitchen cupboard too loudly and she won't look at him while she's preparing the cocoa.

"How did you like the movie?" he asks.

"It depressed me."

"The story is a little depressing."

"Her *life* is depressing," Pamela says, referring to Sylvia Plath. "Allowing herself to be dominated by men."

"The movie wasn't about that so much," he says.

In fact, the male characters all had secondary roles. They weren't depicted with much sympathy. Dale remembers the scene where the boyfriend strips and the heroine looks at his genitals and compares them to turkey liver and gizzards. The narrator's disgust is even more explicit in the novel. Dale wasn't offended by the description. He actually thought the turkey analogy was a little funny. He felt similarly repulsed when looking at male genitals, which he only has accidentally done. No gazing in the locker room. But Pamela seems to like looking at cocks and balls (her words). At least she claims she does. Dale doubts her. He thinks she wants to act that way because she thinks it parallels how men regard women. Actually, he doesn't especially like looking at female genitals. He very much likes looking at everything else on a woman's body, especially the breasts, buttocks, and thighs. But he is less enthusiastic about looking at a vagina, although when he scrutines those explicit photos of the beautiful women in *Penthouse* magazine he rather likes looking at that area. But seeing Pamela's privates up close has been less appealing.

He knows, like most men, that he is very visual when it comes to seduction and sex. He likes looking. But he doesn't think women are as visually oriented. Certainly not the girls he knew while growing up. But Pamela claims she is. She subscribes to that silly *Playgirl* magazine. He still thinks it's for show. He wonders if Regina Wilson enjoys looking at naked men. Most of her nudes featured women. But yesterday when he went to her ranch for a second photo session, she talked him into posing nude. He didn't really want to do it. But that was the favor she wanted in return for using her Lincoln Townhouse during his movie shoot. So, he complied. He went behind the curtain and removed his clothes while she got the camera and lighting ready. He came out and immediately felt foolish. He also worried about getting aroused. But she was so matter-of-fact about the whole thing and initially paid more attention to her camera and lights than to him that he began to lose his self-consciousness. She shot a dozen shots of him, not standing or reclining, but doing something. She said men look better when they are in action or give the impression they are about to act. That was fine with him. He felt more relaxed doing something even if it was just lifting an object or taking an athletic stance. He still didn't like his genitals being exposed but when he did pose with the focus on his front the camera was never pointed directly at his genitals. The camera mostly focused on his shoulders, arms, and legs and what those muscles were doing.

The photo shoot lasted almost an hour and a half and he didn't enjoy doing it. After the initial embarrassment and underlying excitement, it became a job and the whole process was rather tedious and time consuming. It was boring, really. Still, the pay was good. She'd paid him for two sessions yesterday even though he posed only for ninety minutes. He got one hundred bucks. After he got dressed and received the check he asked her if that wasn't too much. She said he'd been a good model. She really wanted to get photos of a young man with an impressive physique to complete her latest series. She said don't worry about the money. Her ex-husband was loaded and he still owed her.

After he thanked her for the pay, Regina said she might want to use him for one more session, for some outdoor photos when it got warmer. Dale said to let him know when she was ready and then they left the studio. While walking through the ranch house, he noticed a young woman sitting in the living room reading a magazine. She glanced at him but said nothing. She was very good looking and she reminded him of the dancer in *All That Jazz*, the lithe blonde with the shapely legs and derrière and the breasts so firm that they mostly stay upright when she takes off her top. Looking more closely at this blonde woman, he remembered she had been one of the nude models in Regina's portfolio. He thought she was the most attractive model of them all. Her nude poses had been the most provocative, too. Nothing explicit but the photos had a sexual energy to them that the others lacked. As they left the house, Regina, who noticed his interest in the blonde, said it was no use. The model was a lesbian. Dale was surprised. How could a young woman that attractive be a lesbian? He never discovered her name. In his mind he just called her Lithe Blonde, after the dancer in *All That Jazz*. But her presence in Regina's home also interested him. Her attitude wasn't one of a guest but someone who was familiar and comfortable being in the living room.

"Aren't you going to say anything?"

It's Pamela. Dale has been thinking about yesterday's event instead of listening to Pamela's denunciation of the men in Sylvia Plath's life.

"I don't know much about Sylvia Plath's life," Dale says.

"Well, I do," Pamela says sharply. "She was a great poet. Mostly under-appreciated during her short lifetime. She subjugated her talent to her husband's. Just another woman deemphasizing *her* life for a man's!"

The subject, like the movie, bores him. "Nobody made her do it."

"Society did. She tried to live her life according to the socio-political and gender expectations of her time, but the anxiety and pain was too much. She couldn't be true to her identity, to her art, to her very self, so she had to destroy herself."

"It's more complicated than that. She was also insane."

"What do you know about insanity?" Pamela cries.

"My mother is schizophrenic so I know a little about it."

Pamela looks startled. "You never told me about that."

"I committed her to the insane asylum the last time she went crazy. I don't understand her illness. I don't think the doctors fully understand it. But Sylvia Plath's problems weren't just caused by society. What you said is probably part of it but there's more too. We don't just live our lives socially. There are

227

a lot of influences and probably the most important influence of all is what goes on inside us. And that's something of a mystery."

Pamela finishes her cocoa and puts the cup in the sink. Dale remembers that two cups are still there, the two cups that he and Mimi used for cocoa four nights ago. He watches her looking at the cups, probably seeing that both had contained hot chocolate.

"At least you're not a slob like most men."

"What does that mean?"

"You keep your place fairly clean. Of course, you probably did some cleaning for your guest."

"How do you know I had a guest?"

"Marsha told me she saw you and Mimi at the movie."

So that was it. From the beginning of their relationship, Pamela made it clear that it wasn't necessarily exclusive for either of them. She didn't want to get involved in some archaic romantic relationship where the woman was dependent on the man. She wanted to be treated as an equal. She wanted her independence. When she wanted to be with him she would be with him. When she didn't she wouldn't. Dale agreed. He never thought of Pamela in any romantic way. She was the one advertising a sexual relationship. She didn't flirt like Mimi; she was more direct: I find you attractive, you want to have sex? Well, he did even though he didn't find her especially attractive. But she was willing. He was wanting. He never had an extended relationship that was primarily about sex. He was interested in seeing what it was about. For a while, things had been copacetic. Now, Pamela apparently wants more.

"Did she stay the night?" Pamela asks in a tight voice.

"Yes."

"Did you sleep with her?"

Dale hesitates. The odd thing was that they did sleep with each other but they didn't engage in sexual intercourse. After Miriam fell asleep he left her unmolested. They slept through the night. When she awoke, she seemed embarrassed, especially about being naked with him. He got up and dressed and left her alone. She did her usual morning routine, got dressed, refused any breakfast and he drove her to Denver. She tried to be her cheerful, loquacious self but after a half-hearted try she grew quiet. They drove half of the trip with only minimal talking. When they drove past Fort Collins she asked him if he was angry with her. He said no. He understood her feelings. He liked her. He didn't want her to do anything she didn't want to do. And he definitely didn't want to bust her and Joe up. She brightened up after that and became her old garrulous self. She talked about how bad her short story for Professor Wilkins' class had been. (Dale didn't say anything; it had been a mishmash of purple prose.) But when she had her conference with Professor Wilkins he'd been patient and helpful in trying to improve her story.

When they got into the Denver metro area, Miriam gave directions and in thirty minutes they arrived in the suburb of Littleton. It was an attractive part of the city but nothing too ritzy. Miriam said that Joe's family lived in the more upscale Monaco Parkway. His father was a dentist with a thriving practice (Jews have such bad teeth!) and that was probably going to be Joe's profession. He was planning on going east for dental school next fall.

Dale dropped her off at her home, an attractive but modest bungalow and before she left the car she leaned over and kissed him in a friendly way on the cheek like she had when she left him at Deb's party. He watched her until she disappeared inside her house then drove away. Since it was a weekday, there weren't any matinées at the Rialto, the Denver repertory movie theatre. Instead, he saw a first run showing of *Tess*, the new Roman Polanski movie. While driving back to Laramie he thought about the movie. He liked it in spite of one obvious flaw. It was skillfully directed and was a fairly faithful adaptation of Thomas Hardy's *Tess of the D'Urbevilles*, a novel that he read a few years ago. The only weakness in the movie was the casting of Nastassja Kinski in the lead role of Tess. She was beautiful and he was especially entranced by her voluptuous lips. But she wasn't a very accomplished actress and she had an odd, almost garbled accent. He guessed she was German or perhaps eastern European. It was a peculiar idea to cast her as the tragic English girl and her distracting voice and mediocre acting abilities undermined the movie.

Now Dale thinks about Pamela's question. Yes, he slept with Miriam but no he didn't have sex with her. He thinks it is ironic that it's the opposite with Pamela. They have sex but he has never spent the night with her.

"We didn't have sex if that's what you mean," Dale says.

"She stayed the night but you didn't fuck?"

He's really getting tired of her obscene mouth. He thinks it's her way of talking tough but it's a rather pathetic pretense because he knows she's not tough. Not physically or emotionally.

"No, we didn't *fuck*," he says so harshly that Pamela is taken aback.

"I don't know if I believe you."

"I don't care if you believe me or not." He knows he's speaking too aggressively so he adds, in a voice more modulated, "but we really didn't."

"I don't know what you see in her in the first place."

"I don't know what you have against her."

"Okay, I'll tell you. She stole my boyfriend. That's right! Such a stupid, cliché reason. The little Jewish bitch shamelessly flirted until she lured him away. It didn't last between them of course."

Dale wonders if Pamela is talking about the same guy that Miriam confessed to being unfaithful with.

"And do you want to know who he was?"

Dale says nothing; he really doesn't care.

"Ward Hughes. The man who came by to visit at the Hogan's cabin."

Dale has already forgotten most of that anecdote. "You mean the guy who works at the Casper newspaper?"

230

"Yes. We were involved for quite a while when he was a senior and I was a junior."

Dale nods. He doesn't really care. He hasn't thought much about Pamela's past. In fact, he doesn't think much about her at all when she's not around. He knows that's inconsiderate but he just doesn't have any romantic feelings for her.

"Don't you care that Ward stayed the night at the cabin?"

"Why should I care?"

"Because he's my ex-boyfriend. We were serious for almost a year. And a few days ago he shows up at my friend's cabin and stays the night with us all. Doesn't that bother you?"

"No, it doesn't. That's your business."

"You're so right! I can do what I want. I don't need your permission or approval. If I want to sleep with another man, I will!"

Her screeching voice annoys him. He's growing angry not out of jealousy but because Pamela is accusing him of something he is not guilty of, not in deed or thought.

Suddenly, she starts crying. And not softly like Miriam three nights ago. Instead Pamela starts weeping loudly, almost hysterically, and pacing through the kitchen with her fingers entangled in her fine blonde locks as if she's about to pull her hair out.

He's appalled at her behavior. He thinks her crying fit is more out of vexation and jealousy than genuine sorrow.

"But we didn't sleep together! So don't worry. Ward Hughes left that evening. He didn't stay over. He just came over to make me miserable. Just the way you're doing!"

She continues to pace and cry but she doesn't pull any hair out. After a few minutes, she starts to calm down. Dale watches but his annoyance with her begins to fade. He realizes that she's genuinely upset and hurt. He says she should get control of herself and calm down. Then he says that he's not trying to make her miserable.

She walks over to him, her face smeary with all the tears she's cried, and she almost throws herself into his arms. He holds her and tries to comfort her but he's not enjoying the experience. In spite of her outburst he doesn't feel any closer to her.

She leaves his embrace and walks into the bathroom. He hears her blowing her nose. She comes back and her eyes are dry and her cheeks aren't wet. But the woeful look in her blue eyes tells him that she's still distraught.

"I hate acting like a typical female," she says. "It's your business who you see."

"I'm not really seeing her."

"But I do wish you cared about me the way I care about you."

"I care about you."

"But you don't love me. And I think I'm beginning to feel that way about you." She moves toward him and presses herself against his chest. "But I don't want to," she whispers.

11

Dale finishes writing his movie review of *Tess*. He adds his by-line, slugs the story, and types -30- at the very end. He likes adding these journalistic flourishes. Even though it's been over a week since he saw the movie, he remembers it fairly well. He didn't take notes, he never does, and he doesn't have a press kit to refer to. So, he has to rely on memory and sometimes he gets a detail wrong. That gives his critics ammunition he supposes, but the *BI* hasn't received any more scolding letters from Dribble and his gang since last semester when CSDS disbanded.

Dale walks over to the copy-editing desk where Dallas is conversing with Felicia. He carries his copy with him and hears the two young women talking about having problems filling space. He thinks they are talking about finding enough news to fill the regular newspaper but as he listens he realizes that they are talking about the special April Fools parody issue.

Felicia says the paper hasn't published an April Fool's spoof for several years now. She would like to revive the tradition. The only problem is that she can't find enough people who want to contribute to make it four pages.

"I'll contribute," Dale says.

"Do you want to?" Felicia asks.

"Sure. In fact, I have over a dozen parody news stories already written."

They look puzzled so he explains that they are the scripts from the radio station's *Buffalo Quotidians*. Dallas doesn't remember hearing any but Felicia smiles and says didn't they hear the show during Deb Pierson's end of semester party last year? Dale says that's right and Felicia says that the parodies were funny. She jogs Dallas' memory by mentioning the "Gas of Wrath." Dallas agrees that the parody was clever. The three of them talk it over and they agree to publish two pages worth. That leaves two pages for the rest of the staff to fill and Felicia thinks they can accomplish that. Dale says he'll bring in several scripts this afternoon but he also wants to write one additional parody news story. Felicia and Dallas agree and he takes leave of them.

Walking back to Gowdy Hall he is pleased that the *Buffalo Quotidians* will see print. No one seems to listen to the radio show. No one has ever mentioned the parodies to him. He is still writing and producing his radio show but starting next week the program is going to broadcast re-runs because he's simply too busy to write new parodies.

In the back of his mind, however, he realizes that this decision to participate in the April Fools issue might be perilous to his standing as a student. That happened before. When he was the campus newspaper editor during his senior year at GNC, he published a special April Fool's parody section. He called it "Smoke and Mirrors" (the newspaper's name was *Smoke Signals*) and its publication got him into serious trouble. In fact, he was removed from his position as editor, although the satires had only been one reason. He also violated a couple of important Nazarene codes of conduct. The parodies didn't contain any scurrilous material; no obscene words or photos or R-rated material. But he attended a religious school and he made fun of some influential campus figures. Worse he'd lampooned an important religious concept and that's what really got people upset. The lead parody news story was about "The Unrapture," a supernatural occurrence where believers' clothes were zapped up to heaven rather than the believers themselves. He was making fun of "The Rapture," the belief that true believers are miraculously transported to heaven just before the start of the Great Tribulation, the time when the Antichrist rises and seeks to control the fallen world. Most people took the rapture seriously at GNC. In fact, during the fall revival an evangelist essentially predicted that the rapture would take place during Easter. It didn't, of course, although quite a few GNC people thought it would. When the rapture failed to materialize Dale thought the non-event would make an amusing parody news story for the April Fool's supplement. Soon after publication he discovered that a lot of people at GNC didn't have a sense of humor, especially about their religious beliefs.

Now he is attending a state university not a religious college. Wouldn't people have a better sense of humor here? Wouldn't they be less likely to be offended in general? He rather thought so. After all, the people at Deb's party enjoyed the *Buffalo Quotidians*. He thought the printed version wouldn't generate much controversy either. And if it did, so what? What could the administration really do to him? Unlike GNC, Wyoming wasn't a private, religious college. As he walks into Gowdy Hall he has a gratifying vision that his parodies will be appreciated by almost everyone on campus. Who knows? He might even win an award.

Grabowski gives a brief rap on Dale's partly closed office door then comes in. He's unusually dressed. Rather than wearing jeans, flannel shirt, and a corduroy jacket (a sartorial style similar to Dale's which Dale does not appreciate), he's wearing an actual suit. It's features an unattractive checked design and the color is a curious brown, tan, and gold but Dale is nevertheless surprised.

"Hey, bud," Grabowski says.

"Hey," Dale returns. "What gives with the unusual garb?"

It takes Grabowski a moment to realize that garb is another word for clothing. He doesn't possess a vast vocabulary. "I've got to attend a special meeting tonight and I want to ask you a favor."

"Okay."

"Would you teach my Intro class this afternoon?"

"Sure, I guess."

"Good."

Grabowski stands there, seemingly lost in thought. The last time Dale noticed that uncharacteristic expression was when his roommate returned from his Mexico adventure. The trip to Juarez didn't turn out that well. Grabowski spent too much money. He stayed at Pablo Mesa's hacienda for several nights but there were so many people living there, not just Pablo's parents but his three brothers and two sisters and his maternal grandparents and even an aunt, that Grabowski took a cheap hotel room for the last three nights. He drunk a lot of beer and tequila. He visited a brothel one night but the prices had been a lot higher than he'd anticipated. He assumed that the whores in Mexico came cheap. He got sick, too. Not a biggie, just a touch of Montezuma's revenge, but that waylaid him for a couple of days. All in all, not a trip he wanted to repeat.

When Grabowski returned, Dale kept waiting for him to say something about a couple of differences he would find, namely, the full gas tank in his pick-up and the six beers in the frig. On the first night of his return Grabowski, as was his habit, went to the refrigerator for a beer and must have noticed that instead of four beers there were six. Instead of just replacing the one beer that Miriam drank, Dale decided to add three brews just to see Grabowski's reaction. When Grabowski came out of the kitchen holding a bottle of beer he asked Dale if he'd started drinking beer. Dale said no. After that puzzled inquiry,

Grabowski let the issue drop. He wasn't one to look a gift horse in the mouth.

The full gas tank in his pick-up didn't inspire Grabowski to make inquiries either. Dale knew his roommate kept track of his gasoline use. He didn't record the mileage or anything that detailed but Grabowski would definitely notice if the pick-up's fuel gauge was lower than he expected. Before he left for Mexico, the gas tank was half full. Dale, in exchange of using the pick-up, filled the tank. He planned on telling his roommate that he'd borrowed his truck for his film shoot once Grabowski asked about the mysterious increase in gas. But as with the beer, Grabowski didn't make any inquiries when he noticed the addition. Dale even walked out with Grabowski to his truck the first time Gary went for a drive and watched as Grabowski climbed into his pick-up, started it up, and backed out of the driveway. Then, for a moment, Grabowski paused and stared in a confused way at the fuel gauge. Dale waited. But Grabowski only gave a shrug of his sloping shoulders and drove off.

Dale wasn't sure how to account for Grabowski's lack of curiosity. Gary rarely showed inquisitiveness about ideas or concepts. However, Dale expected Grabowski to be curious about things he cared about, namely beer and fuel. Grabowski wasn't really religious. His family was Catholic but he never attended mass in Laramie. But maybe Grabowski believed in small miracles, especially the kind that benefited him.

Now Dale realizes that Grabowski is not reflecting as much as he is waiting for Dale to ask him something. But Dale can't think of anything he wants to ask Grabowski at that moment.

"I won't be home tonight," Grabowski says.

"Okay." Dale starts to return to his thesis on his desk.

"I'm going to Casper."

"Is that why you're wearing a suit?"

"Yeah, for the Sigma Delta Chi banquet."

Sigma Delta Chi is the journalism honor society. "Oh, yeah? Are you being inducted?"

"Yes. I won the award for outstanding graduate student."

Dale glances at Grabowski. He stands there in his rather grotesque suit with a small smile on his face. Dale realizes that the Mass Communications Department voted Grabowski the award. What was the criteria? Excellence in displaying a lack of intellectual curiosity? Dale knows he would never win such an award; Comstock alone would see to that. But Grabowski? Why didn't Deborah Pierson win? She actually had intelligence, journalistic skill, and a pleasing personality. But she didn't excel in shameless schmoozing like Grabowski.

"I mean, it's no biggie."

Perfectly expressed, thinks Dale.

He gets up and offers his hand to his roomie. Grabowski shakes his hand.

"Congratulations, Gary. A well deserved honor. And I would be happy to substitute for you in your class. Of course, I know your students will find me a poor substitute but I will do my best to emulate your pedagogical brilliance."

"Thanks, Dale," says Grabowski completely missing the intended irony.

Dale is leaving his office when Comstock emerges from his and holds up a hand signaling for him to wait. Comstock walks over, a grumpy look on his parrot-like face.

"Once again, Dale, it is I who approaches you. I wish you would stop in more often and report your progress with the journal. Did you work on it over the break?"

"Yes," he says. He made it through ten pages before he almost fell asleep. That means he only has two hundred and forty pages to go.

"I'd like to receive the corrected proofs in another week."

"Okay."

"I know you're busy with various projects, projects by the way, that I advised you against. Do you think you'll be able to meet the deadline?"

"I think so, Professor Comstock."

"If you like, you can give me what you've proofed so far."

Dale quickly glances inside his office and sees the stolid stack of white proofs lying unattended on his desk.

"I'd rather wait and give it to you all at once," Dale says. "Sorry, Professor Comstock, but I'm late. I have to teach Grabowski's class."

"Of course, don't let me detain you."

Dale turns and walks away certain that Comstock is casting a critical look at his retreating back.

After the film directing class ends, Dale approaches Wagstaff. He asks him if the only time requirement is that the film not exceed ten minutes.

"That's the only time requirement," says Wagstaff. "We don't want any budding David Leans in class. His films of the '60s were particularly guilty of cinematic elephantiasis."

"So you prefer short films?"

"I prefer concise, well-paced films," says Wagstaff. "Hollywood studio films were quite accomplished at that but of course their subject matter leaves something to be desired, especially for today's cinemaphiles."

"Would you say the shorter the better?"

"As long as it conveys the necessary themes, symbolism, and narrative."

"Yeah, I agree. Length isn't the most important thing. It's the cinematic impact that matters."

"Is that idea one you're developing for your thesis?"

"No. Well, thanks Dr. Wagstaff. I got to get going."

Dale turns and heads out of the classroom, certain that Wagstaff is looking quizzically at his retreating back.

Dale sits in Professor Wilkins office as the creative writing professor reacquaints himself with Dale's latest short story. It's really a short short story. Dale thinks about asking Wilkins the same series of questions as he did Wagstaff but in a literary context rather than a cinematic one.

The story is titled "Marco Polo Is Leaving Town" and it's

a first person somewhat autobiographical account of a college student leaving his hometown to take a journey to Europe and the reaction it produces from his family and girlfriend. It's only eight pages long but Dale sort of likes it. The best scene is where the protagonist mercilessly teases his sister.

While Wilkins peruses the story, Dale glances around his office. It contains a lot of books. Novels mostly. Dale doesn't see Wilkins' novels displayed. Maybe the professor is a modest man. That would be unusual for such a big shot but in class he is unassuming, not arrogant at all. Wilkins was an athlete, an Ivy League graduate, a Rhode's Scholar, and professionally he is an award-winning author. If anyone had a reason to swagger a little it would be him. But he doesn't appear to be arrogant at all. Dale likes that and thinks that sometimes the people who have least reason to be supercilious are the ones guilty of that unattractive attribute.

Other than all the books stuffed in the place, in the bookcases and lying in stacks on the desk and table, Wilkins' office yields little information about him. No photos, no diplomas, no awards, just one small, smudgy window and an old fashioned Underwood typewriter, the kind Dale has which makes him feel a certain kinship to Wilkins. He seems to be a private man and Dale guesses that he uses his office exclusively for work, which explains the lack of personal possessions. He probably doesn't want any distractions when he is busy writing.

Wilkins, now finished with Dale's story, gives him some suggestions on how to develop it into a longer work. He makes a few additional comments on how to improve the quality of the writing. All his suggestions are sensible and Dale agrees with them. Wilkins asks him if there is anything else he can help him with and Dale says no but he would like to ask him a few questions.

"Very well," Wilkins says.

"Why are you teaching at Wyoming?"

"I first came out here with my basketball team to play in an invitational."

"You mean Pennsylvania University."

Wilkins narrows his eyes just a little to indicate he's surprised that Dale knows this information. "Yes, Penn came here. I visited a second time years later. I liked this country. It's very different than where I grew up."

"In Pittsburgh."

"Seems like you've been doing some research on me."

"I was curious. I also read one of your novels. I was impressed by it although I didn't understand all of it."

"Which one?"

"Your second one, *Shooting for the Moon*."

"The sections you had trouble understanding were probably the parts I had trouble understanding, too."

"You had trouble?"

"An author can become entangled in his own work, his fictional world."

"You seem to publish a novel every five years. Does it take that long to write one?"

"It does for me. I'm a slow writer. Perhaps I'm too fussy. Sometimes I work on a sentence all afternoon."

"Wow. I just churn stuff out."

Wilkins grins wryly. "A lot of writers do."

"But you don't. We live in such a fast paced world, with instant entertainment on television, the radio, movies. One of my professors in the mass comm department says that writing is going to become obsolete. I don't think that because I love to read good books. But do you think that books are going to become obsolete?"

"Even if I did, I'd still want to write."

"Why is that?"

"Because it's what I do. I value the act of writing, of creating, of using language skillfully even if no one else does. But there are still a few of us who care about substance over flash."

Dale nods. He admires that attitude. Even though Wilkins hadn't used the word, he knew his attitude exemplified the idea of art.

"Now that you've asked me several questions, I'd like to ask you a few."

"Okay."

"Tell me where you grew up?"

"In Galilee, Oklahoma. It's a small town ten miles west of Oklahoma City."

"What did you do in high school?"

Dale told him that he played sports, edited the yearbook, went on dates with his girlfriends, and goofed off a lot.

"Were there any black kids in your school?"

"No, we didn't have any of them. But we had Indians, including a few full bloods. We also had a Cuban family. And I had a friend who was half-Japanese. So it wasn't just full of white people."

"You never knew any black people?"

"Well, I was sort of a friend with a guy who went to a all-black school. We got to know each other by playing sports. Our schools often went to the same track meets. Our football teams played each other my senior year. He was a likable guy. He had a good sense of humor."

Wilkins nods. Dale notices that his rather large, expressive eyes peer at him in an analytical manner, the same way he will sometimes look at a student who makes a comment in class. As in class, Dale is not certain if Wilkins agrees or disagrees but he definitely seems to be trying to understand.

Wilkins asks if there is anything else he can do for him and Dale says no. They say goodbye and Dale leaves his office. On his way back to Gowdy Hall, he thinks about Wilkins questions and his answers. He said "them" in reference to not having blacks in his high school. He hoped he hadn't sounded rude. Dale wasn't sure how sensitive Wilkins was. Judging from the one novel he'd read, Wilkins was certainly aware of white people's attitudes about black people. Aware and sensitive about it. Living in Laramie, Wyoming would probably enhance his acute perceptions about racial relations and attitudes. Was the fact that Dale had used the rather dismissive term "them" an indication of his insensitivity? Perhaps it was. But how can one be sensitive about something that he has hardly experienced in his life (interaction with black people)?

He wonders if he should have mentioned that one of his favorite modern American novels is *Invisible Man*. Maybe if they have another conference he'll do that.

They lie on her comfortable bed in the nude. Pamela reclines against two pillows reading *The Prime of Miss Jean Brodie*. Dale lies next to her on his side looking over at the stereo trying to identify her albums. On the stereo right now is the Janis Ian album, *Between the Lines*. He hears the beginning of the next cut, "At 17" and he remembers not liking that song back in high school. He listens to it and still thinks it's a paean to self-pity. Janis Ian has a good voice and the song has a simple, plaintive sound to it, but he dislikes the pseudo-poetic lyrics. The one phrase that especially grates on his nerves is "muttering vague obscenities." That's an example of clever writing? How are obscenities vague? In fact, an obscenity is just the opposite of vague. At least, Pamela's obscenities aren't vague. Just tonight she said, after failing to fully reach climax after thirty minutes of trying that she has a "stubborn cunt."

Dale doesn't know what kind of pudenda she has (he, on the other hand, prefers literary if not obscure words to describe intimate organs), but he performed cunnilingus on her until his tongue turned numb. He even did it the way she favored, with him prone between her spread legs while she lies back with nothing to do but concentrate on her own orgasm. From his perspective, the whole act was about as exciting as proof-reading Comstock's damn journal.

She reciprocated but not by giving fellatio. She thought her mouth was too small or he was too big or maybe both. Unfortunately, she had small orifices. She also had small hands but she used one of them to jack him off. It took a while for him, too, and when he ejaculated more out of relief than pleasure he thought he could have more fun doing that himself while gazing at the images of beautiful naked women in *Penthouse*.

Now, he lies on the bed trying to identify her other gyno-centric albums. He sees Joni Mitchell, Carole King, Carly Simon, and several female jazz singers that he's never heard of. He guesses Pamela has good taste in music. But rather than listening to one of them warble, he'd like to hear Cindy and Kate from the B-52s wail "52 Girls."

He wonders how Pamela finances her comfortable apartment and how she buys her albums and clothes and Timberline boots. She's never told him much about her finances. But he gets the impression that her father, who owns and operates a drug store in Evanston, has a good business and he subsidizes her tasteful but modest lifestyle. He wonders what Brother Partridge would think if he knew his ex-Mormon daughter was hanging out in the nude with her dissatisfied lover?

Dale thinks they really aren't suited for each other. Ever since that emotional scene in his kitchen, he's tried to be nicer to her. He even went hiking with her one Sunday. He enjoyed being out in the invigorating spring air and climbing a smaller mountain in the Medicine Bow range but the recreation took too much of his precious time.

In addition to spending time with her that wasn't sexual, he asked her questions about her classes, her part-time work at the *Boomerang*, and other things that he didn't care much about. He even listened patiently as she complained about the injustices women suffered on a daily basis. Why wasn't there any female faculty in the Mass Communications Department? (Dale actually thought she had a good point because most of his favorite teachers had been women.) Why did so many films in the '70s have such weak women characters, almost all of them in supporting roles? Dale answered that rhetorical question: films were external, they focused more on action, and since men were more likely to be tinkers, tailors, soldiers, and spies (and Cowboys, astronauts, cops, murderers, dictators, generals, etc.) films tended to have them as lead actors. She didn't appreciate his answer. You're always too aesthetic, she said. You don't have enough social and political awareness. How will we ever change things for the better, for more equality, if we don't commit to social change?

He told her that real social change had to start with the individual. The idea that elites or intellectuals or politicians could impose social change on the people never worked very well. Besides, he was more interested in our inner lives than our social or political lives. He cared about artistic and philosophical ideas. Pamela thought those ideas were important but not as important as socio-political ideas.

That conversation was typical of their interchanges. They hardly spoke about their personal lives although Dale occasionally asked Pamela about her upbringing. He rarely told her anything about his background or his present challenges and problems. He never spoke to her about Comstock. He knew she liked that strange bird and she wouldn't be sympathetic to his increasing contempt for the mad professor. Pamela sometimes spoke about some of her other friends, in particular the Hogans, the young couple that worked at the *Boomerang*. Since Dale didn't like most of her on-campus friends ~ Dribble, Marsha Martin, Patti Montag, and Robert Baugh – she didn't mention them too much. Sometimes she spoke about a girl named Barbara Hughes, who Dale had never met. Pamela once pointed her out. Barbara was walking on the opposite side of the quadrangle and didn't see them. He couldn't see much detail of her but from the distance she didn't look attractive. She was fairly tall with a rather angular figure. Her hair was brown and cut short, almost to the point of severity. She wore jeans and a brown leather jacket. Her quick gait suggested she was a no-nonsense type on an important mission. Pamela said that Barbara was the most politically astute person she knew. She was very committed to social change. Then he listened to Pamela as she launched into a short diatribe about campus politics and how it was dominated by the frat boy culture, a topic that didn't interest him. It didn't take much to set Pamela off: a newspaper article, a book, a movie, an overheard conversation, almost any kind of information that revealed the injustice of living in a male chauvinistic society.

At least tonight's film didn't launch her on another rant. They went to campus to see a 1969 film *The Pride of Miss Jean Brodie*. (Miriam hadn't been there. She was back in Denver seeing her Joe who had repented of his spring break solo adventure.) Dale saw it before on television, but since the film was R-rated in the theatres he wanted to see the uncensored version. As far as he could tell, the only thing they'd cut for television was the scene where a girl, a student, poses nude for the older male art teacher.

Pamela liked the movie. She enjoyed the battle of wits between Miss Jean Brodie and the scheming girl nude model character. Now, she is skimming the novel, checking for any obvious omissions or alterations from the text, the very thing Dale often did.

He glances at her. She's wearing her reading glasses as she flips through the paperback. He looks farther down and sees a rather long hair protruding from her right breast. The sight disturbs him. Pamela, as with most women, has very little body hair except in the usual areas, so he wonders how that long hair developed. It's just another reminder that he's finding her less attractive the more he sees of her. If he were in love with her such physical imperfections wouldn't bother him so much. Everyone has them. But he isn't in love with her, never has been, never will be, and so physical imperfections definitely detract from her lust-worthiness.

Janis Ian's lamentations come to an end. Pamela leaps up from the bed and he watches her naked body toddle over to the stereo. She looks even more porcine than she did when he first saw her in the buff. Right now as he focuses on her plump and pink butt, he thinks all she needs is a corkscrew tail to match the image of Petunia Pig.

He knows he's being mean. He doesn't want to be. He's just preparing himself for what he knows he will have to do. Extricate his self. He's just not sure when he'll do it. He doesn't want to endure a repeat of that scene in the kitchen.

Pamela puts on Carly Simon's *No Secrets*. The first song is "You're So Vain." She smiles and prances back to the bed. He wonders why she's so fond of being naked. Maybe she thinks it's a requirement of being a natural woman.

"There are several differences in the novel from the movie," she says, referring to *The Prime of Miss Jean Brodie*.

"That's typical. Producers often make changes from the novel. I guess they want to make the story more cinematic. But sometimes it doesn't make sense."

Dale thinks of the suicide scene in *The Bell Jar*. The film changed that scene from the book and the change didn't seem to be for a valid reason. But he doesn't mention it to Pamela. He doesn't want her to think of Sylvia Plath again.

They listen to a few more songs then Dale decides it's time to leave. He gets up to dress.

"Oh, don't put on your clothes," she says. "You're too bashful about your body."

Dale sort of smiles. If only she knew about the modeling. Of course, he hadn't liked it much but he got paid enough to finance his film. So he guesses going through some embarrassment was worth it. O, the ways of Hollywood.

"I'm getting dressed because I'm going home."

"Why can't you stay the night? You never do that."

"I have to get up early."

"You can get up early here. Why don't you want to sleep here?"

"I don't want to bother you. I snore."

"I don't believe it."

"I do. Ask Grabowski. I wake him up all the time with my dreadful snoring."

"I won't mind."

"If you heard me you would. It's like a man drowning. But instead of water, it's mucus."

"Yuck."

"That's why I should go home."

He's exaggerating about his snoring, of course, but it does the trick. He's dressed and he starts to leave when she gets up from the bed and follows him to the front door. Before he opens the door to leave, he looks at her standing there starkers.

"Pamela, what if someone sees you when I open the door?"

"People shouldn't be hung up about nudity."

"All right then."

He quickly opens the door as wide as it will go, displaying the proud nudist to the waiting world. She shrieks and hides behind the door. He's about to leave when she reminds him of something. He leans in and kisses her and then he leaves and she quickly shuts the door.

He walks two blocks to his place and wonders how in the hell he will end it.

12

April Fool's Day 1980. Dale arises early and hustles to campus. On his way, he checks the *Branding Iron* newspaper racks in the classroom buildings and halls. He walks into the Memorial Student Union and sees newspapers stuffed in the kiosks. What is contained in the special April Fool's Day issue is a four-page news parody and two whole pages are devoted to his creations: *The Buffalo Quotidians*, printed version.

Dale grabs a newspaper and goes to the OWR office to read it. He opens the office door with his key, picks up several student submissions lying on the floor (deadline for submissions is today) and sits down at the old wooden desk. He opens the paper to the four-page parody section, called *The Cattle Prod*. He glances at the first page, then turns to the double-page spread where his stories are located. One page consists of several different satires, one of them just composed Friday, and one parody photograph. The other page is devoted to the "Gas of Wrath" saga, stories that were written last semester when the gas crisis was still in effect and broadcast on the campus radio station.

The conceit concerning the "Gas of Wrath" is a reversal of the John Steinbeck novel about Okies leaving Dust Bowl Oklahoma and migrating to California. In Dale's parody, wealthy Californians, nicknamed "Hollies" because most of them originate from the Hollywood area of Los Angeles, are suffering due to the severe gas crisis. A group of Hollies decide to flee their state for the rich oil and gas lands of Oklahoma. Of course, the residents of Buffalo City resist the invasion. Conflict ensues. One family in particular, the Roads, is featured in most of the fake news accounts. Thomas Roads, Sr., a Shell Oil executive and his son Thomas, Jr., and his pregnant daughter, Fossil of Fuel, brave the privations of living in western Oklahoma. The climax of the story occurs when the family is pursued by a crazed mob of Okies. The Roads discover that their Rolls Royce is out of gasoline. But before the mob can reach them, Fossil of Fuel, who had earlier lost her baby, fuels the family's Rolls Royce. Instead of milk, she carries gasoline in her breasts.

Dale scrutinizes the second page. The parody photograph is funny. It's a still of the Monty Python movie, *The Life of Brian*. It shows the Python gang dressed in Middle Eastern garb with turbans. They're smiling at the camera. The cutline below the photograph reads: *The Iranian Revolutionary Council poses for a group picture outside the U.S. Embassy in Tehran. The Revolutionary Council said despite popular opinion they are really a bunch of funny guys. The photo was taken just after 12 thieves were hanged.*

Below the photo is a story about an Iranian invasion force attacking the Washington D.C. area and the inept response by the Carter administration.

The photo and story were satiric allusions to the continuing hostage crisis. Iranian revolutionaries attacked the U.S. Embassy last September and still held fifty-two American hostages.

Other satires included: making fun of Jane Fonda (Dale admired her acting but otherwise thought she was quite silly); satirizing Lenny Bruce (or Benny Luce, the stand-up comic whose routine includes speaking clinical terms for bodily functions and sex acts instead of the now required four letter words); lampooning the concept of palimony by having a high school football player and stud being sued by his former steady girlfriend;

a comic takeoff on the relationship of California governor Jerry Brown and rock star Linda Ronstadt by presenting a Republican version, starring Ronald Reagan and Dolly Parton.

And there's one more parody that Dale especially wrote for the April Fool's issue:

LARAMIE, WYO (IP) – Scientists at this Rocky Mountain university announced today that they had created the world's first talking robot, the SPDRV102, or affectionately known as the Spouting Drivel machine. According to the graduate researcher, Nils Iceberg, the robot is capable of speech although it's often incoherent and jargon-riddled nonsense.

The amazing invention was created by the minds of the technological sciences and robotics division at the university as part of the Computerized Auto Nonsense Talker project or CANT for short. (Editor's note: "cant" is an obscure term for pretentious speech.)

The robot, Spouting Drivel, looks amazingly life-like. It stands six foot tall and has a scrawny frame that nevertheless supports a big head. Scientists added a few additional details to help humanize the machine: large spectacles and a dirty blonde wig.

Researcher Iceberg admitted that the robot wasn't visually appealing but he claimed that he enjoyed looking at it just the same.

Iceberg said operating the robot is quite simple. Just flip the switch and the robot opens its mouth and releases a torrent of nonsense. Occasionally, a sentence will make sense but most of its speech is incoherent babbling and jargon-filled clichés. There is also a special prose adapter that can be plugged into a typewriter and the Spouting Drivel machine can compose reams of gibberish.

When asked what practical value such a robot can offer, Iceberg says that it can serve in a multitude of ways. First, it can substitute for teachers, either at the high school or university level. Second, it can replace most television sports color commentators with a special sports program. Third, by using the prose adapter, it can supersede most newspaper writers, especially movie reviewers.

"With the Spouting Drivel robot we can replace Vincent Canby and Pauline Kael," said the scientist in charge of the project, Dr. Demento. "Or for that matter, almost any reporter, especially those in the arts and entertainment section of the newspapers."

One reporter asked Dr. Demento why the Spouting Drivel robot was called SPDRV102.

"The letters stand for robotic terms but the number 102 refer to Spouting Drivel's artificial IQ of 102. However, we're beginning to suspect that the robot's actual IQ might be lower, perhaps much lower."

Dale thinks: take that, Dribble!

Felicia and Dallas didn't change a word. He thinks it's good to have allies.

He reads the other fake news stories on the front and back pages. Some are funny (Felicia's and Dallas') but some of them are more in the National Lampoon style of humor: crude and making fun of uncool things and people. He leans back in his chair and considers the consequences of his sardonic jibes. He doesn't think many people will object. Maybe even a few readers with an appreciation for satire might think his stories funny. Of course, how many people today can even understand a parody of *The Grapes of Wrath*?

He spends an hour working on the *OWR*, and then heads off to Gowdy Hall. He's walking down the hall, passing Comstock's partially closed door, when the professor dashes out of his office yelling Dale's name.

Dale turns and sees an apoplectic Comstock waving today's *Branding Iron* at him.

"How could you write such scurrilous trash!"

Dale expected Comstock to disapprove but he's surprised to see how incensed the professor is.

"Writing such garbage is unprofessional and unethical! And I'm going to see that the editor, Felicia Fernandez, is appropriately punished."

"Wait a minute, Professor Comstock. Do you know what day it is today?"

Comstock's ire temporarily cools. "What do you mean?"

"It's April first. April Fool's Day."

Comstock glances at the newspaper to make sure. His small eyes blink in recognition. But that rational moment disappears.

"I don't care what day it is! It's completely inappropriate to print such nonsense. A student newspaper should operate like a professional one. Would The *Casper Star-Tribune* print such junk?"

"I don't know. I don't read it."

"That's exactly your problem, Dale Smith. You don't take serious journalism seriously. Instead of preparing yourself to be a responsible reporter, you write adolescent jokes and coerce impressionable young journalists like Felicia into printing them. Well, let me tell you young man, not only will I block the awarding of your degree but also I will see to it that you do not work for any newspaper in Wyoming. I have a lot of contacts, a lot of friends in the newspaper business in this state and I will spread the word that you are a strange, unreliable, jokester. You're as bad as those hippies in the 1971 yearbook. They thought they could pull one over me, too. Well, I saw to it that the yearbook ceased publication. And mark my word, if you talk those gullible young women into publishing any more of your twaddle, I will personally see to it that *The Branding Iron* ceases to operate!"

Throughout the harangue, Dale maintains a calm demeanor. He doesn't take seriously anything Comstock says. He knows the professor is psychologically disturbed. He is a little surprised by Comstock's vehemence. He doesn't like being yelled at. But he lets him finish his diatribe before he responds.

"Is there anything else, Professor Comstock?"

Comstock looks like he's about to explode. His weathered,

tanned face nevertheless increases in color to a glowing brownish pink and his rather small bleary green eyes bulge.

"As a matter of fact, there is. I want you to hand over the proofs to the *Journal of North American Mass Communications Programs*."

"You mean the *JNAMCP*?"

It takes Comstock a moment to decipher the acronym. "Of course that's what I mean!"

"I don't have them with me."

"Where are they?"

"At home. I'll bring them in tomorrow."

"You better or else you'll be sorry, Dale Smith. I'll take action. I'll bring you up on charges before the university's ethics committee. I'll inform Dr. Schneider of your nefarious behavior. I'll –"

"I get it! You want the proofs. I'll give them to you tomorrow."

Dale turns and walks off. He hears Comstock sputtering in rage behind him. Dale isn't sure if Comstock can make good on his threats. He thinks it's mostly bluster. But he needs to work on those proofs. He's not even half way through. But he's not so concerned about that. Because the altercation with Comstock has resulted in an idea: Dale knows how to finish his film.

After his Film History II class concludes, Dale assists Wagstaff with rewinding the film, *A Face in the Crowd*.

"What did you think of the film?" Wagstaff asks.

"I liked it. I didn't know Andy Griffith acted in any good films. I remember him from –"

"Yes, that inane television show."

"Right. I've seen several Elia Kazan's films, *Gentleman's Agreement*, *On the Waterfront*, *Splendor in the Grass*, but I've never seen this one. He's a good director."

"You've seen a lot of old movies, more than most young people. And you're an unusual if not a strange young man in other ways as well."

Dale knows what he is getting at. "Yeah, that's sort of how Professor Comstock described me."

"I heard him berating you in the hallway. I'm afraid my colleague has a loud, braying voice. I hope you weren't too alarmed."

"No, but I learned once again that he doesn't like satire."

"Most people don't. It's interesting that most satiric films in Hollywood history were flops or partial flops. Even *Singing in the Rain*. But as time passes, some of those films are considered among the best in history."

Dale shrugs. He doubts Comstock or any other humorless literalist will appreciate his satires ten years from now. But he has a question he wants to ask Wagstaff.

"Is the movie camera checked out for tomorrow?"

"No, everyone seems to have completed their filming."

"I need to check it out. I have one more scene to film."

"Very well. Just go to the equipment room and schedule your time and pay your fee. And please don't tell me what you intend to film."

Back at home, Dale reads letters from Will Whitaker and Teri Boswell. He'll have to answer them tomorrow night. Right now he has to finish proofing the *JNAMCP*. He doesn't know how he's going to do it in time. He stares at the thick proofs and dreads starting. He hates doing boring work, especially work that is forced on him. He's always been a recalcitrant student when he had to do something he didn't want to do, especially when he felt the reason was arbitrary.

Rather than start, he thinks about earlier that day and the mixed reaction *The Cattle Prod* received. From what few comments he overheard a lot of the students preferred the lower-brow humor in the first and last pages. It seems that most students didn't understand or appreciate the "The Gas of Wrath." He overheard a few students laughing about the Monty Python photo. He realizes most students liked the satires that were more topical. But for the most part, he heard very little comment about *The Buffalo Quotidians* part of the April Fool's edition.

His friends complimented him on his satires: Edward Darby, Felicia, Dallas, and the Von Goebbels brothers. He hadn't seen Mimi yet so he didn't know what she thought. She might dislike the spoof about Spencer Dribble. After all, they inexplicably are friends.

Grabowski arrives. He lumbers into the living room and grins at Dale.

"You've made some people mad, bud."

"Really?" Dale says in a pseudo-surprised way.

Grabowski settles down in the easy chair and looks with amusement at Dale. Grabowski has been even more smug than usual since he won the Sigma Chi Delta award for best graduate student. He traveled to Casper, attended the swell soirée, stayed the night in a swanky hotel, and then returned a hero to the Laramie campus. The award would look really good on his vita. He told Dale yesterday that he'd applied for another job, at another regional college this time in Michigan. Dale said a man of his talents shouldn't limit himself. If he saw an opening at Columbia or Stanford he should apply there as well. Grabowski simply nodded, accepting the good advice.

"I heard that Comstock threw a fit, man," Grabowski says, chuckling.

"Yes, he expressed his disapproval in his usual dignified way."

Grabowski notices that Dale is working on the proofs. He shakes his head in fake sympathy. "Man, how'd you get stuck with that job?

"I don't know. It's a mystery." Dale glances at his roomie who has extended his long legs and now appreciatively gazes at them as if they had grown several inches since the day before. "You can help, if you like."

"I don't like. I'm not any good at that shit."

"Me neither." He goes back to the tedious work.

256

"In fact, I talked the department into letting me use a slide show for my thesis."

"Really? You're not writing a thesis?"

"I still have to write a short paper explaining my photographic methods and describing the individual photos. But it's no biggie."

"How short?"

"Twenty pages maybe."

Dale isn't surprised. His thesis is going to be the regular length, around 100 pages. But the great Grabowski will churn out a mere twenty.

"I've also applied for a summer research assistantship in the department," Grabowski modestly mentions.

"I didn't know there was one."

"Neil Nordberg is leaving after this semester. I'll get his position."

"Nordberg is doing scholarly research for Schneider. What are you going to do? Take portraits of all the professors?"

"I don't know, man. I'm just applying for the stipend. Otherwise, I'll have to take out a loan to finish my degree this summer."

"Well, I hope you get it then." Dale isn't sure if he really feels that way. But Grabowski isn't a bad guy. He isn't mean or nasty. Dale doesn't want his poor slob roommate to go into debt for his degree.

"I guess you won't be around this summer to split expenses?" Grabowski asks.

"No, I'm leaving right after the semester ends."

"Then I'll have to find another roomie, but –"

"No biggie."

Grabowski doesn't smile. He knows he's being made fun of and he, after all, has his integrity. He won the award for best graduate student, after all. Soon he will be Professor Gary Grabowski at some Podunk state college. Still, Dale doesn't want to offend his roommate too much. They still have almost a month and a half to go.

"I saw the photograph you submitted to the OWR," Dale says. "It was good."

That puts Grabowski in a better mood. "Thanks."

"I want to ask a favor of you."

Grabowski shifts in his seat. He doesn't like being asked for favors; he prefers asking for them. "What?"

"I want you to come with me to Comstock's office tomorrow and direct his attention to something out his window."

"Why?"

"It's for my film."

"Why do you need me?"

"I want Comstock to be looking out the window."

"Why?"

"Don't worry about it. I just want you to go into his office and ask him to look out the window. Say there's a book-burning happening on the quad. No, he'd probably immediately rush out there and help. Just make up something plausible."

"Like what?"

Dale almost says: use your imagination but that would be pointless advice. "Isn't Comstock a bird watcher?"

"I think so."

"Then say there's a Yellow-bellied Sapsucker sitting on somebody's head. Just say something to make him go over to the window."

"Are you going to get me in trouble now?"

"How would you get in trouble? You're just pointing out an avian friend. And I promise, I'm not going to do anything that will get you in trouble."

"I don't know."

"Okay, I'll pay you."

"How much?"

"Five bucks."

"Ten."

"Okay, ten. And that's all. Besides, you owe me."

Dale can tell that Grabowski doesn't exactly accept that idea. In his Grabowskian world, everyone owes *him*. But Grabowski nods his head and agrees to do what Dale asks.

Grabowski stands up and stretches. He says he's going to go over to the campus pub. Does Dale want to come?

"I can't. I've got to finish these proofs. It's going to take all night. Besides, I thought you were low on cash."

"I am. But tomorrow I'll have ten bucks."

The next day, as soon as the Mass Communications Department opens, Dale enters and drops off the JNAMCP's proofs contained in a Manila envelope in Comstock's mailbox. He quickly slips out of the department, not wanting to encounter Comstock yet.

He ambles over to the student union and *The Branding Iron*. As soon as he walks into the newsroom, he notices that Felicia looks unperturbed, not at all the way she looked back when the CSDS struck.

"Getting a lot of feedback on the spoof?" Dale asks.

"I'll say. We've got six letters to the editor already."

"All negative, I bet."

"No, about half and half. But there was an especially interesting one from a faculty member. Can you guess who?"

"Not Comstock?"

"He doesn't write letters; he let's you know up close and personal. No, the prof who wrote is Dr. Dribble."

"Let me guess. He especially liked the spoof story about Spouting Drivel, the amazing talking robot?"

"He didn't mention that story in particular but he said the April Day's lampoon was in bad taste and he wondered if the entire staff didn't suffer from some kind of mass psychosis."

"Print the letter and plead guilty."

"I ought to. The other odd thing is that I expected Professor Comstock to express his displeasure to me but today when I saw him outside Gowdy Hall he simply said he knew who was responsible for the April Fool's parody and he didn't blame me."

"Good. I don't want you to get into any trouble."

"He can't exact any revenge. I don't have him for any classes this semester."

"By the way, when you went to his office did he ever offer you sweets?"

"As a matter of fact, he did. It was sort of creepy, like he's some dirty old man trying to lure a little girl into a car. I never understood it."

"Maybe Comstock should make an appointment with Dr. Dribble."

Felicia smiles and Dale says he has to split. He's off to get Grabowski.

Grabowski knocks on Comstock's door. When he hears the professor say enter, he glances over to Dale standing close by.

Dale waits outside the door holding the 8 mm movie camera. He listens to Grabowski as he mentions that he sees an unusual bird sitting on a tree branch near the student union. Dale's amazed that Grabowski is using his goofy idea but it seems to work. He hears Comstock leaving his desk and walking over to his office window.

Dale slips into the office, walking on the tiptoes of his boots. He sees Comstock staring out the window as Grabowski stands to one side. Dale signals his roommate that he can go and Grabowski quickly departs. Dale starts shooting footage. Through the viewfinder he focuses on Comstock as he stares out the window. Maybe there really is some kind of Yellow-bellied Sapsucker tweeting in a tree because Comstock continues to gaze out the window.

Suddenly, Comstock detects something is amiss. He notices that Grabowski is no longer next to him. Dale waits, his camera trained on the professor. This is the shot he especially wants. Comstock slowly turns and sees Dale pointing the movie camera at him. His beady watery green eyes stare into the camera blankly for a moment, and then his expression becomes concerned, then finally livid as if Dale has caught him in the middle of perpetrating some foul crime.

That's all Dale needs. "Thanks, Professor Comstock," he says as he flees from his office.

Dale dashes down the hallway, his fingers tightly holding onto the camera. He hears Comstock lumbering out of his office, shouting: "Dale! Come back here! I want to talk to you, young man!"

Dale continues to run. He memorizes Comstock's clothing, especially the brown, blue and white flannel shirt and the red suspenders. Out of his peripheral vision, he sees the curious faces of the other professors and Deb Pierson appearing in the doors of their offices. He ignores them and throws open the exit door still hearing the agitated calls of Comstock.

As soon as their creative writing class is over, Dale hustles Mimi out of the classroom. He asks if she knows where Spencer Dribble's Modern European Drama class meets. She says upstairs in the comparative literature floor of Roripaugh Hall. He grabs her hand and all but pulls her up the stairs. They arrive on the third floor and Dale looks down the hallway and sees several students emerging from a classroom and one of them is Spencer Dribble.

"Meet me outside beside the bench," Dale tells Mimi.

"Oh, Dale, haven't you done enough to your former friend? It's like Alexander Pope and *The Dunciad*."

Dale leaves her and walks down the hall. He sees that Marsha Martin has joined Dribble. They start moving in his direction but they haven't seen him yet. He thinks they make an odd couple: Dribble with his stylish dirty blonde hair and glasses, Marsha with her bushy dandelion-like dark hair. He notices again that both of them have rather long, bony faces and small eyes.

He walks swiftly to them and his sudden appearances startles them.

"Hello Spence. Hello Marsha. I just have four words to speak to you."

He draws closer and they shrink from him. He stares into their bewildered eyes and says, "Freedom of the press."

He turns and walks away.

The next day Dale enters the Mass Communications department and doesn't bother to stealthily slip past Comstock's door. Instead he ambles leisurely down the hall, waiting for the professor to come flying out of his office. Which he does.

"Dale! I want to talk to you."

Dale turns and takes two steps back to Comstock. The professor glares at him, his beady eyes and beaky nose dominating his face.

"Yes, Professor Comstock."

"Come into my office. I have words to speak to you."

Dale does. Comstock closes the door.

"I don't know what the business with the camera was about yesterday, but I am not surprised by any hijinx you engage in. But that's not what I wish to discuss. First, the proofs you returned showed very little detailed work. Just from glancing through them I noticed that you overlooked correcting several typos and minor errors. Don't you understand that the reputation of this department is at stake?"

"Professor Comstock, you're the editor of the journal, right?"

"Yes, of course."

"Then why don't you hire a professional proof-reader?"

"That's why this department pays your stipend so you can help me edit the journal."

"But I'm doing most of the work."

"And shoddy work it is! But it's too late for me to force you, under some kind of penalty, to revisit your duties. I will have to take over the process."

Dale says nothing. He wouldn't have revisited his duties anyway.

"I also want to express my continuing disapproval of your role in the so-called April Fool's parody. Others participated I know but you're a graduate student and you knew of my sensitivity to vulgarity being reproduced in student publications, so I hold you primarily responsible for that debacle."

"That's fair."

Comstock doesn't expect that answer. He looks to be repressing an urge to shout at Dale. He draws a deep breath and continues:

"I am willing to give you a second chance, an opportunity to keep in good standing in this department. Remember that I am responsible in evaluating your independent study."

"What do you want?"

"I want you to resign your position as editor of *The Owen Wister Review*. I'd also like you to stop writing movie reviews."

"And what do I get in return?"

"A chance to receive your degree. I won't block it."

"We're almost finished evaluating manuscripts at the *OWR*, Professor Comstock. Why is it so important to you that I resign?"

"I don't want to see your name associated with any publication here at the University of Wyoming."

"Because you think you're the arbiter of good taste?"

"And good sense."

"Well, I'll tell you Professor Comstock. There's not a chance in hell I'll do that."

As Dale starts to leave, Comstock starts yelling, "I'm not the only faculty member who considers you a disgrace! There are some in this department and in other departments as well! Dr. Drivel is one. He called me –"

Dale stops in his tracks. "Dr. Drivel?"

Comstock's face turns red. He tries to speak but he cannot.

"Thanks, Professor Comstock. That made my day."

He exits, leaving the stammering Comstock fuming in his office.

Women in Love, the movie version, nears its end. Gerald Crich is dead, having committing suicide by freezing to death in the Alps. His good friend, and wrestling partner, Rupert Birkin, is devastated. In the film's final scene, Rupert confesses to his wife, Ursula, that his love for her is not enough. He also needs to feel love for a man. Ursula begins to understand the implications of his confession. As the camera focuses on her face she stares at him, dumbfounded.

The lights go up and the audience rises from their seats, a low rumble filling the Memorial Union Ballroom. Matt and Mark Von Goebbels, Miriam, Dale, and Pamela stand and stretch. Dale glances at Pamela. She is not pleased that he sat next to Miriam. It wasn't by accident. Dale arranged it with Miriam, Matt, and Mark. He asked them to save two seats and since he and Pamela were almost late they had little choice but to sit in the strategically empty seats.

Dale talks with Miriam and Mark while Pamela refuses to participate. When Mark Von Goebbels expresses some confusion with the movie's ending, he sees Pamela smirking at his unsophistication. Well, Dale thinks, Mark might not be the most perceptive viewer but he's a crackerjack special effects man. And his brother, Matt, performed a valuable function by acting in one scene for Dale's movie. Matt, dressed in a blue, brown, and white flannel shirt with red suspenders, simply fired a rifle out of a window. Dale filmed him doing this with the 8 mm movie camera at the Von Goebbels family junkyard outside of Cheyenne. Dale tried to match the lighting and general appearance of the window with the one in Comstock's office. He shot the scene at the same time of day from the same angle and Matt even added a touch of gray paint to one side of his head at the temple and side-burn. The two scenes didn't match exactly, but they were close enough. He knew because he received the processed film yesterday from the photo lab. Tomorrow morning he would go into the production studio and edit his film into its finished form.

Dale asks the Von Goebbels brothers and Miriam if they would like to join them for a post-film drink. They decline. So Dale says goodbye to his three friends and watches as they leave the student union ballroom.

"Why did you sit down next to them?" Pamela asks.

"Because I wanted to. They're my friends."

"You know I can't stand Miriam."

"That's your problem. I like her."

Pamela stares at him, but her expression is one more of hurt feelings than anger. He ignores her and walks toward the exit. She follows. They start to walk out of the auditorium when Dale sees Neil Nordberg standing near the exit talking to another young man. He notices that Nordberg's friend is a little chubby; in fact, he resembles one of tonight's actors, Oliver Reed.

As Dale approaches them, he moves close enough so Nordberg can hear him. "I bet I know which scene you liked best."

Dale nods and Nordberg grins in a way that is not entirely unfriendly. Dale thinks for a moment that Nordberg is looking at Pamela in an odd way. They leave the auditorium and Dale asks her if she'd like to stop for a drink and she says no she just wants to go to her place. They walk across campus and go inside her apartment. As soon as the door closes, Pamela turns to him.

"Why are you behaving so mean to me?"

"I'm not." But he knows he is.

"You've been rude all evening. And you deliberately sat next to Miriam just to annoy me."

Since that is true he doesn't try and deny it. He sees that she's on the verge of crying. He'd rather she got angry and they could have a big blow out and he could end it.

"I think we should stop seeing each other."

"I knew it! You want to start seeing that little Jewish bitch!"

"No, I don't. But I don't like you calling her that. I just think we're not suited for one another."

"Not suited! What does that mean?"

"It means that we think differently. We want different kinds of things. You like politics, I don't. We have different hobbies, interests, and philosophies."

265

"We *do* have similar interests. I like movies and books, too."

"Different kinds of movies, different kinds of books."

"But don't you like being together? Don't you like the sex?"

He doesn't. Not any more. But he doesn't think he should tell her that.

She rushes over to him. She hugs him. Tears fill her eyes but she fights to keep them from falling.

"I got on the pill," she says. "I did it for you. Now we can do want you want."

She starts crying. She hugs him around his waist and says she loves him. She will do anything for him. Anything he wants.

He considers prying himself loose and walking out. But he feels pity for her and a less charitable emotion, too, a sense of power. He believes her when she says she will do anything for him. Such an admission appeals to him at that moment. It helps to wipe away his frustration over the conflict with Comstock. And her devotion flatters his ego, an ego that had been bruised just a little by Grabowski winning the graduate teaching award and the knowledge that he did a poor job on the JNAMCP proofs.

"All right," he says. He rubs her back. "Don't get upset."

She stops crying and asks if he wants to go into the bedroom. He nods. He knows in the back of his mind that he is making everything worse. But he ignores that voice.

They undress and he waits for her on the bed while she goes into the bathroom. When she comes back she pays special attention to him, caressing him and complimenting him and asking what he wants. She performs fellatio with an eagerness that almost embarrasses him then she agrees to be taken from behind. He's never had coitus with her in that position before and it excites him how she bends over and shows her round ass as he mounts her. His orgasm is the most powerful and satisfying that he's ever experienced with her. But when he reclines on the bed with her in his arms he feels a blot of self-disgust rise inside him. He glances over and sees that her eyes are closed. She seems to have a contented expression on her face. He wonders how she can feel that way. Her behavior was contrary to her sexual principles. Hell, his own behavior was contrary to his principles, too. And yet the Ego inside him enjoyed it.

"How well do you know Nordberg?" Dale asks.

Pamela raises her head. She looks surprised at his question. "Not that well. Why do you ask?"

"You're not friends with him?"

"We're friends but not close friends."

Dale considers her responses. She's never mentioned Nordberg in any of their conversations. But he thought they exchanged a sort of meaningful glance back at the auditorium.

She gets up and puts a record on the stereo. It's the Blondie album, *Eat to the Beat*, that he bought her a few weeks ago because he was tired of listening to her stable of female singer-songwriters. Playing it is another thing she is doing for him. He doubts that she likes the music that much.

Pamela comes back to bed and while they listen to the music she strokes his bare chest with her fingers. He now finds her attentiveness rather annoying.

He listens to the songs thinking that Deborah Harry is the sexiest singer since Linda Ronstadt. He saw her and the group perform on television a couple of times and he felt almost mesmerized by her seductive yet rather haughty performance. Her voice wasn't bad either.

"How did you like the film?" Pamela asks.

"It was okay. There is something about D.H. Lawrence that puzzles me. I've only read two of his novels but there always seem to be something underneath the surface that he is alluding to, trying to dig into, that I never fully understand."

"Have you read the novel *Women in Love?*

"Yeah, a few months ago." Dale decides not to tell Pamela about Nordberg giving him the paperback.

"Have you ever had sex with a man?"

"No, I haven't."

"Did you ever want to?"

"No."

267

"I've had sex with a woman before."

"When?"

"Two years ago I had a fling with a freshman. An experiment. It only lasted for a few months."

"Did you like it?"

"I didn't dislike it."

"Would you do it again?"

"I might if the circumstances were right. I'm not opposed to it on moral grounds."

"That's good to know."

She raises her head and glances at him. "What does that mean?"

"Just a joke."

"Are you opposed to it?"

"In theory it doesn't bother me if women have sex with one another. But I might feel differently if my girlfriend was having sex with another woman."

"Typical male."

"You seem to think that we can change human nature just by issuing political decrees. I don't think it's that simple. For better or worse people are connected to history, to nature, and to morality."

"But you believe in freedom. Freedom to do what you want."

"Yes. But freedom can't be unlimited. Otherwise it leads to excess and decadence."

"You're something of a moralist, aren't you?"

In his present position he knows how contradictory his answer sounds. "I think there is good and evil. And people ought to aspire to do good."

"Well, I believe in doing anything you want as long as it doesn't hurt anybody."

"It's not always that simple."

"It should be."

13

Monday at noon in mid-April Dale takes two letters from his regular correspondents into his room. Dale reads Will Whitaker's letter first. His friend recounts all the academic work that he's doing in the closing weeks of spring semester. He'll finish all his political science course work this semester then finish his thesis during the summer. Will says he's looking forward to Dale arriving in a month. Then he can catch up on seeing movies and indulging in passionate discussions about literature, film, and pop culture.

After Dale finishes Will's letter, he wonders if his friend has a girlfriend or even a girl on a more casual basis. Will never mentions any girls. But then Dale doesn't mention girls, either. He's never written to Will about Pamela or Miriam or even his unrequited desires for other young women like Deb Pierson, Anna Cappelletti, and the Lithe Blonde. So, maybe Will is engaging in his own sexual {mis}adventures and just isn't writing about it.

In fact, Will writes very little about any females, past or present. In one of his earlier letters, Will mentioned that he had a steady girlfriend as an undergraduate at OU. Apparently, that was his first serious romantic or sexual relationship. But she broke up with him during their senior year when she got involved with another guy. Dale wonders why Will hasn't found another girlfriend. He's an impressive guy in a lot of ways. He's not conventionally good looking, but there is nothing objectionable about him. He's not tall but he's not short. He's not athletic but he's not physically weak. Maybe some women don't care so much about those rather superficial qualities anyway. Will is perceptive, good-natured, intellectually curious, and witty. Dale thinks a lot of women would find him appealing.

Dale decides he'll have to ask Will a few questions about his romantic and sexual life when he arrives in Minneapolis. Their friendship has almost been exclusively intellectual but now he's increasingly curious about other aspects of Will's life.

He reads Teri Boswell's letter next. She quit her newspaper job in Duncan. The editor wouldn't give her a regular beat. She moved back to Galilee to stay with her former roommate until she finds another newspaper job. She's already got an interview lined up with a paper in Vinita, Oklahoma, which is located in the northeastern corner of the state. She likes the location. If she gets the job she'll be much closer to her family in Arkansas.

Enclosed in her letter are two newspaper clippings. At first, Dale thinks they were examples of her work, but when he unfolds them he sees that they are clippings from his hometown newspaper, the *Galilee Gazette*.

Both are wedding engagement stories. One announces the upcoming marriage of his old best friend, Rusty Grimes (the announcement uses Rusty's proper first name, Garth), to a young woman named Priscilla Porter. The second one is about another former close friend, Chris DeVille, and his betrothal to Dale's former girlfriend, Amanda Meeks.

It take a moment for that thought to register. He's surprised by how numb he feels. After a moment, he takes in a deep breath and a strange kind of pain surfaces. The ache is deep in his chest. He'd like to reach inside himself and rub the pain away but instead he has to stand over the desk averting his eyes away from the wedding announcements until it subsides.

After a few minutes, he looks again at the two photos. The photo featuring Chris and Amanda provokes more pain but he ignores it as he examines them, especially Amanda. He doesn't want her to look as beautiful as he remembers her. The only reason she doesn't look quite as comely as she does in his memory is because her light brown hair is no longer long but of medium length and her face looks a little plumper, indicating some weight gain. He remembers that she was often worried about her weight. But she still looks beautiful to him and staring at her image brings back a flood of memories that brings tears to his eyes.

After gazing at her photograph for several minutes and examining her facial features, the big blue eyes, the full lips and her philtrum, the pronounced indention between her upper lip and nose that he used to kiss, he forces himself to read the story. The usual info: Rex and Victoria Meeks are pleased to announce the engagement of their daughter, Amanda Elena Meeks, to Christian Brian DeVille. He scans the rest. The date for their wedding is June 21.

Dale glances one more time at the photo. Chris, his second best friend throughout high school and college, looks dapper in his suit. He smiles in a shy, almost incredulous kind of way as if he can't quite believe his good luck. Dale remembers that his old friend always liked Amanda but he never had the gumption to ask her on a real date. Dale hasn't seen either one of them since he left Galilee two years ago after his graduation from GNC. He also remembers that it was his reckless behavior during the end of his senior year that brought Chris and Amanda together. The irony is too powerfully painful for him to appreciate at that moment.

In spite of the pain, he's glad. He knows that he and Amanda could never have been happy together in spite of their love for one another. She was a pious Nazarene girl, devoted to her church, community, and God. He was rebellious and contrary and increasingly frustrated with the narrow world of Galilee and its Nazarene elite. It was much better for her to marry a good guy like Chris. He hopes he makes her happy.

He reads the other engagement announcement about his old best buddy Rusty. He hasn't seen his friend since last May when he visited Galilee for a short time and saw him before heading out to Wyoming. He hasn't heard from him since. Rusty isn't much for writing letters although he is a good writer. But he is an energetic kind of guy, always on the go, and he doesn't take time off to write letters even to a former best friend. Dale thinks he might telephone Rusty to congratulate him on his upcoming marriage.

Dale doesn't think he knows his fiancée, Priscilla Porter. The news story said she is a student at GNC but maybe she didn't attend the college when he was there. He scrutinizes her photo. She's toothsome with blonde hair and big, bright, light-colored eyes. The only thing he doesn't like about her image is her fluffy kind of hairstyle that seems to be in fashion. Rusty looks good in his photo, too. He wears a fashionable light colored casual suit and sports long but well-groomed reddish hair and a neat beard. It looks like he's filled out, too. He was always tall and athletic but now he looks bigger in the chest and shoulders.

Dale paces the room, thinking about his two old best friends and their upcoming marriages. He's happy for them. But thinking of Amanda makes him feel dissatisfied with his own life. He admired her all through high school and when he finally started dating her steady in college his infatuation turned into a deep and enduring love. In spite of his satirical sense of humor, he had a romantic temperament and for the two years he dated her she fulfilled his deepest romantic ideals.

How different it is now! He has a more overt sex life but in spite of the sensual pleasure he indulges in he feels it is nothing in comparison to the romantic ecstasy that he experienced from just holding her hand or looking into her eyes.

He knows he isn't a hedonist or a sensualist or any of

272

those superficially appealing things that the current culture celebrates. He wishes he were a sybarite. He wishes he could dive into the pool of sensation and pleasure and never surface. But there is something inside him that warns him about sensual abandonment. He suddenly feels a searing emotion, one of shame and guilt. He realizes that his behavior with Pamela Partridge is contrary to his ideals. He understands that he is debasing himself and exploiting her. Even if she doesn't think she is being exploited, even if she thinks women can be as sexually focused and emotionally detached as men, he doesn't think that is true. And even if it is true, he thinks it's wrong. He feels ashamed of himself for enjoying his appetites and not feeling at a deeper level. He thinks there is something spiritually warped about indulging in physical intimacy without emotional intimacy. Thinking of Amanda makes him realize with a pang close to agony that there is something deeper and more fulfilling than mere sex. And that something is love.

Dale takes the camera-ready copy and sizes it up on the layout sheet on the light table. Satisfied that the margins are straight, he presses his fingers against the single sheet of photosensitive paper and its waxed back sticks to the paper. He checks to make sure the copy, the first page of a short story, is still straight then does another page. Then another.

He enjoys creating the layout and performing paste-up. He likes the tactile quality of the chore. In fact, this is the part of editing the literary magazine that he relishes the most. He's giving *The Owen Wister Review* a visual identity, a graphic personality. The poems, stories, drawings, and photos are the primary purpose for the magazine, of course, but the way it is visually presented is important, too.

He's working on the last few pages of the layout. It's late, around ten at night, and no one is present in the Mass Communications Department or the photography lab where the light table is located. Dale asked Dr. Holznagle for permission to use the light table and the professor agreed and even gave him a key to the outer room. Dale was surprised that Holznagle had been so agreeable. Dale worried that after his conflict with Comstock all the mass comm professors would ostracize him. But that didn't happen. Dale gets the impression that most of the faculty has experience with Comstock's unreasonable behavior.

Comstock has ceased chasing Dale into the hallway to berate him about the *Buffalo Quotidians* and his poor work with proofing the *JNAMCP*. In fact, when Dale passed his half-open door and glanced in he saw the professor staring intently at student news stories and Comstock didn't even look up.

Just the same, Dale knows Comstock is the kind of man who keeps a grudge. He knows the professor will try and block the awarding of his degree. Dale still has to give Comstock his ten to sixteen page research paper to fulfill the academic requirements for his independent study course. However, Comstock no longer communicates directly with him. All information is relayed by notes. Dale noticed that Comstock's script was both precise and scraggly. It gives the impression that the writer is concentrating mightily to make sure his written words are legible and yet the extra pressure of the hand results in thick, unattractive images.

Dale also responds by written message. Comstock has agreed that the subject of Dale's paper will be an evaluation of other college newspapers in the Rocky Mountain region. Dale will describe the organization, structure, and other basic characteristics of the campus newspapers and compare and contrast them to the University of Wyoming. Dr. Schneider gave him permission to use the department's long distance account to call the different college newspapers and talk to the managing editor and advisor if the paper has one; more and more college publications don't have faculty advisers. Wyoming doesn't. Neither *The Branding Iron* nor *The Owen Wister Review* has faculty advisers. A fact, no doubt, that irritates Comstock. Dale thinks that maybe the reason Comstock has such a narrow-minded and resentful attitude toward student publications is that he isn't an adviser to anything.

Dale thinks there is another reason, a more complicated, psychological one, as to why Comstock is so narrow-minded. Dale theorizes Comstock is afraid of open communication; that he is threatened and disturbed by certain ideas. Why that is the case, he doesn't know. It probably has to do with how he was raised, his early experiences, his family dynamics, as well as other social and psychological factors. Comstock doesn't seem to be an especially religious man so his objections to free expression and open inquiry aren't due to religious scruples like some of the people Dale knew back in Galilee.

The few biographical facts that Dale discovered about Comstock weren't very revealing. Comstock grew up on a ranch outside Worland, a town near the Big Horn Mountain range in northern Wyoming. Comstock graduated from the University of Wyoming with a degree in journalism in 1950. He worked as a reporter and editor for newspapers in Wyoming and Montana for ten years. He then returned to Laramie to get his master's in mass communications with a concentration in newspaper writing and editing. Upon receiving his master's he got a job as a lecturer in the department, then was hired for a tenure-track position. Seven years later Comstock made tenure and was promoted to associate professor. At present he is the only native Wyomingite in the department. He's also the professor with the longest tenure. He's taught at Wyoming for twenty years now. Since he doesn't possess a doctorate, it's unlikely he'll receive another promotion. He'll never make full professor.

All this information came from Wagstaff, the only faculty member that Dale knew well enough to ask information about departmental matters. Wagstaff revealed a few other interesting facts about departmental politics. Four of the seven professors had Ph.D.s: Wagstaff, Schneider, Holznagle (Grabowski's adviser), and Offenbach (Deb's adviser; he taught the advertising and public relations courses). The other three professors only had M.A.'s: Comstock, Jerry Sibelius (who taught radio courses and supervised KUWR), and Jim Swerling (who taught journalism writing, feature writing as well as news writing). Dale had met all the professors at a faculty retreat last fall. Of all the men present, he liked Swerling the best. He found out that Swerling grew up in Oklahoma and even lived for a while in Buffalo City. That fact probably explained why Swerling grinned at him when they encountered each other in the department hallway the morning of the *Buffalo Quotidians* publication.

Because Dale's concentration is in film studies, he's never taken a class taught by Swerling. Dale likes him although they have only interacted a few times. Swerling is a tall, lean man in his late thirties and he has a laconic way of speaking with a Southwestern twang. But even if Swerling became a supporter or an ally he couldn't help Dale much. Swerling, a junior faculty member, doesn't have tenure and therefore has little influence in the department.

Dale finishes the last double page spread. He examines it. The title, *The Owen Wister Review*, is straight. The blacked out space for the photograph is centered properly. The issue number and date is correct. He's done.

Tomorrow he'll take the completed layout to the university printing press. The press run isn't large, just two thousand copies, one sixth of the student body. A lot of people don't really care about reading a literary magazine even if they are paying for it with their student fees. But there is a small group of committed literary types who look forward to its appearance. Among that cadre are some of his adversaries. But while evaluating their submissions, Dale tried to be objective. So in the end, he accepted Spencer Dribble's rather ponderous essay and Marsha Martin's poem. Neither work was exceptional; in fact, Dale thought they bordered on the mediocre. But the prose editors, Virgil Drury and Lee Garth, recommended submission #13 (they evaluated the manuscripts without authors' names on them) and Dale thought Dribble's essay was competent enough to print. The OWR poetry editors, Millie Jensen and Betsy Shore, okayed poetry submission #26 and Dale didn't veto their pick even when he found out the poem's author was Marsha Martin.

Two of Miriam's poems were selected, too. One of Grabowski's photos. And Dale's short story, *Marco Polo Is Leaving Town*, was picked. Lee and Virgil didn't know it was his story and he didn't tell them until they had selected it. He knew it wasn't exactly kosher to have a story printed in the same magazine he edited, but it was only a college literary magazine (although they received submissions from non-students including some previously published authors around the Rocky Mountain region). Besides he liked the story, thought it one of the better ones, and he justified his egotism by thinking of it as payment for all the hard work he put in.

Dale hears the door creak. He'd left it open a crack and somebody must have noticed. He glances over and sees the face of Neil Nordberg peering into the room. Nordberg grins but his cool blue eyes indicate a less friendly attitude.

"Working late on the *OWR*, I take it?"

"Yeah. I just finished the layout."

"As always, I'm impressed with your many talents. My reservations about you becoming editor were unfounded after all."

"What reservations? You said you voted for me."

"I did. But I considered not voting for you."

"Why?"

"The same reason Pamela Partridge almost didn't vote for you. Because you don't have enough socio-political awareness."

"Yeah, I once told her that I was aware of my lack of political awareness. So I guess that means I'm not completely unaware after all."

"Well put. Of course, we both ended up voting for you for similar reasons."

Dale is growing annoyed with Nordberg. He feels an urge to slap his smirking face with the pica pole. But since Nordberg might like that, he doesn't.

"Do you want to know what those reasons were?" Nordberg asks.

277

"Not especially."

"Well, let's say that she succeeded where I failed."

"That's because she has different and more desirable equipment than you have."

"Perhaps Pamela and I aren't as different as you think."

Dale doesn't answer. He's rolling that assertion in his mind. He recalls how Nordberg and Pamela looked at each other two weeks ago at the screening of *Women in Love*.

"At least I had a reason to embarrass you by stealing those *BIs*. I don't know what Pamela's reason was."

"I don't believe you."

"She was on the *committee*, too. Along with me, Spencer Dribble, Marsha Martin, Patti Montag, and Robert Baugh. But don't worry. We won't reconvene the committee to interfere with the *OWR*. I don't suppose you'll have anything in the magazine anyway."

"You know, Nordberg, you make a really good Quisling."

Nordberg's insinuating smile vanishes. He's well read. He knows whom Dale is referring to. Because of his ethnic background, it's an accurately shot insult and Dale notices it hits Nordberg straight in his traitorous heart.

"Fuck you," Nordberg hisses.

"No, fuck you, Nordberg. And I mean that in the worst possible way."

Nordberg slams the door shut. Dale hears his footsteps for a moment then they fade into the almost eerie silence of the still department.

Dale suddenly feels a jolt of anger. He almost wants to chase down Nordberg and punch his smug face. But he realizes that he's not only furious with Nordberg. He's even angrier with Pamela, his erstwhile girlfriend.

He brings the *OWR* layout home and notices that Grabowski isn't in. It's almost eleven, a half-hour past his roommate's usual bedtime, so he wonders where he is. Probably at some girl's place although Grabowski usually brings his chicks to their place. Not so much lately. Perhaps Grabowski has run through all the eligible chicks in Laramie. It doesn't matter; Dale's not interested in thinking about his libidinous roommate. In fact, he thinks his behavior in that department really isn't much better than Gary's.

Dale, still vexed, tries to calm down by pacing in the living room. He's too agitated. Maybe Nordberg was lying. But he doesn't think so. He remembers asking Pamela whether she joined in with the CSDS gang and she denied it. He believed her because she was obviously an accomplished liar and because he wanted to believe her. Thinking of her lie almost produces a fury inside him.

Part of his anger is directed at his own behavior. For two weeks, four weekend encounters, he's gone along with their warped relationship. In fact, he enjoyed it in a perverse way. It reminded him of the time in high school when his girlfriend, Wendy Wainwright, became enamored with him. He hadn't understood her passion and because of his naiveté and inexperience he didn't take advantage of her. Part of his reluctance to sexually exploit her feelings was the social mores of their hometown. Galilee was a conservative, religious place, and even though Wendy wasn't a Nazarene, she was a religious girl in her own way. He didn't want to hurt her even if he had enough callousness to do it.

But now he thinks he is developing a kind of callousness. He cares more about his sexual appetite than he does for someone's feelings. Even though from the beginning Pamela indicated that they were undertaking a frankly sexual affair with no strings attached he doubts that she really, deep down, believed that.

Therefore, he thinks he's more responsible, more to blame, than she is. He doesn't want to become some callous bastard who sexually exploits women. According to Pamela that wasn't possible nowadays. Women were capable of engaging in sexual adventures just like men. But he doesn't believe that. It is more socio-political rhetoric. Men and women are different; they

279

have somewhat different sexual natures. When it comes down to a sexual contest with no deeper feelings involved, where the woman has more desire for the man than he does for her, then the woman would lose. It sort of amazes him that an intelligent young woman like Pamela doesn't understand that. The way a woman didn't lose was when she acknowledged her sexual difference, accepted that she had a deeper emotional nature than a man, and used her sexual attraction to exact a commitment from him. That approach might not work in the end either but it gives her more protection than the "equality" approach.

Ever since he read about Amanda's engagement, Dale became determined to end his affair with Pamela. But now knowing she lied to him gives him an extra incentive.

He walks out of the townhouse and strides two blocks over to Pamela's apartment. It's a weeknight and late but he can't wait. He walks up to her door and knocks. She answers the door.

"Dale, why are you here?"

"Can I come in?"

She nods and he walks inside. He notices she's not dressed for bed. She's wearing her usual attire: jeans, an outdoor shirt, but no Timberland hiking boots. She's taken them off and instead is wearing a pair of blue sneakers.

She looks at him in an inquiring way. He's never just showed up out of the blue. He hesitates only a moment.

"When you told me that you had nothing to do with stealing the newspapers with my movie review in it, you were lying weren't you?"

Her blue eyes don't blink. She stares at him without any guile, which almost makes him doubt the truth. But he continues to stare at her and after a few moments her eyes flicker away from his.

"Yes, I lied."

"Why did you do that?"

"Lie or steal papers?"

"Both, I guess. But let's start with the lie."

She walks over to the small bookcase and strums her fingers along the spines of the books.

"I didn't want you to get angry with me."

"But you must have known that I would find out eventually that you were with them."

"Maybe not. If no one told how would you find out?"

"Well, someone told."

"Let me guess. Neil?"

Dale nods. "Now tell me why you did it."

"All of us had been drinking at a pub. We started talking about things, people, the BI. Spencer mentioned how he hated your reviews. Marsha didn't like them either but her real motive was that she heard your radio show making fun of her father. Robert and Patti joined in. But the real instigator was Neil Nordberg. He was sitting not far away, overheard us, and came over and said he had an idea. We should steal some BIs and hold them ransom until they fired you. Everyone thought that was funny."

"Did you think that was funny?"

"Yes, I laughed too. But I was half drunk and I didn't know you well then."

Dale shakes his head. It's one of those revelations that surprises him: that people talk about him, dislike something he does so much that they want to hurt him. Knowing that he was considered an object of scorn to some people wounds his ego.

Pamela walks over to him and touches his arm. "That was last semester when I didn't know you well. When I didn't care for you."

"If you really cared about me then you would want to understand me."

"But I do want to understand you."

"You don't like my way of thinking, do you?"

"Not especially."

"We disagree about a lot of things. That is, if we talked about them in any depth."

"Maybe."

"So what is the point of all of this?"

"The point of us? It's to be together. To enjoy each other."

"That's not enough anymore."

"So now you want to end it? Because you're feelings are hurt? Because I don't like your damn movie reviews?"

"It's more than that."

"You're just like a man. I thought you might be different. But when things don't go your way, then you want to quit. I've been giving you everything you want, haven't I?"

"And that bothers me, too. It's not healthy." She stares at him in an offended way. "I mean, it's not healthy psychologically. Spiritually."

"What the hell does that mean! If you like it, then what's wrong with it?"

"Because it's not based on love."

"But I love *you*. You're the one that doesn't love."

"That's partly right. And that's why it's unhealthy."

Pamela starts to pace the room. She thrusts her hands into her hair. But this time she doesn't start crying.

"I don't know what else you want! You want more sex? Less sex? Different kinds of sex?"

"That's part of the problem. Everything shouldn't be based on sex."

She stops and glares at him. "That's what I *want*! You're the one who wants to exploit me. You've made me betray my principles. You've made me act like a stupid bitch. Getting jealous over a Jewish twat like *Mimi!*"

"I warned you before about talking that way about Miriam."

"And what are you going to do about it? Beat me? That's what men do when they start losing an argument."

Dale waves his hand at her. He starts walking to her door. Pamela rushes over to him, and grabs his arm.

"Don't go. I'm sorry I said that. But you're hurting me. Whatever you want, I'll give it to you."

"I want to end it."

She shoves his arm away and begins crying, almost wailing.

She reaches for her hair again and this time starts pulling it. He goes over to her and grabs her and tells her to stop acting crazy.

"You're driving *me* crazy!" she wails. "Why don't you love me?"

"I'm sorry, Pamela. I shouldn't have let this go on for so long. It's my fault."

She breaks away from his grasp. "Go then! Get the hell out! You're just another disgusting man. It was all a game. I didn't love you. You didn't make me love you!"

He goes over to the door and opens it.

"You're nothing special! Just another prick! I had more orgasms with *Barbara* than I did with you!"

He leaves but doesn't slam the door shut. He's not angry. He just wants to get away.

From behind her door, he hears her shrieking. After three strides, the noise fades away.

14

Sunday evening in early May and Dale sits at the editing machine cutting, splicing, and taping his 8 mm epic. Even with the additional footage he shot, the film clocks in only at two minutes and twelve seconds. However, the mini-film has a lot of edits. It's taking longer than he anticipated and tomorrow evening is Premier Night for the Film Directing class. He finishes the last edit and puts the film on the edit wheel and rewinds it. It's a very short film but all rolled up on the reel it looks deceptively long.

He worried all week that the second part of his movie wouldn't be processed in time. Every day he checked his mailbox. He knew he was cutting it close sending the film in when he did, but he didn't think of an idea to embellish his original film until after the Comstock controversy. But it looks like it's going to work out. The processed film arrived Friday and he started editing it over the weekend. He took time off, of course, to see the last two campus movies. He sat with Miriam and the Von Goebbels brothers. Friday they watched *Carnal Knowledge*, an early '70s Mike Nichols film. Basically, the film was all about sex. There wasn't much nudity (although Ann-Margret, an actress he always found appealing, made an appearance in the buff) but the characters, especially the ones played by Jack Nicholson and Art Garfunkel, expressed themselves in graphic terms. More than once, Dale glanced over to Miriam to get her reaction. She didn't seem perturbed.

On Saturday, they watched *Butch Cassidy and the Sundance Kid*, a film that Dale had originally seen at the drive-in with his mother and sister, back when his mother still took them to movies. His mother began to dislike seeing movies in the late '60s because of the explicit violence, sex, nudity, and profanity. But he remembered her liking *Butch*. On a second viewing, Dale still liked it even though he thought the film had such a late '60s sensibility that the western setting, in spite of the comedic intentions, seemed oddly incongruous at times.

Miriam didn't ask why Pamela wasn't sitting with them. In fact, Miriam didn't ask about her at all and Dale told her nothing. But when Miriam saw him walking by himself over to her and the Von Goebbels brothers she smiled one of her delighted broad smiles.

Dale hasn't heard anything from Pamela. She hasn't called; he hasn't called her. The encounter was over and it wasn't either brief or one to remember. He feels ashamed of himself for what he did. He thinks he let the whole thing get out of hand. His Nazarene friends would be shocked if they knew about his behavior. When he thinks about it, he feels rather astonished with himself, too.

But he doesn't completely regret the affair with Pamela. He thinks he learned something about himself, sex, and maybe even women. He isn't sure how representative Pamela is as a modern woman, but he knows now that the implied offer of no-strings sex isn't always made with a full understanding of the consequences. He also learned that people can think one thing and feel another. Of course, he knew that already but not in a sexual context.

As for departmental matters, Comstock and he were still communicating through written missives. Dale turned in his independent study paper last week. He hasn't heard anything from Comstock. The paper was boring to write but he got it done. He is also finishing up his thesis, an analysis on Billy

Wilder's major films, including *Sunset Boulevard* and *Ace in the Hole*. He feels more motivated by that kind of writing and he thinks his thesis has some perceptive points in it.

He and his staff got the print run for the *Owen Wister Review* a week ago and put copies in all the bins and kiosks on campus. When he last checked, all copies of the literary magazine were gone. He received some compliments from his friends, a few acquaintances, and some professors. Dr. Woolfson, the dean of student services, complimented him as had Professor Wilkins.

The last week of classes start tomorrow and all he has left to do is hand his thesis to Wagstaff and show his mini-movie at the Film Premiere Monday night. He doesn't have any final exams so he can leave Laramie anytime after that. In his last letter to Will, he estimated he would arrive in Minneapolis in mid-May. He will call once he gets to Oklahoma and give him more specific travel plans. He is going to drive down to Oklahoma first and see his parents, grandparents, sister, and half brother. He won't stay long, however. He no longer thinks of Galilee as his home. It will always be his hometown but it is no longer his home.

His film all finished, Dale puts the reel into the protective case, turns off the lights to the editing room, and walks out of the basement of Gowdy Hall. He doesn't feel like Cecil B. DeMille or Billy Wilder but he thinks he's accomplished an important goal.

Dale walks into the Mass Communication Department office and checks his mailbox. He notices a folder containing clips of his movie reviews and his independent studies paper sticking out in his slot. He grabs the folder and on his way to his office he notices that the research paper is covered in circles of red ink. He sits down and flips through the twelve pages. Every page has red circles on it. When he looks more closely, he sees that certain words are circled. Pronouns. At first glance, he doesn't know what he's done wrong.

But Comstock apparently thinks he did something seriously

wrong. On the last page there are no comments, only a grade: F.

Dale hardly believes it. He scans the paper again. Dozens of sentences have a red circle over the words "they" and "their."

He doesn't understand. He scrutinizes every page. Red circles are everywhere. There are a few other mistakes; a couple of typos, a misplaced apostrophe, two misspelling of words, but the vast majority of circles are around those two pronouns.

Dale knows he shouldn't be surprised but he is. He didn't think that even Comstock could be so petty and vindictive. Nevertheless, he wants to know what those red circles mean.

On the way to Comstock's office he notices the office door is slightly ajar. Even though it is eight in the morning, Comstock is in. He's always in. For a brief moment, Dale feels a touch of sympathy for the professor. He remembers what Pamela told him many months ago: that he had a troubled marriage. That partly explains his long office hours, he guesses. But that momentary sympathy evaporates when he thinks about the professor's meanness.

Dale knocks on the door. Before Comstock gives permission to enter, Dale comes in. This is the first time they have met face to face since the *JNAMCP* fiasco.

Dale sees that Comstock is not pleased to see him. Dale walks over to his desk and shows the professor the paper. He asks what all the red circles mean.

"I'm not surprised that you haven't figured that out. You obviously aren't proficient with the AP style-book."

"I know what it is," Dale says. "I sometimes referred to it when I worked at the newspaper."

"That is not apparent from your term paper."

"Professor Comstock, what do these circles mean?"

"Errors, my boy. Errors."

"What kind of errors?"

"Errors in pronoun usage. You are supposed to refer to newspapers not in the plural but in the singular."

Dale examines his paper. He notices that the circled pronouns are plural. Instead of calling *The Branding Iron* "it" he referred to it as "they." He glances at Comstock, who has not turned his way but has a rare small smile on his leathery face. Dale grabs the AP style-book from off Comstock's desk and looks up the section on pronoun usage. Comstock is right. Newspapers should be referred to in the singular.

"Okay, I made a mistake. But it's essentially the same mistake throughout the paper. And it's an error that really doesn't result in confusion. I mean, a lot of people misuse pronouns like that."

"Not a responsible journalist."

"So that's the reason for the F? Because I made one mistake about AP usage of pronouns?"

"It's just not one mistake. It's dozens of mistakes!"

"Not really. It's one error that's repeated throughout the paper."

"Yes, repeated over and over."

"But isn't that like misspelling one word. Even if a writer uses that word a dozen times in the story it's essentially the same error."

Comstock grabs the paper from Dale's hand. He starts counting the red circles. He counts six on the first page. He flips the page and counts five more. He continues the process until he comes to the end.

"I count fifty-six errors. How can I not fail a paper with that many mistakes!"

Dale knows it's no use. Comstock, the curmudgeon, the stickler, the narrow-minded censor and puritanical prose-master, will never admit that his real motive is vindictiveness. Dale defied him by writing satires and getting them printed in a publication that Comstock considers his intellectual property even though he has no official authority over it. Dale did not proofread the two hundred and fifty pages of the *JNAMCP* with due diligence even though a professional proofreader would have found it difficult to complete the task in the time frame he had. But worse of all, Dale did not bow to Comstock's egotism and megalomania. He did not treat the silly man with deference, did not try to emulate Comstock's paranoid fear of creative expression.

"Is there anything else I can do for you?" Comstock says in a voice that isn't so much scornful as gloating.

Dale looks down at the professor. He's looking away. Comstock hasn't turned his bleary green eyes to him at all during their conversation.

"I do have one additional question."

"What is that?"

"Why are you such a miserable, narrow-minded bastard?"

Comstock gives no indication that he heard the question. He stares straight ahead, his beaky nose dominating his profile. Dale walks out of his office without giving the professor a glance. Now he's glad he made that change to his film.

That afternoon Dale goes into *The Branding Iron* newsroom to hand in his next-to-last movie review. With this review and the last one he will write for the Friday paper the total number of reviews he wrote during the two semesters on the newspaper is fifty-two.

He enjoyed seeing the movies and writing the reviews. It took quite a bit of time. With practice, he got better and faster. He wrote this next to last review, about *My Brilliant Career*, in just twenty-two minutes, perhaps his personal best. He'll try to break that record Thursday when he reviews *American Gigolo*.

Felicia Fernandez is at her desk. After handing in his review of *My Brilliant Career* (he mostly liked the movie; it was about an Australian girl in the 1920s who rejects a suitor in order to pursue a writing career and live as an independent woman) to the copy editor, he goes over to Felicia to say hello.

"Did you hear about the big story?" Felicia asks.

"No."

"Three students were found guilty of trying to stuff the ballot boxes during the student council elections two weeks ago."

"Who found them guilty?"

"The student council ethics committee. Now the students will have to appear before an administration disciplinary committee."

"Who are the three students?"

"Well," Felicia says with an embarrassed wince, "you know one of them. Pamela Partridge."

"Pamela? Really?"

"Yes, she was one of the three." Felicia gives the names of the other two perpetrators, a guy and a girl that he doesn't know.

"What's going to happen to her?"

"I don't know. She'll find out Wednesday when she meets with Dean Parsons and the other committee members. But it might be serious."

"How serious?"

"Since they were caught before anything happened, maybe not too serious. Didn't you read about this two weeks ago?"

Dale shakes his head no. He's been so busy of late that he hasn't read much of the campus newspaper. No one told him about it either. Not even Nordberg.

Felicia gets a telephone call and Dale signals to her that he's leaving. But before he goes, he walks into the morgue where past issues of the paper are filed. He finds the newspaper of April 23rd and flips through its pages until he finds the story on page three of the eight-page paper. He quickly reads the six paragraphs. It recounts mostly what Felicia told him: Pamela and two other students were caught attempting to stuff the ballot box in Tuesday's student council elections. They were carrying dozens of previously filled out ballots. They hid them under their clothes and appeared at the polling places just before the election period was to end. When they were caught all three claimed it was a joke. They weren't going to stuff the ballot boxes but since all the ballots had been filled in for the same candidates, in particular, the female candidate for president, a junior named Barbara Hughes, they were reported to the administration and the student council ethics committee.

He's surprised that Pamela would pull such a stupid stunt. She's more intelligent than that. But he realizes it's not a question of intelligence as much as character. He thinks about the date of the misbehavior. He broke up with her Sunday night. The election was Tuesday. He doesn't think there is a connection.

Then he thinks about the name Barbara Hughes. He realizes that she is the girl Pamela occasionally mentioned, once telling him that she was a close friend. But how close? As he remembers what Pamela screamed at him as he left her apartment, how she had more orgasms with *Barbara* than with him, he understands that she must be the girl that Pamela had a fling with a three years before. That idea is weird enough but then he recalls that the guy who works at the Casper newspaper is named Ward Hughes. Are Barbara and Ward related? Brother and sister? If so, Pamela's affairs with them (but at least they occured at different times) were unwholesomely semi-incestuous and he is glad that he ended the affair with Pamela before it got even more perverse.

He leaves the paper's morgue and walks out of the newsroom. He wonders how Pamela is reacting to the news that she'll have to face the administration's disciplinary committee. The whole debacle must be keenly embarrassing to her. He wonders if he should contact her. He thinks not. Even though he wants nothing more to do with her, he hopes nothing severe happens to her. He knows from recent experience what it is like to get into trouble and it's no fun.

Then he stops in his tracks and thinks: if that's true then why am I risking more trouble with my film?

That evening at 7:30, Dale joins six other students and several guests, including the ones he invited, Edward Darby, Deb Pierson, and Miriam, and two faculty members, Dr. Wagstaff and Professor Sibelius, as they sit in the film lab's screening room to watch the student director's final cut.

The films will be shown according to a pre-arranged order.

Dale's film will be shown last.

The screening room is fairly small and the forty people take up nearly half of the seats. Dale sits in the back row next to Darby and Miriam. Not far away, Deb and Wagstaff recline in their theatre-style seats.

For whatever reason, Dale isn't especially nervous. He's seen his final cut only once but he worked on the film for ten hours straight so he knows every scene. Instead of worrying that something will go wrong like a splice might tear or the film will get stuck in the lens carriage and melt into a bubble of goo on-screen, he leans back in an almost indifferent manner, a fatalistic calm settling over him.

The projectionist starts the first film. It's entitled "Frat Feud." The film begins with a shot of a second floor window at a fraternity house. The camera zooms in and six frat boys appear and start to pillow fight. Dale quickly gets the idea. It's a parody of the sorority sisters' pillow fight in *Animal House*. But instead of attractive girls, the combatants are frat boys dressed in boxer shorts and T-shirts, except for the star who only wears jockey shorts. The idea is sort of funny except that after the first few seconds it's obvious that the camera operator is more interested in the handsome star rather than the comedy of frat boys pillow fighting like girls.

Dale glances down a row where the film's director, Russell Burke, sits. Dale recognizes Burke as the guy who was with Nordberg at the screening of *Women In Love*. Burke still looks like a younger version of Oliver Reed. Burke is sitting with the star of his production, the handsome young frat boy. Burke and the star exchange grins.

Well, Dale thinks, it could be weirder. Burke could have filmed a nude wrestling scene like the one in *Women in Love*.

The second film, "Clowning Around," is more convention-al. It's simply a film of pantomime, with two clowns acting like Marcel Marceau. The mimic each other skillfully but the film doesn't have much cinematic inventiveness.

The third film is Von Goebbels brothers production. Dale

glances down to the first row where Mark and Matt sit. Their posture is erect and at full attention. The film starts with the title, *Blowing Up*. Dale glances at Wagstaff. He has a grin on his face, no doubt thinking the film is a parody of Antonioni's 1966 masterpiece, *Blow-Up*. But it's not. The film shows a young man, dressed all in white – pants, shirt, jacket, Panama hat – running through a junkyard. Another young man, dressed completely in black, is pursuing him. There's not a lot of cutting, just the camera following the two young men from a middle distance. Dale plays the fleeing character. (He reluctantly agreed to play the Young Man in White to return the favor of Mark and Matt appearing in his film.)

Dale's glad that his face isn't shown. Mostly he's just a white figure running past the twisted iron and metal debris and rusting hulks of old cars. But apparently a few people recognize his form. He sees Deb and Wagstaff turn his way with small smiles on their faces. Miriam and Darby give him a quick, amused look, too.

The Man in White races out of the junkyard toward a dark sedan in an open field. He jumps inside the car and tries to start it. Meanwhile the Man in Black raises a bazooka (a weapon that the Man in Black hadn't been carrying previously) and takes aim. A moment later, the dark sedan explodes.

The film has an unsynchronized soundtrack but the explosion is loud and sounds authentic even if it is coming from a tape. Everyone in the audience jumps at the explosion. The Von Goebbels brothers raise their hands and cheer. The explosion is a real one. Fire bursts out of the car's windows, glass shatters, and the driver, obviously a dummy, is engulfed in flames.

The violent end to the film agitates the audience. Dale hears them murmuring. He can't tell if it's positive murmuring or negative. Miriam leans over and whispers, "I'm glad you survived that."

The audience grows silent as the next three films are shown. Nothing especially interesting. Just short films about campus life: a clumsy comedy set in one of the student cafeterias; a backstage drama set in the wings of the university stage; and a film about baseball with unconvincing parallels between a real game and a Mighty Casey who strikes out during his team's last at bats.

Then Dale's film, entitled *The Sniper*, starts.

FADE IN:

INT. - ROOM. DAY.

A medium shot of a man seen obliquely from the side. He wears dark trousers and a blue, brown, and white flannel shirt with red suspenders. A brown fedora covers his head. He carries a rifle case. He walks into a room.

CUT TO:

EXT. - CITY STREET. DAY.

A dark Lincoln Townhouse convertible drives slowly down a city street. Sitting inside the car are the driver, wearing a navy blue business suit and sunglasses, a woman wearing a pink skirt and jacket and a pillbox hat, and a man wearing a black business suit. A United States flag flies from the radio antenna at the front of the car.

CUT TO:

INT. - ROOM. DAY.

The man peers out the window then attaches a silencer to the end of the rifle's barrel.

CUT TO:

EXT. - CITY STREET. DAY.

The convertible cruises down the street. The man and the woman in the backseat smile and wave. In the background are three people waving back.

CUT TO:

INT. - ROOM. DAY.

The man hoists the rifle and presses the stock against his right shoulder. He moves the tip of the rifle barrel out of the open window and takes aim.

CUT TO:

EXT. - CITY STREET. DAY.

A briefer shot of the man and the woman waving. A park is in the background. A few people are seen at a distance in the park.

CUT TO:

INT. - ROOM. DAY.

A close-up of a finger squeezing the trigger of the rifle.

CUT TO:

EXT. - PARK. DAY.

A medium shot of a brown gopher (obviously fake) being shot. A bloody explosion rips a gaping hole in the gopher's chest and it topples over.

CUT TO:

INT. - ROOM. DAY.

The sniper shakes his head in frustration and readjusts his aim by moving the rifle to his right.

CUT TO:

EXT. - CITY STREET. DAY.

The convertible continues to cruise down the street with the man and woman waving and smiling.

CUT TO:

INT. - ROOM. DAY.

Close-up of finger pulling the rifle's trigger.

CUT TO:

EXT. - PARK. DAY.

A gray squirrel (obviously fake) clinging to a tree trunk is shot. A bloody hole appears in its fur on its back. The squirrel falls off the tree.

CUT TO:

INT. - ROOM. DAY.

The sniper tightens his shoulders in frustration. He aims again.

CUT TO:

EXT. - CITY STREET.

The convertible moving down the street with the man and woman waving and smiling.

CUT TO:

INT. - ROOM. DAY.

Close-up of the finger squeezing the rifle's trigger.

CUT TO:

EXT. - CITY STREET.

A yellow bird (fake) is perched on a tree branch. A red hole appears in its feathery belly. The bird clumsily falls from the tree branch.

CUT TO:

INT. - ROOM. DAY.

The sniper shakes his rifle in frustration. His begins to remove his hat.

CUT TO:

EXT. - CITY STREET. DAY.

The rear of the convertible as it drives away. The man and woman share a laugh.

CUT TO:

INT. - ROOM. DAY.

A close-up of the sniper's face as he turns to face the camera.

The leathery, wrinkled middle-aged face is livid with anger.

CUT TO:

BLACK BACKGROUND.

Credits in white appear on the screen: Starring Edward Darby, Miriam Morgenstern, Mark Von Goebbels, Matt Von Goebbels, Virgil Drury, Lee Garth, Millicent Jansen, and Betsy Shore.

Screen goes totally black for a second then in white letters: Special Guest Star Cyrus Comstock. Written and Directed by Dale Smith. An Oswald Production.

When the film ends no one claps. In fact, there is no sound audible at all but he whirring of the projector for three seconds. Then Miriam laughs. Mark and Matt Von Goebbels begin to clap. Miriam joins in. A few more people begin clapping, too. The overhead lights in the studio come on.

Several people turn and stare at Dale. When they see he is wearing a blue, brown, and white flannel shirt with red suspenders Miriam and Darby in particular guffaw. Dale nods to acknowledge their mirth but he's aware that several other people, including Professor Wagstaff and Deb Pierson, are gazing in astonishment at him.

Wagstaff stands up and says, "Let's give all our student directors a hand."

He starts applauding and the rest of the audience does the same. People rise from their seats. The student directors talk with their friends, answer questions from other directors and audience members.

"Dale, how did you ever convince Professor Comstock to appear in your movie?" Miriam asks, a big smile still on her face.

"I didn't."

Miriam looks puzzled. Before Dale can explain Ed Darby walks by.

"I'm glad Comstock isn't my advisor," he says with a wry grin.

Dale returns a wry grin and watches as Darby leaves the screening room. The Von Goebbels brothers appear and they and Dale and Miriam converse for a few minutes. Dale compliments the brothers on their excellent special effects not only in his film but especially in their disaster epic. The brothers agreeably nod. Matt says they are going to the campus pub to celebrate and asks if Dale wants to join them. Dale tells them he'll stop by later. More congratulations are exchanged and Miriam, Matt and Mark take their leave.

Deb walks by and says she enjoyed watching his film but she says it in a more polite way than a sincere way. Dale's sure she finds the inclusion of Comstock to be in poor taste.

Dale sees Wagstaff is still in the screening room talking to Burke and his Star. When those two leave, Dale walks over to him.

"I wish Professor Comstock could have been here," Dale says. "I sent him an invitation."

"Did you really?" asks Wagstaff.

"Yes. But once again the professor demonstrates his anti-art attitude."

"Art? Only in the most generous of terms."

"You didn't like the movie?"

Wagstaff grins in spite of himself. "In my official capacity as a member of the faculty I have to say no. But in an unofficial role as movie watcher, I enjoyed it very much."

When Dale arrives home an hour later he finds Grabowski stretched out on the couch watching television. Just like his roommate to prefer the boob tube to watching a movie, even if the movie was a student made one.

"What's up?" Dale asks.

"S.O.S." Grabowski replies.

Dale thinks he will miss Grabowski's gift for gab. He walks over to the couch and glances at the TV to see what his roommate is watching so avidly. Is it a sporting event? No. It's it an inane sitcom? No. Instead, he's watching something vaguely educational, the PBS science show *Nova*.

Dale is almost amazed. Grabowski actually feeding his brain instead of his belly (or libido). Dale watches some of the show. It's about Eskimos hunting whales and a group of environmentalists trying to dissuade them of that ancient but ecologically disruptive act. He thinks the show is a little boring. Certainly no *Nanook of the North*. As the show ends he sees the title: *Umealit: The Whale Hunters*.

"Thinking about moving to Alaska?" Dale asks.

Grabowski rises from his reclining position. "Now that's the life. Living in the wild hunting your own food."

Dale doubts that his roommate would find such a life agreeable after about one day.

"Didn't you get my invitation to the film screening tonight?"

"Huh? Oh, shit, I forgot. Sorry about that, bud."

Dale is tempted but he refrains from saying the Grabowskism.

"How'd it go anyway?"

Dale shrugs. "S.O.S." He starts to head off to his room.

"I got some bad news today," Grabowski says.

"What is it?"

"I didn't get the research assistantship for the summer."

"That's too bad."

"Yeah. Deb got it instead."

"Really?" Actually, Dale is glad. At least she has some actual research skills. Dr. Schneider must have picked competence over schmoozing when it came to something important, such as his book. "Sorry about that."

"Yeah, well, no biggie." Grabowski shrugs.

"What are you going to do this summer while you finish your degree?"

"Guess I'll have to borrow money." Grabowski gives him a knowing look.

"Sorry, Gary, but I don't have any money to spare. In a few days I'm leaving for Minneapolis. I'll need all the money I have for the trip and finding a place to live."

Actually, Dale had saved almost a thousand bucks during his one-year stay. He, like his roommate, has frugal habits; even more so because he doesn't drink beer. However, he really does need all his money. He's saving up for the Big Trip that he and Will Whitaker aree going to take in the near future. Besides, he doesn't think Grabowski has any reason to resent not getting a loan. They argued over this month's rent. Since Dale is only staying ten days of the month he wanted to pay just one-third. Grabowski thought he should pay the whole month. That's how rent was paid, month-to-month. So they reached a compromise. Dale would pay one half of his share of the month's rent, $100. Now, Dale feels a little like a cheapskate but then he recalls that Grabowski has always benefited from sharing expenses half and half. No longer the food because Dale changed that deal once he saw Grabowski's gargantuan appetite. But they still split utilities and the cable TV bill. Since Dale has no interest in watching television and therefore wouldn't have gotten cable TV in the first place, he thinks paying for half of it is somewhat unfair. But he never complained. He just paid his half. He knows without TV Grabowski would be a lost man. He might even have to read a book.

Grabowski shrugs. "I guess I'm going to have to borrow from the university then."

"The interest rates are fairly low," Dale says, offering encouragement.

"At least I found someone to replace you."

"You mean you found another roommate so soon?"

"Yeah. A friend of Neil Nordberg, Russell Burke, needed a place. The house he was renting was sold."

"Lucky you." Dale says, on his way to his bedroom. "I think you'll like having Russell Burke as a roommate."

15

"When are you leaving?" Miriam asks as she and Dale walk out of Roripaugh Hall. Their last creative writing class is over.

"Early Saturday morning."

"How sad it is not to have any more campus movies to go to. What will I do without your expert commentary to guide me in my movie viewing?"

"Read Halliwell's."

"What's that? Some kind of magazine?"

"No, it's a reference book that gives a short synopsis and critique of almost every movie made in the last sixty years. Of course, the reviews aren't as astute as mine but they'll have to do."

Miriam smiles but he sees in her brown eyes a shadow of sadness. He begins to feel a poignant swell inside him too.

"So what are you're plans this summer?" he asks thinking a practical question will help quell that feeling.

"I'll hang around the house for a few weeks recuperating from an arduous senior year! Then I suppose I'll have to find some kind of job. But what kind? What kind of job does an English major hope for?"

"A girl Friday job."

"What's that?"

"It's a job where the girl goes to work only on Fridays."

"Oh, you! I always play the straight woman for your jokes."

They stop walking. She has one more class in a different part of campus. She reaches into her purple purse and grabs a small notepad and scribbles her address. She rips the sheet of paper out and it gives it to him. Then she hands him the notepad.

"Now, write your address down so I'll have it in case you lose mine."

"I won't lose it." But he writes an address in her notepad and hands it back to her. "That's my grandparents address in Oklahoma. I don't know where my address will be in Minnesota yet. But they will forward my mail."

"Now I want you to write me! I want to keep in touch."

"Okay, I will."

"I got to run now for class."

Suddenly, she throws her arms around his neck and gives him a big sloppy kiss on the cheek, not quite as sloppy as the one she gave him at Deb's party, but close. This time Dale doesn't mind. She lets go and says "bye" and hustles away. Dale watches Miriam walk away, and as if reading his mind she gives him a quick glance back then starts gyrating her hips, mimicking the sexy walk of her movie idol, the divine Marilyn Monroe.

Dale grins and waves at her. He'll miss Mimi.

While walking across campus toward the student union, Dale sees Professor Wilkins across the quad. The author takes longs strides. His hands are jammed in his dark trousers and his head is bent in thought. Dale wonders if he's thinking about his novel, the one that is taking a little longer to write than his previous ones. As Wilkins walks out of sight, Dale remembers reading his second novel, *Shooting for the Moon*, and being impressed by its artistry. He enjoyed his conference with Wilkins, too, and admired his dedication to his literary work. The primary reason Dale came to Wyoming was because it was a fairly small campus with a film program. At the time, he thought he might like to be a filmmaker. He loved books, especially novels, but it seemed that the written word was becoming passé. Film seemed to be the dominant art in society. Dale remembers that discouraging discussion with Wagstaff and Nordberg, the one where they declared the novel to essentially be a defunct art form. But as Dale watches Wilkins striding away he thinks he is a writer that refutes their argument. None of his novels have attracted a sizable number of readers. Certainly not an audience to rival even a mediocre Hollywood movie. But does that matter? What matters more is the integrity of one's creative work. And Dale thinks that Wilkins is the embodiment of the true artist; one who creates out of a principled need to communicate the truth as he sees it. Dale thinks that's more important than all the schlocky Hollywood films put together.

Dale decides to enter the student union by the side door on the west end and he's about to open it when he sees Pamela Partridge on the other side. He opens the door for her and she slips out. She glances at him, an embarrassed smile on her pink, plump face. She's not wearing her usual outdoors clothes. She's dressed in more refined clothes, tan dress slacks, a forest green blouse and a tan vest. She starts to descend the three cement stairs when Dale asks her if she is all right.

"What do you mean?" she says.

"I heard about the trouble you got into. I was just wondering if everything turned out okay."

"No, it didn't turn out okay. I was just leaving the meeting."

"What happened? They didn't kick you out?"

"No, nothing so dramatic. They are allowing me to graduate."

"That's good."

"It's not good at all. They are going to put a negative citation on my transcript."

"That doesn't sound so bad."

"Not so bad! What about when I apply to graduate schools? I might not get into the program I want."

"Yeah, that might be a problem. But it could be worse."

Pamela shakes her head, her blue eyes tearing up. "Yes, it

could be worse. I suppose you think it should be."

"Not at all. In fact, I'm sorry this happened to you. But it is your fault."

"Yes it's my fault. Everything of late has been my fault. Well, Dale, I must go. I'm late for another meeting."

Dale nods and watches her walk away. He thinks he shouldn't have said it was her fault. Of course, it was. Trying to stuff the ballot box to rig an election? Where did she think she was? Chicago?

Still, he feels sorry for her. He wishes he could do something to make her feel better but he knows any of his efforts would just make things worse.

Friday afternoon and Dale sits in the wooden chair in Wagstaff's office while the professor peruses his thesis. Wagstaff performs his task with his characteristic quickness or carelessness. He flips from page to page as if he's using the manuscript to fan the air. He's not reading it for final evaluation. He's just browsing through it to make sure there aren't any significant problems (like pronoun usage) before Dale departs campus.

"From my cursory reading, I'd say your thesis is in adequate condition." Wagstaff tosses the 109-page manuscript on his desk. "Of course, I don't know why you bothered to finish it."

"Because I wanted to." Dale knows that Wagstaff would prefer he not complete the manuscript. Less work for him.

"It's a *tache inutile*," Wagstaff intones.

Dale can only guess what the French phrase means from it's context. He guesses it means something like "there's no point." Wagstaff is certainly well educated for a Ball State man.

"Maybe not," Dale says. "I'm going to see Dr. Schneider about the F in the independent studies class.

"I doubt that you will find any success. Department chairman really have little authority in such matters. He can't force Comstock to change the grade."

A week ago Dale showed the failed independent study paper to Wagstaff but he barely scrutinized it. He agreed that the grade was severe. He agreed that Dale essentially repeated one mistake. But grades on written work were not exactly objective in nature. Comstock could claim other reasons why he gave the paper the F. Wagstaff advised Dale to forget the matter. He could stay in the program for another semester and make up the one failing hour and perhaps then receive his degree. But Comstock would make trouble about that, too. Academic departments didn't like conflict. Fellow professors preferred equanimity with their peers. Rather like the United States Senate, an academic department emphasized courtliness, good will, and cooperation on the face of things while privately they enjoyed savaging one another.

Dale definitely doesn't want to stay for another semester. He won't even have a place to stay after tomorrow. Nordberg's friend, Russell Burke, is going to move in on Sunday. And Dale has no interest in a male only *Three's Company*.

Besides he's eager to join Will in Minnesota. They have a lot to catch up on. Dale kept him appraised about his cn-going struggle with Comstock but it would be more satisfying to denounce the censorious professor to Will in person. Plus there were movies to see, books to discuss, and plans to be made about The Trip.

"So, you really don't think there's any use talking to Dr. Schneider?"

"That's correct."

"And even if he was able to convince Comstock to change the grade he might only raise it to a C, which still wouldn't count for credit.

"A very likely possibility."

"And even if he raised the grade to a B, Comstock would still raise hell in the department about my receiving a degree. And his fellow professors would be reluctant to engage in the debate especially since some of the professors hardly know me and some others are not happy with my performance in certain areas."

"Your analysis is astute."

Dale shakes his head, but not forlornly. "I'm still going to see Dr. Schneider."

"You are a stubborn young man but I do like your taste in movies."

Wagstaff points to his thesis. Turns out that Wagstaff was a Billy Wilder fan, too. However, Dale knows Wagstaff to be a capricious creature. More than once he heard Wagstaff praise a director then two months later change his mind after re-viewing a movie. Wagstaff is also a unpredictable grader. Dale heard students complain about receiving a high grade on one paper then receiving a low one on the next. Wagstaff always awarded him A's except once when Dale wrote an analytical paper for his film history class on Frank Capra. The paper was just as well written, insightful, and documented as his other ones, yet Wagstaff gave the paper a B-. Dale didn't ask him why. He just changed his thesis topic from Capra to Wilder.

"Did you ever have a difficult, unreasonable, emotionally disturbed man for a professor?"

Wagstaff raises his vague eyebrows. His bald head seems to shine as if brain activity produces a sheen on the skin of his skull. He fingers one long strand of his Fu Manchu mustache.

"During my doctoral studies I encountered a man that might fit your description. I had a few early confrontations with him. He had to be on my doctoral committee too because of his specialty. So, I asked another professor I was on good terms with what I could do to alleviate the situation."

"And?"

"He said discover something that the professor especially likes. And use it to my advantage."

"And what was that?"

"Cigars. I gave the difficult professor a box of Cuban cigars. And don't ask where I got them. I must protect my sources."

"And from that point on, you had no trouble with the difficult professor."

"That's correct. He became my champion in fact. As long as he received his Cubans."

"Well, the trouble is that I don't know what Comstock likes. Maybe nothing except punishing pupils with pronoun problems."

Wagstaff grins.

"Comstock does like bird watching," Dale muses. "Maybe he likes candy because he gives it out to his favored students. I guess I should have asked you before about appeasing a difficult professor. I could have given Comstock a Tweety bird and a box of lollipops and I wouldn't be in this mess."

Predictably, Dr. Schneider offers no encouragement.

Dale presents his case. He shows the department chairman the independent study paper. But Schneider gives the same reasons for his impotence as Wagstaff predicted.

"Besides Dale, several of us in the department are disappointed in your poor effort with the *JNAMCP*."

"But Dr. Schneider, I'm not a professional proofreader. I told Professor Comstock and Dr. Wagstaff that I don't have very good skills in that area. I'm a writer not a proofreader."

"I understand your point, but part of your GTA was based on assisting with that task."

"Yes, assisting but not doing it all. Did you see how thick the proofs were? Is it reasonable to expect a graduate student without specialized editing skills to spend fifty hours proofing such a detailed document?"

Dr. Schneider lifts two upturned hands. "What can I tell you, Dale?"

"And Professor Comstock didn't even read and evaluate my movie reviews. There were twenty-five of them. That was objective in taking the independent study course in the first place: to write movie reviews."

"Well, movie reviews," Schneider says in an unimpressed voice.

Dale remembers that Schneider's specialty is mass communications theory. Therefore, he has little interest in the more practical aspects of journalism. Dale took two courses from him: research methods and professional ethics. He earned A's in both courses. But it is obvious that Schneider feels no sympathy for Dale's current plight.

"So there's nothing I can do about this?"

"You could petition the graduate school appeals board once your grade is recorded by the registrar. You could also speak to Dean Schmeltzer, the academic dean. But I doubt –"

"He would change anything."

Dr. Schneider turns up the palms of his long, thin hands again, not in supplication but in indifference.

After Dr. Schneider's pep talk, Dale checks his departmental mailbox for the last time. He notices there's a manila envelope in it. He grabs it and walks to his office.

Along the way he notices that Comstock's office door is completely shut. He's still in there, however. Dale sees a wedge of light emanating from under his door. Besides, Dale *senses* Comstock's presence. The same way Dr. Helsing senses Dracula's proximity.

Dale heard nothing from the other professors about his film and Comstock's guest starring role. Dale wonders if Wagstaff, Sibelius, Deb and Edward Darby mentioned the professor's guest starring role to someone and then they mentioned it to someone else and so on. That's how gossip wildfire starts. But if that happened, he hasn't felt any heat.

He opens his office and sits before his desk. He thinks its rather odd that he's received so little feedback, well, positive feedback for his many creative efforts. He wrote movie reviews, wrote and produced a radio show, edited the literary magazine, and created a film. And yet only a few people, his friends, complimented him or even acknowledged his efforts. Talk about an artist living in obscurity!

Dale opens the Manila envelope and pulls out three 8 x 10 photographic prints. He's the subject in all three. At first, seeing his image embarrasses him. But as he examines the prints, he decides he has nothing to be really embarrassed about. His face isn't shown in any of them, which is a relief. Two of the photos aren't very revealing and all three are tastefully and artistically done. His physique is just one element out of several: texture, light, shadow, and composition.

A note is attached. It's from Regina Wilson. She thanks him again for taking the time to model for her. The note also informs him that she's having an exhibit tonight at eight o'clock at the Rocky Mountain Gallery in downtown Laramie.

He thinks he will go.

Dale decides to get there late so there will be fewer people. He doubts that anybody will recognize him from the three prints that he expects will be displayed in the gallery but he doesn't want to take any chances.

He leaves his place at twenty minutes to ten and walks alone to downtown Laramie. He didn't mention the exhibit to Grabowski or anyone else. His roommate is at the campus pub washing away his sorrows.

As Dale approaches the entrance to the Rocky Mountain Gallery, he notices that a small group of people, four women and three men, are milling in front of the door. Some of them carry hand-made signs of protest. One unattractive middle-aged woman's placard declares: *More Skin, More Sin.* A husky middle-aged man's poster says: *God Wants People to Wear Clothes.*

Dale nods at the Laramie seven and starts to duck into the gallery. The man holding the sign waves it at him.

"Young man, don't go into that den of iniquity."

"The gallery isn't that. It shows visual art."

"Art? It's smut!" declares the woman.

Dale points to her sign. "I like your sign. It rhymes."

For a moment, her prune face smiles. But when she sees him enter the den of iniquity, she shakes the sign at him.

He walks inside the small but handsome gallery. He sees several people he doesn't know gathered around the front where most of the refreshments, cheese and wine, were consumed. Otherwise, there aren't that many people in the place.

He starts to walk into the first section of the gallery when coming in the other direction is Regina Wilson. She smiles when she sees him.

"I'm so pleased you came, Dale."

"I had to get by that gauntlet of protesters first."

"Oh them. They're some primitive church group that is offended by the exhibit."

"That one sign seems to have it backward. According to Genesis, Adam and Eve were naked in the Garden of Eden. You might say God was the first creator of nudes."

"I don't think they would understand the irony of your point."

"No, they don't seem to have much appreciation for subtlety."

Dale notices that Regina is all dressed up. She's wearing a purple dress, a necklace, and her normally wild and flowing hair is more under control. She's also wearing more make-up than usual. She looks attractive in her Earth Mother kind of way.

"Well, take all the time you like looking over the exhibit. We're supposed to close at ten but I think we'll be open for at least a half hour longer than that."

"Okay," Dale says as he prepares to go.

"Oh, by the way, Dale," Regina says. "I meant to mention this to you during our last session. If you're interested in doing more modeling I can arrange for you to see an agent in Denver. You probably could pick up some work in a few weeks."

"Thanks, Regina, but I'm more comfortable on the other side of the camera."

She beams her broad, becoming smile. "I understand."

They exchange farewells and Dale pauses before he walks away. He looks back and sees Regina walking over to a tall, lissome blonde young woman. Dale recognizes her: Lithe Blonde. He's never seen her this close before. She looks as lovely as the last time he saw her one month ago, although now she's wearing clothes, an attractive red dress. The previous time he saw her was when he arrived early for his last modeling session and decided to take a walk around Regina's ranch. He ambled around to the back of the house and as he approached the studio he saw Regina photographing Lithe Blonde through the large studio windows. Lithe Blonde was gloriously nude. She stood with her back to him, her head tilted to the right, her left leg bent at the knee, her right arm held in the air as if she were holding something. Her pose reminded him of a scene from Greek mythology. Maybe Aphrodite offering herself to Adonis (or Sappho). Dale took as long of a look as he dared. He didn't want them to observe his unintentional peeking. Maybe he looked at her for only five seconds but they were perhaps the most thrilling five seconds of his eyeballs existence.

Dale enters the gallery, especially on the hunt for a print depicting Lithe Blonde's memorable pose. After passing by five prints, he finds it. Surprisingly, the photo doesn't match the image in his memory. It's a great photograph. And the model looks fantastic. She's fairly tall and lean but with a definite female shapeliness especially the long, curvature of her hips, the dimpled buttocks, and the supple thighs. However, the black and white photo has a different context to it. His memory of that pose includes a larger perspective and color. The photo is an artistic rendering of that memory. It's in its own world.

Dale thinks it's a great photo and not just because of the model. He looks at the price tag. Damn, if he could spare $200 he'd buy it.

He examines all the other photographs in the first part of the exhibit hall, seeing five other photos of that model. They're fascinating photos, all of them are nudes, and they combine an artistic detachment with genuine erotic energy. They are shots of Lithe Blonde from the back, the front, and the side. None of them are explicit, although the one frontal photo shows some of her pale pubic hair. But even in that one the intention is to depict her image in relation to the other elements: the setting, light, shadow, composition, texture, etc. He notices that all five of them have been sold, too.

He moseys through the exhibit, quickly assessing photos that don't interest him as much and taking more time with ones that do, like the blonde's photos. He notices that two other models, both women, are used in the other photos but those images are not as spectacular as the blonde's. The models aren't as attractive and they appear clothed and partially nude.

Then he sees one of the photos with him as the model. Even though he saw the print a few hours ago, seeing the photo in the exhibit creates a different reaction. His image is now being shown in public and he's not sure he likes that. This photo is a torso shot, showing his shoulders, chest, and stomach with his arms flexed in front of him. At the bottom of the photo he can see the beginning of his Levi's, a detail that makes him feel less self-conscious.

Farther down the wall he sees a second photo. It shows even less of him. He's holding a hammer, about to strike a plank of wood. The camera focuses on his arm and hand. The image of his closed hand is so clear that he can see the creases in his knuckles. His arm muscles impressively bulge. The photo is detailed enough that he can see the rather sparse hair on his flexed forearm. The stylized photo almost takes on an abstract quality. Arm, hammer, plank of wood, and surrounding darkness. Dale likes it.

Dale knows there is one more photo of him on display. He rounds the corner and enters into another area when he sees it mounted on the wall. This photograph embarrasses him a little. He sees a small group of people assessing that photograph as well as two others photos hanging next to it on the wall, photographs of some of the ranching implements Dale remembers seeing in Regina Wilson's barn.

Two people leave the small cluster of observers, and Dale recognizes one of the remaining art lovers. He takes two steps closer.

He looks at the print he's featured in. He's photographed from the back. His arms are raised above his head as he lifts a beam of wood above his head. The action pose reminds him of some artistic rendering he once saw of Atlas holding up the world, although he doesn't have the massive musculature of the mythic Atlas. The muscles in his neck, shoulders, arms, back, butt, and thighs are all flexed. He's nude which gives him, now a viewer, a curious, ambivalent feeling of embarrassment and excitement. It's not a sexual photograph though. The camera is focused on the taut muscles and the swarthy skin and how it contrasts with the white, knotty wood. Still, he doesn't like the fact that he isn't wearing any clothes. His image is revealed from the outstretched hands to mid-thigh. He remembers Regina telling him that if he had longer legs he would have almost perfect proportions. Well, that had always been his obvious physical shortcoming. Thankfully, the viewer can see very little of his face in partial profile, just a glimpse of his chin, jaw and forehead.

When three more viewers leave, Dale quickly walks over to the remaining observer. Dale sidles up to Nordberg and when his former friend turns his way Dale pretends to be assessing the photograph with professional detachment as if he were a mechanic examining a car's engine.

Dale glances over to the surprised Nordberg and grins just a little.

"Looks like I loosened up after all. Eat your heart out, Nordberg."

Dale turns and walks away, certain that Nordberg is staring at his retreating back.

Six in the morning and Dale is all packed and ready to go. Before he gets into his Chevy Monza he stands in the empty street and looks at the dawning of a new morning. The air smells fresh and dewy. Rays of sunshine seep into the sky from the dark horizon. He likes how the evergreen trees stand tall and give off their musky scent. He thinks he will miss Wyoming.

It's been almost one year since he arrived in Laramie. Even though he knows he's leaving without his degree, he doesn't think it was a wasted year. He learned a lot. He saw over two hundred movies. He got involved in several student activities and that proved educational too. He met different kinds of people. He experienced life in ways he never experienced it before. Those experiences changed him for the better. All in all, not a bad way to spend a year.

He climbs in his car, starts her up, and drives down the street. He turns on Highway 287 heading south. As he speeds up the car, he pops in one of his homemade cassette tapes. It's the album by Bram Tchaikovsky, "Strange Man, Changed Man."